Jewish
Latin
America

Ilan Stavans
series editor

MESTIZO

RICARDO FEIERSTEIN

Translated from the Spanish by Stephen A. Sadow
Introduction by Ilan Stavans

UNIVERSITY OF NEW MEXICO PRESS

Albuquerque

Library of Congress Cataloging-in-Publication Data
Feierstein, Ricardo.
    [Mestizo. English]
    Mestizo / Ricardo Feierstein ; translated from the Spanish by
Stephen A. Sadow ; introduction by Ilan Stavans. — 1st ed.
    p. cm. — (Jewish Latin America)
  Originally published: Mestizo. Buenos Aires : Planeta, c1994.
  ISBN 0-8263-2115-1 (alk. paper)
  ISBN 0-8263-2116-x (pbk. : alk. paper)
  I. Title. II. Series.
  PQ7798.16.E36 M4813 2000
  863—dc21   99-6319

                                                  CIP

Other titles in the *Jewish Latin America* series:

> *Jewish Gauchos of the Pampas* by Alberto Gerchunoff
>
> *Cláper* by Alicia Freilich
>
> *The Prophet and Other Stories* by Samuel Rawet
>
> *The Book of Memories* by Ana María Shua
>
> *The Fragmented Life of Don Jacobo Lerner* by Isaac Goldemberg
>
> *Passion, Memory, and Identity: Twentieth-Century Latin American Jewish
> Writers*, edited by Marjorie Agosín
>
> *King David's Harp: Autobiographical Essays by Jewish Latin American
> Writers*, edited by Stephen A. Sadow
>
> *The Collected Stories of Moacyr Scliar*

Translator's Notes and Acknowledgments

Mestizo's author Ricardo Feierstein is one of my closest friends. We have met in person only seven times, in Argentina and in the United States, but we have developed a relationship that is professionally productive and personally deep. I have long been very familiar with his trilogy of novels *Sinfonía Inocente* and his many volumes of short stories. With the American poet Jim Kates, I translated and edited a bilingual edition of Feierstein's poetry entitled *We, the Generation in the Wilderness*. Through the interchange of many letters, I accompanied the creation of *Mestizo*, watching it develop from thousands of miles away. I shared the excitement when Editorial Milá published the first version of *Mestizo* and then the satisfaction when the Argentine division of the prestigious Spanish publishing house Editorial Planeta put out a revised edition with an eye-catching, multicolor cover. On that occasion, I wrote a laudatory article for the Jewish-sponsored weekly newspaper *Mundo Israelita* in Buenos Aires.

Years later, I convinced Feierstein to take me to Villa Devoto, the Buenos Aires neighborhood where he grew up and where he set much of the novel's action. I stood on the exact spot where the protagonist David Schnaiderman would have witnessed the murder, met one of the real Grimaudo brothers, a model for a minor character in the novel, and saw the remains of the Anaconda theater and many of David's hangouts. Feierstein was distraught over the changes that had taken place "in the neighborhood." I was delighted to cross the line between fiction and reality, if even for a few moments.

One event thrust me into the task of translating *Mestizo*. On July 19, 1994, a car bomb destroyed the AMIA building (Asociación Mutual Israelita Argentina, Jewish Mutual Association of Argentina), the seven-story structure housing the Jewish community headquarters. Eighty-six people were killed and two hundred injured. Feierstein, who worked for the AMIA, lost many colleagues, most poignantly, his secretary Mirta Streir. While not hurt physically (his office was in another building), he was psychologically injured in ways that are only slowly healing.

Back home in Boston, I felt the shockwaves of the explosion. From such distance, there was not much I could do to help in the rescue effort or to comfort the victims. For me, translating *Mestizo* became my way of protesting the bombing, of responding to the terrorism.

The wide use of words and expressions found only in the greater Buenos Aires area complicated the translation of the novel. I sent long lists of queries to Feierstein who replied with dictionary-style explanations. Also, the novel contains many Yiddish and Hebrew phrases. Fortunately, I can handle those languages. The utterances in Ukrainian, though, did send me looking for a native informant. The inclusion of poems, comic strips, movie scripts, and many other formats within one novel called for a continual search for equivalent modes in English.

I would like to thank those who have helped me with the lengthy task: Ricardo Feierstein; Jim Kates, who is my co-translator of the poems "Old Jews" and "Argentina 1983," and who helped me smooth out the chapter entitled "A Guided Tour of the Neighborhood"; Andrés Avellaneda of the University of Florida, who loves *Mestizo* and who read the manuscript so carefully; and Jeanne Prevett who checked the details. A special thank you goes to Annie Clark, who found the time, while preparing for her wedding, to help out with the final draft.

Mario Szichman of the Associated Press; Edna Aizenberg, Marymount-Manhattan College; and Isaac Goldemberg, Hostos Community College, SUNY, helped keep my enthusiasm high. Rita Gardiol, Indiana University, gave me much-needed advice. Cola Franzen, Mark Shaffer, and the others of the New England Translators Group provided me with encouragement when I most needed it and helped me with technical problems in the text.

Professors Holbrook Robinson and Harlow Robinson, successively my chairmen in the Department of Modern Languages of Northeastern University, supported the project enthusiastically. My ongoing discussions with Professor Jim Ross, former chair of Northeastern's Jewish Studies Program, helped me clarify my ideas about Jewish writing in the Diaspora.

Special thanks are due to Ilan Stavans, series editor of Jewish Latin America, and author of the introduction to this volume. He is both a dear friend and an astute teacher. At the University of New Mexico Press, it has been a pleasure working with Dana Asbury, acquisitions editor, who keeps things calm and on track, and Elizabeth Varnedoe, manuscripts editor, who, it seems, can handle anything and everything that arises, and Susan Walsh and Chris Crochetière, designers, who used their amazing repertoire of technical skills to construct a text that is complex in its layout and its content.

And much love to my wife Norma and my daughter Beth who were so understanding of my need to spend so many hours working on this enormous jig-saw puzzle.

Stephen A. Sadow
Northeastern University

INTRODUCTION
Ilan Stavans

"There is mist that no eye can dispel," writes the German novelist W. G. Sebald in *The Emigrants*. The sentence, so ethereal, so acute in its description of the type of abysmal solitude brought upon us by the displacements of modernity, strikes me as fitting to describe what Ricardo Feierstein does, also admirably, with a stroke that automatically places him as a leading voice in contemporary Jewish fiction, in his commanding *Mestizo*. The mist that results from emigration: Sebald's characters—Dr. Henry Selwyn, Paul Bereytner, Ambros Adelwarth, and Max Ferber—are all expatriates, wanderers forced to depart, to live in eternal transit. They have gone from Lithuania and Germany to England, Switzerland, France, New York, Constantinople, and Jerusalem. Their personal odyssey is about silences, about the search (and research) into the chambers of memory in order to reconstruct *das heim*: the place once called home. Home—*el hogar*—is at the core of Feierstein's semifictional investigation too, but the quest of David Schnaiderman, his protagonist, an unemployed, forty-year-old, married Argentine Jew, with children and a B.A. in sociology, is, unlike Sebald's, inward looking. He isn't exactly an expatriate; he isn't even an immigrant. Born and raised in Argentina, he is very much a sedentary creature, but only physically, for he is a nomad in the spiritual sense, an eternal wanderer: the consummate Diaspora Jew. What makes his pilgrimage bewitching is the way in which Schnaiderman's ghosts refuse to leave him alone. Not until and unless he acknowledges them does he become a full person.

It doesn't seem fortuitous to compare Feierstein to Sebald. I remember thinking, just after I finished *The Emigrants*: How terrifying a book this is, plotless, amorphous, announcing its overall message only by omitting it! *Mestizo*, in Stephen A. Sadow's lucid translation, has a similar effect on me. It is about absences and omissions but of a different kind. Exile in it is not geographic. Schnaiderman is, from beginning to end, on his own turf: his Argentina. But is it really *his*? As a Jew, he is a Diaspora dweller, a polychromatic Diaspora ruled by a God that allows his creatures to shape their existence through chance. In Buenos Aires, he is, has always been, a guest—a permanent guest perhaps, but a guest nonetheless. To feel remotely at home he needs to piece together the puzzle of his own transhistorical pilgrimage, from Poland to the Southern Hemisphere and Israel. His own patronymic is the clue: in Yiddish, Schnaiderman means "tailor"; or metaphorically (and far more appropriately): "cut-and-paste man." Indeed, that is what he is designed to be: an assembler, the kind of person who, as Isaiah Berlin once put it, "feels condemned to wither when cut off from his familiar environment, and so he resigns himself and begins putting two and two together. . . . "

Deception is one of Feierstein's leit-motifs. He deceptively models the structure of his novel after detective fiction. The time is 1983, although the overall tale takes the better part of the twentieth century. At the outset, a crime occurs: Sheila Abud, a Lebanese, is assassinated in Buenos Aires. The only witness is Schnaiderman, but instead of speaking out, he abruptly enters a state of temporary amnesia. The recovery, of course, only happens after he reappropriates his past, but this act of reappropriation is slow, fastidious, peripatetic, and surely painful. Multiple voices impregnate his convalescence, from the many Eastern European newcomers to the New World at the turn of the nineteenth century to the fortification of their successors, what Feierstein calls, fittingly, "the generation of the wilderness," the offspring of those immigrants (Schnaiderman included) whose identity is, as the title claims, *mestizo*.

The term *mestizo* has concrete connotations. It sprung out in New Spain—today's Mexico—during the seventeenth century to refer to a caste crossbreed by Spanish and Indian blood, and *mestizaje* is understood to be the process of social formation. It was, even after independence, a derogatory word to denote people of lower strata without social attributes. Above in the hierarchy were the Spaniards and Creoles; below, the Indians, mulattos, and *sambos*. Argentines are whiter in skin color. Unlike in Mexico, this whiteness precluded the emergence of a mixed race, what in Spanish American jargon is described as *ni de aquí, ni de allá*. In truth, there were plains Indians in the region when the Spaniards arrived, who were annihilated by the Argentine army in the 1870s, about the time of the Indian wars in the United States. In sociological terms, the long-term effect of this genocide was the same as if there had been no pre-Columbian population. The equivalent of the *indio* is the *gaucho*, and while early *gauchos* were part Indian, *mestizaje* was comparatively minor when seen against the large-scale phenomenon in Mexico and Central America. Along this line, Feierstein clearly refers to a cross-fertilization that is cultural and not hereditary. For him the word *mestizo* denotes a person with Jewish ancestry born to Jewish immigrants in Argentina and almost paralyzed by the duality.

The duality is of selves, of loyalties, and plurality of scope, since Schnaiderman's reappropriation of the past is incredibly ambitious. To foreign readers, the term *mestizo* might also be assumed to refer, at least at first sight, to the zigzagging Sephardic-Ashkenazic relations. It is a mistake, though. Passing references to Sephardim aside, Feierstein's main characters are all prototypes—perhaps "archetypes"—of the Eastern European heritage of Jews in the Southern Cone. This, I should stress, is not unique. In spite of its *converso* and crypto-Jewish past in the colonial period, the modern Jewish population in the Americas, to a large extent, has Yiddish and Europe as its sources. By the time the waves of Ashkenazic immigration arrived in Argentina, in the 1870s and onward, the Sephardic component in the native population had all but disappeared as a result of persecution and assimilation. The *nuevos judíos*, the new Jews from *shtetls* in the Old World, saw themselves as first settlers, utterly ignoring, unconsciously at least, their Iberian precursors. It wasn't acknowledged until the

1960s when another Sephardic immigration arrived in Argentina, mainly from Syria, Lebanon, Turkey, and Iraq. The connections between it and their Ashkenazic counterparts are tense, although not as intense as in other nations in the region. (In fiction, a more direct encounter between Sephardim and Ashkenazim is still to appear in the literature of Argentina and also the Spanish-language Americas. In fact, I can only think of a single case—Mexico's *Like a Bride*, by Rosa Nissán—where such an "interrupted dialogue," to use Albert Memmi's words, takes place.)

The character of Sheila Abud, a Christian Arab whose peripatetic life first makes her emigrate to Lebanon and then to Argentina, is emblematic: her love affair with an Ashkenazic Jew is a passionate if explosive matter in Feierstein's novel; it draws attention, even if tangentially, to the interfaith connections between the Jews that descend from Eastern Europe and the heterogeneous people of the Middle East, not only within Israel but from the nations surrounding it.

Mestizo is built with architectural breath: it is made of three parts of almost equal length, plus an epilogue. They are deliberately compared to the parts of a three: its roots, trunk, and branches. Major events are described from the viewpoint of various character—the fall of the Austro-Hungarian Empire, World War I and II, the creation of the State of Israel, the Cuban Revolution of 1958, and the so-called Dirty War in Argentina, complete with its guerrilla heroes and military rulers. Schnaiderman's counterpart is his grandfather Moishe Burech, a patriarch born in 1868 in the town of Yarchev, on the Polish-Russian border, and dead in Buenos Aires in 1951. Along comes a cast of many: Doña Sara, an immigrant widow settled in Argentina in 1913 with her eight children; León Piatigorsky, of Schnaiderman's same generation, just like Teresa and Ignacio (he is Sheila Abud's lover); Isaac, Schnaiderman's father, and Eduardo and Ruth, his own children.

Detective fiction, thus, is used only as an excuse, a subterfuge, because what is clearly in store is far more Proustian. As the homicide is sorted out, the reader comes across a huge confederacy of onlookers waiting to be noticed by Schnaiderman: ghosts from his childhood in the Villa Devoto neighborhood and his young adulthood in a kibbutz in Galilee; apparitions he reconvenes from his exposure to Argentine fascist groups like the Tacuara; and, also, Palestinians acquaintances he meets during the search in the capital. But he eventually realizes, as does the reader, that memory—his own personal one, and the mythical memory of his people too—is never pure. On the contrary, it is a cul-de-sac, a game of mirrors from which he cannot emerge without a sense of distortion. This prompts the philosophical questions: Is there such a thing as truth, be it historical or mythical? And what is a human life if not a chain of lies conveniently interpreted? Incisive questions, no doubt, specially for someone who belongs to an era of self-doubt and self-absorption, and to a country where history is easily and frequently manipulated to serve the objectives of the powers in vogue. Also, Feierstein, born in 1942, belongs to a literary generation in Argentina that came of age reading *Hopscotch*, a labyrinth of a novel, in which *lo real*, factual reality, is perceived from various perspectives, none fully satisfying. *Mestizo* owes much to Julio Cortázar: Schnaiderman, like Horacio Oliveira, is a divided man; and his odyssey makes sense only when transposed against an throng of photographs, inserted to make fiction more concrete.

Hopscotch never actually reproduces photographs. Neither does it reproduce the throng of clippings so essential to its last part, it only quotes them; Sebald's *The Emigrants* does, though: clippings and photographs. And what effect do they have? Simply, to make exile more visual. In *Mestizo*, on the other hand, their function is far more complex: the maps, newspaper clippings, and numerous photographs call attention to the limitlessness and ephemerality of literature. Their suggestiveness makes the reader wonder if what is at hand is a *testimonio*, an accurate account of Jewish life in Argentina, and not, as the suggestion is made earlier on, a full-fledged tale of the imagination. In the end, of course, truth and legend, fiction and history, are made into one and the same as Feierstein announces, convincingly, that only by teasing ourselves, by accepting that memory is a form of fantasy, are we truly capable of grasping our own true essence.

Argentina holds the largest Jewish community (200,000 souls strong) in the Americas after the United States. It is also the oldest and most ideologically diverse, with many prominent public diplomats of Jewish background. Most of its members are urban dwellers, and Buenos Aires is their stronghold. Their strength and status, not surprisingly, have inspired the most notorious anti-Semitic attacks in the whole continent, from the *Semana trágica*, a full-fledged pogrom in the early part of the twentieth century, to desecrations of cemeteries, vandalism in synagogues, and the terrorist car-bombing of the AMIA building, the Jewish community center, in 1994, in which eighty-six people perished. Feierstein's is a working-class background. In his youth, he was involved in Hashomer Hatsair, and as an adult he has worked for AMIA itself and for a Jewish publishing house. This novel, published in 1994 and his first to appear in English, is based on extensive archival research done on Jewish immigration and released in a volume he co-edited entitled *Integración y marginalidad* (1985). It is also arguably the best and most accessible installment of a tetralogy, not released sequentially and known under the banner of *Sinfonía Inocente*, that includes *Entre la izquierda y la pared* (1983), *El caramelo descompuesto* (1979), and *Escala uno en cincuenta* (1984). But, most important perhaps, it is among the most technically complex novels about the so-called identity wars, and about the Jewish experiences in the Spanish-language orbit, ever to appear, a stunningly polyphonic piece.

It signals, I'm convinced, an engaging counter-life to modern Jewish letters. It is a response to the type of literature, sarcastic, clever, at times self-denigrating and often self-referential, produced by Philip Roth and his successors. As I reread Feierstein to write this introduction, I keep on asking myself: What is his place on the global Jewish literary shelf? How does he compare to American-Jewish and Israeli authors? At times he calls to mind the A. B. Yehoshua of *Mr. Mani*, but without his cinemascope technique taken from Faulkner or his chronological regression à la Harold Pinter. His keenness is far more intimate, his attention to detail much closer to the Delmore Schwartz of *In Dreams Begin Responsibilities*. Feierstein's brainstorming also recalls the Saul Bellow of *Herzog*: lucid, inquisitive, unstoppable in the quest to discover his wholeness, if not his holiness. But these comparisons are misleading (that is, deceiving) for his is clearly a very personal literature, rooted to the core in Argentine soil. Not accidentally has Feierstein has come to represent, by virtue of his courage and insightfulness, a leading literary voice of Argentina's postimmigrant generation, one that followed the founding figures of Alberto Gerchunoff, César Tiempo, and Bernardo Verbitzky. Still, it seems far more fitting to link him to Cortázar and Sebald than to those predecessors: to Cortázar as a result of his experimentalist "private I," ready to destabilize literature in order to make it more truthful; and to Sebald in the way that Feierstein embraces deception and impurity. His poignant novel is about the recognition that emigration is not a status but a condition. "Bastard memory!," Schnaiderman seems to shriek. "I try to unveil your mysteries, but your mist always defeats me."

To feel, to believe that the roots push from your feet and run and hesitate, like aggressive snakes toward some subterranean source, where they settle on the sand, and again unite, you, living thing, unknown tree, unidentified tree, that produces the fruits that you yourself will pick.
—Jean Joseph Rabearivelo,
   Poetry from Black Africa

As people, our appearance is quite different from that of a tree. There is no doubt that we perceive the world in a manner that is quite different from that of a tree. But at the basis of everything, in the molecular nucleus of life, we and trees are identical.
—Carl Sagan, *Cosmos*

Woman Shot to Death

Only witness suffers a shock which affects his memory

An event surrounded by strange circumstances, apparently caused by passion, occurred yesterday afternoon where Campana Street and General Mosconi Avenue meet, on the northeast sidewalk, in the Federal Capital. At approximately 5:30 P.M., the neighbors were surprised by some shouting —apparently the result of brief discussion—and the sharp sound of several shots. Near the corner, Sheila Abud, Lebanese, 43, lay in an immense pool of blood. In spite of attempts of several passersby, Mrs. Abud died before reaching the hospital.

An examination revealed that there were four wounds, each made by a .38-caliber bullet, two in the chest, one in the face, and the other in the left forearm, with which, it appears, she tried to protect herself from the attack. In the purse that she was carrying were found her documents and a large sum of money, which makes robbery unlikely as the motive for the mysterious execution. Red spots are still visible on the wall and the sidewalk. Some circumstances, as yet unclear, make the killing more extraordinary. Near the dying woman, sitting on the sidewalk, was found a man, about 40, from whom personal information could not be obtained. Somewhat stunned,

it seemed, the result of blows to the forehead—on which could be seen mud stains and an open wound—the only witness to or protagonist in the matter is under the effect of an emotional shock, that has provoked, according to several police sources, a partial amnesia, because of which he cannot remember anything, not even details about his own identity. In addition, several people who, by chance, were in the area, insist that they saw a young man, carrying a huge kitchen knife, run down Carlos A. López Street, some hundred meters from the place where the perfidious attack, which caused the death of Mrs. Abud, occurred.

The victim, who lived near there, was well thought of by her neighbors, who commented repeatedly on her singular beauty. Wife of a prosperous merchant in the district, she lived for more than twenty years in our country, all that time in the neighborhood where she died. The investigators trust that the unexpected emotional shock experienced by the man now in custody will be overcome, and, that with his testimony, they will be able to shed some light on this confusing episode. The case is being directed by Officer Santa Cruz, Precinct 47, the Villa Pueyrredón district.

PROVINCE OF BUENOS AIRES
JUDICIAL BRANCH

REPORT OF THE FORENSIC PHYSICIAN,
DOCTOR SERGIO LEV, ABOUT
THE STATUS OF THE WITNESS N. N. IN PROGRESS

<u>Presentation:</u> He appears to be a person in a perplexed
state, as if in a situation of being alienated from
himself. His expression appears glassy. From time to
time he enters a state of psychomotor excitation, acting in ways that lack precise definition. In response
to questions about his identity, he smiles in an unmo-
tivated and vacuous way, without being able to be precise about it and through an awkward sort of language.

<u>Antecedents:</u> From other people and witnesses who were
on the scene, it is known that he was found in a state
of self-absorption, immersed in his thoughts, during a
rain and hail storm. That he struck the curb, after
seeing an episode that caused a quick and unexpected
impression on him, possibly the homicide in progress,
and the posterior trauma provoked by the shock of his
head against the pavement.

<u>Psychological examination:</u> Unstable attention. Un-
pleasant istmia, depression, irritability. Slow and
incoherent thinking. Total amnesia of evocation. Confused conscience. Agitation. Global disorientation of
self and in time and space. Psychomotor excitation.

<u>Conclusion:</u> N. N. finds himself in a state of memory
loss, without the ability to concentrate nor the consciousness to orient his actions and guide his thinking. His mental state is decompensated owing to an
earlier period of lowered defenses (anxiety, self-
absorption, depression) prior to the traumatic
situation. He could not tolerate the blow, and it
translated into a loss of identity, disorientation,
and confusion of his conscience and of himself.

1. Roots in I

To be original is to return to the origin.

—Antonio Gaudi

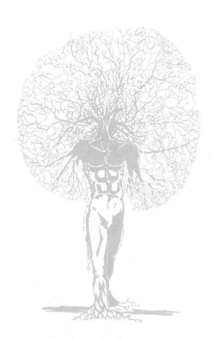

family tree

An incident, a memory, a photo. That's all I know. That's why I've come to see you. You're a doctor, right? Your job is to penetrate the mystery, clear the fog, pull aside the shades. Get to work, then.

Who was Moishe Burech really? Why is his grandfatherly figure, fascinating, yet unknown, the heart of the enigma? What use is a family photograph, forgotten for generations and found by chance in a large chest filled with yellowed papers,—if chance exists in circumstances such as these—during a search for which I had barely two weeks, given the deadline set by the judge.

Why this need by the police to know my identity so quickly? Who other than myself is troubled by my lack of an identity?

Yeh, yeh, I understand your impatience. You want facts, not talk. It's your job. Okay, here we go.

The incident.

To tell it straight out seems nonsensical. I went to apply for a job. The ad said that a resume was needed. I had been out of work for three months, and my situation was . . . almost desperate. Since we returned from Israel, several years ago, things have gone from bad to worse. I haven't been able to fully readjust, to know who I truly am. No, don't get me wrong. I've already figured out my name, that kind of thing. I'm referring to that . . . look, I have degree in sociology that I got a decade ago, and I was going to apply for a job as a clerk, a pitiful clerk. As if I were handicapped. But what could I do? There were discussions at home with my wife and the kids, confusion. . . . So I put together an enormous portfolio, my identity card, my transcript, diplomas from high school and the university, papers from the Registry, my kids' birth certificates, papers from my former employers, recommendations, bits and pieces, CURRICULUM VITAE—bah! It was my whole life.

I could never have predicted that it would be Fall, that it would be raining hard, that I would run as I got off the city bus, trying to make the green light, that crossing the street, a gust of wind and hale would scatter the folder of records that slipped from my arm; that diplomas and identity books and evidence of my life history would take flight at the precise instant that the traffic light turned red. That I was able to get my footing, to stagger across to the sidewalk, filthy, battered and bruised, sloshing around in the muddy and foul-smelling water of the gutter, soaked by that passing dark truck while dozens of vehicles surged ahead, wailing down Mosconi Avenue, some zigzagging, with their lights on. I remember that cloudy and gray afternoon, gusts of wind, my trying to get up with the help of the boy from the newspaper kiosk on the corner, while papers swirled in the pavement cracks, a light blue and white city bus, obstructing my vision for a moment, tree leaves scattered on the ground, my sense of desperation at being airborne, without a place to get my balance nor a solid support to hold on to, my past and my history and my surname spread over the sidewalk, stuck to the tires of some car, flattened in an unseen corner.

Do you understand me? I am still nobody. When another person looks at me, on a police summons, in line with those looking for work, *I am nobody*. In Buenos Aires, words and smiles don't count: only the facts. I can't verify my name, what I have done in my life, what stitches of guilt and innocence embroider the story of my life.

I don't have a history. I don't remember anything. I'm tied to reality by this one old family photo that seems to be close and disturbing. But I can't reconstruct an identity from something of which I, more than anyone, am doubtful. Without familiar pictures, papers stamped with India ink and worn by my fingers, bits of parchment that show years of work and study, I myself don't know who I am.

And I need to know who I am. Overcome the resistance of memory. You can find me again. I am lost.

The rest is anecdotal. There is a story, possibly sordid, of adultery. There is a woman in that store on the corner across from where I'm lying after my fall. My head hurts, I can't see well. There is a man, shouts, loud discussion. Everything happens in an instant. There is a revolver, several shots, blood that splatters the yellow wall of the building, the sidewalk, my hands, my face. There is also, it seems to me, a knife, the adolescent who leaves running from the same house and rushes at the man with the revolver. There is a slippery spot, and I fall again, a blow to my forehead, confusion.

And now, a judge who gives me provisional liberty and a deadline to discover my identity, to reconstruct with your help, the cardboards bearing photos, the lost diplomas, that evidence that I am in fact a person of flesh and blood, a solid being and not a phantom separated from himself, the only witness of a crime—who can't remember the face of the murderer.

You don't believe me. Are you already convinced that I'm making this up? Okay, think that. Your opinion is not important. I need your services, not your compassion. Make me speak once and for all.

VOICES AROUND THE STOVE

Our house had two stories, and we lived on the second floor. In the first, there was a butcher, a certain Hitl. *The day of the pogrom, many hooligans met outside. We had a large iron door in front that wasn't at all easy to open. All the men met in the first floor apartment with hatchets, knives, sticks, whatever there was for self-defense. The women and the children stayed upstairs on the second floor.*

Just then, he came, the owner, who was at a son's house, at about that time. The Poles wanted to get inside. They threw a grenade against the door, and they blew a hole through the metal, but they weren't able to open it. Next door there was a store that had an open area. I remember that it sold kerosene, candles, soap, it was a general store, it was part of the house, and it had a door that opened to the premises. Do you remember? Eleven o'clock at night. He was a Yid too. It was nighttime. He didn't realize what was happening, and he wanted to go inside. They said to him, "Ah, you have the key." Then they opened the divider, and they stole or broke everything in the store. And they got into the house through the backroom.

We were horribly frightened. When they got in, they went directly to the first floor apartment and the fight began. Everyone was shouting, and we were crouching on the floor upstairs, trembling. The arm of one of our men was slashed with a saber, but our guys killed a soldier, a Polish officer, they were all Polish volunteers who did the pogrom, they were brutal.

I was a five-year-old boy, but I still remember the fear we felt, the butcher's blood-covered cleavers and knives, the alarms, the sweat and the noise, the blows, insults, someone who cried for God.

After all, they weren't able to get upstairs. We defended ourselves well, and the others left. Then the Jews themselves formed a militia to protect the building.

I remember it as if it were today. They burned houses and synagogues. They killed many Jews. This was in Lemberg. The Poles were two kilometers from the city, and the Ukrainians were in the city. A Jewish deputy, a Zamerstein, formed an army to defend the place. The Poles were on the surrounding heights and watched everything. Shortly thereafter, they entered the city, fighting, and the chiefs gave the soldiers twenty-four hours to do anything they wanted—rob, rape, kill.

So that "the boys have a good time," as they used to say. The government authorized that for one day, they could do what they felt like. A group reached the building. We lived in a Jewish neighborhood, it wasn't a ghetto, but rather a part of the city where poor Jews lived. The rich lived in other places, farther from downtown, mixed in with the Poles; there they weren't going to carry out pogroms, but rather in poor Jewish neighborhoods: Niodove, Poltevne, on the outskirts, between the mud and the slime. They went there, where the majority of the residents were Jews. On the other hand, the wealthy Jews, the businessmen, lived in the residential district, but they made up only a small portion of the neighborhood. The rest were Poles, so the Jews could pass unnoticed. Yes, we had a great time as kids, it was lovely to live between the mud and the anti-Semites.

From the window of my house the Poles could be seen. Our porter, who was a Ukrainian, let our people enter and shoot from the hallway, keeping the door shut. I remember papa who had only recently returned from the trenches, shouting at us, "Children, on the floor and in the kitchen," when fierce shooting would begin, because they were shooting at our house. We were dragging ourselves, on the ground, to the back of the house. After that, we stayed put, and there were shots into the pillows and the headboards. By chance, we saved ourselves; if we had stayed in bed . . .

Yes, we are survivors. Since childhood, we survived by chance. We are here, others could have been.

In my village is told the story of the *melamed*'s son. There was one who had a brother, around 1900, and all of them gave beatings; it was like that then, the father, the mother, and the teacher beat the children. The educational system was like that. Even the cultured people who brought teachers from Vienna, they hit as well. Education meant corporal punishment. My mother who was small and couldn't hit, scratched . . . had to take care of it somehow. And then the *melamed's* wife died and left eight or ten kids, and he married again. All the children got out of there, the oldest went to America, and another was a bookkeeper in Vienna, and so on for the rest until only the smallest was left. And the stepmother threw him into the street, and this child was half wild. He made his way to a den of thieves and scoundrels, carrying all that pain with him; to say the least, it wasn't a good environment. There he grew up, tall and handsome, very strong, he could trounce twenty men, he was so wild, a very special Jew.

That was until the war. I met him in 1914, they sent him to the front, but he was there only two or three days, and he escaped, he wasn't one for discipline. He returned to the outpost of thieves and deserters, until one from the "family" turned him in, and the police came and took him away. Two days passed and he returned, they had beaten him so badly that they almost killed him, because he was a savage fighter. The 1914 war ended, and he was always in hiding. Then, when the Polish army was formed, he volunteered because there was a lot of opportunity to steal and kill, it was 1919 or 1920, and they went to fight the Bolsheviks. Right away, they promoted him to corporal and came to town on a white horse, so beautiful, in my life I had never seen such a horse.

A wild man, *nu?* In the tavern, they recounted his deeds. It was said that one time, the Bolsheviks entered an estate, and then he arrived with his company and killed all of them. Then Heller, in Poland, formed an army with all the prisoners, and one day, they were traveling on a train, these savages, and Jews were also traveling there. And a soldier began to cut the beard off a Jew, it was the Poles' favorite sport, they always did it. Then Shimon, as the *melamed's* son was called, got up from his seat and said to the soldier: "Are you crazy? What are you doing?" And the other man answered him, "What does it matter to you?" Shimon didn't say anything more, and he gave him a terrible blow, other soldiers jumped up and a brawl broke out, blows flew, and Shimon took out his revolver and killed the soldier with one shot and threw two more through the train window. They discussed it in the town for a long time after that, what he did with those who considered themselves lords of all Poland and did whatever they felt like. Finally, someone put them in their place, for once they had to pay.

They arrested him to put him on trial, but the mistress of the estate, whom we had once saved, went and used her influence. Since they had to give him some sentence, he got a year in prison. He appealed, and he got two years.

Finally, however, the government offered him a job as a mailman, the kind that traveled with their carts from one town to another, carrying letters. And all this happened, as I said, after the Great War, when we were coming and going from one place to another trying to survive. And there were many stories like this one.

I remember well the day that the Great War began. I was ten years old. Our little village belonged to the Austro-Hungarian empire, and there, Franz Joseph gave the Jews great privileges: they could become officers in the army and things like that. And, well, the war broke out. In these small villages lived only Ukrainians and Jews. We were all in the frontier zone. The Ukrainians were anti-Semites and very privileged, but all the important posts were off-limits to the Jews, they were the ones who ruled, and they never did anything for the benefit of the Jews. Since they held all the power in their hands, they didn't respect the Austrian laws. The only thing the Poles and the Ukrainians had in common is that they called us "Jew-lepers."

One Wednesday, the war began. And war doesn't choose, it kills all, German or Jew or Pole. Two days later, the next Friday, the Cossacks were already in our town, about one hundred kilometers from the front. The Russians entered the war, and sent out about four million Cossacks against the Poles, who were prepared to march in a holiday parade, not to fight. The Hussars were also there, those pretty boys from the Hungarian cavalry, but the Russians destroyed them in a jiffy.

Then the rich folk escaped toward Vienna and the middle class fled to Lemberg, now it's called Lwow, *nu?* And us, the poor folk, we escaped as far as a town about six kilometers from our village. Born there, and we lived there, and we went to that town, Guine. We arrived, and they fed us, I think we were there for a couple of hours, and during the night they wake up my papa and me, and it's a Cossack. They asked for food, but they didn't do anything to us, they only said to us, "Why don't you return to your homes? Nothing will happen there." Then we grabbed the packages and the bread, and we walked back the six kilometers to the place where we lived. And on reaching the town, everything was completely in flames, and we didn't know what to do. Because those who lived in the village, the *goyim*, were robbing shamelessly from the abandoned houses, and after that they burnt them. The Ukrainians from the town were with the Cossacks, and for them the war was the greatest glory in the world, at last they were able to avenge themselves on the Poles and the Jews. For that reason, I want to say that the war kills everything it doesn't respect, it's terrible, but for them it's a party, what do I know? Yes, yes, in Yarchev, the same thing happened. When the Russians and the Ukrainians entered, they burnt down the entire Jewish neighborhood. We were eight days in the cemetery, among the grave stones, hidden there, and the shots and explosions passed over our heads. At night we went out to look for a little water, but during the day we couldn't move.

Because if an army enters a town, it needs the inhabitants, if they are going to burn, it is bad for them, but this general who sent the Russians was an uncle of the Tzar, he was the biggest drunk in the whole world, he was drunk night and day, in the most common way. And he was the one who commanded that army.

I too was ten years old when the war began. We stayed in the town for a few days, hidden, and then we escaped to the nearest big city, to Lemberg. We had at home a brick cellar, and there, half of the Jews from the town left all of their things, and they built a wall to close it up. But the Russians came, burning the houses and later the Ukrainians behind them . . . They stole everything from us, everything. They discovered the cellar, and they took everything, even the window frames, they stole everything, everything, everything.

My father and my grandfather and many generations before them had been born in this town, but there was always hatred between the Ukrainians and the Jews. I remember when I did my military service, and I went into a town, we were on maneuvers. I wanted to eat ears of corn, so I went with a young fellow who was something of a thief to an estate near the village, and we picked ears of corn. I went and asked a woman: "May I cook this corn?" She answers me: "Yes, of course, you can cook it here with straw."

"With straw?"

"Here everything is cooked that way. Straw is used for fuel."

So I tried to cook, and I ended up completely black from the smoke, and the corn was still raw.

"How can it be, ma'am," I asked her, "'that having such forests around the town, down where we are having our maneuvers, that you don't have stuff to cook with? Even bread is made with this straw as fuel . . . "

"Yes," she answered me. "But those forests belong to Polish landowners. Last week, a nineteen-year-old boy went in there to cut a few branches, and they shot him. They killed him, understand, the Polish landowners killed him."

For that reason, they hated the Jews in the villages. Because the police officer and the priest and the overseer were anti-Semites, they had an interest in turning aside the gaze of the landowner, diverting it. So they told the common people, "the Jew is to blame, he's a bloodsucker, a dealer," and now everyone sees them in a bad way; and what's more, no one defended them, it was worse.

At times the peasants and others confronted the landowner, but since he was protected by the policeman and the priest, only the Jew was left for them to deposit that terrible hatred upon. Later, a bit of culture came to the town, I was working in a house where already there was a university student. A medical student, I think, in the fourth year. And they wore caps of different colors: for example, the medical student would wear a green cap, the veterinarian, a blue one, you saw them in the street and, in a glance, you knew the profession. Even the high school students wore uniforms.

There were politicians too. Before the elections of 1923 or 1924, there were campaigns, that's the same everywhere, the charlatans went around speaking in the towns. They said that you are poor for this reason or that, because the Jew has a restaurant. But a boy got up from the audience, a Bolshevik, and he shouted, "The landowner is the one that has everything, and not the Jew, owner of a restaurant, who is only a servant of the powerful owners of the fields and the forests . . . " And the orator got up from the table, and there was trouble, they arrested the young guy.

In my town, in Yarchev, there were some three hundred inhabitants, of which half were Jews and the rest Poles and Ukrainians. In the town council there were thirty-two representatives: sixteen Jews, eight Poles, and eight Ukrainians. That zone now belongs to Russia, but it was always the border of something: after 1918, the Ukrainians came, and they were there for a few months. They threw them out, then the Poles were there from 1920 to 1940, when Hitler came in. And in that year, 1920, in Lemberg, there was a *pogrom*.

All the *goyim* are anti-Semites. Don't trust them, at some moment will flower the Nazi that is inside.

Among *yiddin*, it's different. Even if you don't know them, you feel that you are among family.

Yes, it is something different. You don't have to be so alert.

There was always a great division between Jews and *goyim*. It's also true that when Jews would pass in front of a church, they would cover their heads or spit. That they learned in the *cheder,* they would enter there when they were very young, three years old, it was all very obscurantist and with a great deal of fanaticism from both sides. Some of them made fun of the others. The Ukrainians were nationalistic and volunteered for the army, they didn't want Poles or Jews. But we went to school together: for example, when they had "religion," we went to the patio and stayed outside.

We were in the same grade, for sure, but there was a terrible hatred between the Jews and the non-Jews, we fought. One time, I punched Leibko and almost killed him. And Yushki, I remember how he feared me, because we weren't intimidated, he grabbed a knife—he was my seatmate—and stabbed it into the bench, again and again. He was Ukrainian, it all went over his head, so he made up for it by stabbing the wood of the school desk.

In the classroom, we were seated, Poles with Jews, and each would pinch the other, but outside nothing doing, we didn't mix. Moshé Jutz, who later sold himself to the Nazis and informed on the Jews of the town and its hiding places, had a *tallit,* and the Polish kids pulled the fringes.

I, who did my military service in Poland, can say that there were some who know how to get along with others, you don't have to exaggerate and say that all were anti-Semites. I shared with some as if we were brothers, they were anti-Semitic only because the government was. The Ukrainians and the priests, who didn't have a government, were more anti-Semitic than the Poles, and they possessed greater power.

We couldn't leave here either. We were only forty kilometers from Lemberg, and many people from my village didn't know that city.

The poverty was so great, so great, that we didn't have ten cents for the trolley car, nor could we even dream of traveling. We didn't know about it, and it didn't occur to us, we lived submerged in misery, it's somewhat difficult to understand in this time of trips throughout the world.

I didn't experience such extreme poverty. Moishe Burech was a tailor, and he had enough work. The trade had been in his family for generations.

But papa was very ambitious. His error always was to try to do more than he really could. His friends would ask him, "Why don't you save up enough before you start building?," and he would answer, "If I wait until I have the capital, I'll never build anything."

Then he began to build. He worked from Monday to Friday, and when he delivered the suits and collected for them, the bricklayer, carpenter, and others were waiting at his door, and finally he was left with nothing. He spent his time building. He made there two cellars and a barn for the cows, I don't know why he did so much.

But there were other tailors, such a Yussi Schnaider or Zalman Schnaider, who really were starving to death and who didn't have work, wearing themselves out there in the dust and the mud of the town, dark streets, and wagon drivers' shouts.

A friend of papa's once said that he was poor because he lacked ten cents. For in that place, from Monday to Friday, they ate anything, but on the Sabbath, this friend prepared a special meal, and he didn't have ten cents to buy the candles, so he couldn't act like a rich man. Simply put, he couldn't make it, that's the way it was, he couldn't make it. This Zalman Schnaider was a good tailor, but . . .

It was awful. In the winter, the children went barefoot in the snow. There was another neighbor, also poor, a butcher, but his trade was better than the tailor's. At least, from time to time, he had a bit of meat or soup, and he gave some to Zalman's children, so that they wouldn't die of hunger. In my house, when we children cried because we were hungry, mama would put us to bed and always say, "Be quiet, go to sleep, tomorrow I'll have bread for you."

Ambition and the desire for progress, the search for a way out that we see now, just didn't exist. You walk in front of a store and stop to look in, and you think what did this fellow do to achieve this, perhaps I could do the same. There were stores in the town, and you passed them from a distance—since nothing was within reach, nothing was of interest, you didn't worry about it.

My wife, for example, came from a very poor place, they didn't pay rent because that shack belonged to them. What did they lack? They made ropes for pulling carts, all kinds of ropes. If they had had a little more ambition, during the week they could have made a lot of rope, carry it to the city and sell it there. But no, they were sitting in that hut, and a peasant came to buy rope from them, and he gave them a coin or a kilo of potatoes, and it's a deal. They sat there until another customer arrived. It didn't occur to them to try to better themselves.

Papa had a lot of work, he was a very well-known tailor. For example, they would bring him an overcoat to repair, and he always said yes, and he threw it on top of the clothes basket that sat in the corner which we jokingly called *toit shtible*, the death house, because the pieces of clothing stayed there and nobody touched them for three months. Everyone wanted their clothes for the holidays. *Pesach* was drawing near, and they begged him. "Moishe Burech, are you going to make this jacket for me?" He said yes to him too, and when that guy left, he would say, "V*orfes haran en toit shtible*," and, pum, it would fall on the "the little house of death." When the day arrived, half of his clients came in tears, begging him to do the work.

He didn't know how to take advantage of the situation, get some workers, and take charge of things by having them make the suits . . . No, he sewed by himself, or at most, with his children, and after that he used to go over to chat with his friends or play dominos.

We also had a few cows that gave us milk. From time to time, we went to help the peasants with the harvest, and they paid us with part of what the land gave them. We went to dig potatoes, and they gave us in payment about forty bags of potatoes, we had a basement full for the winter, that was in good times.

Yes, because in bad times, when the war came, my brother died when he didn't have a potato to eat. And there were others who were always bad off, always starving, without milk and without potatoes or anything.

Papa had both Jewish and non-Jewish clients, they respected him. But nevertheless, when the war came, the same ones who had been his clients came to rob and loot, taking advantage of the fires and the disorder. Not all, of course, but some were thieves by custom.

Almost all, bah, Mechl had a restaurant, and he put a jar of candy at the entrance, and he left it and didn't keep an eye on it. Each *goy* who entered stole a piece of candy. Later on Mechl charged them more for each beer. Leaving the candies for them was part of the deal, they liked to steal.

The *goyim* were also, for the most part, very poor. I had a Polish friend, Krantz, who once brought me a pear as a gift, because he had pear trees. The pear was so pretty, almost all of them had dark skin, but this one was very beautiful. You have to understand the importance of a pretty and juicy pear in that misery. Krantz told me that what was in the tree had already been completely sold except for the one he brought me, and they only ate the ones that fell on the ground. They couldn't touch the others. All this brought hatred with it, resentment, the desire to kill.

Mechl's father, the one with the restaurant, was a very capable Austrian. He dedicated himself to many different things; he sold land, he was a wig maker, and above all, he was very good with his mouth, he was a great charlatan. He did everything by talking. He always talked about fortunes that he had made in other towns, and that he brought to Yarchev, although, in reality, he was hardly able to get married, and he didn't have enough to rent a room.

Papa, then, lent him a room provisionally, until he could find something else. He came with all the odds and ends that he had, piled up on a small cart, he set up a barber shop in the same room in which he slept. But when he began to speak in the town's tavern . . .

Do you remember? Poor Moishe Burech. The other guy told how he arrived in Yarchev with an enormous amount of luggage, in two wagons, coupled together, each one with eighteen wheels, with velvet sofas and a dozen chairs from Vienna and so on. Papa was sitting and listening, and the guy asked him from time to time: "Do you remember Moishe Burech, those velvet sofas?," and he went on making it all up. What could papa answer him, if the *schvitzer* seriously believed in what he was inventing?

Mechl, the son, came out the same way. He wasn't a meter, fifty in height, but he claimed that he'd hit all the drunks in the town, that he had a dirty punch and stuff like that.

Once, he said that, while doing his military service, he was washing his hands in the sink and two huge Poles, cavalrymen, bothered him, hitting him on the back of the neck. He said to them: "Stop joking," but they kept on bothering him; so, Mechl grabbed their heads, and brought them together so they hit each other, he left the two of them on the floor unconscious, and he left.

In that café that they had, the restaurant, the Jews went to chat and tell stories, but the customers, in general were *goyim*. Every so often, there was trouble, fights between drunks, then they rushed to call Carlos, and he came and he gave them a thrashing and threw them out of the place, like in the movies. And later, Mechl would say that he had thrown them all out, he said it so many times that he believed it himself, he repeated the details of the thrashing, the same way Carlos would tell it to him. It was funny.

With all that about the poverty and the persecutions, what do I know, it was nice to spend your days there, to live in those small villages. We lived there, we grew up there. You can't turn history around and start anew.

family tree

Now, the photograph that I kept on my night table. I made a copy for you, doctor. Here it is.

What do you think? Doesn't it say anything to you? I, on the other hand, can't look at it for more than a few seconds without my eyes filling with tears. I don't know why, I can't control it. An inexplicable feeling of infinite tenderness, the only and the sweetest connection with reality left to me. I have already ascertained that my name is David Schnaiderman, forty years old, two children, a degree in sociology. And? Everything else is missing. Knowing who I am, not who others say I am.

The photograph was taken about 1928, in Yarchev, a village on the Russo-Polish border. Bring over this magnifying glass: if you push the button, there is a light. There, that's it. Now, look carefully.

The source, the first place. The floor of tamped-down earth, not passable when first rains come, snowmen and children's games in the snow. Do you understand? Every detail leads to childhood stories, anecdotes heard near the stove, sounds of a music that I can scarcely perceive.

They are dressed in their best get-ups, but the house is extremely poor. It's a family of tailors, each one owns *one* suit for "going out." Not two, one. If it tears, backside in the air until it's sewn. What you see in the back is the outhouse, grooved metal pieces on the roof and walls made out of wood that will burn like a tinderbox during the Great War, in the *pogroms*. And rebuilt again and again. Strong and resinous wood from the nearby forest. That metal roof, where at night Chagall's fiddlers will pass by, is not enough to hide the fact that the bathroom is found outside the house, in the patio, with a door that doesn't reach to the floor and through which the cold Polish wind filters without being considerate, with flute-like sounds, chilling the women's' bladders and kids who run there before going to sleep. Keep using the magnifying glass: the wall behind them, bricks that are barely on top of one another, without plastering. Dividing wall with the neighbor, marker of that earthy patio where my roots were planted, so poor and at the same time so full of dignity and joy.

Do you understand, doctor? Let's begin with the faces. The details. Push the button so that the light helps you visualize the image enlarged by the glass. That's it. Look at that shawl on the great-grandmother, the one who sells vegetables at little town fairs, with shouts, interjections, movement of the carts, smell of horses. That necklace on the grandmother, at her side, and the light eyes and the face without wrinkles. The climate of repressed emotion in those strong faces, full of vitality, brought together for the last family photograph before beginning the breakup, the trip to America, the chimera of a wished for and improbable meeting in the Argentine pampas. The place where, many years later, I would go on without knowing why I like to eat French bread smeared with butter, raw onion, some salt, as my favorite food. Or my blood would encounter louder echoes in the turbulent gusts of winter, hard and obstinate, than in that bland and dulling summer that drowns me, while, at my side, everyone seems to enjoy the damp perspiration. Summer is almost inconceivable in this dirt-filled patio that I look at as someone hypnotized.

And Moishe Burech, my grandfather. Seated at the center of the photograph, hatless patriarch, undefined smile, almost Leonardo-like in its expression. See his eyes with the magnifying glass, please. The mischief and decision that are there in his gaze. Now, view slowly, with the glass, each one of the other faces. Obviously, you don't know them as I do. But don't you read a possible story in each one of them? Can't you recognize will and pride in those thick lips, pushed forward? Perhaps a bit of tameness, even humiliation, in that other face? Sensation of not fitting or being tired of living or obstinate and creative faith in that fist, that gesture, that flower on the lapel or that tip of a handkerchief emerging coquettishly, re-splendent? Signs, in all, of an illusory reality, frozen in its splendor and, for that reason, revealing.

My entire story is in that photograph, although I would only be born many years later, on this side of the Atlantic. That undefined smile of Moishe Burech would repeat in the stories that, uselessly, he would try to tell me in a tiled patio in Villa del Parque. He seated, with a cripple's chair and a Slavic-accented Yiddish, full of consonants. I couldn't understand him, entrenched in an exquisite Spanish that he would never understand, condemned to not communicating, to never being able to exchange a word, only friendly gestures and affectionate kisses. Each of us speaking in his own language.

I never understood him, and now I miss him. What would my grandfather have wanted to tell me, doctor? What events would he evoke, what connections could he have transmitted to me in that unintelligible language?

I am sure that, if I had understood then, everything would be much simpler for me now.

PATER FAMILIAE

All my family were tailors. Tailor after tailor. And like all tailor families, we weren't well off. At home, each boy had only one pair of pants, there were many brothers . . . there was racism in the Polish school, it was very difficult to enter, they only accepted five Jews a year. Even so, those who were able to be admitted had to put up with a Catholic ceremony before class. One of my brothers, who still was very young, wanted to go to the bathroom during the ceremony, and since they didn't let anyone leave until it was over, he wet himself. When he returned home, he had to wait, sitting on a stool, until my father made him a new pair of pants. That's how we lived.

We were about ten in our family and my mother was a very hard worker. She made the bread herself, washed the clothes, fixed up the house for parties. She worked a great deal to take care of all of us . . . On Friday, she got up at three in the morning, prepared the white bread for Saturday and the cake, we kept on sleeping. She woke us up and brought fresh cake to the bed. She was so good.

We had two cows, hens, ducks. In order to eat, we would go to the hen house. We would wait for a hen to lay an egg, and so, still warm, we would break the shell and suck. Uncooked, raw. All of that was great. And later they would milk the cow and they gave us some right there, with the rest of the milk they made cheeses and butter. It was so in the good times, during my childhood, before the war. We were poor, but we ate well. We went to play ball, on Saturday for example, four or five hours of play, we returned home hungry, and mama brought in some large pots of curdled milk which she got from the cow we had, and she also made potato *varenichkes*, we ate everything all together, and we filled ourselves well. And we were satisfied.

My house was very large. It was growing by bits and pieces. There were about six rooms and something like an attic, I don't know how to say it in Spanish. Food was kept there for the cows in winter. We left the bedroom empty, and we went there because the aroma of the dry straw was so nice, we threw ourselves on to it, and we slept on the hay without anyone bothering us . . . it was better than being in bed.

We were ten children, but three died when they were little. We also had two dogs, a bitch and a puppy. They were named Bianca and Luck. They searched for their own food in the forest, and one day they came home with bullets in their sides; the forest warden had shot them. Fortunately they weren't hit in vital spots, they came home bleeding, but they recovered quickly, by licking their wounds.

I mentioned the school a moment ago. I finished the school in my village, in Yarchev. There were four "popular grades" and then three more grades, which were taught just like high school over here. Anybody who wanted to study more had to go to Lemberg, which was the district capital. I learned languages: Russian, German, Polish, of course, Yiddish which we spoke at home also. There is History, Geography, Mathematics, and all that. There, all the children went to *cheder* until nine or ten at least, later on they study Talmud and all that stuff. It was a tiny room, pretty filthy, there were tables separated one from the other where we sat until nightfall. The *rebbe* used to collect the children; he would call for them and pick up into his arms those who didn't want to come, and he sat them down on benches around a large table. The room was part of his own home, everything was small, hardly a shack. And that's the way it was.

All the religious men wore curly *paies*, hats, those large capes. And for the Sabbath, they wore fancy hats made from fox tails. When they got married, they bought that sort of hat for the groom and cut the bride's hair—because she wasn't allowed to continue wearing it—and they put a wig and scarf on her. They bathed every so often. There is a joke that was told there: One day this guy goes to the public baths, and when he is about to leave, he says, "Oy, I forgot my undershirt." You know when he found it? The next year, before

Pesach, when he went to the baths, he found he was wearing it. It's a joke to show that they never bathed or changed clothes. There were many sects among the religious folk, each had its own *rebbe*. And each time that the *rebbe* came to visit, he came in a cart, then the fanatics untied the horses, they hitched themselves to the cart, and they dragged him to the village, singing Hasidic songs and dancing . . . Fanatics . . . They were really fanatics.

Well, I was talking about the school and I went off in another direction. I did the first five grades in Lemberg, because we went there when the war began, and I finished through the seventh in the village, as I said before—when we returned. In the upper grades, anti-Semitism was stronger. Boys and girls went to school together. Among the girls, there was only one Jew; among the boys, I was the only one, eight Ukrainians, four Poles and me. That was my grade. I attended school without books of my own. I would pay strict attention to the teacher's explanations, the girls would lend me books, and later I would let them copy my homework. For that they lent me the books . . . The studies were difficult, lots of languages. The younger Jews spoke Yiddish at home, but in the street they were embarrassed and spoke Polish among themselves. But we in the high school weren't intimidated; all of us were big and strong. Carlos was always the strongest of the brothers, though Jacobo wasn't far behind when using his fists. He had so much strength in his wrists that there wasn't anybody who could beat him in arm wrestling, not over there in Poland and not here. But Carlos is the biggest overall . . . Well, he was sitting in school as quiet as could be when he heard some snickering, and he went over to see what was happening. Some boys were harassing a Jewish schoolmate, they were pulling his hair and throwing around his *kippa*, shoving and laughing. We weren't religious, but we were Jewish. So a terrible fury gripped Carlos, when he saw what they were doing to the poor boy. He grabbed an inkwell and slammed it down on one of the boys; he did it with such force that he split the fellow's head open. The teacher expelled him from the high school, and on the way home, he imagined he'd get a good beating, but when he got there and recounted what had happened, Moishe Burech congratulated him.

Another time, I remember, a teacher was about to hit him, I don't know why, and the basement happened to be open. Carlos jumped aside, and she went after him and she fell down the basement steps. Yes, we were all very cheeky. At Christmas time, Polish students came down to our neighborhood, "little" boys in uniforms and hats like the rich kids over here, they carried canes and they came to beat us up, to enjoy themselves, hitting Jews. They would put a razor blade on the point of the cane to turn it into a weapon, and when they saw a religious man, they shook him hard and cut off his beard with their knives. At that point, the cart drivers, the butchers, some of us Jewish boys got together, with stones and chains, and we gave them what for, even though the police helped them out. Once they even brought revolvers and scared us off with their shooting. Then, in the tumult, a rock split open the head of one of us. We used home remedies to cure ourselves, putting bread and butter on the wound, and then back to the fight. But they couldn't chase us away.

My father too was very brave. Violent, huge, very strong. They used to say at home that newly married, he left the temple to stroll by the . . . no, no, it wasn't a plaza. I'll explain what the villages were like; he walked into the area where you bought things like . . . a marketplace, yes a marketplace. And the houses of the Jews and their stores were around the marketplace. Those who came to market, the peasants, left their horses and carts there, after selling their fruits and vegetables, they went to buy at the stores, at all the Jewish businesses that were nearby. And it happened that one of the peasants, after selling his things, got drunk and began to take a swipe at every Jew he met. He grabbed them by the beard and threw them to the ground, or he smacked them hard, he broke store windows. He was a huge man with an enormous physique, a savage. The Jews began to close up shop, they were afraid. My old man walked over and saw what was going on. He said to my mama, "Let's see, Hettie, let me go, *Luzmir nuj de ant*"-because they were arm and arm. She was frightened.

"What are you going to do, Moishe Burech, if you please?"

"Not a thing, be calm," he says. "Let go of my arm."

Then he comes up to the guy and says to him,

"Are you the son of a bitch who's hitting folks?"

"I am," says the guy, a bit surprised. "Why?"

Then my father gave him such a wallop that the guy fell to the stone path. Sparks seemed to fly. And lying on the ground, he said: "I'm tough to have taken such a blow!"

But he wasn't going to hit any more Jews on that day. For his efforts, they gave my father fourteen days in jail. The police had come to see what was going on, and the fellow sat with his face torn apart. They were newlyweds, the night before, so Moishe Burech spent the two weeks of his honeymoon in jail, with his wife alone at home.

We were all like that. Really violent, or else we would have died young, we wouldn't have survived. Another time that I remember, a peasant brought a cart of potatoes to sell and got into a dispute with my papa, I don't know why, and he called him something like *Yip*, which means something like "stinking Jew." He grabbed the horse's whip and from atop the cart, he hit my father. Carlos was inside, sewing with the machine, and the neighbor children came in and said to him, "Hey, they're beating up your dad." Carlos ran out and when he saw the guy with the whip, he went crazy. He grabbed him by his clothing, pulled him down, and beat the shit out of him. One punch left him bleeding and unconscious on the ground. Then he returned to the sewing machine and sat there as if nothing had happened. The police came. "Who hit you?," they asked the peasant because the police only came when they were beaten, not when they beat up Jews. He was still half out of it, he said, "I think it was the tailor." They come inside and they ask. Carlos says, "Me? I never left here. I'm sewing on the machine. I don't know anything." And they couldn't do anything, but that peasant would think twice before hitting Jews.

Over there you had to take what you could find. For example, I got along by mooching bread and butter from some kids we played with. The kids' father had not been in the war because he was missing an arm. He was in the black market, importing and exporting meat; in those days they had everything. The scheme worked so: four or five of us were playing and four or five of us including Jacobo went to the bathroom. When we got back we made hissing sounds so that the other kid would feel like pissing; we told him to go and do it. "You're not going to piss with bread in your hand," I would tell him. "Give it to me, and I'll hold it for you while you go to the john." And so he went. And we ate all the bread and butter and marmalade. When he came back, there was nothing left. Then the fellow began to cry, and he went home. His mother realized that I had done it because I was so hungry, so she said to him, "Don't cry." She gave him another piece of bread with butter and marmalade and invited me too.

The same with sleds in the winter. We used to borrow them, to slide "just once" in the snow, and good-bye, they never saw them again. They got angry but not too angry. They wanted us as friends because we defended them from the Ukrainians and Poles who wanted to beat them up. And the stamps? I'd get a fellow to take out his wallet to trade stamps, and when he began looking at them, Jacobo came running by and grabbed them up in a scarf he carried. Later, we divided them up.

I also liked to go to the movies a lot, but I never had the money. In those days, you could get in by bribing the usher (as they call them here) or even the janitor. We didn't have enough money to do even that, so I took some tin buttons from Moishe Burech's tailor shop, and I put them on the trolley rail, when the car went by, they were flattened so that they looked like coins. Then, I went to the movies when the picture had already begun, I gave the usher a used ticket, and a bit of metal that seemed like a coin tip, and he let us in. As many boys did the same thing, when they turned on the lights, they had no way of knowing who had given coins and who bits of metal. You understand? That's how we went to the movies.

You had to "arrange" things, as they say here. We would go to the orchard that belonged to the parish priest, and we would steal pears from the cellar where he saved them for the winter . . . like the refrigerators we have today . . . a storehouse. We would put sticks through an air hole, spear pears, and take them out one by one. You don't forget the taste of those pears. I've eaten in many restaurants in many countries, but nothing has ever equaled the tasted of those stolen pears.

In Yerushe Nove, there was a market where they sold animals. So, to buy them cheaper, two Jews made an agreement and would act in this way: one would go up to the vender and ask him. "What are you selling the hen for?" The fellow would answer, for example, "Ten rubles." The Jew would say, "I'll offer you three rubles." He would make a sign, and the other Jew would greet him, "Sholem Aleichem. How are you? How are you doing? Are you going to buy this hen? At three rubles? Are you crazy? Don't you see it has a *nedel*? Are you really going to buy a hen that has a *nedel*?" It was a made-up word. It didn't mean anything. Finally, when they had driven the seller so completely crazy, he let them have it for three rubles, convinced that he had sold them the worst animal in the world.

Another way was if they noticed that the hen was about to lay an egg. In that case, they would say that they had to feel the hen to see if it were any good. They pretended to check it, and they put the egg in their pocket, and then they returned it, saying they didn't want it. We lived that way. Poverty sharpened our wits.

Another time I remember, we were in the synagogue, it was some holiday or other, and a policeman entered to arrest a Jew for having deserted from the army. He was a friend, so papa grabbed the policeman and shook him while his buddy escaped. Result: two more weeks in jail. As if Moishe Burech were a permanent client of the police station.

But Carlos was even worse, because of his unmatched strength, and he never thought about the consequences of what he did. His hobby was to toss the drunks out of the tavern, next door to the house, Mechl's place. I remember that once there was a family, famous for its seven huge brothers, Ukrainians and ferocious, the Chismitsky's. They were so bad that if you wanted to insult somebody in the village, you'd call him a Chismitsky. One of them, who was about one meter eighty tall, found himself in the bar on a day when Carlos was kicking a drunk out. The huge fellow got angry. "No Jew is going to hit a Christian in my presence!" he roared. Carlos grabbed him quickly and dragged him to the sidewalk and hit him with such a blow that he flew across the street and bounced against the railing of the front walk. That Chismitsky ended up deaf and with three less teeth. The next day, Carlos went out armed, with a revolver in full view, and every time that one of the brothers came near, he would say to him: "Come in, come in, so I can put three shots in you and leave you dead like a dog." Finally a Jewish harrier, who was a client of the Chismitskys, acted as a go-between and arranged for a "Peace Treaty" between the opposing sides, and we all finished it off by toasting with beer in the tavern. It had to be there.

Another time, we went to recover a pigeon that they had taken from Carlos, who, since he was little, had worked with birds. He knows how to speak to them, he raises them, he feeds them, he cures their illnesses better than any veterinarian, sixty years dedicated almost exclusively to the birds. Well, when we arrived at the thief's house, the fellow had hidden an iron rod behind his back, held so, and when Carlos began to protest, the guy suddenly took it out and smashed him in the head. When he tried to repeat the blow, Carlos, still dazed, grabbed the iron bar and, like a crazy man, began beating the man with it. There was no way to stop him, I had to throw myself over the guy's body and stay on top of him to stop the blows, otherwise, he certainly would have killed him. My brother was like that.

Life made us hard. Anti-Semitism was stirred up by the government, the police always intervened on the side of the others, we couldn't count on anyone. We had to defend ourselves. The taxes, for example; when someone couldn't pay, the inspectors came and took everything; they were terrible. The sheets, the overcoats, the blankets—which were very thick there as it was very cold—they took everything out to the street and carried it away with them. They would take a peasant's last cow, which meant death for poor people.

Once an inspector came to ask for a bribe, just as they do here. He said something or other to my papa, that he give him money or he would turn him in: Moishe Burech looked at him, dropped his trousers and said, *"Vis guelt? Kishmir in tuches."* "You want money? Kiss my ass."

These inspectors didn't frighten him. You have to imagine the situation, not just anyone would have dared. The fight with those people was like that, they were so bad. Because of all of that, first my brothers, and later I came to Argentina. You couldn't live there any longer. The anti-Semitism was unbearable. In the university, they put in quotas. I think that they called it "numerus clausus" or something like that. They ruled that for every hundred students admitted, there would be ninety-four Poles, four Ukrainians, and two Jews. And law was the only thing Jews could study, that's why there were so many Jewish lawyers. They weren't allowed to study medicine or engineering, they just couldn't enter those fields. And they made life impossible for those who were admitted, they hit them, they avoided them. The tension was constant.

Moishe Burech lived with those nerves, always, he spent all day at the sewing machine, sewing and cutting, you have to imagine such a large man with so much energy, keeping it all inside, every so often he would explode. One time two large fellows, Polish grenadiers, came to pick up a suit. I re-

member that it was a Sunday morning, and the work wasn't ready. So one of them pounded on the table and shouted, "What do you mean that it isn't ready yet," and he cursed my father.

My papa, without showing any emotion, said to my mama: "Hettie, efnmer of detir."

She opened the door—the others hadn't understood, of course, because Moishe Burech spoke in Yiddish—and my papa grabbed the first one by the lapels, raising him into the air, then with one punch he knocked him out of the house. He gave the second fellow a terrible beating. The two of them had to escape through the rear of the house, because people were returning from church, they'd been to Mass, and those fellows were embarrassed—they were just teenagers—that people see that they had taken such a beating, their faces, their noses covered with blood.

The story stayed with us. We would say, "Hettie, efnmer of detir." And everyone knew the rest. But he wouldn't pick a fight, never. He only defended himself and didn't let anyone put him down. He had his pride, that was it. He didn't like to fight.

Precisely because of that, they respected Moishe Burech in the village, despite it being full of anti-Semites. Even your enemy is thrown off when there is dignity. At the time that they were putting up a slaughterhouse in the village, they demanded a huge bribe. The commission was formed of four goyim and my papa. They stole, they stole everything, and they said to him, "Don't be stupid, drop off a truckload of bricks at your house, the town will pay for it." He never took anything, never. Later, the plan was discovered and a group of officials came to investigate, and the director came over to congratulate my papa, he was the only clean one of the whole group. He was straight, very straight.

Mama took care of the house. She hit us and stuff like that, but she wasn't violent. Once when Abraham came in crying because the teacher hit him, papa got up from his sewing machine, went to the school, grabbed the teacher, and shook him, two swift blows; there was a cellar there, he threw him down into the cellar. He spent three

35

weeks wasting away in jail for that one. Mama took care of the household; but defense was papa's job.

He didn't let himself be provoked nor be taken advantage of, so he was a calm man, very calm. He worked silently with the machine, and his fights were always with his fists, he never used arms nor practiced with them. But from the moment he got angry, he was like that, really wild.

Moishe Burech wasn't very religious, but he went to *shul* on Friday night and Saturday. He was very advanced for his times, not at all fanatical. Everyone in town thought highly of him; when there were municipal elections, there were sixteen Jews and sixteen gentiles, and he was elected councilman in both races, that's to say the two lists. They liked him that much. In town there was a saying that was often repeated: "You want the truth? Go to Moishe Burech." He was a moral authority in the village, they respected him because he never lied, he had principles. He knew the area well, because we had been there for several generations, and he also had some knowledge of engineering, surveying, and things like that. So, whenever there was a lawsuit over a piece of land or the boundaries of a lot, they immediately called on my father to resolve it. He was very fair at those things. It could have to do with his best friend, but if the other person was in the right . . . he would judge in his favor. He was like that.

When he was little, the city burned from end to end, and then it was rebuilt. He remembered all the plots, the boundaries of every lot. Once there was a lawsuit between a woman and her neighbor—about a small piece of land, a common event—and the man was rich, a client of my father's, and the neighbor was a poor widow. In those days, disputes were settled by a *mensch*, one man was named for each side. And the widow chose my father, and the guy knew that if my father was there, he lost. You had to be there, half of our income depended on that man and his children. The guy came over and said to him, "Moishe Burech, I want something from you. I'm not going to ask you to lie, I know that you are not going to do that. Only say no, don't be the mediator and let someone else do it." He answered, "No. I have to defend the widow," and he went there, and the woman won the case. The man never brought us any more work.

Because of all that, my father refused to ever leave the village, he was very attached to Yarchev. Everybody loved him, he was a big shot there. An engineer, for example, would call him when they were building a city structure, he came to ask for Moishe Burech's measurements, he asked him advice. He had the village in his head. Like a walking archive, that's how he was. Several generations of our ancestors were born there, my father went to Polish school, and to the *cheder* in the little village. There was a neighbor there, Marash, the one from the bar. After supper on Friday nights, the most progressive fellows got together, and I went to read the Polish newspaper to them.

They discussed politics there, papa, Marash, and three or four got together to fix the world. I don't know why they were so progressive, because of their formation or what they were born with.

Of course, there were no rabbis at these meetings. Moishe Burech had little or no religious belief. He had a paid seat in the *shul*, like all the families, but he rarely went. His parents weren't religious either. My grandfather was a tailor too, and my grandmother had a stand in the market, she sold fruits, vegetables. More fruit. She always said to the old man, to her husband, that he ought to give up his trade. "A *soifer*, a scribe, can work into his seventies, as a *schnaider* you can't reach that age." Because of the eyes, of course. And she was right, the old man saw himself obliged to leave the trade, and he helped her in the market.

Now there was also a branch of the family that went to the United States. One brother and two sisters of my papa. We never knew anything more about them; for us, it was like a legend. I know that they got rich there, because they bought land where oil began to pour out, so they gave them a fortune for it, they earned a lot of money. They separated themselves from us, and it was partially my papa's fault, because he was very proud. Such pride can't be described.

After the First World War, when Moishe Burech and Abraham returned from the trenches, the brother and the sisters sent him an enormous package from the United States, with gifts and money. My papa, without opening anything, returned it to the senders. He didn't want to have anything to do with them.

They were angry because of an old story; we built the house on a large piece of land, half belonging to my grandfather, half belonging to my father. Papa said that he bought it, and they said he took it from grandfather, those family stories. Then they got angry. Moishe Burech couldn't tolerate anyone doubting his word. Throughout the entire village, it was known that he never lied. He could allow himself to kill before he could lie. Then he broke off from them, and he didn't want to know anything more. Another time they wrote to my mother, sending her a photo of my cousin who had been a beauty queen, MISS BOSTON. But it was the same, papa never let us answer. I don't know what happened to them.

family tree

I can only guide myself by the images that that great old man left in the others: one of my cousins remembers him shortly after he arrived from Europe, walking with difficulty, with a cane, his back rigid and the violence of his character intact, still restrained, like bubbly steam that finds its container too oppressive.

I spot him near the curb on the way to his work, an autumn morning. The cane tapped rhythmically, that uneven walk that kids would maliciously call "the gimp." An enormous rat, running in the gutter of Cochabamba Street. The grandfather isn't disturbed, he keeps up the rhythm of the cane, and almost without looking, he quickly takes advantage of the falling stick to distract him, and with a sharp blow, he disembowels the rodent. He continues walking unperturbed, violent, almost brutal, but tranquil.

Other stories existed, too. The one in which Moishe Burech refused to immigrate, to abandon that little village where he had become a respected patriarch. For that reason, he never could adapt to Argentina or learn the language. That he was always a good-for-nothing, with little taste for work, obliged by his wife to return to tailoring, the sewing machine, and the needle every day. The story that he was an extraordinary man (the image somewhat idealized by the distance, perhaps), a valiant Jew who never bowed his head nor turned his gaze away, even if he was dealing with the highest authority or the risk of death. Of his almost superhuman, pious wisdom that allowed him to confront that death when it arrived, with enormous dignity. Of a soft moralistic Jew, advanced in a time of backwardness and fanaticisms, natural leader of his group. The one about a person who, with ten generations of ancestors in that place, had to live close by to Polish and Ukrainian neighbors who yelled "Stinking Jew" at him. The one about the religious man of the last few years, sitting in the sun on the patio, crutch and cane leaning against the chair; or pleading to God that he cure his legs or let him die like a man.

Who was he really, the grandfather? I notice, doctor, that seeking him—in Europe and here, in Israel, at the trial where I have to appear—I will find myself. I will be able to understand and prolong our survival, to know why I am alive, what I should answer, who I am.

Incident, memory, photo, crime which is dubious or invented, in your opinion. Police citation, psychotherapeutic treatment. The figure of Moishe Burech. I myself, my children. Roots, trunks, extremities of the tree that I must decipher. I am lost among my own echoes: Argentine, Jew, past, present . . . Interrogate the other old folks, engrave me with them, make me take on the personality of the speakers of my memory, witnesses of my childhood. Study my loves and my dreams, please. And discover that common denominator that the judge demands of me.

Here's a check, as an advance, for your work. Come on, don't look at me that way. Help me.

PATER FAMILIAE

Religious people and progressives. It wasn't as simple as it is now to separate them, but . . . you could see, you knew that you weren't the same. My mother Hettie was always a bit more religious. Papa was, for his time, a very advanced man who didn't accept explanations like "God wants it so" and "He knows why." He made us say the morning prayers but without checking on us, hardly murmuring. In contrast, my uncle from Lemberg, when we were there, made me recite completely all the prayers, out loud, so that I didn't miss a single syllable.

Mama lit the candles, she always went to *shul* with us, then we went home and said the prayer with the cup of wine and all the kids. On Saturday, we acted like the religious people, you didn't cook or turn on the lights, it was sort of sacred. In comparison with the fanatics, we weren't very religious, but we were observant, we followed the traditions half way, like those on the outskirts.

Saturday morning, we would get up early. We would wash and put on special clothes for temple, then, when we got back, mama prepared breakfast. Once in a while a *goy* came at noon and heated up the food, but most of the people did it this way: Friday afternoon, they lit the oven and the firewood burned slowly. On Saturday, when they took out the lunch, it was cooked and still hot. A little later, in the afternoon, when we lit the candles, we would light the fire again.

There were religious people who were liberal and those who were strict, for there were many fanatics. There were also Zionist groups, many were formed . . . From argument to argument, Saturday mornings we got up early, I slept in the attic—and we went to steal apples from the priest. The Catholic Church had its own orchard with lots of apples, and we went there when it was scarcely dawn, and we made packages with our pants and shirts, we filled them all with apples, and we tied them up. We escaped by jumping over the wall. Then we would go up into the attic and eat them. Once the parish priest sent the dog after us, and we couldn't get down from the tree. It was dangerous, a huge dog, like a German shepherd. He kept us up there in the branches for more than an hour.

Okay, let me go on about the religious Jews. All the food was *kosher* there. Ham, we never touch. We had a lot of milk from the cows and mama made cream, butter, cheeses . . . all week, because in that place, you only ate meat on Shabbat. There were two Jewish butchers and one *shohet* who slaughtered one or two cows for the Sabbath, and that was sold to the Jews only, only the part from the rump was sold to the *goyim*.

There were two temples: one belonged to the fanatics and the other to the progressives. We went to that one, a beautiful building with benches. Moishe Burech had bought his seat, and we always went with him, we stayed beside his bench. The women were in the balcony, like an opera, and they looked down, they heard the cantor, everything, but separate. In the other *shul*, the one belonging to the fanatics, the women didn't enter, only the men, and their women went to the progressives' temple. Their *shul* was smaller, filthy, how to explain it, you couldn't compare. In ours, there were bathrooms and everything. You left rested. Every so often, they called my father to read from the Torah. On the holidays, those who read gave a donation and with that the synagogue was maintained. The rich made large donations, the poor whatever they could.

We were there every Friday and Saturday without fail. And on Saturday nights, we went to the other one, the stricter one, because they chatted in the dark until the candles were lit, all the men got together and talked.

Also, we celebrated the holidays: *Hanukkah*, *Pesach*, we collected all the crumbs of bread, we looked everywhere because they spread them on purpose, a bit of bread here and another little bit there, we put everything in a ladle and then tied it up, everything is a custom, to clean the house before the holiday . . . and *Shavuot* and *Lag BaOmer*, when we went with the *rebbe* to the forest, and there we sang and played, as if it were a picnic. On *Hanukkah*, a candle was lit for the first day, two the second day, and so on, on the side of the candelabra was put the *shamesh,* a little candle always burning, that was used to light the other candles. Papa always sang a prayer and then played cards. In the *cheder* and at home too, over there, the game was called "31," here we play "21" and the *dreidel.*

Pesach, for sure, was a lovely holiday. We burned the crumbs that we'd collected, and the everyday plates were put away, we used *Pesach* dishes, all new, for eating, drinking, everything. Papa by himself searched for the bread crumbs and burnt all of them at nine in the morning, more or less, and at noon we ate potatoes with butter, and we waited for that night, for at the *seder*, we really ate. There was chopped fish and meat and *kneidlach* and stuff like that. Beforehand, the floors were washed, the house was painted, we had a woman who came to help us, it was a complete cleaning. We bathed and changed clothes, everything was new to celebrate *Pesach*. We didn't forget that it was the holiday of the liberation, when we left Egypt.

After *Yom Kippur* came *Sukkus, Sukkot* in Hebrew. On the side of my house, we had a bit of land, and so my father built a *sukkah*, a hut. We would go to the river and look for reeds, and we made a roof, then we took a fruit which here I think they call a melon or something like that, we cleaned it and we made some holes, and we put candles in them. They looked like lamps. We hung up the four melons with candles, we decorated the *sukkah*, it was something to behold. We put up other decorations, and at night, we went there to eat and to pray. We made the roof with holes in it so we could see the sky. We brought in a table with chairs, and there were neighbors who didn't have any land, so we ended our singing, and we lent them the hut, so that they could celebrate too.

Before *Yom Kippur,* my mother would always prepare soup with *kreplach* that she made with chicken giblets. My children say that I always remember the food, when I speak of Poland or of the holidays, but they don't know what it is like to be really hungry, the war. Everything is terrible, you always feel hungry, that you are never going to have enough to eat, that you could eat forever without stopping.

Okay, I'll continue, in the morning, they did *kapure* with the hen: you grab it by the neck, say a prayer in Yiddish (something like "let all of the sins of the year go with you"), you twist the neck, and you throw it. The men with roosters, and the women with hens. Then the slaughterer cuts their throats, says a prayer. We take them home; with the giblets the *kreplach* were made, and with the rest of the chicken, the soup for *yontif*, for the holidays. At five in the afternoon, more or less, you eat well and you fast until the next day. Males over thirteen years old too. Not the children; they only fasted until midday.

The holidays were very nice, but a bit strange. At the marriages held by the fanatics, the men danced with the men and the women with the women, they didn't mix. Among them, when a woman was here and another opposite, they shout, "Away, away, stand aside so I can pass" because they don't walk between two women. In the prayer that they say everyday when they get up, there is something like "Thank you, God, for having made me a man and not a woman." They are so backwards. The women take care of the business, work, and the men go to the *shul* of the fanatics to study. Sons of bitches they were.

Because the women over there took care of the house, the business, the children, the husband, the women wore themselves out working. And they, assholes, would say to a woman, "If your husband studies, and you take care of him well, when you die, you'll go to paradise, because God knows that you fulfilled your responsibilities." And the poor one killed herself working and the men sat there, talking about anything whatever, politics, gossip, a verse of the Talmud. They passed the time, and when noon arrived, they went home, had a good lunch, said so long and went to the temple to study and talk until night, like lords. And the next day, the same. Everyday.

Not the progressives, they worked, traded. Over there the fanatics, for example, would have a daughter who they wanted to marry off. Then they went to their *shul* and sought out a boy who was studying there, they took him to their daughter as a son-in-law—of course without asking her if she liked him—and they would give five or ten years of room and board like a king. And the guy would get married and return to the temple to continue studying, son of a bitch, while his wife wore herself out working. They were like that.

So, I'll tell you again, we were respectful, but at that time and at that moment, being a progressive was to oppose all of that, to fight for modernization, to free the women from that slavery, and also cut one's hair shorter, without *paies,* to be able to go to a Zionist club, to sing and dance. My papa always was independent in that. And we followed Moishe Burech. Always.

The war came and we had it pretty bad. I was five years old when everything began. We had to escape from the village toward Lemberg ahead of the Russian attack in 1914. When we returned, the Ukrainian peasants together with the Russian invaders had cleaned out all the houses, they didn't leave anything. We began to work again, with papa and the brothers, to raise ourselves a little bit, but then Austria and Germany counter-attacked, and the Russians, before withdrawing, stole and burned everything. They left only dust and ruins of our houses. And that's how it happened that we stayed in Lemberg, the largest city nearby. A long time there. Meanwhile, the Austrians took my father into the army, my brother Abraham too, because they mobilized every man from eighteen to forty-five years old. All the men had to go to war . . . and we, the young, stayed with mama in Lemberg.

When the army began to recruit men for the war, they made them show their ability with a rifle. They told my father to shoot in any direction or pretend to be nearsighted, he was just at the age limit—forty-five years—

and with a pile of kids to support. But he was very proud, everyone knew that Moishe Burech wouldn't be a coward in any way; then he hit six bullseyes with the rifle, and they took him immediately. He had never carried a gun before. He left his wife and kids, and they sent him to the Russian front, in a company that had Hungarians and Czechs. He didn't understand anything, so he bought a pair of dictionaries, and he began learning two languages, so he could speak to the other soldiers. They kept him until 1916. At first, he dug trenches, and that caused an illness in his legs, rheumatism or something like that. When he returned from the front, he was still sick—and then he went to work in a tailor shop and made the uniforms for the officers and for the army in general.

He began and ended as a private. He never liked stripes, military salutes, parades, and all that. He couldn't put up with any fanatic.

When papa returned, he still walked more or less okay; a few years later, when he arrived in Argentina, he had to help himself with a crutch and a cane, and over the years, he got worse. But having just arrived in this country, he would go alone to the port, walking. It was forty blocks, but he wanted to know everything, hear the language. Nevertheless, in spite of the fact he arrived in 1936, and he lived fifteen years in Buenos Aires, he never could learn Spanish. A bit strange, really. Well, at that time in Lemberg, there was terrible hunger. The hunger was such that you can't describe it. One of my brothers, Joel, who I loved so much, was sick and asked if someone could bring him a potato, it would save him. And he was so weak, the poor fellow. Now it seems ridiculous, but we couldn't even get hold of a potato. And Joel died.

Another time, Jacobo saw some rats that were carrying away pletzales, bits of bread, from the ruins of a bakery that had been destroyed by the bombing. He went into the rubble of what had been the cellar, he fought with the rodents until he scared them away, and he collected several pieces of bread to share with us. Someone who's never been through something like that could never understand it. We took advantage of the pauses in the shooting to run over to the

46

cadavers of the soldiers and take the chocolate that they were able to carry in their pockets.

With the desperation that comes from hunger, we ate anything. One time, Carlos was able to capture some cats and we cooked them, what were we going to do. My mama had gotten hold of a kilo of something to make soup, I don't remember what, but it had an awful taste. We would eat a spoonful of it each day, each of us, from that horrible soup. And Hettie would say that when the war ended, she would make that meal from time to time, to remember the hard times.

In 1918, papa returned, and a little later, Abraham. But right away, they broke up the Austro-Hungarian empire, and the Poles fought for their independence, and the Ukrainians besieged Lemberg, fighting the Poles. We were condemned to war. Much later, I was able to see some World War I maps, and then I understood where we had been. They came through from the East to the West, and then the counter-attack came from other direction and us always in the middle; they smashed us when they came and smashed us when they left. We were a no-man's land, a frontier.

And we had a pretty rough time of it there, they had cut off the water, and we didn't have any to drink; we went out at night, dragging ourselves to the ponds, or at times we filled a bucket with snow and kept it in the house until it melted, and with that we kept going. Three weeks they had us under siege in Lemberg until the *Hellerchis* arrived. They were called that because they were soldiers of General Heller who organized the Polish army, no . . . it was in support of the Poles—with soldiers who were prisoners after the war. Anyone who wanted to signed up and was given food and a new uniform, so that they would fight the Ukrainians and later the Bolsheviks. The Westerners aided that army.

My brother Abraham was a prisoner of war, he was in a camp in Italy. Then he enlisted in that army, but when the train passed through Lemberg—it was going to the Russian front, toward the

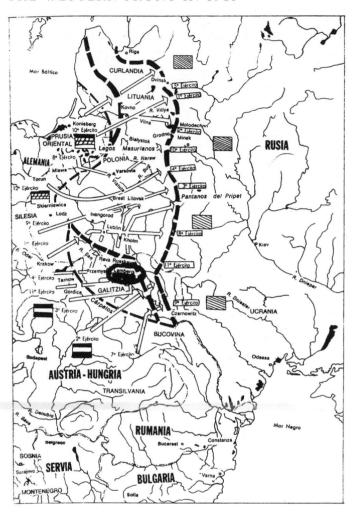

Before the attack of the forces of Germany and Austria in May 1915 (indicated with the arrows), the Russian army, not being able to maintain its positions (fine broken line), on January 19, 1915, began to retreat. In mid October, the Tzar's troops were able to consolidate in the front marked with the thick broken line, that goes from Riga to the locality of Czernowitz, in the Rumanian front.

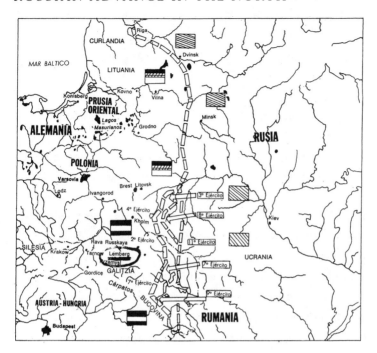

In June of 1916, between the swamps of Pripet and the Czernowitz, Russia placed a million men under the command of Generalissimo Brusilov, whose overwhelming attack surprised the Austrian forces. Germany had to approach in support of its allies, transferring fifteen divisions from Verdun and putting them under the command of Hindenberg, who was able to take the offensive. The arrows indicate the advances of the Russian troops.

Bolsheviks—he deserted and went home. He burned the uniform and dressed as a civilian. We all thought that he had died. When he knocked at the door of the house, we couldn't believe it. Mama hugged him and wouldn't let him go for the entire evening. She feared it was all a dream. Then Abraham went to hide in his fiancée's house, Sarah's, and when the military police came to look for him, we said, "He isn't here," and after a while, they didn't look for him any longer.

There were other times when we saved ourselves. Papa and Abraham went to look for hay, and they ran into some Cossacks who harassed them. They hid in the grain pile, and the Cossacks took their lances and started sticking them into the grain, and they couldn't move to avoid the jabs, to keep from being discovered, but luckily, none of them harmed them. That was near the village that was called Yerechutz Nove; although it was called Yarechev, a nickname *Nove* came because there was a Yerechutz *Stare* which means "old" because fifty years before, the whole city was burned down, and it was necessary to build it from scratch. It wasn't possible to save anything, they had to build it again, so they gave it the name Yerechutz Nove, since *Nove* means "new."

We were in Lemberg from 1921 or 1922. My papa returned to Yarchev to rebuild the house. With my brothers and a mason, they rebuilt it, and we moved again to the village. Once again to work hard and rebuild everything; they hadn't even left the foundation. I was thirteen years old when we returned to our native village.

In the village, they formed a soccer team. The majority were Ukrainians, I was the only Jew who got on the team because I played well at forward, number 9. And then they came from another village, some huge fellows, they came and they stopped at our house. We gave them a place to change clothes, and when they left for the game, they said:

"Are we going to play with these pipsqueaks? We'll score ten goals at the very least."

But it turned out that in the end they lost four to one, I made three goals off them. They left with their tails dragging, they didn't know what to say.

But I remember too that once, while on the team I had to kick a penalty kick.

I kicked and missed, and my teammates yelled at me: "What are you doing, Stinking Jew!" That made a great impression on me. My family lived there for as many generations, perhaps before many of the ancestors of these Ukrainians and Poles, and nevertheless, they saw themselves as rulers of the country, and they yelled "Stinking Jew" because I missed a penalty kick. There and then, I understood that we could never be equals. The Jews would never assimilate in those lands.

When we grew up and were already adolescents, we went to a Zionist Society that existed in the village. The fanatics called us *goyim* because boys and girls went there together, and we sang Hebrew songs, we talked about Israel, all that stuff . . . About the *kibbutzim*; the first ones had just been formed . . . How to do so with Polish Jews who didn't know how to work the land, the majority were artisans and merchants, but of the land nothing . . . nothing . . . nothing. There in the Zionist club, they began to report that in Israel, we Jews could cultivate the land, have animals, dairies, all that could change the life of a Jew.

When I was sixteen or seventeen years old, I was about to leave for Eretz Yisrael. In those days, you formed a *kvutzah,* a group, but from Lemberg, they told us who could travel, they gave us two tickets every three or four months. Two *Halutzim* could travel, no more. All of us couldn't go, they wouldn't have had enough for the passage; perhaps there was an arrangement, I don't know. So I didn't get my chance, but everyone wanted to go. We learned to build roads, to work hard.

Here is a picture taken when we began to have *Halutzim House* in the village.

We did everything energetically, full of enthusiasm. Everything to go to Israel. Here we're putting in the foundation of the building by hand.

We were like a separate part of Lemberg, from there they would decide and would choose, we would continue with the activities, later on we rented a room, and we met there. When the anniversary of Hertzl's death came, we went to the temple and lit candles. Then the fanatics got angry and put them out, they fought with us. That was serious business, they used stones and sticks, they split open our heads with their blows; in general they took worse than they gave. They said that we were all *goyim*, that we couldn't do this . . . that they were waiting for the Messiah and that what we were doing wasn't Jewish, to be Zionist was to be a *goy*, a betrayal. You had to pray and nothing else, and meanwhile, the anti-Semites killed us all. Here we are: all the boys with the portrait of Theodore Herzl. Yes, we're all here. It's 1920 and something.

In those days, Carlos, Jacobo, and I were in the Zionist movement. Not the two older brothers, because this was only for the

young, directed by two or three adults, who were definitively on top of the new ideas and arrangements. There, they organized the *Halutzim* who would go to Israel, they began to work in order to learn. I was in a group called *Algemeine Zionistas*, something like "Popular Zionists." The majority of the youth of my age were Zionists and not religious, there were only three or four of the *Misrachi*, we fought the orthodox. All that was exclusively for the youth. The adults didn't get involved in those fights with the fanatics who wouldn't tolerate Zionists.

The land for the movement building, as I said before, was donated by a Jew from the area. They made these foundations upon which to build it; we all worked, but they weren't able to finish the construction, there was no money to continue. Then we rented a room from one of our neighbors, and later on they told me that the Russians occupied that house and ours too, and they put the headquarters of the *Komosol*, the communist youth, in it.

We were poor and backward in an even poorer and more backward village. Few of us liked to read. I, from my earliest days, was crazy about books, and I spent all night reading: Tolstoy, Dostoevski, the writers of that time translated into Polish, although I knew Russian and German too like many there.

So I spent hours and hours with the lamp burning, a kerosene lamp, of course, there was no electricity in that area until 1930. When I left, there was still no electricity. And when Abraham, the oldest, got married, I would go at night to his room and stay there reading. It's something you can't talk about: I was so involved in the reading, I was there all night as if hypnotized. My mama once came down at four in the morning and saw the light burning, she came in to check on me, since it was time for sleeping. And she took the lamp from me. Then I got a candle, and when everyone was asleep, I would light it, and stay there reading, night after night.

For that reason, the progressive Jews chose me to read to them, on Fridays, all the Polish newspaper of the week. The meetings were run by my father Moishe Burech, and they discussed news and politics there, instead of spending *Shabbat* praying in the synagogue.

Moishe Burech's mother, who appears in the center, had a fruit and vegetable stand in the market. A very special old lady, as I re-member her. She went to the doctor when something hurt her, for example, and he prescribed a medicine; then she would go to the pharmacy and buy the remedy, and then she would go home and throw it in the garbage. Moishe Burech would say to her, "Mama, what are you doing?" and she would answer, "What do you care? I went to the doctor because he has to live, I bought the medicine, be-cause the pharmacist has to live from something, and now I throw the medicine in the garbage because I also have to live." This was my grandmother, an old horse trader, a character.

In the back, you can see the bathroom, outside the house. There was a bit of land—some eight meters—and water was drawn with a hand pump, right there. The toilet was a black hole. The bathroom wall you see here, then the metal roof and the neighbor's garden wall. They took this photo because Jaime and Abraham were traveling to

Argentina without their wives. The children too stayed in Poland but just for a short time.

We were well dressed. My mother Hettie appears with her own hair, because my father didn't allow her to cut it and wear a wig; she has light blue eyes and is very blond, a real Pole. Sara appears without a wig, at about that time she stopped wearing one. My parents got married in 1895, in the last century; my brother Abraham was born in '96, he's second to the left with the children. My sister, who appears in the center, was married in Poland, her husband, who was from Lemberg, appears at the left, and she met him when we lived there from 1918 to 1923 more or less.

In my house, there were two cellars, the bedrooms were above them, two rooms with a bedroom in between, then came the living room . . . the house was large. For the business, they used the entire width of the lot, with a large window facing the back, and next to the shop. You don't see any of this in the photo, it's taken from the front. Jaime is seated at the right with his family. Carlos, the tallest, is at the left. I'm next to my brother-in-law—looking to the right—and Jacobo.

55

In the shop worked apprentices from the village and the surrounding areas. They weren't paid, they came to learn the trade. We also worked as tailors. One of the apprentices was a cousin of mine; two others—a Jew and a *goy*—came from farther away. There was another tailor in the town, Zalman, who was sort of the competition. We called him *pisht in der kurt,* because he didn't get up from the sewing machine even to go to the bathroom. And even we did that.

Moishe Burech really didn't want to go to Argentina, but what was he going to do? His older children left, and then I went, then Carlos with my sister. Who stayed? No one except Jacobo, who came with them in 1936. When they left, there was already civil war in Spain. They got out just, just in time. In Poland, other relatives remained, uncles, cousins, we never learned anything about them. The Lemberg zone was severely punished during the Second World War. The Germans entered there. They told me later that they had made my village a total disaster. There was a massacre in the center, the market area, where the Jewish families lived. They didn't do anything to the Ukrainians, because they were with them. But not one of our relatives remained alive.

Luckily, we left early enough. We said, "Don't go there anymore, the future is death." And we left.

family tree

It has a lot to do with it. But I'll leave it to you to judge. Aren't you a psychiatrist? Your job is to decipher my fantasies. And it doesn't matter to me if you use yours to do it. You chose this meddlesome occupation, to try to figure out other people's lives so you can understand yourself better, perhaps. Yes, yes, don't be impatient. I'm going to tell you the dream.

I advance along a very curvy dirt road. It is narrow, and at the sides there is underbrush, shoulders that descend, dark rough spots. Certain danger. I get on a rather simple wooden vehicle, like a child's car or a dark brown wooden scooter, not at all shiny and a bit worn (some nails or metal clasps can be seen between the outlines of the boards). The vehicle has two pedals and cords, one on each side, that serve as the steering, tied to some wooden planks that are higher on the two sides. There are two of us. I can't identify the other, perhaps she has something to do with my daughter.

I drive and we go forward. The road is winding, and we constantly have to turn; despite the enormous number of curves, the limited speed and the strength of the cords allow me to steer without wrecking myself. At the end of the road, the bushes and plants grow denser, always a green and untended, natural vegetation. At that point, there is a small stopping area, just before a very odd crevice.

It's a type of crack, a cut in the earth, that advances in a twisted line; in some sections, it is very small, and in others it gets larger. What's evident is that, looking downward, this cut has a terrible depth, you can see only darkness, if one falls, it is impossible to survive. In any case, it isn't easy to slide through that scar toward the emptiness, unless you are careless.

Getting off the vehicle, my companion turns around and goes

back toward the path, acting now like a driver (in truth, it has to do with a driving test to get a license, to be authorized as a driver, "to legalize" your knowledge; she will take the test in a little while, as soon as it is practical). How does this relate to me? I ought to cross that ridiculously narrow precipice and go over to the other side. We are four or five people who are crossing and on the opposite edge, there are several robust men—who work at this—whose job it is to help out those who are trying to cross, to keep them from slipping downward by imprudence or distraction (somewhat similar to those who from the dock help raise a launch, on the broad strip of water that separates the vessel from dry land). They aren't really necessary, but I accept their cooperation: I take the hand extended by the one standing in front of me, forcefully setting his feet in the earth so he himself wouldn't slip, and I cross on tiptoe this opening in the earth. One of my feet, perhaps because of a distraction, slips a little, and a few grains of dirt fall toward the precipice but, except for this minor worry, I make it to the other side without further problem. I thank the workman—who is already returning to help the next one cross—and I continue my route. The scar, dark and deep, is at my back, defeated, a thin precipice where you would have to fall sideways to be able to pass.

I feel relief. But part of me was left on the other side. I write a short poem on the stone wall in black graffiti that says: *I'm disintegrating.*

I'm losing the best part of myself.

Do you want to take a piece?

VOICES AROUND THE STOVE

It was near the end of the war, in the central plaza of Yarchev, when they killed this Bolshevik boy. I saw him. And everyone was talking about him in the village and in my family, many years later, in 1918 immediately after the October revolution. He was hardly more than an adolescent, he would have been about seventeen; he lay hurt on the ground, dirty and bloody with feverish eyes. A boy. A Polish officer approached him, with a revolver in his hand, and pointing at him, he said, "What are you doing far from your country? Did you come to fight here?" And the boy answered him, "Svobodoi." It meant "For Liberty" in Russian. The Polish officer got angry, many people in the village were watching him. He hit the Bolshevik in the head with his revolver and threatened him, "If you say that again, I'll kill you. Why are you fighting, you Russian dog?" The fellow looked around and shouted, "Svobodoi."

And the officer squeezed the trigger and blew his brains out. The story was long told in the village. We were very impressed by it—and especially in Yarchev, there were not many communists, I think the only one was the wigmaker, perhaps two or three more. There were more Zionists.

We were always in the middle. When the Russians came through, they burned everything, then the counterattack came from the others, and they burned the village again. A no-man's-land.

I remember that the Bolsheviks were there for a couple of weeks, they had taken another village, seven or eight kilometers from Yarchev. After the battle, they entered with bloody sabers. My aunt had a toothache and had her face tied up in a handkerchief, I don't know if this helped her at all, but it was the custom there. The Cossacks went right to my aunt's house, right after the fighting, covered with blood, and they wanted tea. She told them that she didn't have any sugar, so they took out a bag full of it and gave it to her: "Have some sugar!" My aunt took a lump, and they told her, "No, take more, take ten lumps." They ate and they drank, and when they left, they left behind the sugar as a gift. She complained that her tooth hurt, and then one of the Cossacks showed her the bloody saber and said, "Cut it out. If it hurts, you have to cut it out." But they didn't do anything to her, they ate and they left.

There weren't many problems in the village with the communists, because of their politics. On the contrary, between the Zionists and the religious people, there were.

Zionism was curious in Yarchev, an orthodox community. Both parts had to be there, you couldn't easily separate them: the tradition was very strong, the *yeshiva* and all that. The Zionist youth would shave underneath their sideburns, the *paies*, and they did it in this way: during the day, to go to temple and in daily life, they wore their curly sideburns, but at night, when they went to the Zionist center, they would lift up their curls with their fingers, and put them behind their ears, and so they would change themselves into modern emancipated Jews. They were both things at the same time.

There was a great deal of religious fanaticism in that Poland of the 1920s, especially among the older women. One of these old ladies, before *Pesach*, did a *humetz,* and then she put rags on the hens' feet to keep them from making a mess. When her husband, who was a *shohet*, exclaimed that nowhere in the entire Talmud nor in the laws of *shachrut* was it written that it was necessary to put rags on the chicken feet, the old woman replied something like, "If I paid attention to what you say and what the rabbis say is written in the Talmud, my house would be full of impurities. You are not to be trusted."

The same thing happened with illnesses. On the Sabbath, for example, in spite of the fact that a woman was old and sick—Lázaro's mother-in-law—the rabbi authorized her to take medicine for her illness, even though it was *Shabbat*. In spite of that, not only did she refuse to eat because it was the Sabbath, but she wouldn't take her medicine either, and so she died, that very same day, a Saturday.

Yes, it was a very closed world, fanatic. You had to be very brave to try to challenge it. When Moishe Burech married Hettie, my mother, there in 1890 . . . she had a turned up nose and blond hair, long, which it was the custom to cut off (when the religious Jewish women got married) and replaced with a wig, so that no one other than her husband could ever again see her own hair. The day of the wedding, in the morning when the traditional wigmaker arrived to cut off her hair, Moishe Burech made the table shake with a blow of his fist, and he threw her out of the house, yelling that his new wife would not go out into the world with her hair shorn.

One time, to play a joke on me, you guys made me step on thin ice, and it broke. I fell into the water, I was dressed in a cardigan and shoes for the snow, I weighed a lot. I wanted to get out, waving my arms, but the ice was very thin and kept on breaking. Finally, I was able to grab on to a thick piece, about twenty centimeters thick, and I climbed out, soaking wet and dripping.

Yes, I remember too. You went to the synagogue . . .

Of course, I wanted to dry myself in front of the stove. I sat by the side of it, shivering, in silence, but someone went to tell my father who came running, and he dragged me by my ear. He made me stay in bed all Saturday afternoon which was a terrible punishment for a boy in those days.

Later, with the Zionists there, everything evolved a bit. But even among the Zionists, there were fights, during the elections and things like that.

Tzvi, for example. He was crazy to go to Israel, and he wasn't able to go. And now that he lives in Argentina, he would be able to go. No longer. He doesn't go. He stays here.

In those days I was eighteen years old. Now I'm somewhat older.

The Polish army put up posters that said, "Flea-bitten Jew. Go to Israel." And then they didn't let him leave. You couldn't understand it.

I was selected for military service, but I escaped, because if I didn't, the word was that I would die. I was chosen for the cavalry, two years. And the chief of police of the village, the cop, was angry with my papa, he always said that he carried my photo in his pocket to help him catch me. And my father would tell him jokingly that if he got a hole in his pocket, he was going to lose my photo. He laughed in his face, because he already had a letter saying that I had arrived; they were looking for me in Yarchev, and I was living in Uruguay.

That policeman was pissed with Moishe Burech over an old matter: when he was made chief, he wanted them to give him a hectare of land, so he could build an estate. When they debated the matter in the village council, the plan was presented, and no one got up to say anything. There were thirty-two neighborhood representatives, they all had tongues, but no one was moved to open his mouth.

"An oks ot a langue tzing, en kenescht bluzen a shofer." "An ox has a large tongue, but it can't blow the shofer."

Everyone was afraid. Papa was the only one who got up and said, "I don't agree with this and this." He expressed all the historical and legal reasons for not giving the land. Always calm, without getting irritated. Then the other guy, the police chief, got up, furious, muttering, "You'll pay me for this." And Moishe Burech answered him in front of the council: "I'm not afraid of you. You are afraid of me, because you are in the bar drinking beer during your shift, but I'm not a thief, so I'm not afraid of you."

Around 1916 he was sent to the war, to the Russian front.

The army would pay a pension for that, a very little one. At that time, mama and an older sister worked making cigarettes for the soldiers, with a little machine, for a company that was selling them to the armed forces. We, the kids also worked at that, once the tobacco was put inside the paper and the paper rolled up, we cut off the ends of the cigarette. They were made by the thousands: if normally an average woman made two hundred an hour, for example, mama made almost a thousand, that was the comparison. That chubby one worked hard.

It was a little metal machine, she placed the tobacco just so, the paper, she closed and finished. It had to be very full, it took skill, because if you put too little tobacco, it was a soft cigarette, it had to be hard and at the same time not come apart because of too much inside. That was in Lemberg. We worked a great deal, we made them one by one, night and day.

At that time, you couldn't deal in tobacco nor with food, everything was illegal. Black market, *nu?* And one of my friends was walking with a small sack, carrying merchandise, and a guard stops him and says to him, "Hey you, what are you carrying there?"

"What am I carrying? I'm carrying dog food."

"Let's see. Show it to me."

The guard opens the bundle and sees that it contains tobacco. He asks him, "And the dog is going to eat this?"

And he answered, "And so, if he doesn't like it, he won't eat it. It's his problem . . . "

You remember the jokes, but you can't forget the hunger. We were always hungry and were in bad shape in those years. I remember that there was a terrible battle, in 1919, they killed more than one thousand soldiers, the combat went on all day. And we went running through the firing, every time that there was a pause, to take the chocolate and rations off the cadavers. That you never forget.

Yes, life was hard in Poland. Here they say it is dangerous to get involved in politics, with this killing that the military has done lately, they say that they have made thousands of kids disappear, a terrible thing. There in Poland they sent you to a prison in the city, and *chau, pinela,* no one returned. They tortured them and they killed them, that happened to anyone who got involved in politics.

Those of the *Bund* were Jewish socialists. Here in Argentina, there was one named Pinie Wald, who published the daily *Di Presse;*

in 1919 they accused him of wanting to create a soviet here during "La Semana Trágica." There were *pogroms* and many dead, it was something terrible.

One time, a man went to the center of town, there in my village. It had to do with a butcher who was very drunk, a *yid*, who was drinking a great deal. He entered the first dive, and they gave him a glass of vodka, they already knew what would happen. You used to drink in tin glasses so the amount couldn't be faked, you understand? They were marked at an eighth. Drinks. He entered, drank, paid, and left. And in Yarchev there was a bum who went after him, a *goy*, who followed him from dive to dive, and the butcher left a bit of his drink in each glass, something, and the other guy, the bum, drank up these drops, and soon he got drunk just from the drops that the other guy left him. But you know how these things are. In this life, everything comes to an end. The butcher drank so much for so many years that he finally became ill; the doctor told him that he could drink only milk. For him milk was *drek*, disgusting, but he put up with it for two or three days and then, once again, went into the village. He passed by the first bar and called them all sorts of things, time and again he insulted them, dirty words, I'm not coming here again, it's your fault and so with everybody. He passed by every one of the bars, and he insulted their mothers but without going in. And so on until he reached the last one on the street, and then the owner came out to the doorway and said to him, "If you were capable of passing by so many taverns and you didn't go in for a drink, you've earned a good drink as a prize," and then he accepted, drank a vodka, and got completely drunk again.

Yes, I remember them. The butcher of Yarchev. Everyone was poor there, but he had great luck. All the women shopped in his butcher shop, an incredible thing. His son was a stupid ass, but he also had a lot of money. How did he do it? By luck, always the same way. He would buy cows, for example. He was going to go and buy a dying cow. But suddenly he had a headache or caught the flu and he didn't go, just when the deal would have cost him. Or meat went up in price after he bought it. Always something like that. Luck. The weather, circumstances, everything helped him.

His name was Moishe, I chatted with him once. I said to him, "What luck you've got Moishe, you're always making money." And he answered me, "Look, you believe in God? I certainly do. Because without money, I'm worthless, I'm an ass." And it was the truth. The father was an important fellow in the school, a member of the Municipal Council and who knows what else, and the son a loser. "If I didn't have money, what would become of me?" he confessed to me. "I'm not worth anything. Look, God gave me this because He knows that I have nothing else."

There were about five butcher shops, but his was the busiest. It was incredible. They brought meat once a week, a cow, and then sold it for several days. Freezers and refrigerators weren't necessary there, it was so cold: you slaughtered on Wednesday afternoon, Thursday you sold, and then you ate, and so it was. The other days you didn't eat meat, it wasn't like it is here in Argentina.

The peasants ate meat only two times a year, at Christmas and New Year's. There wasn't money for anything more; some couldn't even eat that much, the general poverty was terrible. The exploitation by the Polish landlords, Ach! . . . horrendous.

One time, I remember, a fat guy entered Marash's restaurant. He drank a vodka and ate a sandwich of Krakow salami, he spent about five or six pesos. He was a landlord, and one of ours, a socialist, began to argue with him, how was it that he paid the peasants so little. And he answered, "What do you mean that I pay little? I give each peasant . . . (let's say, in the money of those days when milk cost 20 cents) I pay him a peso a day. And he buys for himself a liter of milk, he buys a kilo of flour and he makes a loaf of bread, all with 55 cents, and with that he eats all day and he has 45 cents left over. And if a Polish peasant has money left over, he doesn't want to work any more. And so he's earning too much, I'm paying him too much. . . . "

You ate a lot of potatoes, not that much meat. Some chicken, potato doughnuts, potato *latkes*, everything made of potatoes, the cheapest. There was a song that went: "Monday, potatoes, Tuesday, potatoes, Wednesday, potatoes, Thursday, potatoes, Friday, potatoes and Saturday . . . potato cake . . . "

Hunger and poverty. You remember that.

And, in spite of that . . . we couldn't emigrate until many years later. The situation was getting worse all the time; the Polish government was more and more anti-Semitic. We weren't afraid of them, we would wait for them with rocks and break their heads open.

We were the only Jews in Europe who fought. Including in the ghettos. They didn't get away with it.

But the police always protected them. There was a Jewish store there, and they put up a barricade, so that no one could go in to shop. They broke the windows, the signs. Everyone went to protest to a Jewish senator, Schraiber, and the government promised, through him, the Interior Minister would speak to the village on the radio. Everybody waited to hear what he would say. I remember each Polish phrase, as if it were today. Even the modulation of the voice and the adjectives that he used, I remember. And he said exactly this: "You shouldn't beat the Jews, I'm opposed to that. But to boycott their businesses, I agree with that." That was the Interior Minister himself, I believe his name was Racowski.

In that climate, we were living. Some said this and others that, but over there anti-Semitism was official policy, the Interior Minister himself proclaimed it.

To me, it comes to mind that there in the village was a Ukrainian doctor. And there were doctors who were very good, who studied a lot. And this one wasn't a very good doctor, he paid more attention to politics, against the Jews. And so, once the wife of this anti-

Semite's partner got sick and needed a doctor, and he called for the best doctor in the village, a Jew, he was very good there. When this Ukrainian learned of what had happened, he called his partner immediately, he said to him, "Hey, we've been going around speaking against the Jews, and you call this doctor for your wife . . . " The other fellow answered him, "When my wife is sick, I don't get involved in politics."

Yes, the climate was very difficult there. Jaime was the one with the most initiative: in spite of the fact that he was healthy and worked in Lemberg and all that, he felt that Poland wasn't a place for him, that there was no future. He took his wife and children and immigrated to Cuba, the only country in America that was giving visas. He was two years fighting, and he returned to Poland because he couldn't take the tropical climate, he got sick. They didn't let him enter in the rest of Europe, and there also was a crisis at that time. They were the first in the village, the pioneers of that flight.

My story was different. I was going with a girl there, in Yarchev, but I was poor. And the relatives, the people, began to ask me, "When are you getting married?" I began to look for a place to live, I wanted to rent from that guy whose son killed Aisik later on. A room, to set up a tailor shop. All of us were tailors there, I came from generations of artisans, a pride of work. But I couldn't earn a living, Zalman-Schnaider was starving to death. I said that I was going to the city, to Lemberg. And there you had to give a deposit, pay for the key, when you wanted to rent a store. It cost, for example, 500 pesos for the key, and I had . . . bah! in truth my fiancée had, I didn't have a penny; she had, let's say 200 pesos. One of their sisters and her husband, good people, got involved and obtained, finally, one which asked only 200 pesos, he has my last name and was also from Yarchev. Precisely one room with a kitchen, all that I needed, and with folks from Yarchev. It was a great joy. I had everything worked out and I could get married and have a *hasene*, a wedding. But then, when they heard this, my acquaintances around the corner, the ones from Yarchev, asked the landlord not to rent to me. Because they also were tailors and were afraid that I would take work away from them. They were rough-it-out tailors, for the peasants. Not tailors to measure, fine. I write a letter to my fiancée, and she sends me ten dollars for the gesture. When I go to see the landlord he says to me, "No, you have to forgive me, Lázaro, but I can't rent to you for this and that." He killed me. That place was as . . . if it were at the distance, let's say, Avellaneda is from downtown, very isolated, on the outskirts. I leave angry and very sad and I go to work, what could I do? On the way, I meet a friend on the street. A communist he was, but a first-class tailor, first class, and very advanced and cultured. He says to me, "Lázaro, why are you so sad?" And I told him. And he says "How stupid you are, what are you going to do here in Lemberg? As soon as you can't pay the rent, they'll throw you out. There are always more poor people here, don't you see. I'm leaving for Argentina."

It was about 1930, some had gone already. And in Yarchev, they received beautiful letters, from Montevideo, and all that. There, here.

Of course, fine, that morning I didn't want to work anymore and my friend, instead of taking the trolley, walked with me for thirty blocks. And he told me everything: that he had a fiancée in Argentina who had left with his father-in-law, a vest-maker whom I knew; he told me about the unions there, how you worked, that I could go as a presser. So we arrived at the Immigration Office. We went in and waited a little while, and they called us there, the director came out, and it happened that he is one from my village, an intellectual, son of a lawyer, a family of the highest quality but assimilated, they didn't even know how to speak Yiddish.

Yes, I remember that family.

"Luzer, what are you doing here?" he asks. I knew him well because once in the orphanage—I grew up in an orphanage—the father helped out there, and he did exercises with us. My companion says, "He wants to go to Argentina." I didn't say anything, I didn't even know what to think. The fellow says, "Good, sign here on this application and leave it, I'll arrange it for you." I then write to my fiancée telling her everything, dying of fright, and she answers me, "It's the best thing you could have done." She was sharper than I!

What a development!

I returned home and I found a call from the army. I had to do reserve duty, five weeks of military exercises. I did them, and then I got married, a nice wedding, and in October, I traveled alone to Argentina. I remember it as if it were today. My wife couldn't come with me, because my mother-in-law was sick. Just at the moment that the papers arrived there, the mother died. Then, she came.

Everyone went to meet her at the boat.

Yes, there were about twenty of us on the trolley. An Italian who worked with us, who we called "The Maestro," went to meet her. Among the immigrants, we helped each other, everyone went to meet her. And what did I have? I bought a bronze bed that cost me forty pesos and "paisano" Sruel sold me a table for sixteen pesos. I ran out of money. A friend gave me an oilskin tablecloth, and on the bed without a mattress—I didn't have enough for a mattress—I put a quilt. I borrowed chairs from Leibl; another "paisano" lent me a very small clothes closet with a mirror in the middle. So then, we arrived together at my room, on the trolley. I had gas and everything in the room. And when my wife entered, she saw the wood floor, the furniture and all that, she got all choked up and began to cry. Then she called me over to one side and said to me, "Lázaro, really *all of this* is yours? All of this? Then we must be rich." We spent the night hugging and crying. You can explain that to anyone. . . .

Yes, it was very hard for us in those days. He who had a bed and clothes closet was already like a millionaire. I don't know how we ever managed with the language. Yes, until now, fifty-five years later, I can't learn Spanish, you have to imagine how it was at the beginning. Working little by little with the Italian, he would say to me, this is "iron," that's called water, and so, little by little.

I came to Argentina on Monday, on Tuesday they showed me everything, on Thursday I was working for an Italian tailor. Mechl came in to ask if they needed a clerk, and he arranged everything. He knew a few words. And on Saturday, I collected my wages, and I sent ten dollars to Poland. I gathered them peso by peso, it was 1930, and our money was still worth something. Everything was so cheap that I wrote to Poland that people were crazy to say there was a crisis, if I was buying a kilo of dry biscuits for sixty cents, a dozen bananas for ten cents. Food was very cheap. And we were starving to death when we came from Poland.

Absolutely, instead of eating bread twice a day, with half a kilo of cakes we had enough for midday and for the evening. Now they sell you the cakes one at a time, not by kilo.

What feasts I made for my wife when she arrived, for all the years we'd suffered from hunger there. Pans of greens, pots full of tomatoes and onions with cream, with *smetene,* and bread of those made by Panificación Argentina. We ate six loaves of bread the day she arrived. You couldn't compare Poland with Argentina. Here you threw yesterday's bread in the street and you bought new; I constantly passed by people carrying shopping bags of bread. There in Yarchev we ate old bread, and that was when there was any. At times there wasn't even stale bread to eat.

I came in 1937. We were among the last who were able to leave Poland. I remember that here, one time, I went into a restaurant at Lavalle and Rodríguez Peña. Immediately, they put bread on my table with oil and vinegar. Of course, I looked at that, and I ate all the bread that there was, dampening it in vinegar, and then another piece of bread. Then the soup arrived, a good soup. We are from a small town, and we know how to grab, when the waiter brings the tureen to serve us. With the soup spoon very full, thick. That soup cost fifteen cents, no more. And I was already full, I wasn't hungry any more, but it was a shame to leave then, so I ordered beef with fried potatoes, although I couldn't eat any more. And a jug of wine. And I paid sixty-five cents for all that. Ah! And a piece of fruit too. And although times were hard, I earned four pesos and could live on it for the whole week. And eat, eat anything I wanted to.

I remember the Italian tailor's wife. He lived next to the police station and he would invite me for supper, to help me save money so that I could bring my wife from Poland. They were good people, our problems were similar. In those days, for us it was a paradise, a *gan eiden*. To even think of having a heater to warm tea or a coffee with milk, that was a bachelor's dream. In Poland, it was unimaginable. I bought a heater for seven pesos and a maté cup and a liter of milk. I could make a whole pot for myself, if I wanted to, to drink while I worked. In contrast, over there in Lemberg, it wasn't easy to get them to make you a glass of tea, and even with it, we were left hungry.

I arrived in 1930, two months before Isaac. And we sent the papers.

I arrived in 1932, already married. But he arrived a bachelor. I got married and spent my honeymoon on the ship, I can't complain. We traveled for eighteen days.

That was good. I traveled in a freighter, French. Thirty-one days.

I took a ship in Danzig, and I traveled to Cherbourg, twenty-two days all told. First four and then eighteen more to get here. Television didn't exist then, but the trip wasn't boring. It was full, full of people, it was like a village.

I helped a friend of mine, we did our military service together, get a job in the tailor shop. He didn't know the trade, but I recommended him and he got in. And afterwards, another new one arrived, and it bothered him a lot. I asked him, "Che, why does it bother you?" And he answered me, "It's that I've suffered so much since I arrived, and I got to where I am, what do I know?" I told him, "There's no reason to be resentful, the fact that you suffered has nothing to do with it. I suffered when I entered, you suffered less, and the one who comes now even less, it's a question of progress." But of course, this depends on the character of each person.

So there we were: working, suffering, enjoying, immigrants and young people, full of life, confident in the future. We read the newspaper in Yiddish; for that reason we didn't learn Spanish well. That way we learned the news from Europe. We formed committees here during the war, and then with the birth of Israel and all that.

But we were already old-timers, we "carried" the newcomers. They called us "the bad Poles." Like the old man Shmuel, he was always a brute, he made a lot of money, but he continues being a brute. Right now, in Miramar, he goes to the beach and urinates on the jetty, the rocks. His prostate couldn't take it. So I would always start to applaud and to yell: "Good! Bravo!" And so everyone who passes by there looks at him.

Yes, he's now a multimillionaire. But he's still such an animal that he didn't learn to speak Spanish, and he's forgotten his Yiddish. By now, he doesn't know how to speak any language. He just grunts.

Why would he need to speak, with the money that he has? And he also has a hernia which is so big, gigantic. It hangs from him like a purse. We tell him to keep his jewels there when he goes on vacation.

When Shmuel came from Poland, we always played jokes on him. He was stupid and didn't understand the language; he worked in a tailor shop. He didn't even know how to greet people in Argentino and that make him angry. One day he came and he said to me, "Che, teach me to greet people in Spanish, at the very least I want to say 'Good Morning' when I come to work in the morning." So I told him that in Spanish "Good Morning" is said "the whore who gave birth to you." The fellow goes, studies all night at home—he had it written down—and the following day, he greeted people, "The whore who gave birth to all of you." The others wanted to kill him, they thought he was insulting them.

Yes, he's very dumb. When we play dominoes on the beach, each turn takes him half an hour, he scratches his legs and his head, sits there for a while, as if thinking about which strategies suit him. And then he says, "I pass, I don't have anything."

For sure he never read a newspaper.

My wife liked to read in Spanish, *Radiolandia* and all that, and so she learned the language better. Even today, I read everything in Yiddish, books, newspaper, everything. . . .

I got involved in politics immediately, almost without knowing the language. There was a tailors' strike, and I was on a picket line against the bosses. The police tricked us and we fell. I didn't know how to speak, so I did it with hand signals to show that I didn't understand. . . .

It was dangerous to speak in those days.

"Vus ba klign of der link, ba a nar of der tzing." "What a wise man keeps in his throat, a fool has on his tongue."

I would say another version from the Ukrainian: *"Durnel no pohaduiut, mudre nopovischt."* "What the fool doesn't know, the wiseman doesn't say."

There in jail there was a punk who worked for the police and interrogated us; we called him the "Russian sow." He was a master of Yiddish, and Polish too it seemed, and he took a job with these police. An ordinary sort, from that type of people. . . .

But we weren't very much afraid of him. We were never scared of him. We were workers, and we fought for what was ours.

family tree

I have the sensation, Mister Schnaiderman, that we are not getting anywhere. Babbling memories, anecdotes that are more important to their protagonists than to anyone else, the mythic figure of the grandfather Moishe Burech who appears like an idyllic superman.

It's a tour without a guide, blind. I don't understand what you're getting at, except a review of ancient complaints and present confusions that go on surfacing, of parents, relatives, paisanos, old folk who are no longer alive except in the memory of a story, trying to recreate an experiential and human climate that no longer exists. Inventing ideal characters as objects for identification. To find your roots, go up through the branches. Very complicated.

What is the meaning of this search? You ought to present yourself as a witness to a crime and get over a partial amnesia. And there doesn't appear to be much to be proud about in these dry, fibrous, insubstantial roots that lack the sort of outstanding elements to which we are accustomed. There are no family archives here that one could consider conserving. There are no documents from some leader who is even associated with those places, there are no medals or decorations, private diaries, correspondence of historical interest, zones of "connection" that might permit the presumption of a genealogy tied to the destiny of the country.

Nothing of that. I only find and imagine village people, average Jews, humble artisans, Poles at one time or Austrians or Russians depending on the season of the year and their relation to the offensives of the armies at war, at one point on that moving and triangular frontier. An impure war, in truth. They don't even possess a defined nationality.

I know, don't tell me; it is precisely that characteristic that I'm not able to sort out that is the object of the investigation, that's what you pay me for. I have tried, for example, to find some connecting thread in the plot: objects that are family property—a samovar, a set of glasses for drinking brandy, an ancient edition of a sacred book, a dagger—that are passed down from one generation to another and acquire a life of their own, help the interpretation of your hypnotic delirium. What do you think? But you don't have them, your present family doesn't either. Everything reduces to bits and pieces. What can distinguish you people from the crowd, if you *are* the undifferentiated crowd, the masses, if in your family tree there are no heroes or rabbis or generals?

I don't want to offend you, but I am very professional in my work, and for that reason, I should warn you: in the testimony collected until now, I find only some family stories that go on repeating from fathers to sons, from relatives to friends, forming something like the mythic substratum of your family name.

Do you understand me? Like the supposed bravery of your grandfather Moishe Burech, or the hunger they suffered during the war, or the family pride in not ceding to the aggression of the others. Since you were children, that past of misery and horror that surges forth from the stories has been beautified for you, to compensate for your not having a real tradition.

I'm trying to be hard but sincere. I will continue collecting stories to see if the panorama improves.

Now concentrate. I'm turning on the tape recorder. Speak. You bet on the possibility to *see yourself be born*. Do you catch the beauty of the idea? To watch oneself looking at life, blossoming, opening a new chapter in this infinite series of trees that we finally are.

PATER FAMILIAE

At twenty, it was my turn to go for the physical examination for the Polish military service. As I was very tall and strong they sent me to the grenadiers. My friends, in my house, they all began to tell me that service in grenadiers lasted twenty-five months—normally it was only eighteen months—that you have to take care of horses, keep them clean and who knows what . . . I said to myself: "I'm not going to do my military service." In any case, I was about to immigrate, so I asked my cousin for his documents; he was four or five years older than I, we were very close friends. We took this photo before the trip. In the stable.

He had already done his service, and with his passport, he was going to cross the border into Germany to seek treatment for an eye ailment. I grabbed the document, I made myself look like him, and I escaped from Poland. I took the train that was going from Krakow to Berlin. Before crossing the border, when the police got on to check documents, I hid in the bathroom, I closed the door, and I stayed there until the train left the country. In those days, I wasn't afraid of anything.

Just after I entered Germany, I tore up the passport so as not to implicate my cousin. Then I arrived in Berlin as a deserter, and they gave me fourteen days in jail for crossing the border without permission. They locked me up as if I were a common criminal, with the other prisoners. The Jewish Society of Berlin intervened to keep them from sending me back to Poland.

In the prison, I was in a very small cell, everything closed off. It only had a light grate three meters high, and you couldn't see out. I was going crazy. I began to protest, to pound on the door. They gave me a Bible to read, and I refused it, I wasn't in the mood for religious books

. . . Then I asked for work. They asked me what I could do, and I told them that I was a tailor, and that I could do everything. They sent me to the workshop. I worked making covers for the prisoners' food platters, trivets for the hot pots, everything . . . anything so I didn't have to be locked up!

Soon after I arrived at the workshop, I became friends with another prisoner who was a braggart, which here we call a "big shot."

"You'll see how well you're going to do here. I've been here for eighteen years, and I have twelve years to go. They gave me thirty years!"

"What did you do?" I asked him.

"I stabbed my wife, and I killed my sister. Nothing more," he answered.

I pretended not to understand. Immediately, he brought me a meat sandwich and a coffee with milk. He treated me well, he was a prisoner with influence there; he was able to get even bread and butter, and at five we stopped working.

After the fourteen days, they let me go, and I went to the Argentine consulate. My two older brothers were already here. But I couldn't go, they weren't giving visas. So I went to the Berlin Jewish Council, that was like the community mutual association here, and it was on very good terms with the police. I couldn't return to Poland as I was a deserter; they would give me two years in prison and military service afterwards. The President of the Council looked at me and said:

"What are we going to do with this one?"

They thought I was a communist. Another one from the Council said, "Better to keep him far than near."

They asked me which country I wanted to go to, and I immediately said "Argentina." But he told me that there are no visas, that the only place I can go is Montevideo, where they let you enter without a visa. Okay, they gave me a passport for there. They asked me if I had money, and I told them that I didn't, even though I had a hundred dollars. A guard got me the passport for nothing. The idea was to send me far away; to them I was a communist and they were afraid of me, because of their relations with the German police and the name of the community and things like that. But they helped me, you can't say anything, thanks to them, I made the trip.

They gave me the passport for Uruguay with only an exit visa. Something that would take me far away and not let me return. I left for Hamburg, and I took a French freighter, the *Aurigne*, and from there I stopped at many ports. It went on stopping at all of them. I passed by Antwerp, then Marseilles, Lisbon, Rio de Janeiro, some thirty days until arriving at Montevideo. At the start, we were in the third or fourth class, I don't know, the lowest one. We were some thirty-five Jewish immigrants from Poland and Lithuania, I could speak with them in Yiddish, and the captain had a Kosher kitchen for us. But it wasn't a big deal. There was no wine to drink, so that on the third day, I went to eat with the sailors, and I did just fine there. Also traveling were about two hundred Spanish immigrants on the ship. We had songfests and dances on the bridge, among all of us, we made ourselves understood with signs and a few words. There was a great celebration when we crossed the Equator, it is a tradition to baptize the sailors that do it for the first time. It was a great party.

And so I arrived in Montevideo, after the 1930 revolution. I couldn't go to Buenos Aires yet. Where was I, in Pocitos, in a little hotel on Rincón Street, those who had been against the revolution and the military dictatorship were arriving. They were Argentines, and they told me that they had to escape because the police were after them. They were Jewish boys, sure, but from here.

I didn't know anything about America. They told me that in Argentina you lived very well and that a General Uriburo led a coup and took power. They were in the opposition, and they had to flee.

And so life went. I was a month in Montevideo. I looked for work, and I began as a tailor's helper. I lived in a pension. I was sewing for about eight days, and then the boss came and told me there's no more work, and that he doesn't have the money to pay me. And he didn't pay me, and what was I going to do to him? They took advantage of the immigrant. I didn't know the language or anything, I couldn't protect myself.

I wrote a letter to my brothers here. The answer came immediately: that I shouldn't dare to enter Argentina illegally, that I shouldn't move from there, that they were arranging for the immigration papers so I could enter legally. Because those guys who take you across, once they get the money . . . out at sea, if the papers aren't in order, if the Prefecture launch comes close, they throw you overboard to keep from getting involved. That I don't risk it.

But I didn't pay any attention to them. I went out to the Jewish section of Montevideo. I realized that they were Jews by the letters on the posters and the synagogue that was there. I spoke with a guy, and he told me that for one or two hundred dollars, there is a passage to Buenos Aires. They gave me an Argentine-type passport, from those who deal in these things. I didn't have to do anything other than memorize the name on the passport.

The document cost a hundred dollars, but I said that I only had twenty-five, and they gave it to me just the same. I made arrangements with the smugglers, and they took me across in a launch with another guy who'd been vouched for. If over here they were to ask me, I was to say that I came from Uruguay "swimming," what could they do to me?

I went through customs with the false passport. It said there that I was foreigner, resident for three years in Argentina. I had only learned the information that was shown. When my turn comes, the policeman asks me, "What's your name?"

I repeated from memory the first and last names. The other guy who came with me, told me later that they asked me, "How old are you?"

That I didn't know what to answer, I didn't understand anything. I said something under my breath, who knows what, and then he pointed at me and said to his companion, "See, these Russians are dumb bastards. He's here for three years, and he'll never learn the language."

Finally, he let me go through. When I got off the boat and was able to enter, I grabbed the passport, and I had to send it back by mail, so that they would take off my photo and put the original one back on, so that the Jew who was involved in this would be able to return.

Then, at last, I arrived in Buenos Aires. Without money, without the language . . . what could I do? I didn't have a cent, I didn't know anything. I began to walk. I see a taxi and I ask him with gestures if he could take me to San Miguel, where my brothers were. I show him a piece of paper with the address. He says yes, "Do you have so much?" I get him to understand that no, money I don't have, but I can give him my mesh watchband. It was a nice watch. He says no, all in gestures. No deal, he wanted five pesos and I didn't have a cent. I ask if he can take me to Cochabamba Street, close by, where my friend Mechl lived, the neighbor from my little village who owned a restaurant there. But he refused.

I set out to walk through the port area. I see the face of someone passing by there, who seemed to me to be Jewish. I quickly went up to him, and he was a bit surprised, and I ask him, *"Du vist a yid?"*

"Yes, how did you guess?" he answered me, in Yiddish.

"By your face."

"What do you want?"

"Look, I just got off a ship, and I don't have a single peso, and I don't know how to speak the language. At this address, Cochabamba Street, at the 4100 block, lives a paisano. Can you take me there?"

"Of course . . . This is Cochabamba Street, right here. Let's go . . ."

I thought we were going to take a trolley, but he didn't have any money either. We went from the 100 block of Cochabamba Street to the 4100 block of Cochabamba Street . . . "We came walking," he says. It was the 17th of January 1931, a very hot day it happened to be, okay, what do I know? We walked the forty blocks. The fact is that he carried me along.

We arrived there at about noon. Mechl himself was at home, because he worked as a *cuéntenik*, one of those who sell on credit in the street. He'd been there for six months, and when he saw me he got so happy, made coffee, and went to buy drinks. He invited the fellow and me.

Okay, I had lunch with him, we said good-bye to my companion, and then Mechl says, "Now let's go to San Miguel."

But we rode on the 86, on the trolley, and while we were going through Devoto, another paisano saw us.

"Where are you going?"

That fellow was already a "big shot," he had been in the country for about two years, he knew how to take care of himself well. Mechl explains to him that he's taking me to San Miguel. Then the fellow, while we were going toward the train, called my brothers on the telephone—he already knew how to speak on the telephone and all— and he tells Abraham and Jaime, "Your brother arrived in Buenos Aires, and now he's on his way to your place."

When we arrived at the station, an entire multitude had assembled: my two brothers, my sisters-in-law. Luzer, other paisanos, everyone was there, waiting. You can't describe that. The reunion in the new country was just so emotional, we all cried for joy.

Okay, I arrived. I was with them a few days, after that, I found an ad in the paper where they were looking for tailors and I went to work. I found one in Devoto, who would give me three pesos a day if I wanted to work. Then I looked for a place to live; I rented a pretty big room for fifteen pesos, and I was set up to live in the capital. In those days, on three pesos a day, you lived well, and you saved money. Every month, I sent about ten dollars to my parents (that was about twenty pesos). I went to the Polish consulate, and from there I would send the money, it arrived perfectly.

I rented a room with Mechl himself, that one on Cochabamba Street. In those days, that was how it was done, we paid for it between the two of us, and he worked in his part. It was in that room at the corner of Beodo Street and San Ignacio Street that I began to learn Spanish. Just coming here still makes me very excited. I remember that there was a political rally on a corner, a few days after I arrived, where Alfredo Palacios was speaking. I approached to see the red flags and the people. I didn't understand the language yet, but I did understand the meaning of the event. It made me remember the Bundist rallies in Poland, the leftists and workers over there. For that reason, I stayed there listening, but in a corner, almost at the end of all of it, to be able to escape running, if the police or the cadets with sticks with nails on their points arrived.

But nothing happened, and that thrilled me. The rally ended, and the people left and no one dispersed them, no one struck. I said to myself: "This country is a dream, it's a marvel, it just can't be."

I remembered that, soon thereafter, a tailors' strike began. I am in among the leaders. I don't know the language well yet, but there is a great deal of suffering, a man can't see that without reacting. In that period, I wasn't really communist, but socialist, I read Di Presse. The others weren't the same, the cuénteniks and other businessmen who read the Idische Zeitung, were more to the right. But I am a worker, my place was there. In that period, that of the strike, I started to work for myself, and I moved to a room on the 300 block of Uriburu Street. I was still a bachelor, and I worked together with my brother Carlos for the Hercof Company, at the 700 block of Corrientes Street.

They paid us seven pesos for each jacket. And to make a jacket, we had to work for at least two days, each one of twelve hours work. It was a pittance, on the other side, they were still paying twelve pesos a jacket, which was low, but it was the going rate at that time.

It wasn't a partisan thing, everything was mixed together, from several parties. Spaniards and Argentines and Jews and even Italians. We were all tailors, that united us. We called the strike, but there were "big shots." It was for an indeterminate period of time, until they raised the price, seven pesos for a jacket was too little. A pittance. When the strike began, I boycotted my older brothers too, since they gave me part of the work, but I couldn't betray the others, nor let myself be seen working. A strike is a strike, isn't it? That caused me a problem with my brothers.

There were a lot of strikebreakers because of the terrible conditions. Some had workshops and would bring in packages with the makings of ten jackets. There wasn't a chance. We couldn't win. The strike lasted eight days, but it failed. They threw the strikers out of the places where they worked. There were reprisals. The owners were bastards, too, they beat the shit out of all of us.

The owners agreed not to pay any more, and the cutters were with them, they made a deal. At that time, those of us employees who worked outside called the strike, they gave us the jackets, and we returned them finished. It was a large business where I worked, it had some six cutters—who were with them—and us in front.

We went on strike and in order that the "big shots" couldn't enter, we set up a picket line. I was one of those who made sure they don't go through. But the bosses called the cops. As soon as I step forward to stop a strikebreaker, and barely grab his lapel, three or four policemen jump me, grab my arms, and put me in the paddy wagon. The "big shots" didn't understand that if they didn't break the strike, they would have to raise our commission.

They took all of us from the union leadership to what was called the Special Section. I believe it was on Urquiza Street at the 600 block. I was held for six days and from there they sent me to the Police Department. On Moreno Street. As we were incommunicado, they separated us into halls, those with bunk beds hanging on the walls, one on top of the other, mixed in with common criminals. Just like it was in the ships. Bunk beds, a dirty blanket, rats. As I was a foreigner, they threatened to send me back to Poland. I answered with gestures, I didn't even know the language well. There I met "the Russian Sow," Jacobito who worked for them and took the statement in Yiddish.

"You are a communist?" he said to me for openers.

"No. I'm a Polish Jew, I don't understand Spanish," I answered him.

"What do you mean you don't, if here is your ad in the communist newspaper?"

And he shows it to me. It was my brother's doing. I pretended not to understand.

"So what? It's in the newspaper from the religious school, Cardinal Capello's, I also took out an ad. That's business. I'm neither communist nor Catholic."

"We'll send you back to Poland for being a communist," the guy tells me. "We don't want communists here."

"No, I'm not a communist nor a Catholic. I put ads in for business reasons."

I was of course familiar with the Party's newspaper. But to protect myself, I had to say that . . .

The "Russian Sow," a fat guy . . . a Jew who had sold out. He came and began to speak Yiddish, getting friendly, so he could find the truth in the lies, but we already knew, we were warned that you didn't have to say a word to him, because the guy was a sell out. He belonged to the police, they paid his salary. He gave me "advice." He told me not to continue with those "things," that they were going to kill me, that it was all for our own good. And, years later, they came to see me from the same Special Section, because of another ad in the Party daily. They said to me, "So you're still fucking around, communist?"

After it all, we lost the strike. They broke it, they didn't raise our commission. They had many "big shots" on their side because in those days, there was little work. But they didn't break us, we kept on fighting.

To tell the truth, I lied to the police . . . because I spoke Spanish, I knew it already. Yes, some months had passed already . . . Because when we rented the room with Mechl, there was a family of Italians. The old lady didn't know Spanish, but she had five or six kids whom she spoke to in Italian, and they answered her in Spanish. And from there I began learning the language.

The suffering was so great at that time, the abuse from the bosses too. A few years later, for example, the payment for a jacket was twenty-four pesos. I made two jackets for a large firm, one that made clothing. I go to collect, and they want to pay me . . . nine pesos. I tell them no. I go to report it. I went to the Union and from there to the Labor Ministry, and I made a complaint. I still haven't been paid for those jackets.

It was exploitation. It caused that strike, in 1933 or 1934, and later the fight continued in the union. But the bosses were very strong, the government was with them. It was very tough.

With all that, we worked and we worked. Like beasts, day and night. The needle stole our sight. I always worked as a tailor, until I rented space in Boedo Street, and there, I went into business with

my other brother—had he arrived from Poland? Yes!—with Carlos, and we also arranged for the papers and brought over our parents and Jacobo. Then we rented a house with business space on Nicasio Oroño Street and papa stayed there with Carlos, and I stayed with Jacobo on Boedo Street. And so we worked, until I got married. Abraham and Jaime also worked as tailors, we were a full-fledged clan. "Canaro with his Orchestra," they would say to Moishe Burech, when he went out with his five sons, we filled the sidewalk. We progressed little by little, some more, some less, some of them bought a house. And so. Our only entertainment was to go to the river once in a while. We would swim, remember Yarchev, sing in Yiddish and in Polish. Nostalgia, *nu?*

We were able to get my parents and Jacobo out on the last ship that left from there, before the start of the Second World War. After that, everything was an inferno in that area. Before leaving, Moishe Burech donated our house to the Zionist Association. Later, when the Nazis entered, from my entire village, only two brothers were saved, who fled for Russia when the Red Army came through. The rest of the Jews, they killed them all, they turned them into dust.

I met these brothers again around 1950 when they traveled to Argentina. They described how my house had been the headquarters of the Zionist committee, and, after the war, the Communist Party Committee met right there, since the entire village was then inside Russian lines. That house was a symbol. Everything happened there.

A little while ago, another paisano of ours returned from Lemberg. After the war, not even he knew how to save himself. And he says that nothing is left in Yarchev, they didn't even leave the ashes. So they must have rebuilt my house. They say that today you can't recognize anything there, it's as if you were dealing with another country, another planet. The little village exists only in memory now. We carry it inside us.

When Moishe Burech arrived in Buenos Aires, he began to work as a tailor, cutting in the Boedo Street business with me. Later it was that he rented the Nicasio Oroño locale, with Carlos and Jacobo, he set up another tailor shop. He only worked in the workshop because he didn't know Spanish, and so couldn't deal with the clients.

So I spent several years, working, until I met my wife at a Zionist party, I believe it was for Herzl's birthday. I went and she was there. But that was much later, when I was all grown up, when I already had the business on Boedo Street.

Of course, it's not right that I say it, but I was a quite a fellow. One day we went to a party held by another paisano, soon after arriving in the country, I say, and I danced, and I had a good time. The daughter of a certain Polak was there, Dr. Polak, and when I left, she comes and says, "Who is this boy? I like him a lot!"

And they told her, and then she exclaimed, "Too bad he's a greenhorn, a gringo! And he speaks Spanish so well. I really like him!"

So, that's the way it was. She was a "criolla" and to those who had been here for many years a Polish immigrant wasn't such a good

thing, they wanted a "doctor" or an "Argentine." It gave them status or something. But we didn't cause problems. In this photo, you can see all of us Poles when we arrived, in the Palermo gardens.

Later I got married, and my two children were born. All of the brothers were already established, so we decided to retire papa. Therefore, we put together a bit of money every month, and we paid a pension to the old lady, a "private retirement fund."

When Moishe Burech arrived, he went to live on Boedo Street because Carlos and Jacobo didn't know how to do cutting in the tailor shop, only sew. He had to show them, he was the teacher. Later on, as it was too large a house for my mother alone, they moved to Cochabamba Street, a room with a separate kitchen. In the meantime, Jacobo wanted to break off his arrangement with Carlos, and so he rented a work area with a house on Nazca Street, of which he had to sublet a section because it was very big. That was in 1946 more or less, around August in that year. By that time, Moishe Burech only did cutting, he no longer had the eyesight for sewing. Besides Cochabamba Street, he would go over to cut in the Boedo Street tailor shop. He walked two or three times a week from one place to the other, and there he would cut. The fact is that, finally, the parents went to live with Jacobo, and the brothers paid the rent for the room and kitchen that they had, there in Nazca Street.

Moishe Burech walked with difficulty; because of the infirmity in his legs that he caught during the war, he used a cane. He would arrive here, rest a bit, cut two or three suits, and return home when he felt like it. He was very old by then. He worked all that he could, but always inside the shop. He didn't deal with the public.

He had been born in 1870 or 1872, more or less. By the time he went to Nazca Street, he was already seventy-four or seventy-five. From the time that he moved, he got progressively worse, he also let things go, and the days pass, he didn't take care of himself. The only thing that he liked was the sun, he would sit in the sun in the patio and say that this would cure him. Once, when he went to *shul*, he grabbed one of the walls and shouted something that came from deep inside, he asked God to please cure him, because he couldn't walk anymore. He was more of a believer as an old man than he was when he was young. At the end he let himself believe a lot.

After the Second World War, the battle for the creation of Eretz Israel began, here too, in Argentina. We were communists, socialists, but very Jewish too, you couldn't separate it, we were practical Zionists. We fought with the Nazis here, as we had with the anti-Semites in Poland. We would collaborate as we could, it was all like a dream, I remembered how I was a *halutz* in my little Polish village. There was a *Palestine Cultural Broadcast*, that's what it was called on Radio Libertad. Later it was changed to *Israel Cultural Broadcast*, when the State was created. I remember that well, because I still have a letter from that period, among the old photos in a drawer of the highboy. They broadcast every Tuesday and Thursday between eleven and eleven fifteen at night, and they sent letters to inform us about the broadcasts and to get us to tell those we knew to listen too, how they fought for the State and Jewish culture. You had to organize and all that. Israel was always very small, and it had many enemies.

When one sees everything together, it's difficult to understand. I suffered a great deal in Poland for being Jewish, and when I came here, I saw that there was freedom. I didn't want my children to be different and I sent them to public schools, always. We lived in Villa Pueyrredón, a distant neighborhood, next to Villa Devoto, almost without Jews. And after all, you return like a glove.

My son David became a Zionist, he was already grown, and he went to live in Israel for a while. He has blamed me to this day, he told me I was a bad Jew. What does he know about Judaism? He already wanted to go at the time of the Six Day War in 1967. I was able to convince him not to, his wife was pregnant and about to give birth, it was crazy. It was a very difficult discussion. I had a lump in my throat that day, I couldn't speak, I almost wept. A shame. I told him the truth, what I thought: that I would go too, that if we had to die like Jews, at least let us die together. As a family. It comes down to the fact that it is always, as they say here, difficult to be Jewish. My son left for a *kibbutz*, some years later.

In 1948 Israel was founded, and Moishe Burech died soon after. In 1951. I was quite upset. He always was a man of few words, even more so here, in the language that he never learned. He was lucid until the final moment. He wasn't quiet because he didn't understand, but because he was that way. In Europe, he also spoke . . . word by word. Few words. That which was necessary and nothing more. When he answered something he went directly to the heart of the matter. He didn't waste time going around the subject. He always repeated a proverb: "to speak is silver, to keep quiet is gold." And he followed it.

At the end, when a person dies, it is because he has no more life inside of him. My children will say I am backward, but this is so. . . . Some overcome an illness or a difficult condition because they still have that kind of inner reserve. Others don't, at a certain moment, it is used up, and then they die. It's that simple. When they say that "he was destined to die," it means that it's something natural, the accumulation of life that one carries inside, good-bye, it's over. One carries a quantity since birth, and uses it up.

Here are the two of them; a good-looking pair of oldsters, worn by life. This is one of the last photos that they took together.

I'm never going to forget Moishe Burech's death. My papa's, it was the first day, I think, that I cried without shame, even in front of my children. He was lucid until the last moment, as I said, and he was always very brave. Before dying, he realized, one should realize that it's ending. He called his children to the bedside, one by one, and he said good-bye to them. Taking his leave, so, and we were crying and

he, tranquil. Then when mama came into the room, she began to cry and grieve, she couldn't contain herself. She grabbed his hands and yelled at him,

"Moishe Burech, why are you going? What are you doing? Where are you leaving me?"

And he answered her, serene but without strength, always with few words: "And where am I going?"

family tree

I quit. If you want, I can explain why. But I quit. Either I haven't understood you, Mr. Schnaiderman, or I haven't found what interests you. I feel like I have failed. And you cannot continue depending on me.

I am a professional, and I have worked conscientiously. Tape recorder, papers, questionnaires: here are two filled folders. But I collect words and not actions. Fragments of life instead of pulsating scenes. Dates and stories chopped up by the passage of time and that, taken together, offer some vague hints about the spiritual climate of the times. But.

I have found, above all, anecdotes. Skipping among the interstices of memory, distorted by the oblique lens of nostalgia. It is necessary to look backwards to assure its transmission, but an identity of the sort you are seeking, friend, is not constituted of memories alone. For that reason, you prove to be suspicious.

No. An identity requires dramatic action, personal experiences, actions. Drama, in sum. A tree that is something more than a drawing, or the photo of a grandfather with whom you could never converse and who was transformed into a mythical figure, unreachable.

You endeavor to decipher that transmission, that message from the roots, passing through a country in formation. It's an unlikely mix. Personal, unique. And moreover, Schnaiderman, you ride roughshod over it, when in your forties, that age of existential disruption, where the developed consciousness of your own mortality appears.

You should define your relationship with the old Jews of your story, those voices near the fire who beautify a life that is often miserable, forging visions of the past that are so uniform that they end up believing them.

Don't you want to speak directly about this ambiguity? In that case, I can give you a bit of advice: write down your impressions, alone. You seek yourself, not them. Lock yourself in a room, take paper and pencil, begin with a title—something like *Old Jews*—and let your associations flow freely. Let's see what happens.

Because speaking only . . . even the language is blocked by that extreme rationalization, deformed by desire. It takes a tradition of courage and heroism that, turned on its head, can be read as a defense of violence. One side doesn't operate without the other. Those repeating thrashings of others explained by anti-Semitism (I'm not anti-Jewish, but you folks have the habit of exaggerating that point) hide the other factor in the equation: insensitivity, brutality, subjugation.

Clinical experience tells us that there is always a bit of sadism in that moralizing: the nonviolent intellectual is in some way a person carrying repressed violence. He ought to look over his instinctive world, his morbidity, his repressed temptations, the sexuality, that which explains the other side of your family and of you, yourself.

Neither do I see, in the material that we have collected so far, the influence of the maternal side. It's as if you'd wanted to select, whimsically, the bits of history that fit an image that does well for you, that fits you: honest, brave, sensitive in the face of injustice. Now you are lacking everything else. I can't accompany you, if you, yourself close off the way.

Do you understand me? These are the limits of my ability to help. It's not enough to recall situations, it's urgent *to act on them*. Drowsing in the orchestra seats, my good sir, will never equal being a protagonist in the scene, that although close by, slips between the fingers. Forget all that has been heard and associated until now and ask yourself what you feel facing all that. Look at your longtime friends, those two or three people that one meets during adolescence and with whom it is possible (and with them only) to speak without masks or hidden intentions. Return to your childhood neighborhood, see your former neighbors, your image reflected in the eyes of those others who knew it.

Here are my papers, that which I've figured out until now. I'm not going on with this, it's not my style. Wake up. Act. I can't do it for you. You leaned over the well of nostalgia and you fell in. Don't accept living in the past, a less fixed time, more plastic, one that can be molded. No, my friend, the present time is harder, rigid, implacable. Take these folders and set yourself straight.

Don't worry about the fee: I'm satisfied with the advance that I have been given. Now, only you can continue the work. Take a stand. Gamble.

The ball is in your court. I've finished with this matter. The young lady will accompany you to the door.

MATER FAMILIAE

The year was 1919, the year of *La Semana Trágica*. I had been born a little earlier, here in Argentina. We lived on Belgrano Street, where my father had a shoe shop, set off from the workshop. Suddenly, I see the caretaker of the building lower the curtain and come running. The shop was in a large hall, and behind it were several rooms; the caretaker lived in one of these former dining rooms, that were left over. She saw a column of workers coming down Entre Ríos Street, and she was stunned. She called my mother and told her that it was dangerous to be there in front, with the two babies—Cecilia and me—and with my father. We all went inside.

Many of the neighbors got together in that enormous dining room, and they began to discuss the situation. There weren't any Jews except us. The majority were Spaniards and Italians, a typical immigrant apartment house. Many young people armed themselves so they could join the demonstration that was heading toward the Vasena Ironworks. My father wanted to go too: he took out of the clothes closet the revolver with a mother of pearl handle, the .38 short that we still own, he loaded it, and he wanted to go out. Then my mother grabbed him by the neck, and she began to cry.

"You can't go!" she yelled at him. "You have two little babies. Stay here!"

I held on to my mother's sweater, and I cried too. That scene was burned into my memory, the large man, pulling away, with the revolver in his hand, and the women who would not let him go. Cecilia wasn't even two years old, and she cried too. We were the babies of the house, all the women came out of their rooms and put themselves in front of him so that he couldn't leave. He said that it couldn't be, everyone had left and not him. With such struggling, he finally had to stay. Luckily—because they turned the demonstration into a massacre, they killed dozens of workers that day.

My father made parts of shoes, and my grandfather was a shoemaker, they shared the locale; one made repairs off to one side, and the other sold men's shoes. There was also a workshop on the other side where six or seven men worked, those were the ones who went to the demonstration. I think they killed one of them.

My father arrived in Argentina when he was thirteen years old. His three younger brothers were born here. He spoke Spanish well, and he got married here, when he met my mother, at eighteen or nineteen years old. It was arranged by the paisanos, as these things always are.

It happened that Hanna, my mother, arrived together with her sister Rifka, when they were both girls. Since Aunt Rachel cried a lot when she arrived here, she didn't have any family, we sent the two girls to her in 1910. Since they knew a bit of sewing, Hanna immediately went to work as a tailor's assistant, in a shop belonging to a paisano, and my father saw her there—he had arrived a long time before and so was Argentinized—when he once went to visit there, and he fell in love with her. Now the problem was that the two of them were underage; his parents could sign for him, but she didn't have anyone. But in those days you could do most anything, since the older folks didn't have a marriage certificate from here, only a marriage document from Russia, as they came from Besarabia.

It was like a novel. The two were very young, and they loved each other, according to what my grandfather swore to the judge. Moisés was twenty-two years old and Hanna twenty-one. They were of legal age. They looked for other witnesses among the paisanos to back up this declaration and so, in 1911, they were able to marry. For that reason, my mother repeated during her entire life that the age on the document was not her true age.

My mother's parents lived in a little village in Russia. My grandfather had an attack of appendicitis, and he was very sick. My grandmother Sara put him on a cart and took him to Odessa to try to save him, but the roughness of the trip caused him to suffer peritonitis, and he didn't return. Sara was left a widow and with eight children, alone: the two daughters, Hanna and Rifka, were already in Argentina. Once, much later, Hanna found in her older sister's house, under the gramophone, a letter from Russia, in which was told the death of her father (that Rifka had hidden). It was something terrible.

Then, soon thereafter, Sara sold everything that she had, some relatives helped her, and in 1913, she left with all her children for Argentina. I had just been born, they went to live on the 500 block of Frías Street, that I remember.

My grandmother Sara was a very advanced person, with left-leaning ideas. She subscribed to the daily *Di Presse* and she would always comment on Botoshanky's articles. Whenever she had a free moment, she spent it reading, she took care of herself very well, in spite of her lack of high culture; she stood out among the women of the period; cultured, independent, taking care of her children, a hard worker, a good cook. Here she found a new partner, and she married again; for us, the grandchildren—she was something wonderful.

The second husband was named León, and he loved us a lot. I was the oldest granddaughter. We always went to visit her with Cecilia and Rosa; as soon as he saw us, the old man would begin to sing and dance, to yell in Yiddish, "Here are my pretty *pupis*! My pretty dolls!"

Every once in a while, Grandma Sara made a spread and invited all her grandchildren. Everything she made tasted of honey, I can't forget it. We lived a block from her house. Once I went over there, and my grandmother offered me peaches in syrup. And I tasted such a rich flavor that even today—at that time I couldn't have been older than seven—when I think about it, I can taste those peaches. And every time that I would visit her, she would offer me something that she had made, she was so skillful. She would bake a priceless *strudel*, I've never tasted anything like it since.

Once, they came to choose several children to sing at the Teatro Colón. They included me as the first voice, I don't know if I deserved it, but I went. On the stage of the Colón, there was a kind of riser, and we came from three schools: a boys' school in the center and two girls' schools on the sides. We were only a few from each school.

We sang two very pretty folk songs and the *Aurora* march. My grandmother told me—I was small and thin—that the President of the Nation, who was present there, was surely taken with me. She said it in jest, of course, because for all grandmothers, their grand-daughters are the most beautiful.

As for my grandfather on the other side, he didn't get along well with my father, because the old man had a minor vice. He drank a lot. Already in Odessa he drank an incredible amount, it was incurable. For that reason, after a while, Moisés opened a small shop, for repairs, on his own. My grandmother was a very small woman, she had a very soft voice, so that she could hardly be heard. She made *humentaschen* for Purim, and she always asked me, "Do you know why you make the empanadas with three points? Because they are like Haman's hat."

She cooked them with *mun* and honey, those cakes had a very special fragrance; she, poor dear, didn't have an oven, they were very poor and got by with a little wooden kitchen set. They would borrow a brass oven for the holidays. She was a very constrained person, and with her immense crop of children, she didn't last long, she would have died around 1939, and she was already a widow by then.

For my other grandmother, Sara, after my cousin Bernardo, I was the oldest, she always came and brought me hair ribbons. When she saw that a ribbon was getting old, she went and bought me another one. I had seen a spectacle with ballerinas, I think it was in a movie, so I laid out a rug on the floor and did some steps, and some shakes,

I was six and I did everything I could to entertain her. Grandmother applauded me and said, "This is the grandchild who is going to be a great artist."

She was crazy about me, and I about her. She would always repeat a proverb that had to do with her grandchildren: "*a titz un dus a hitz*," "a dozen, and this one the favorite," and she pointed at me.

"You love your grandmother Sara more than you love me, don't you. You love her more, isn't that right?"

I said no, that I loved them the same, but in truth my Grandmother Sara was the favorite. She bought the ribbons for me, she adored me, she inspired me. And I needed that because of the problems at home.

I have always been apolitical. The only thing I remember is when they kicked out Yrigoyen, in 1930. Those were bad times for the worker, because then it wasn't like now. The fashions didn't change so suddenly. The manufacturers produced an immense stock, and then they cut their staff. At that time, I was fifteen years old. My father didn't have a shop any longer, but rather a large workshop, with operators. He had machines and everything, but the factories made goods to store away—because shoes don't spoil—and when they reached a certain limit, they kept the workers on, giving them bits and pieces of work, and paying what they felt like. They went along selling off the stock at ever higher prices, and meanwhile the workers were starving to death.

When there was a lot of work, you did well, but not everybody knew how to save for the bad times. The cycle was: three months of intense work, three month of little work or unemployment, where you eat from what you had saved, or you had to go to others for help. I remember having had to go several times to borrow some pesos to pay the rent or in order to eat.

I worked with my parents since I was twelve, I helped my brothers—because we were so many—and I helped in any way I could. I had a little sister who died of meningitis, after Ana was born. A bad doctor got hold of her, and she died immediately, at ten months old. My mother was left half crazed because they had told her that she couldn't have any more children, because she had had a severe hemorrhage. She had lost babies between Cecilia and me, one never knew why they died, perhaps incompatibility in the blood or something like that, who knows? The fact is that when Cecilia was born in 1917, it was terribly cold, and it had snowed, it was wintertime. In the children's hats they put pieces of cotton to muffle the cold from their ears, and they were afraid that this little baby girl would die too. For that reason, they took care of her as if she was a crystal goblet.

Cecilia was always very nervous. When she was little, she bit my arm. I remember it even now. Once the girl who lived next door said to me, "Your little sister is so pretty," and I answered her, "Yes, yes, you are right. It's a pity she's so bad."

The truth is that my father made distinctions. I remember that one time the two of us went out to walk along the street, he took us by the hand. I was always skinny because I had hardly been born when my mother became pregnant again and weaned me, so I didn't know how to eat or to suck from a bottle. I rejected everything. When one of those little babies, who were born after me, died, I didn't want to eat with my mother. I went to a neighbor, and I chewed dry bread. Like a hunger strike, right? My parents then bought me the best cakes and pastries, but I preferred the neighbor's dry bread, it was like a rejection that I made to her in return for what she did to me by getting pregnant. For that reason, I always grew skinny, too thin, while Cecilia, who they hovered over so she wouldn't die, looked like a cabbage. Besides that, she was blond and I dark.

So we went out for a walk, and we met a gentleman, a friend of the family. And the man asked my father, "Are these your two daughters? Isn't the little blond one so pretty?"

"Well, yes," my father answered. "The blond is pretty, the other one so, so."

Of course, I was *the other one*.

This was etched in my memory forever. It was my father's ignorance, he who clearly had a preference for her. Cecilia was always the spoiled one. Around the corner from my house, there was a doll factory that in those days made porcelain dolls, and my father would buy them for her. She would play for two or three days and she'd break it, so papa would go and buy her another doll. I, on the other hand, don't remember ever having had a doll in my life. As I was the older sister—I was six or seven years old—"I didn't need it."

I never had a doll until, already grown up, I bought one for myself. I bought a doll, one of those that comes in pieces and you put it together, and afterwards I kept it in a closet, and I never had time to complete it. Because I was acquiring it part by part: first the body, then the little shoes, the head. . . .

And fifty years later—I bought it when I first began to earn a paycheck—at sixteen or seventeen years old—my children took advantage of one of my trips, and they threw it in the trash. According to them, "They cleaned up." And "for me" they threw away the doll.

Later on I bought another doll for my late sister Ana, when she was twelve and so sick that she almost died. She had an infectious rheumatism. Her legs were all swollen, as was her stomach. We put her into the Hospital Israelita, she was the youngest, and I loved her a lot. What did I do then? I put on a white smock, to disguise myself as a student, and I went behind those who were following Dr. Malamud, who was the chief of the wing and taught in the Medical School. That was my first vacation, and I spent it inside the hospital. I met my boyfriend at the door there, we had a cup of tea on the corner, and then I went back to my sister.

Of course, I wanted to know how she was doing. So I got myself behind a line of students in smocks, and we went into the room. She stopped at each bed, the doctor, that is, and she explained the case. When she got to my sister, she reviewed everything, she examined her, and she said, "It's necessary to stop the rheumatic infection so that it doesn't spread to her heart, because that is the greatest danger with this sort of illness, if it touches the heart, that's it. Therefore we're going to change her diet completely and give her injections in her veins."

And she was right. Ana got more strength and she improved.

My first job was two blocks from my house, with a dressmaker. I didn't want to be with my father all day long, on the machine, since he didn't sew but instead made shoes. I didn't like that work. In those days, shoes were made with stitching, it was done with cardboard, and I had become a specialist in the process. Not just any worker could do it, it was difficult. But I got tired of being at the machine all day. Also, I had to make deliveries.

I wished for, I don't know, something better. My father wanted me to go to the factory where he got the work, but I didn't want to be a factory worker. It seemed to me a bit degrading, shameful. So I went with my mother, a block from my home, where a seamstress needed an assistant. They had me making hems and finishing, easy stuff, until the political situation calmed down; but when payday came, they paid me one peso fifty, which was a joke. My father would pay three or four pesos and to the good workers he would give as much as five a day.

Therefore I saw that this wasn't going anywhere. And I went back to work with my father. In school, I took two separate programs: the one for twelve to fifteen year olds was a three-year course in "cutting and dressmaking." Those under fourteen years old weren't permitted to take these courses. When my teacher found out that I was only twelve, she wanted to throw me out, and I began to cry. As I was one of the best pupils, she gave in. But she said, "You can stay under one condition. If an inspector comes around here, you are fourteen years old. If they ask for your parents' marriage booklet, they lost it and are in the process of getting another one. Remember that I'm taking a chance with my job."

So that's how it was, and I was able to finish my course. At fifteen I graduated as a teacher of sewing and cutting.

I liked dressmaking a lot, and I did it at night—because during the day I worked with my father—so I could make my little samples. My Uncle José also had given me a booklet of coupons, so that I could have twenty-five lessons (because when he bought a sewing machine, they gave him that little booklet for lessons), and then I took the course in embroidery with the Singer machine. By fifteen, I had already finished the course and the twenty-five lessons, everything on embroidery and dressmaking. I was eager to progress and improve myself. I went and signed up for handwork, and I also completed that course. There was a girl who lived in front, a very delicate girl, who was a teacher, I envied her! Because to be a teacher would have been my greatest wish. My father sent me at twelve to learn the piano, in the house of the factory foreman's daughter. He did it so that her father would give him more work; I mean to say that my father not be left without work during the difficult periods, so she gave me free piano lessons, to get along.

This teacher explained to me that Theory and Solfeggi were the same for the piano and the violin. And as my father scratched a little on the violin, and he loved the instrument, and I did too, he wanted me to learn that instrument. In those days, grandmother Sara would come over to my house. And there were "The Young Ladies' Orchestras"; it was a style, three or four badly made-up girls, and one would play the violin. When my grandmother learned of them, she said to me, "Go on, go on with the violin. You'll end up playing in bars and cafes, for sailors. And when you get married and have a baby, you'll bring him along and rock the cradle with one foot while you continue playing."

Of course it frightened me, this business of working there, and with all those men watching. Because the majority of those who went there were men. I didn't continue with the piano or the violin. I started to look for outside work, so I could leave my father's shoe factory.

My sister Cecilia accompanied me. She always found work

through the ads. She was employed as a saleslady by Imperial House, at the corner of Diagonal Street and Suipacha Street. I found a job at a large furrier that did import-export, at the 700 block of Carlos Pelligrini Street, which doesn't exist now because they widened Nueve de Julio Avenue. Then I went and got out my seamstress diploma, and the owner said to me, "Yes, there are many who have diplomas and don't know anything."

Cecilia, who was a quick thinker, answered him immediately: "So, give her a try."

"Okay," said the guy. "Then you bring me a certificate that you have been a saleslady."

I went to ask Solomon, the Turk, the one whose wife smoked with a *narguile* and everything. He didn't want to give it to me because he said it was too dangerous for him, that the inspectors would come and so on.

What could I do? I remembered that the "Palace of Style" belonged to a sister of my Uncle Isaac, and that her husband was a good man, "salt of the earth." We went there. He looked at me—he was named Marcos, they called him Marquitos—and he said to the clerk, "Give a certificate to this girl."

Just like that, without a fuss. I go with the paper, although I didn't know that this gentleman had a branch on Carlos Pelligrini Street on the 600 block. I quickly went in to work there because of this recommendation that came from a "neighbor," practically. But I didn't understand anything about furs. Any time anyone came in, my knees knocked.

The first day a lady came in. In those days French was in fashion.

"How can I help you?" I said to her. And she answered, *"J'envais un chanté."*

I looked at my partner, and I said, "One moment please."

The girl whispered "Silver fox." Then I went, and I showed her what she wanted.

I learned rapidly. At two years, I was patternmaker and was making as much as my friend who had been working there for sixteen years. She went in to protest and they raised her salary, but they raised mine too, they gave me the difference secretly, as a "pattern-maker." Which means that I made more than she did. I made the patterns. Once they even sent me to the movies, so that I could copy the furs worn by a movie actress. And they brought me designs from Marcel Pouner, the one who dressed Evita, who was a client of the store. The owner of the furrier also did importing. He brought me models and I would make a full-sized pattern on heavy paper. They made that model with fabric, and they tried it out.

All, all of the clients had to pass through my hands. I was the patternmaker, and the owner also did fittings. I fitted the *toile* (that's "cloth" in French). I knew which was the red fox, which was the do-mestic fox, I learned a bit of everything. Also, I had an especially good memory; in high school, I hardly studied, I heard the explana-tion from the teacher, and I repeated it.

It's that you get a trade by working, there isn't anywhere to study that. You have to know a lot about fur cutting and be precise, be-cause furs are sewn side by side, there can't be any mistakes. After the fitting, I had to recheck the *toile* and the pattern before the cutter worked, because the fur had to fall perfectly, it wasn't something that could be corrected like work done by a seamstress or a tailor.

The decade of the thirties was very difficult for the workers. You'd work for three months and you'd be unemployed for three months. When I started, I gave half of my salary to my household. A part, a good part. Even so, many times, I had to ask for credit because in my house money was always short.

When we began to work, my parents' furniture was already twenty years old. Aunt Rifka's father, who had a factory, had made them. All carved wood, all very nice. We had a set with six chairs and the bed where Cecilia, Rosa, and I slept. I got Cecilia excited about refur-nishing the place, and we purchased a Chippendale dining room set, two sideboards, a large oval-shaped table, two large chairs, and other chairs. All of it was second-hand, but it was like new, impeccable. We made curtains for the dining room windows, and we put up another curtain as a separation, because the girls slept in a divided part of this room. We bought a radio, one of the first that came out, with an attachment for records. In short, we tried to live a little better.

Even when I left, they gave me double pay, and they told me that that job would always be open for me. But I had already formed a family—I had a daughter, obligations with the home, I couldn't. Here we are in the patio of my father's house, on Castro Barros Street, all my father's family and my mother's family, at my daughter's third birthday. We were quite a few, as you can see. My husband has David in his arms, he's a few months old. He was my second child.

In those days, social life was very restricted. In the *shul* on 24th of November Street, they had formed a club, for the children of the members of the *shul*. My father was also a member there, because we went to the parties. They always had meetings, theater. Once my brother Bernardo sang in the chorus with the *hazan*. They gave him a prize, I don't know if it was ten or twelve pesos, he was a little kid.

Then he was asked if he didn't want to donate it to the *shul* and my father said yes. The guy gave him a receipt, and my father donated what Bernardo had won. We had our first social activities there. There they had founded a club that was called *Jorge Brandes*, and it was for people a little bit older. You paid fifty centavos a month. When it started to have a few members, they rented, just around the corner from where we lived, a hall and a vestibule. That was for meetings, you spoke about everything including politics and Nazism in Europe, because many of the kids were students. One was the fat Moscovich, my husband and I met him years later while walking the streets of Mar del Plata. I asked him if he was married and he answered me, "Who am I going to marry if women find me disgusting?"

There was also a beautiful library, where we could take books out in Spanish: Dumas, José Ingenieros, Dostoevski. For members only. They gave us a period of time to read the book, and if we didn't return it, they would charge us a small fine, nothing more. And there I began to read, to put a lot of attention into reading. And besides that, I bought *Leoplan* and *Para Ti* because I had to travel almost twenty minutes on the trolley, and if I was able to get a seat, I would read. I asked that they recommend titles, and I polished them off on the trolley.

Also, they organized dances. The members paid very little, and with the admissions paid by the nonmembers, they collected funds for improving the library. Later they moved next door to my house, a bigger place, on the second floor with a balcony. It was fantastic. Then another club appeared, *Enrique Heine*, which doesn't exist anymore, and another one that began to compete with it. Since so many clubs were opening up, the number of people attending was dropping. But there were very nice dances, even some with orchestras. One time, in the Rural Society, they hired the Jazz Band; they paid so much for the place and the orchestra that they were left with nothing. But that was the type of promotion they did. We girls went to the *Enrique Heine*, which was on Ayacucho Street and competed with the *Hebraica*, but in the end, the *Hebraica* won out, because it had an enormous library, incomparable.

There I practiced Swedish exercises. I did it after work, I arrived home with my legs trembling. I left late, and I was worn out, I worked all day on a shortened schedule. I had a bit more than two hours of traveling, and at noon, they gave me two and a half hours to eat, just enough time to go home, eat, and return. And before the employees weren't allowed to sit down, the Chair Law wasn't in place yet, Palacio's, that came later. We had to be always standing. People who came in had to see that we were not only standing, but busy: the counter was piled with twenty or so enormous cases, and there were placed the cheapest pelts. Not the fox but the rabbit or the hare. And then we had to act as if we were working, as if a client had just come in: take out a whole case, dust it. Straighten it up and return it to its place . . . And so, all day long.

I remember that around that time a lady, whose father-in-law had been president of the nation, came in. She had a last name made up of two last names. I never understood this mania for putting together last names to make them longer; we, with just one, fill up a whole line. In those days, few women drove cars. She had the little car key in her hand, and she would always twirl it. A lovely woman, young, very pretty. She always asked for me, and if I wasn't there, she wouldn't buy. She brought in many patterns from her fashion designers, for ornaments on the wraps, and she was so accustomed to me that she wouldn't let anyone else wait on her.

When there was tourism, we had very many Chileans who came to buy here, carloads of skins, fur blankets. I believe I remember now that that president's wife was Señora de Figueroa Alcorta, a tall, dark-skinned woman, very fickle. I was okay in that store, they were very upright and they paid me on time. They didn't like to be asked for advances, which unfortunately I often had to do because of my sister Ana's illness and other things, until I got mad and said, "Enough." My father took out a loan for forty pesos from a cooperative to buy things for the house. He had to pay monthly, and he never had enough.

They are sufferings that one endures. I, in those days, did well and I could handle whatever might occur. My other sister called me then *the millionairess*; she was dying of envy because I earned four or five times what she did. With all of us, we managed. We came out of nothing, by struggling, we could emerge from the depths. A few times only were we able to enjoy ourselves at the river. That was a party. From then, I have this photo, with my aunts.

Soon thereafter, I met my husband, and I got married. My children were born, and that's another story. As for Moishe Burech, my father-in-law . . .

Yes, my memory of Moishe Burech is very clear, especially with what the old lady told me. Because old Hettie was a good woman, a bit quarrelsome, may she rest in peace. In front of my sister-in-law, when I went into the kitchen to help her, she said to me in Yiddish (since she never learned Spanish), "You are my best daughter-in-law."

"*Schuiguer*," I answered her. "You say that because we've never lived together, you don't know me."

She insisted, "No, you are my best daughter-in-law. When speaking of a son-in-law, you say in Yiddish, *man geneidem*, man from paradise. As a joke."

Moishe Burech told me, "For a woman like you, it's necessary to search the whole world, because when one is good, she's good for everything. . . . " I was the only Argentine, all the other sisters-in-law had come from Poland. I was the "native."

Why did they say to me that I was the best daughter-in-law? Because I once made her a robe, because when sugar was scarce, I never went to visit her without bringing her two kilos as a gift (whatever the price). I did the same when you couldn't get flour, I always brought her little things that you generally couldn't find.

When there were disagreements in the family, Moishe Burech always tried to calm the tempers, although he never spoke a lot. He would play dominoes. A bit later, when he died, the children played poker. People of his age speak little, and what's more, he didn't go out. There was the old man, Mechl's father, who had been first his tenant and later his neighbor in the village, the one that had a bar. But he stopped seeing him because, when he arrived in Argentina, the guy became a religious fanatic, while in Yarchev, he was such an atheist that . . . once he saw him smoking on the Sabbath, so later he asked him, "You, who are you kidding?"

Moishe Burech went to *shul* on Saturday, but he wasn't so fanatic. For that reason he didn't respect Mechl's father as a person. He was always the same phony, he used to say that in the depths of winter he would go out in his shirt-sleeves and not feel the cold, because under that shirt he wore a fur vest. It's funny now to tell it.

When we were married, we took a photo, all together; there were the two of us, my parents, my in-laws and my two grandmothers.

Both grandmothers were sixty-six years old. Hettie, who was

sixty-five at the time, was quite pleased because she thought she was the darling of the group.

When I had my civil wedding, my husband made me a cocktail dress: jacket, silk lapels, and a skirt. Moishe Burech sewed me a vest with a little plaid collar, with some imported corduroy he had bought. He didn't sew for women, he did it only for me. Such was the perfection of that vest—he was a man who loved his trade, he did it very well—that when I later went to a first-class dressmaker, in a boutique, a client of theirs wanted them to make a wedding dress like that for her. She asked me if I could bring the pattern for the dress and the vest. I told her that I could, but when I went to ask Moishe Burech, he answered me, "Tell your dressmaker to go to the academy to learn."

He was a first-rate tailor, detailed, better than his sons. He learned to sew in Lemberg. Also, Jacobo, his younger son, studied to be an electrician in that city because he was too near-sighted to sew, and in those days, there weren't many eyeglasses or opticians. For example, he heard less in one ear, and they wouldn't believe him, so they would throw a coin on the floor, and since he turned around, they

told him he wasn't deaf and that he should stop faking. That was over there, according to what they say. And in Lemberg, they learned trades.

Moishe Burech was sixty-five years old when he arrived in this country, but he seemed much older. He walked poorly, he had arthritis, rheumatism in his knees. He wasn't in very good shape. He was left that way by the war, his leg problems began in the trenches of '18, and he didn't have specialized treatments. In those days, one didn't get cured, he was deteriorating.

From time to time he read *Di Presse*, but he didn't go to his associations, he didn't go anywhere. He wasn't speaking. His world had stayed there, in Europe. He never completely understood what he was doing over here, in this place, with these incomprehensible people and languages. Neither did he travel. He didn't know how to make his way in the city. He knew how to walk, with a cane and all. At times, he held himself up on a chair, because he had weakness in his legs, but he would make twenty, thirty, forty blocks. Little by little, gritting his teeth, very slowly, but he would walk them. He had a strong character, a great will. But he couldn't travel.

Later on, his children together paid for his retirement. But there is a very wise proverb in Yiddish that says: *Az eltern guibn di kinder, lajnzei beide; ober az kinder guibn di eltern, veinenzei beide*. That is, "If the elders give to the children, both laugh; but if the children give to their elders both cry."

He died because he had a little bit of everything: arthritis, a transfusion which seemed to mix urine with the blood, kidneys, and all of that. He was already sick from before. In the end, in the hospital, he didn't have enough strength to open his eyes. He died in 1951, at eighty-three years old. According to Hettie, she said that he died because they gave him the evil eye, when he celebrated his eightieth birthday, someone who found out and was jealous. In the photograph, he is there with those who gave that party, in Jacobo's house. It is exactly twenty years after that photo from Poland, before the

first ones left for America. You can look at both and compare each person, in one and the other.

There are stories and stories: someone told me that since Moishe Burech liked to play billiards over there in Yarchev, and he was something of a tough, he would spend his time playing with his friend Marash. One time, Hattie got tired of the fact that her husband didn't come home, and so she went to the bar, grabbed the billiard cues and broke them over the table. Hettie was tiny but fiery. Moishe Burech only would look at his children, and he would still dominate them, without hitting them. But when Hettie would call them, and they didn't come immediately, she went out with an iron rod and yelled louder and louder, and as they entered, they already knew that there was going to be trouble. They came in, one by one, to protect themselves better.

Chubby and small, but she fought with the big ones. Once, when Abraham was already married, he slapped his son, for he hadn't been behaving himself. Hettie went, took her turn, and gave Abraham a slap. He was confused.

"Why did you do that?" he said. "Can't I hit my own son?"

"Because your son is my grandson," she answered him. "And if you can hit your son, I can hit mine."

Very tough, the old lady. They told me that once when Carlos had done I don't know what, and she threw a scissors at him, that if she had hit him, she would have killed him. And here is the strangest thing: Moishe Burech never once hit any of his children, and they had an incredible respect for him, while Hettie, with all her hitting, they didn't respect. No one knew why.

Moishe Burech was always a very respectful man. When Hettie yelled at him, he would say, "Let her go, let her go, it will pass." He would keep his place, he would try to calm things down. "Let him stop talking," he would say. I don't know if he was a great worker, about that I've heard differing versions. But there is no doubt that he was intelligent. Very intelligent. Hettie, toward the end, got angry and shouted at him in front of everyone, "Old Animal," "Old Ox," and things like that. She had the poor old man in her power. And he put it all aside with a movement of his hand, he downplayed its importance.

"It's nothing," he was saying. "Let her go. It will pass."

family tree

Old Jews

Survivors
swallows barred from ever going back
landed from Lodz, Odessa and Vilna
Prague and Lemberg, maybe even Vienna
with the skies of Europe in their eyes
bobbins from a mislaid skeleton
bewitched by something at our back
and seeking farther along
distracted by their yearning for blue
orphaned in spite of the strain
of thrusting the bent chin up and forward
of tremors sometimes held in check
of studied vowels opening out
like casements on the infinite.

These are the old Jews
hardworking cannibals of affection
poets who share in the history
and prison and the bread of great men
in a glorious past, under
laceworks of European constellations
in petals of Yiddish sifted through
like the odd piece of luggage
no longer wide streets and the groan of wagons
no longer drunkards and snow on the windowsill,
no longer the tavern with its rackety chairs
no longer those rabbis of the Cabala
their characteristic language

of thorns and quavers, groomed by daylight.
And then the others:
Litvaks who embroider unfamiliar threads
kosher butchers with shadowy beards
the outlandish workmanship of hatters
peddlers from Istanbul and Damascus
roster of Jewish occupations
of strutting divers into the surface
and all, all of these
loud and lithe as dolphins
saunter through the streets of Buenos Aires
nothing to smoke, coddle, kiss or sing
hand on their ribs, as if just now
they realized they'd misplaced something
in their immigrant wisdom.

Children riveted
by their witless amazement of being alive
lost among the conspiratorial winks
of a city wide open, and no longer grasping
these are the old Jews, faithful flotilla
of pirates stripped of their main and master
who artistically compose expectations
into echoes of shock.
And that one, who on the streets of Warsaw
may have been a politician of subtleties
now picks out grubby little deals
or speculates with his wealthy compatriots
in a dull and paralyzed culture
to swerve around the potholes of hunger.

And who, really, would not
be moved to compassion at seeing those mastheads
shake with fury on either side

filled with the inert sounds
foreshadowings and honed prescriptions
and turbulent gatherings of Yiddish
illuminated only by the ashes of
fires ignited years ago
in a far-off wilderness alongside the Rhine
and still another without tinder
radical passengers in the night
owners, in spite of everything, of our deficiencies
in the Hebrew seedlings of a garden
we didn't plant and yet continue to love.

Oh, my old Jews
passports of thick diphthongs
of foreign clothing and shifting eyes
of hurried walk, as if some
geometry of shadow might be lying in wait
running through the mechanism of time
with brusque and rusty whispering
ties clumsily knotted
among communities of inhabitants
and stout philanthropists of asylums
who spit sideways and restrict
the pulsebeat of irrational grievance
standard bearers of lost causes
always refugees in the eyes of the world.

Stubborn peddlers
clamorous with grievance and even envy
blind, allergic to joy
so distant from me, so speechless
and blocking the progress of the new
setting history against enterprise
and making themselves hated by their awkward

manner of being evil
and, nevertheless, when I consider
everything they could have been
if the wind had not torn them up
cut short a newborn ascent
when I imagine the wasted land
and their sad, bleak roots,
oh, how I love you, you old Jews.

2. Trunk and YOU

There is nothing more sublime
for life than a memory
especially of childhood
—Fyodor Dostoevski

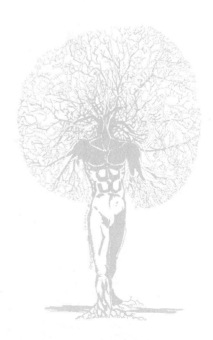

The clerk with the throaty voice looked at you from the other side of the window and said, "Are you the interested party?"

"Yes, sir."

He took out a blank application, placed it on the table, and picked up the ball-point pen.

"Last name?"

"Schnaiderman."

"Again?"

The eternal story, experienced since elementary school (where you were "David," "S.," "Schaiman," "man," "the tricky one," and similar variations) and copied exactly during scholastic experience of your children. But now it affects a job that you need; it must not ruin things right from the start.

"Schnaiderman," you repeat.

"Look, I . . . "

"I understand, don't worry. Don't get nervous. I'll spell it for you: S for Solomon, C for Carlos, H for Horacio, N for Napoleón, A for Arturo, I for Inés, D for David, E for Ernesto, R for Ramón, M for Manuel, A for Arturo, N for Napoleón. Schnaiderman. It means 'tailor.'"

You rapidly spit out the string of proper names, because you have said them on an infinity of occasions. The man is able to get a bit beyond the middle of the last name, including two errors: he omits an I and he adds an unnecessary R. . . .

"No, no," you say. "Look, I'll spell it for you again."

"It would be better," he answers, handing you the application, "if you write it yourself. I find it difficult to copy *foreign* names."

Your friend León "Try Anything" Piatigorsky used to say that you were overly sensitive about this subject. Could be. And that you don't even have *his* name. Your face reddens from nervousness, and it occurs to you that, most likely, it would be useful, now, to chat with León about what is happening. He would help you. He always got along better with his environment.

"What is your name, sir?" you ask. He is surprised.

"Hector García. Why?"

"And your last name is not 'foreign' but rather 'Argentine'?"

"Yes . . . Yes, sir."

"You mean to say, then, that you descend from a tribe of Mataco Indians. Or Tobas. Or from the Querandí Garcías. Perhaps Cailfucara García, an Araucano chief. Lautauro García, of the Diaguitas?"

His cheeks turn red. He is a bit tense.

"No, sir, I wanted to say that I am 'Argentine' because I was born here. In this country."

"I also was born here."

"In Buenos Aires. In the neighborhoods."

"In Buenos Aires. In the neighborhoods."

You seem to echo him, but your tone is mocking. People have begun to crowd behind you, and they are in a hurry.

"My mother too is Argentine," the clerk adds with less firmness. "I am a second-generation Argentine."

"My mother too is Argentine. A native of Buenos Aires, to be exact. Second generation."

He blushes again and smiles, perhaps looking for an amusing aspect of the issue.

"But my father came from Europe like all the immigrants."

"Mine also came from Europe. In any case, you wanted to say that 'both' had *foreign* surnames, only from different places. Yours is from Spain, mine from Central Europe. The two of them, immigrants. The land of origin, practically neighbors."

"But my father arrived here fifty years ago. In 1933. He's like any Argentine. And he's naturalized."

"My father too is a naturalized Argentine. And I'm sorry to disappoint you, but he arrived before yours did: in 1931. All these details are of little importance. But that's the way it is."

There is a silence. Some in the line protest in a lowered voice, checking their watches. Unemployed who are looking for work, graduates in sociology who have lost hope in their profession, jackets with frayed sleeves, and thick eyeglasses. The clerk seems to understand that it's not in his best interest to get upset.

"You don't understand me. To be Argentine is . . . I don't know, the language, to be Latino. That's it. Latino."

"The language? I believe that you lose on that one, my friend. I am an editor of scientific works in Spanish. So if it depends on a grammar test . . . "

"No, no. You don't understand me. I was referring to the length of the surname."

"You are right. I don't understand you. Your prejudices define everything that is different as *foreign*. I want you to explain to me why the name 'Schnaiderman' would be foreign and yours, García, would be *Argentine*. All last names here are either 'mestizos' or 'foreign,' if you wish, because those who came to conquer these lands destroyed without mercy those who were native to the place, they stole their riches and exploited them like animals. There will be, at the most, a question of numerical antiquity—names that possess two or three or five more generations—which, as we know after the last few years, doesn't mean much: those who sold out the country during the military dictatorship, are, for the most part, irreproachable surnames that date from the Spanish conquest, and that stand to sing the Hymn. Which is to say, they descend from those criminals that Columbus or Solís took out of the jails to bring them, as adventurers, to the conquest of a new world. I don't see much lineage in that direction."

The man began to get obviously upset. Several in the line, now, listen attentively.

"It's evident that you don't understand me," he says, finally. "But I won't speak to you about the Fatherland or the 'essences.' I'm referring to the fact that yours is a 'difficult' last name. Do you understand me? Lots of consonants and vowels together. Here we don't know . . . We are not accustomed to that."

"Do you mean to say that your linguistic ignorance draws the distinction between 'Argentines' and 'foreigners'? Because you don't know languages of that section of Europe, I become a second-rate citizen. If you were illiterate, then, 'Argentine' surnames wouldn't exist. In your view, the 'Argentine' is not a sum of the diversity, the inevitable pluralism and mixing of a country of immigrants, but only that which is the same as you are. The 'others' are the 'foreigners.'"

"No, no. Don't get me wrong. It's also a matter of religion."

"Of religion?"

"Of course. We, the Catholics, are the majority here. And we constitute one of the pillars of this society, as the declarations of the Church and the Armed Forces state. This country was born Catholic. And we have simple surnames, Spanish and Italian. On the other hand, you the 'Moishes'—and I beg your pardon, I mean no offense—have some awful names that can't be pronounced or written. At least here, in Argentina. Do you understand?"

"No."

"What do you mean, no?"

"An architect friend of mine, whom I have to see later is named *Luis León*. Another of my acquaintances, a renowned psychiatrist and writer is *León* Perez since his birth. Both are proud and self-confident Jews. Do you want simpler names? On the other hand, there is an extremely important bishop in the Argentine diocese—famous for his antediluvian beliefs—who is named Ogneñovich. Not to mention the Pope himself of your Catholic flock: Why don't you write for me now, on a piece of paper, without making a mistake, *Karol* Wojtyla? It's the name of his Holiness, Pope John Paul II, I don't know if you knew."

You begin personally to fill out the application. Hector García watches you while you write, indignant. Those in line sigh. There's no longer not much chance for this job. You turn in the form.

Here it is. Argentine surname, as good as anyone's. I don't feel like a second-class citizen nor do I allow anyone to treat me so. Think about it. It's *your* problem.

You are beginning to find yourself, as the psychiatrist recommended. To not keep quiet. But in reality, beyond the verbal pyrotechnics, this is also *your* problem. You are the Jew, the minority, the marginal one for many.

The clerk doesn't answer. He considers the unexpected dialogue to be finished. Looking over your head to the one who is behind you, he barks, "Next, please."

family tree

He entered the bar, bumping into people as before, as always: "How are you, David? Do you recognize me, after so many years?"

The slightly lost expression, the abdomen that advances notoriously—"I have gained fifteen kilos," he will immediately confess—the hands with thick fingers, without rings and with well-chewed finger nails. The past hits you in the back of the neck like an enemy. There at a distance. The sweet and forgotten adolescence.

"León . . . It's been so long since . . . I wanted so much to see you. To speak . . . "

"Of course, of course."

"I've got problems. I . . . "

"I know. I read the papers: The murder of Señora Abud and all that. Calm down, David. Your old friend is going to help you. The cops want to bother you: you in particular, an innocent who hasn't yet come out of his shell . . . "

You feel comfortable, protected. As before.

"That's the reason I made an appointment with you. We are the kind of friends you can't make when you're older."

"Something stronger than time unites us, David. Although we haven't seen each other for about ten years. Isn't that right?"

You order another coffee, this time with a few drops of cognac.

You don't know how to proceed. Only a few summers have passed, what you have in common cannot be watered down. León had been living in Israel. It is a good place to begin.

"What did you do in Israel, León?"

The smile danced in his eyes, surrounded by small wrinkles, on the deeply tanned skin: he always knew more, he had the ability to surprise with an unexpected response.

"I looked for a Sephardic woman with cash."

"You're not serious."

"Totally serious. I put ads in the newspapers, I wrote to the matrimonial agencies. To sum it up, just that."

He pats your back, an accomplice.

"Let's agree that I didn't find exactly what I was looking for. She's not very pretty—not very smart either, you're not going to believe it—she doesn't have money. But she does have Arab cousins. You know what I mean?"

"No."

"The family. Arabs. That allowed me to begin my planning for the development of communal settlements. LOS CHAMA. I urgently had to learn the Arabic language."

"What are you talking about?"

"If I never told you about that, it's too complicated to explain it to you right now. Returning to your question: to support myself, I had to use my wits. For a few months, I was a *shomer* . . . "

"That is . . . "

"Guard. Caretaker, bah! In the international hotels. They give you a gun, and you check out the garage or the entrance lobby, connected to the Concierge. After a short time, I started a business. Look, to tell the truth, I have thrown myself into 'holiness' . . . "

León hands you a yellow box with inscriptions on it and two small brown stones, one of them very coarse and the other polished until it has the texture of satin.

"What is this?"

"*Ness International Limited.* My company. With its headquarters in Tel Aviv."

"'Ness' in Hebrew means . . . miracle. And this . . . "

"These are, in effect, holy stones. Miraculous. You have here the certification in three languages: Latin, English, and French. Read it."

There is a stamp, a signature, and printed above: "Attestatio Benedictionis, ex Ordire Fratrum Minorum huic perinsigni Santuario Navitatis D. N. Jesu Cristi inserientium formula adhibita, benedixi haec pia devotionis in quorem fidem . . . " et cetera. Below the stamp, "Hoc testimonium dator tantum peregrinis, et quidem, GRATIS, postquam objeta religiosa in sacrestia benedicta fuerint." He doesn't let you ask.

"The little rough stone is the one that comes from the ruins. The polished one is worked with a machine that I bought there. This is very serious, David, they bring luck. You have to carry it in your pocket, and, from time to time, rub it. It calms the nerves, too."

"You're kidding . . . "

"What are you saying? You're crazy. They are 'holy stones.'"

"Where did you get them?"

"There's the secret. My new Arab cousins. I am involved with two of them who are big shots. Each has a team of masons working on restorations: one group works on the Wailing Wall, in Jerusalem; the other on the Church of the Nativity, in Nazeret. Do you know of anything holier? First-class Jewish and Christian relics. They bring me the rubble, after each repair. I divide and classify the bits of stone, before polishing them . . . "

"And later you sell them?"

He shot you a pitying glance.

"If you do business, the little stone loses its value as something holy. I give them away: to pilgrims, tourists, monks, to all those who send in requests by mail. I have clients in Italy and Spain, collectors, Benedictine friars . . . "

"And what is your business?"

"Very simple. 'International Miracles,' David. I ask four and a half dollars for shipping expenses. I invest a dollar twenty in packing materials and postage and, with the difference, I can support myself, make donations to both religions, and carry forward my project of settling with the Arabs. I am a practical man, an entrepreneur. Even the best ideologies need fuel . . . "

He laughed again, and his abdomen shook.

"That's all. I am also involved in a sanitary business. That's the reason I come to travel out of Israel."

"Sanitary?"

He took out some folders and spread them on the table.

"Portable bidets, that you place against the toilets. Ass-cleaners, bah! You may know that in the Middle East, the bidet doesn't exist. And with this AIDS business that's beginning to appear, the boys are desperate about hygiene. When you want to use it, you place it in the middle of the toilet bowl, you sit down, you start the water going in the toilet and . . . with a good wash, let AIDS come. Isn't it brilliant?"

"I think that . . . "

"The little apparatus has a spout, like a showerhead, and it sprays upward. I buy them here for five dollars and sell them there for twenty. I'm hoping to be able to corner the market in the Arab countries by means of an Italian front company . . . "

All of this seems quite pleasant to you. You forget the reason for this meeting at a bar on Saenz Peña Street.

"Now I'm working on the oil project," León went on. "My head is a computer."

"Oil?"

"Grape oil. I don't know if you are aware that it burns away cholesterol. There's a kind of craziness, there in the Mediterranean about that matter. It's very, very expensive, it costs about ten dollars a liter. I can get it here for two dollars, I send it in cans—inside a shipping crate—and I bottle it over there, I put on a new label and into the purse. Do you see how many businesses can be set up? Or did you think that the land of Israel would defeat old León?"

He hits you on the back, laughing again. You return to reality.

"León, it's time that I explain things to you. I'm in big trouble . . . I lost part of my memory, it seems, and there was a murder that . . . "

He rises out of his seat. He takes your elbow.

"I know everything already, don't explain anything more. And leave that watery liquid, I will treat you at home with good Arabic coffee, with grinds. Now let's go right away. Didn't you need witnesses?"

"Will you know what to say? Because I . . . "

"You don't need to think so much *before* each movement. Man of action, not talk. I will go, I will explain to the official that I have known you forever, and I will guarantee that you are a good fellow and that you don't have anything to do with Señora Abud's crime. And after that, we will go looking for some chicks to screw: my tongue has been dry for a while, and I want to moisten it. Come on, don't look disgusted. In the Middle East, one learns many things like that . . . "

You agree. While you cross toward the Police Department, your memory—like an auto which has stopped for a long time—sputters and begins to function, but not without effort.

THE FASCINATION OF "TRY EVERYTHING"

You've gone mad, León. A floodgate went up, and your past exploded like a flag flapping in the wind. You talk and you talk.

I don't want to end up like Tolstoy, whose fixation on one idea led him to sexual abstinence and the lack of contact with reality. I want to "try" a little bit of everything, to experiment with my desires and not have a taboo that can make me sick.

You enumerate: you practiced thirty-seven sexual poses—you kept records—for and against nature. You smoked marijuana, you got drunk, you climbed a mountain, you grew carrots, you tried to ski, you tried all the orifices, you studied theater and graphology.

That mania for action, to do and to do, without stopping. Everything, always, once, twice at most, when you weren't sure of having completed the experience. As if to live was a series of tests, you say, that have to be resolved as quickly as possible. The secret is to get the pleasure out of you and then to be able to dedicate yourself to your true passion: to collect minibus tickets with reversed number and to found a new concept. As always, it's difficult to know if you are speaking in jest or seriously.

The officer observes you, immutable behind his poorly trimmed mustache. He keeps on asking: what is your relationship with Mr. Schnaiderman, since when have you been friends, what do you do, why have you come forth voluntarily to testify? You answer with a certain pride, but without mentioning *Ness International*.

"Some of the activities that I undertake—for example, stamp collecting or chess—I find interesting at the beginning and a bit ritualized later. Others, like aerobics, leave me frankly indifferent. A few, like coprophragia or incest, are somewhat more than repugnant, and I abandon them soon after I begin."

The instructor doesn't seem to have a sense of humor. Another officer looks for and compares some cards from the file.

"Schnaiderman has been my friend for more than twenty years," you finally say, when the air is becoming tense. "I recognized his photo in the newspapers, and I came to put myself at your disposition. His memory problem, surely, is something temporary; you're dealing with a good man. I guarantee to you that he could never have anything to do with the murder of that Señora . . . Abud. David's wife is named Gingi, you ought to know that. They have two children, he has a degree in sociology . . . with little prospect of employment these days. You recommended a doctor to him." Here you show a smile. "Thanks to which . . . "

"Don't waste time with unnecessary information."

"He has been able to remember something," you proceed, as if you hadn't heard. "Concerning his ancestors, his European roots, a mythical figure in his life in the form of his grandfather . . . and some more things. This is the whole story."

You pause. Your clothing is disheveled, a bit dirty. The great bald spots have uncovered a bulging and wide forehead, tanned by the sun. A multitude of white hairs invade the long, reddish thick hank you comb toward the back. Your eyes, protruding a great deal, denote mischievousness, but also inspire fear. The policeman remains very serious.

"On what occasion did you meet Mr. Schnaiderman?"

You show your uneven teeth.

"In those days he wasn't a mister, but only a little kid. We were neighbors and classmates in high school for a couple of years. Then, we were together in the *Halutzim* movement."

The other man looked at him, questioning.

"Ah, you don't understand. It means something like 'pioneers.' From the Zionist movement, do you understand? We were going to go to live in Israel, to liberate our country, build a new man and all that. If you aren't Jewish, it's difficult to explain."

"It interests me exceedingly, Mr. León Piatigorsky. Tell me about that."

With clarity, the scene appears to you, but you know that you are going to tell nothing about that which now circulates in your retinas, as if you were living it again; the building's caretaker, old Sara—that crazy woman who later would marry Ignacio's father, the other Jewish neighbor on the block—a glass of tea in hand and shifty eyes, leaning on the door frame and chewing on something. You separate the sticks that are still piled under the stairs.

"Firearms, no. That would be very serious."

Tzvika, thin, with eyeglasses, approaches you.

"The Nazis are really going to attack us?"

His innocent air softens you.

"Yesterday they threw a tar bomb. They know that we meet here, that we are the only ones ready to oppose them in an organized manner. They can come or not. We'd better be prepared."

You call two comrades whom you trust. The vehicle traffic now roars outside, beyond the metal curtains. Inside, a worn-out wooden floor, the staircase with a carved railing, multicolor murals that scream from the wall of the construction of socialism in the country, the plow with the rifle, the circle dances with *kibbutz* caps and golden spikes streak throughout the composition. Echoes of music float in the air. And of communal dance, too.

When the attack began, you opened the window and jumped out, with half the group. The rest, behind me, through the door. Being afraid doesn't matter, comrades; we also need to acquire pride. For two thousand years they've been coming to hit us. The moment to say "enough" has arrived.

You transmit a sense of security and a bit of juvenile craziness. You call David and Leo.

"While the others prepare the sticks, let's discuss Chava's problem, we have to set up the rotation."

You feel yourself protagonist in a heroic story. Was it Antek, that mythical figure—participant in the Warsaw Ghetto uprising against the Nazis—who had said it, placing his hand on your forearm in the middle of the meeting, in Yiddish, a deep register that wasn't used for making jokes?

"León, there need to be more. A thousand, at least. They should protect the Jewish community from the Nazis. You are the spine of the self-defense. We can't let ourselves be intimidated, not an iota."

Chava had been threatened by telephone. Several times. "We are going to kill you." "Dirty Jew." "We will put swastikas between your legs," all that. You organize the comrades in four-hour watches: every day, you study Chava's program of activities, so that the boys can always follow her. They have a manner of communicating with the headquarters, and another with a larger group, for emergency cases. Not a single moment transpires in which Chava, outside of her home, is allowed to be alone, without some comrade nearby. It is exhausting, but it contributes to the return of the adolescent's tranquillity. The agitated decade of the sixties, faraway and unforgettable.

That slow methodical chore of gathering information and intelligence makes you nervous. Once, and enough already, as in everything. You ask to join an active group.

The question, now, is far more concrete: training, a great deal of training. To await the instructions. This afternoon, that one with the black jacket: Monday night, the three blond guys with their greased hair slicked back who walk toward Santa Fe Avenue: one armed with a pistol, the others with knives. You are left with a sore foot when your boot smacked against his jaw, you are splashed with teeth and blood. Everything is like a flash: to hit and escape, break heads or take what comes. Without asking, knowing the least possible. This is not a joke or a novel.

Not everyone can: a group of "intellectuals" trains for four months and finally David, one of them, breaks a collar bone while practicing, without ever entering the action. Others proclaim themselves pacifists or incapable. It's okay: in these matters, no one is obliged. It isn't military service.

A Friday night, they assault the headquarters in Villa Crespo.

They arrive in two cars. They are the same ones, surely, who were responsible for the tar bombs. They throw rocks against the metal doors. They yell: "Filthy Jews! Communists! Come on out, cowards, motherfuckers!"

Inside, there are four comrades and several children from the recreation center. You distribute the sticks with concise orders and an odd trembling between your legs.

"Let's go out, boys. We have to chase them away from here."

The others look at you. Schnaiderman's brother—hardly an adolescent—is there, with lenses with thin frames which don't quite hide his near-sighted and frightened eyes.

"For the kids," you add, signaling them with a gesture. "What's more, it's educational."

Two more terrible blows on the door: chunks of paving stones, without a doubt. You forget the window tactic, and all go out by running through the front. There are a dozen from the Tacuara, armed with chains and brass knuckles. The tussle is short: David's brother lies on the ground, they step on his glasses, kick him in the head. Another boy got a blow with a chain in the face. As the beating got worse, the neighbors began to arrive, a police car's siren could be heard.

There are a few disturbances, and everything seems to end. Almost as soon as it began.

You ask the organization for an immediate reprisal. They agree. They order you to wait two days to collect information. "They" too are organized into cells, and they had terrorized the Jews and the political militants in the neighborhood. It was necessary to impart a "heavy" lesson.

The order arrived on Tuesday, for that night. They meet at the appointed place and divide up poles and pieces of iron. El Tata will

135

carry a revolver, for any emergency. Large clouds darkened the sky after a hot and humid day.

"Like a Romantic novel," you joke. "A storm before the action."

Scarcely a smile in response. In pairs, they walk toward the bar that the "information" had indicated. You carry the long bludgeon under your pullover, your hand contracting, white knuckled, the tremor coming from the pulsing of your blood. You think about the kids last Friday, almost victims of these animals. You remember photos of the concentration camps, carefully studied these days. There is no mercy for them: they are murderers, beasts. Monsters hidden under human flesh. The European business won't happen again to us.

They arrive at the bar. From outside, David's brother, his eyes still black and blue, points out the table. There are about ten, smoking. Young men, in general: the oldest looks about thirty.

"Follow me, comrades. Six million murdered Jews are watching us. Don't fail them."

You enter with a firm step, right to the table, while you take out the stick. The others sense something, as they begin to empty the seats. You don't plan: in action, he who thinks, loses. You raise the club and you smash it, without speaking and with all your strength, on the head of the nearest one. A dry "crack!" is heard, and with a drowned-out yell, hardly audible, one of the Nazis collapses.

What happens next is like an explosion. Chairs fall to the floor, screams, the sound of bottles breaking: two groups trying without mercy to kill each other. There are some sighs from the women who watch, from the other tables, covering their mouths with their hands, not understanding. Two other broken heads hit the floor, blood is spilled in the corners, injured boys flee in desperation to the street, risking their lives in that melee.

It doesn't last more than three minutes. They chase them onto the sidewalks of Villa Crespo, some fifty meters. After that, you order a retreat. This is a skirmish, not the killing of anyone. There are two police informants among them, you don't have to irritate the uniformed authorities. A cold wind starts up, prelude to the rain that will come. The neighbors crowd together.

You run down a side street, almost without breathing. There is no one on the next corner, and you take advantage of the moment to throw away the club that has blood stains and hair stuck to it. You enter the plaza from an angle, and you cross the rough grass, chunks torn out during the Sunday soccer games by the boys from the nearby factory. A strong thunderclap precedes the rain. The wind stirs up a filthy cloud of dust from the gravel paths. The statue of some hero, or perhaps a gray stone fountain, rises in the center of the plaza; you can't see clearly, the storm has brought the night early. You seem to see El Tata who is coming from the other side of the monument and you go towards him, your lips together, you heart turning over, the excitement that resists leaving you. The error is terrible. It is not El Tata, although he is approximately the same age. When he springs, you recognize him; he was in the group in the bar, he was the one in charge, the older man. Tall and broad shouldered: "an expert in wrestling and karate," you had been told by those with the information.

You are desperate. You try with your fingernails, teeth, kicks. You receive a strong blow to the stomach which knocks the breath out of you; you pant, feeling the breath and the hatred of the other man over your body, you sense that you are going to die there. You strike, and they strike you. Again a siren is heard.

You are blinded and you shout. He does not; he wants to strangle you silently. The two of you roll, mashing each other on the grass. You discover the murderous face to be at your reach and you push a finger into his eye, in desperation. He groans like a madman, he tries to hit you in the testicles. You break out in tears, in a panic, but you go on twisting his eye to one side, because your life depends on that. The police car arrives, they shake you to separate you, they arrest you. The rain is now ferocious, everyone is soaked, and your hysterical shouts mix with the wailing, the water that falls, the terrible wind that shakes the bodies.

You are lucky in the court's judgment: "Assault." Two adolescents with concussions, the leader who lost an eye. You repeat everything your lawyers tell you: you claim innocence, to be to the right politically, circumstances, an attack of hysteria, the pressure of the moment, you state your regrets on a document that you sign. You are able to leave. Two years on probation. For many months, you live outside of your home, changing your residence every night, because they are looking for you so they can kill you.

You don't tell any of this, which had flashed through your mind like a camera on fast forward. But they keep observing you with distrust, while you testify about Schnaiderman. You begin to regret having come, for having let yourself be carried along by an impulse, that almost suicidal omnipotence.

"You were in Israel, correct?"

You try to win time.

"Why do you ask me that? What do they have to . . . ?"

"Here we ask the questions, sir. I repeat: you lived in Israel? Do you still live there?"

"Yes, sir."

Your voice recovers its normal tone, after the very brief interval of distress. Only the eyes change, something in your glance: one eyeball is larger than the other and the red veins are noticeable, your forehead is knitted.

"Can you explain to us what you do in that country?"

You smile knowingly.

"It's a long story . . . "

"We're not in a hurry, we will hear it."

You clear your throat, you look toward the ceiling. Mental concentration. A pause.

"Let's begin with my original plan. A moment came, it would be six or seven years ago, in which I separated from my wife. She couldn't understand me, she is Sephardic. Turks, you call them. The daughter of Jewish Arabs, Syrians. Different cultures, that is, we came from different families."

The officer thumbed the cards.

"My plan was simple: I go to Israel, I put ads in the newspapers, as they do over there, to marry some old lady with a lot of money. So, I could live without working—or running some business to keep from getting bored—and I set out to carry out my proposal: *CoHESION*.

"What proposal is that?"

"That's the part that requires a more extensive explanation. If you . . ."

"Speak, please."

"Good, my project is developing under the acronym *CoHESION*, which stands for 'Coincidences of History, Evolution, and Society In the Order of Nature.' I've been working on it for twenty-five years, since my youth. It deals with taking advantage of natural resources and resettling the population in an economical fashion in the entire world. For which it is necessary to legislate a new juridical system, the *REGA*, 'Regulatory Entities with Growth Affirmation.' Don't make jokes about López Rega, like everyone else . . . "

"I'm listening to you."

"In *REGA*, participation is divided like this: Capital, 30 percent, Labor, 30 percent, Defense, 8 percent, Education, 8 percent, and Autonomous Coordinating National Office, 8 percent. The dividend would be divided in other percentages, guaranteeing a minimum, adjustable, living wage. This mechanism is perfectible.

You begin to get excited about your own speech.

"This complements the *CHAMA*, that is, the 'Complexes of Humans who are in Autonomous, Mixed Agro-business-Industrial units,' that is the final result of a process of Community-Colony-City-Complex to foment the settling of human nuclei in a planned way. It is a first step, the geophysical space for these settlements is determined by the border areas that go on conforming the 'skin' of the national being (and here is where I find some connection with the early *kibbutzim*, the communes that contributed to the establishment of Israel). Each member of this community that I propose agrees to work on three levels: primary exploitation, as in agriculture and fishing, industrial processing, and social labor. This last, without any remuneration."

"This sounds rather similar to the communist idea."

"It is in that way that we succeed in debureaucratizing the political function, and we go along preparing the people . . . "

"Preparing?"

"Of course. As managers of a Social Being, of harmonic growth."

The policeman senses that you are pulling his leg. His furrowed brow, nonetheless, possesses a certain satisfied attitude.

"It is all very interesting. Tell us now what you did during your stay in Israel."

"I'm getting to that. I am a good salesman, I don't know if I mentioned that to you. For fifteen years, I made my living selling everything, from rags to ideologies. It is something in my family, you know, it's in my blood."

You stop, convinced you said something stupid. He takes notes, impassive.

"Well now, my product, the COSAS, or 'Cells that are Organic, Social and Arranged Systematically' doesn't 'exist' yet in a way that it could be 'shown,' although I'm sure of having eight million clients by the year 2000. Essentially, what I do is make use of the idea of a living organism as an analogy, with its natural structure, studying its internal processes and the relationship with the environment.

"Your activity in Israel, please."

"Yes, I'm getting to that. I have there, after my marriage, many new relatives, including some cousins and neighbors of my new wife, with connections to the underworld. We spoke in Arabic and we immediately understood each other. But don't get me wrong: I said to myself, in order to put my plan in practice, I need to go there. Here, in Argentina, they wouldn't listen to me; it doesn't have anything to do with the military government, it is that here they have another set of problems. More urgent.

"You've already arrived in Israel. Continue."

"I dedicated myself to various businesses without importance, to make a few pesos. Already married, I went to see the Arab relatives, and I proposed to them my model of social dynamic organization, the COSAS: its area of development would be the lands that currently make up Israel's present borders with Lebanon, Syria, Jordan, Saudi Arabia, and Egypt, with a depth that oscillates between seven and sixty-three kilometers on both sides of the line. In fifty years, the COSAS would transform this "no man's land" into a keystone for the cohesion of the countries in the zone, since they carry in themselves an esthetic and scientific message. Each one of the COSAS is a cell and an organism at the same time, but its action isn't marginal . . . "

One of the policemen stops writing.

"The imperfection of the frontier lines, greatly inferior to the fine weaving that I would create, is one of the principal causes of conflict, because from both sides, there are misshapen growths that meet at a point in common. The organisms rebel against this situation, and begin to develop in an infection-social process . . . the subversion that you mentioned before, exactly, that debilitates the organism. But communism doesn't have anything to do with this. These cells of fifty to one hundred families, with an optimum number of seventy, are the best antidote for the question . . . "

You smile internally; now you have them in your hands, you think. You caught them.

"You're dealing with the original embryo of the future organic Cities-Parks that will be organized on a hexagonal plan that has kabbalistic value. With that form, you guarantee the psycho-physical health of the country and . . . "

"Enough already of your idiocies! I have listened to you too much. You are completely crazy."

You shake your head, you add a gesture as if to say, "I knew that you weren't going to understand me." He who had consulted the cards moved his hand.

"No, no. This man isn't crazy."

There is a long pause.

"Don't try to confuse us, Piatigorsky. We're not neophytes at this. It can be that Mr. Schnaiderman doesn't remember much of what he saw, but your presence here is not coincidental."

You look at David: what does this guy want? You see something surprising.

"Señora Abud, the murdered woman, came from Lebanon, that is true, but in reality she was the daughter of Palestinian refugees. Her parents brought her to Beirut in 1948, when they fled the war from the Galilee zone. We have checked this information with her husband. Señor Abud conceded that it was true."

The officer continued without varying his tone of voice.

"You joined Jewish shock troops in the sixties, you were tried for assault, and you were on parole for two years. After that lapse, you traveled to Israel about . . . "—he consulted one of the papers—"about 1973. Shortly after the *Yom Kippur War,* as you call it. You returned after two months, according to what Immigration has told us."

"Yes, I had forgotten it. But it was a seminar about . . . study of the Hebrew language. The other officer had asked me . . . "

"He will speak later, sir. You traveled again in 1978, but not because of that absurd plan that you have told us about. Possibly the part about your Mafioso cousins is true, but the rest is fantasy. We want you to tell us the truth."

You pale. You sit up in the chair.

"I assure you that . . . "

"It would serve you not to lie anymore. We interrogated the young Ahmed Abud, the son of the murdered woman. It was he who chased the attacker with a knife, though without reaching him. He has just

142

confessed, too, his membership in a shock group of young descendants of Arabs, identified with Palestinian groups and Arafat's people. Terrorists. What do you have to tell us now, Mr. León?"

You sit back down again, swallowing saliva. Downcast perhaps.
You make a gesture of estrangement. For once, the situation is getting away from you. The policeman's voice continues monotone,
without inflection.

"I'm letting you know that you are under preventive detention."

family tree

To unite the dispersed cords, David. You study the folders that the psychiatrist gave you, its pages numbered and clipped with an obsessive mania. Clinging to those roots now spreading out—discovered, through an almost hypnotic state, in the obscure depths of your memory—you slowly return to reality. You know already where you come from, the infinity of blows that you took in first person in order to incorporate them, to fill yourself up with those voices that resound near the burning fire and the circle of family. To never again deny you nutritive sap. The grandfather Moishe Burech is one of the firm legs upon which you can base your mestizaje.

Now, how to go on? The judge and his rush, the police, you never stop learning what they know, the appearance of León (his words open paths to the memory, but these split up in such a way that, like a delirium, they turn out confusing you.)

You are now suddenly frightened, after that long evocation that brought you back to the story. An unfortunate woman murdered in front of your eyes, whose face—disfigured by the shadow of death—is nevertheless near to you, incredibly mixed in a war of gangs that you refuse to recognize.

You lack life experience, the friends, the people of your generation. The circle could be closing itself through the involuntary witness of your past. Desperate search to restore a logical order; the opposite is the unimaginable nothingness of not knowing who you really are (not those that others tell you that you are). Anguish. Nausea.

To write these notebooks, once and for all, was an attempt to make sense out of the chaos. To reestablish an imaginary harmony and to sew together the disparate pieces. To work them into an embroidery in order to hide the meaninglessness of an existence which slides on the toboggan of the everyday experience. You look at the mirror León suggested to you, as if to say "don't play games," but you can't get yourself to begin. You only look. You have to sweeten the memories. You want to construct a closed and perfect world, in the image and shape of a god, and because of that, unbearable.

Can you replace the psychiatrist with your old friend León? How much is there of the real and how much of the mythical in that nostalgic highway? Is the truth of a remembered fact more important than the sensation that it has left in your memory? Only pain brings understanding, though the nostalgia may help you to live.

León is no longer like he was: the fascination that he awakes in you cannot hide the hints of adventurism that you surmise in his speech. And then?

Will it be that childish fantasy? The victorious little boy, strong and brave, that the others admire and at whose feet the women fall. "Everything one does in life is for chasing chicks," León used to say. You make a correction: it is the need for feeling, the desire to seduce in order to be loved, even if it comes mixed together with social struggle, and the brilliance of the intelligence. Everyone needs the feeling of others to be able to exist.

That perfect world of León, of action and of passions, a life of resolve and answered questions, leaves you out. It doesn't fit with your present full of doubts and failures, unemployed, amnesiac. It is something smaller and more limited, your own body, whose pain books don't cauterize.

You stop. You lean your hand on your head. You feel yourself doubting León, in some way, and you don't know how to go on. You are about to break into tears.

What would the grandfather Moishe Burech do in this situation? A man doesn't define himself by ideas alone, but also by his actions. He would have investigated, you answer yourself, the heart of the matter. Like the time he defended that widow, in the lawsuit she had with his best client. The *zeide*, the tailor with wide hands and strong character, the one who carries the memory of your heritage. The truth is the first issue, the beginning, before whether God exists or not. He gives it a meaning, a taste of life.

You go to Teresa's house, after a call from Gingi to alert her. She married a year ago, but from her courtship with León there are memories and letters. Above all the missives sent from Israel interest you, the mysterious part of the story. Either your friend is crazy, as one of the police thinks—and that is the reason he challenges the investigators—or you enter in an intrigue whose unexpected threads lead to confusion. Each memory approaches the present and dilutes it. It's necessary to reconstruct, too, the others' history, from the foggy moment when you abandoned them.

You are invaded by the sense of foreignness that characterizes those whose past is more important than their present, obliged daily to infuse glory and heroism of bygone years into a mundane routine, sometimes a miserable one—which you can't tolerate. The favorite student of Gino Germani in the sixties, you have become an unemployed sociologist. Master León, brother in arms, brave Jew who fought for his people as a youth; what does he have to do with this present day murdered woman, murky business deals, delirium, police inquisitions and witnesses who make it all suspicious?

You push the doorbell at Teresa's house. You don't have to speak much; she seems to understand the problem, Gingi's telephone explanation has been convincing. She goes toward the library, takes

146

out a thick file with the dated and well-organized cards, you look in the letter "L."

"We always think about you two, with Oscar, my husband."

Such a stable couple that you and Gingi had become, for so many years—she said unexpectedly, while she sorted a group of papers.

"Yes, it's true," you answer, as if you were repeating a lesson. "In some way, we owe it to you, Teresa. If it hadn't been for you . . . "

She had arranged for you to meet years ago, and that was what she wanted to hear. It doesn't cost anything to give her the pleasure, you think. It is part of a game whose rules everyone shares. Teresa goes along with the simple mention of her centrality, and she hands you the material.

"Here it is," she says. "I sorted the cards that León sent me from Israel and which refer to that absurd project. Read them calmly. I'm going to make coffee."

Your hands tremble slightly. There is a certain shame in stirring frozen time, dry and fragile leaves where the memories melt drop by drop, until they become unrecognizable . . .

The mood already is present in the first letter, dated in Jerusalem, November 17, 1978. Evidently, by that time you had already lost contact with León.

I have written an ambitious theatrical work, that is being translated into Hebrew and English. Also, a composer of Argentine origin is transforming it into an opera. It's called *María Hebrea*, and its central character is María, the sister of Moses, will later become María, "the alchemist of the first century of our era" and whose story is confused with that of Jesus Christ's mother, to become María, "the predestined," a woman who cannot be herself for millennia and who, renouncing immortality, is transformed in our times, into a revolutionary leader. And, paradoxically, she, who has fought against idolatry, is used as an idol. Besides that, I am going to describe to you a curious phenomenon: in Israel, I feel "at home" and I consider the others to be "foreigners." That is, perhaps, the effect of my successive wives (Syrian-Lebanese/Jewish-Egyptian) and of my present command of the Arabic language, that each day I speak more fluently, which permits me—and obliges me—to frequent circles hardly seen by those who want to assimilate. I found branches of my family that connect me to some two hundred "cousins," located in distinct corners of this society. However, their oriental mentality, pragmatic and mercantile, is very far from my idealism. . . .

The letter is charming, but it doesn't clarify much. Your old friend serves the coffee in porcelain cups, on the little table.

"Teresa, did León ever speak to you about a certain Señora Abud? Do you remember the name?"

She smiles: she isn't pretty, but her hair, short and dyed black, her olive-tinged face, the dimples in her cheeks and those teeth, just a bit too big, help her to maintain an adolescent expression, capricious, like that of twenty years ago.

"No, David. I never heard that last name. You seem frozen in the past. It's been many years since I've seen León, these letters are almost relics. My life has advanced in other directions."

Her husband is a prosperous dentist who wears eyeglasses with fine gold frames and never takes off his tie. One of his daughters, an adolescent, was a beauty queen during the last carnival. Being militant within a movement belongs to another time, most surely, but you just can't explain that, precisely, it is there that you left the traces that explain the present. It would take too long to explain, and she wouldn't understand.

The following letter is dated the 23rd of December 1978, and contains a more pessimistic tone, though it does clarify things:

The activity related to my projects has suffered a halt, given that my backer for the community center left for Mexico. But—

you won't believe this—an Argentine fellow got involved with my biggest project (the settlement) and is already forming a multiparty political action group, whose title is *Shituf Peulah* "Cohesionism" (Interaction—Cohesionism—Bomb of Peace). This man is secretary general of the *Herat* in Ashkelon and he has a great reputation in the Party, especially in the Latin American section. But there are also people from *Sheli, Avodah, Mapam, Ratz,* and independents, too. We are drawing up a program manifesto which will, in its critical section, propose a national coalition for the Third Republic. You probably realize that the concept couldn't be crazier, but my ideas are too. I feel myself called to the great conclusions, to participation in transcendent projects. Our comrade Natan, here in Israel, has convinced me that we, a Jewish self-defense group, were the ones who put the brakes on the anti-Semitic developments in Argentina in the sixties. More than political campaigns or elections, the boys that we beat up had to back down from their Fascist projects.

You continue looking through clamped folders. The next letter is from the 25th of February 1979:

With each day that passes, I am more enthusiastic about my decision. I haven't had a single day that wasn't like a vacation, and I am learning to appreciate the value of my philosophy of life. Instead of a widow, whom I was seeking, I won the grand prize: a writer, madly in love with me and my ideas; she is more extraordinary than I am. And that is only one of the miraculous things that are happening. An Arab boy who works at the hotel where I pretend to be working as a guard told us that his family owns four hundred *dunams* near the Jordan, below the Allenby Bridge, of which they can only farm one hundred, since, for security reasons, they are prohibited from using the other three hundred which are on the riverbank. Talking with my team of people, we see the possibility that this place could be converted into the first attempt of *Shituf-Peulah* (Interaction) and that, given the conditions, it will serve to measure our strength against the speculators and bureaucrats. On several occasions, there were Jews who wanted to buy those lands, but we would rent them from the family of this boy with the option to buy, though the idea is that the Arabs participate as partners. (. . .) In another area, the political combination is a fact: we work in a cell-like arrangement (each representative meets with me, together with the other representatives, and acts in an autonomous way inside of the partisan group). When the time is right, we will form a general constituent assembly. It's the mechanism of the *Koach Coetzia*—Cohesion Force—so that no one can try to devour another, whatever wealth may be available. As I told you, I include Arabs and also a powerful feminist sector. My companion does *transcendental meditation* and, because of it, I already have relationships, which may become interesting, with groups in other countries. They tell me that they are forming a team to found a commune within our project. (. . .) Perhaps this may sound like nonsense to you, but here life isn't at all difficult for me. If I wanted to make millions, at the cost of leaving aside my project, I could do it. But it doesn't interest me. I am, as always, trying something new and sticking to it in order not to get bored, which understandably annoys a lot of people. For me, Israel is a party. Forgive the scant poetry of my letters, but I limit myself to informing you, in the most succinct way possible, some of the contexts which I move in order to obtain my objective. Do you remember? The COSAS for the Co-HESION of CHAMA, that is, "the COHESIONISM, the highest level of Zionism." This will be the title of one of the essays that may serve as a declaration of the movement's principles. I have already named Ignacio, the little fat guy from Villa Puerrey-dón, who was my childhood neighbor and the first disciple I ever had, as my personal delegate in Buenos Aires, with wide powers signed and sealed. . . .

Teresa observes with worried eyes, while you are finishing the reading. Then, having lost a bit of her composure, she grasps your arm.

"David, why did León tell all this to me, *to me in particular*? We were lovers and comrades in the movement for only a couple of years and since then more than a decade has passed. Why to me, who never understood theory? What did he want?"

"Perhaps to impress you," you answer. "You were the only woman who decided to leave him, before; always, he would do it."

"You know the story: my father insisted, he said that León was a madman. I was eighteen years old, I didn't know what he wanted, I was confused."

"It's okay, Teresa, you don't have to explain anything to me."

A question occurs to you that might lower the created tension.

"Why did he choose Ignacio, and what is this business of 'personal delegate'?"

Teresa laughs, a bit hysterically.

"You still ask? Because the two of them are completely crazy! The extremes finally touched each other, as the military said. I was never with them, you can imagine, but in some things . . . "

"What do you mean that they are . . . ?"

"Crazy, David. Megalomaniacs. One with his absurd plans, who attempts to hide the failure of his original plan, the *kibbutz*-utopia. All made-up verbiage to cover up his delirium. Wouldn't it be simpler to admit that adolescence had ended and we'd better face reality? The other one, Ignacio, took on that madness—even worse, because he never went to Israel and he took all the blame—through the religious route. . . . "

"Ignacio religious?"

"You didn't know?"

"No, no . . . It's been years since . . . "

"Religious and fanatic. 'The way of return,' as they told him. The former Marxist rediscovered his grandfather the rabbi, and now he is found between *kipot* and *tfilim*, eating only kosher food, and praying in the synagogue. What do you think? He transformed his youthful faith in a mystical search, with the same level of devotion. It's said that Sara, his stepmother, is completely crazy, and she pushed him in that direction."

"Sara? The same one who . . . ?"

"Yes, you remember her. The caretaker of the building where the youth movement operated. She got together with Boris, Ignacio's father, when he lost his wife. And it seems that, in addition, Sara's story is quite strange, tinged by dealings in white slavery in her youth, when she arrived in the country or they brought her here, no one really knows. A murky past."

"Complicated, for sure."

"If it is as I say . . . the extremes come together. For that reason, David, you've got to maintain your equilibrium: middle class, moderate pretensions, moderate sensibilities. . . . Everything normal, under control. I . . . "

To shorten Teresa's disquisition, you open the last letter, without being able to avoid that a certain resentment remain floating in the atmosphere, and slid over the upholstered chairs (with slipcovers) in the living room. It is dated the 6th of May 1979:

I have decided to finalize the religious divorce with my former wife; I left her in Argentina. Ignacio will take care of those matters, he likes to deal with Arab women, even if they smell bad. It isn't a reproach, Teresa, she left me alone in this adventure, and now that I have Sophia, I appreciate the difference with that poor woman, interested exclusively in my money. I, on the other hand, continue with my plans. Ten days ago, I had an interview with an elderly sheik from Jericho, the supposed former

landowner—with 6,000 *dunams*—from which they have left him
60 *dunams*. And they refuse to let him complete the house that
he had begun to construct for his family. He looks with sympathy on a project which entailed the cooperation of Jews and
Arabs, such as occurs in my settlement program. But what was
more interesting was the relationship—in the same place—with
a guy, a teacher in the Terra Sancta High School. He is the first
Arab intellectual that I have been able to contact, and he has
become interested in the COSAS idea. The possibility arose for
the creation in Jericho of a School-Farm-Factory. We will see
what happens. (. . .) I quit my job as security guard at the hotel
and I live, thanks to God and to my companion, who wants me
to dedicate myself completely to the task of writing and acting
in pursuit of the objective that led to my immigration to Israel.
This country is like an apple, half sweet, half bitter, so as not to
bore you. Our movement is important because I can rise, if we
make enough noise, to levels which are difficult to reach. And
with a place to stand, I will move the world. I have decided to
lower my guard and be, like these "cousins of mine," pure feeling.
Each day now seems like a week to me, as it does to children. I
enjoy each instant, I make plans, and I speak in Arabic all day. I
am also beginning my integration into Hebrew and to meet high
level entrepreneurial colleagues, because many politicians lag behind them, and it's better that they come seeking you, and not as
I did until now, me chasing them. That is in the Jewish sector. In
the Arab sector, I make out quite well, and I haven't even begun
with the Sephardic sector. . . .

You put your eyeglasses on the small table, next to the cold remains of the coffee.

"Was this the last one? He didn't write to you again?"

"No. Never. The truth is, I never answered the two that you just
read. His delirium was beginning to tire me. Recently, I found out

that he was back in Buenos Aires, but I never tried to see him, since you can imagine that my . . . "

You hesitate for a moment.

"Also, David, he represents *the past*. Worse yet, the part of our history that went mad. He left the tracks. Do you understand?"

The memories appear mixed up, as if you had reversed to a different part of the same movie.

"We grow, David. We can't go on living in our adolescence, that's sick. In the meantime, we have had . . . experiences. You know, you're a bomb thrower at twenty and a fireman at forty. Your parents are right in certain things, they weren't as stupid as they appeared."

You agree, confused. Your silence inspires her to continue.

"Tell Gingi to call me, for a long chat. It will be pleasant to remember old times, the movie dates, the graduation dance . . . the trips on the subway to meet you. Do you remember? We could spend a weekend in the 'country,' my husband makes a very good *asado*. Definitely, but without politics, you understand? That word has been erased from this house. Because our daughter . . . "

You say good-bye with a few words, while Teresa, suddenly loquacious, follows you to the street entrance, expounds her new world view—social success and those who resent those who arrived and channel their failure into protest and violence.

You walk. You have to get a handle on what it is that you are trying to find. León, Arabs, Señora Abud, impossible projects, divorce of the first wife, Ignacio as "personal delegate" and now a religious fanatic.

You try to concentrate. What happened before the shots and your fall to the sidewalk. The police theory about the confrontation between shock troops seems absurd to you. Although you evoke the ghosts, you let them circulate as in a card game: Teresa, León, Gingi, your children, the *Halutz* movement, the Villa Pueyrredón neighborhood that right now begin to draw themselves in front of your eyes as if the most distant were the first to be evoked. Two Jewish families live on that block, Ignacio's and yours. Ignacio is an insignificant little fat kid, who wore eyeglasses from the time he was very young. A follower, timid in all the adventures, an admirer of León when he arrived on the block. And several Arabs, that's true: Miguelito, the one from the handkerchief factory: the Syrian from the store, short with a thick mustache, "very anti-Semitic," according to Don Boris. Edo and Roberto, sons of Lebanese, pals in the games and pranks, with whom you invented complicated battles in the tiled alley, that always ended with "I'll tell my papa and he'll kick your father's ass," "I'm sorry for you, little kid, mine has a punch that no one can handle."

And also the Italians, Galicians, the Portuguese from the bar, the "Baldy"—he works as a bartender and wants to play around with all the domestic servants on the block—Caetano, the fanatic fan of San Lorenzo; the short Maciel, tango singer. Alba practices Spanish dance. Pallarotti resigns himself to being a mechanic so his brother can study medicine. Your father makes calendars for the tailoring trade (pocket calendars, with photos of Floren Delbene, Tita Merello, and other movie stars printed on the back). And Anchoíta, that skinny guy with the mustache that suggests his nickname, humiliated by the neighbors, who didn't forgive him his mother's whoring. Anchoíta's mother; yes, sir: dark-skinned and somewhat obese, breasts like melons and hips that bounced up and down above very high spike heels, showing shamelessly—while on the bakery line—that Cingolani, the tycoon, had had her 'big and curved on the top' and had been very generous in payment (which caused a scandal, because Mrs. Cingolani presided over the Ladies Society of the parish). That same Cingolani, aristocrat of the neighborhood, with his green Henry J automobile and the quick trips to Mar del Plata, that the neighbors would know about, in spite of his pretenses, from the beach sand stuck to his shoes.

Anchoíta's mother: in the butcher shop, again, facing a hanging display of small sausages that provoke in her an irrepressible attack of hilarity, because of associations that could motivate, if they were known, several dozen bouts of masturbation among the adolescents in this block of Villa Puerredón. You also were inspired erotically by the cutie with light blue eyes from the bicycle shop or the baker's wife—dark-skinned, with large hands and eyes that were always sad—grown-up females, impossible love, caused by an awakening sexuality, a crazy desire.

Essential mixing of the "little Russians" and Basques, the Yugoslav from the paint shop and Aranda, the painter of letters (who once crossed the avenue at full speed chased by "the Italian" Mendía, who had an enormous kitchen knife in his hand). You were an atypical "neighborhood Jew," David, with the sounds of tango, the "café-bar-billiards," the bar on the corner where cards were traded, the Lunfardo dialect, the Tito pizzeria next to the Aconcagua movie house and those sidewalks whose paving stones you recognize from the city bus, looking out the window, without needing to pick out buildings or street numbers.

The nostalgia submerges you in an irrecoverable and idyllic past: the sidewalks of Mosconi Avenue, Cuenca Street, Helguera Street—with its little plaza, where you would take the children to enjoy the pallid autumn sun—Teqendama Street and its elementary school, the Syrian-Lebanese Hospital, the Catholic high school, Our Lady of the Orchard (where a domestic servant went to tell the Mother Superior that you wanted to rape her). Everything, everything mixed together, from the religion to the offices and the ideology, and, nevertheless, so ample in possibilities, so full of dialects and customs.

Memory's tricks: the memories appear in blocks, in pieces, and you put them together by means of big stitches. Roots that bring you to that frontier town—Polish?—raked over without pity from all directions by the wars, the mix of dialects and nationalities. Jews with Ukrainians, Poles with Russians, Austrians with Hungarians in the empire that was disappearing: the flags that followed one after the other, at times sharing the school flagpoles. From there to the Latin American *mestizaje*, that childhood fatherland in Villa Puerreydón.

(Or Villa Devoto? Always a border). Populated by Croats and Lebanese, Syrians and Italians, Creoles and Jews, Spanish and Portuguese, all mixed in that *porteñismo* of Buenos Aires that put them together like a thick salad, throbbing with odors and textures, meals, and the linguistic inventions that came from the inevitable retarded fellow Pascual to the bored guys in the bar, who count caps from soda bottles or bet on the ending of the license plate of the next car to pass, immobile travelers of boredom, meeting in the tables spread along the sidewalk.

And, to finish, the experience in Israel, the sun quickly appears stronger to you (even though it is almost night) in the memory of those mornings picking grapefruit in a *kibbutz* in the Galilee, a meeting place with a marvelous and unrealizable utopia. But, in León's inconclusive letters, in the expression of admiration that you imagine Ignacio to have, there remains the invisible presence of those Jews whose faces are hard and gentle at the same time, born under a Middle Eastern midday, speaking a language full of musical cadences, and risking their lives through the streets of Jerusalem or Safat that are, you were now feeling, an unexcisable part of your heart.

Let them mix, truthfully. If you believed in God, everything would be simpler, but thus. . . . Yourself freed, you begin to walk, hands in your pockets that mark time for the march, David Schnaiderman, son of Isaac, the tailor, grandson of Moishe Burech, the tailor, husband of Gingi and father of two children, forty long years and unemployed sociologist, adolescent friend of the suspicious León, amnesiac witness of a murder which occurred on a Buenos Aires corner.

They had warned you: the forties mark a dangerous period, memory and balance of what you will no longer do and what you did, accompanied by a sharper presence of your own finiteness. For that, in that age also, insomnia begins. The cognac, you smile. You never liked alcohol much, but a little glass before going to bed, now, helps you get to sleep. You understand your uncles, your oldest brother-in-law, Raúl, the shopkeeper, all toasting with their eyes, establishing complicities that, untransferable, only in this instant, reach the retinas of your reality. The same as in novels of love.

Love? Yes, love even if it sounds romanticized and ingenuous. You go on discovering yourself, capable of being moved easily, of longing for a woman with a certain fixation, of trembling before a tragedy of jealousy, abandoned children, an unhealthy passion. Twenty years ago—you remember, in less time than it takes to tell it—you claimed to offer a biological explanation, of which you were certain, for the attraction of the sexes, such and such hormones, certain nerve strands, sensations of helplessness, simple enervation of the genital organs. This would stop the desire for a certain woman, provoke erections, orgasm. The ideological was the important factor, the class struggle, the inhuman exploitation of man by man. That ideal, that objective, justifies a life and a heroic death. *If there is no God, only the utopia gives sense to the world.*

Now you are softening, perhaps the product of the same confusion. You constantly need your wife more. You smile with tenderness on touching the combination knife and nail clipper that contains, folded, a short little knife.

One memory brings another, like the beads of a rosary: you travel to the Argentine south to celebrate your twenty years of being in love and your first camping trip together. You visit with Gingi the same places as you had on the first trip, a generation earlier. During the excursion through the wooded island, covered with arrayan trees with their tobacco-colored wood, a lady on the launch ventured that it was likely that pumas lived in the sometimes impenetrable foliage, Gingi went pale without saying anything; but at the beginning of the hike, she came near and murmured into your ear, "You brought the knife, didn't you?"

You can't avoid laughing. That infantile belief that the attack of a wild beast can be stopped with a pocket knife is symmetrical with her visions of anger: when she fights with you, she sees you transformed into a bear or a lion. It can also be the gossipy hairdresser converted into a snake, or the bartender into a rhinoceros. Monstrous animals that scare her, even making her cover her eyes. Much of this has passed, but the amazement that captivated you still survives in her.

You enter a bar and, without thinking, you ask for a strange sandwich which takes you back to eastern Europe: bread, butter, a lot of raw onion, and salt. You eat in large bites, anxious, hungry, while the past is entering your blood, through the strong taste of the sandwich that your father consumed daily. Can there be anything better than that savage and odorous grating of raw onion pleasing your palate?

León and Jewish self-defense, the dead woman who was a Palestinian Christian, the son Ahmed in Arab youth groups . . . Teresa and that bitter resentment for the paradise lost with which she tried to associate you, the now religious Ignacio as "personal delegate" in a lunatic project. . . .

Ignacio. The trail goes that way. He lives very close to the zone where . . . You are going to consult with Gingi, and she will say yes. You get up and ask for the telephone book. There he is: he is the only one who remained in the neighborhood, who didn't marry, who didn't go to Israel, who didn't do many things (except this late return to religiosity, so disconcerting).

When you close the telephone book, a girl with long blond hair and insolent eyes is observing you. You want to appear confident, but stunned, you are the first to lower your gaze, intimidated by the youthful impudence. Do you feel like an old man, no longer up to these rough and tumble adventures? Are you afraid, ashamed? Do you have ethical objections? The unpleasant aftertaste of that adolescent extremism, as Teresa would say?

family tree

The invitation—celebration of the twenty-fifth anniversary of graduation from the high school—arrives precisely when you are retracing your steps. Never having returned—in all that time—to the high school nor to have seen your former classmates, you find yourself in front of the doors of the "Reconquista" High School, hardly renovated at all, with same swinging doors and the glazed windows that look out on the plaza.

Traces that shake sleeping nostalgia, hard slabs that time and changes have formed around.

You step on the doorstep as if entering a tunnel made of time: you are in 1958, you occupy a seat of wood that is worn-out and covered with inscriptions etched in with pen knives, in rooms that *now* seem to you to be strangely small; or you cross a patio of which, barely, a worn picture made of paving stones stays in the corner of your memory. Presentations, meetings, longings. Words.

Giménez remembers an experiment in chemistry class that ended with the test tube smashed on the roof, like a mortar shell. Almós and "the German" Meter remember the strikes of that year, the conflict over public or religious schooling. Mr. Suárez recounts his suffering as a poor soul who still can't retire (before, in another time, with his loud voice and his character, he was the terror of this division of adolescents). Ferri, the one from anatomy, now very old, reveals human values that you never imagined during a lecture course, given in the auditorium. The eternally smiling music teacher—whom the years had hardly affected, like a light shadow between the teeth—directs the student chorus that intones, in honor of your class, a shared and deliciously primitive song.

What is happening to you? Your classmates emerge from a nightmarish picture, illuminated by a sensation that increases the "strangeness." Some are as they were, frozen; they inhabit tree-lined streets, with low houses in Villa Urquiza, they sip maté on the sidewalk, their sons play the quinela in the same bar, they buy clothing and shoes in the shops that remain completely the same. You could say that they are the happiest, solid in their simplicity, only darkened by that air of neighborhood boredom, from a calm life, without uproar. Others have changed so much that it is impossible to recognize them: bald, gray-haired, fat. How do you appear to them? You compare each face with that on the old photo that you clasp to your chest like an invaluable treasure.

Here the addition of a beard, there bags under the wrinkles on the forehead, thicker glasses. Where have the smooth and firm expressions of adolescence gone? Where are the short haircuts, fine ties, colored plaid scarves, expressions that seem to swim in crystalline water, big winter overcoats, collective masturbation, the insolence of that unrepeatable age fixed in an image, innocent rectangle that locks up under inviolate key everything you want to know?

Who were you? In the transgressing look of the others you find the reflection of your own adolescence, so far from this confusing present: the youngest of the group (having skipped two years in primary school, bored by the figures that you knew by heart), small and chubby body, innocent. Shy to desperation, almost insignificant, just as you appear in the photo. You began secondary school as the first of the row, and you end up the last in the fifth year, going through that impressive physical spurt that replicated—according to what was said in your home—the height of your grandfather Moishe Burech whom you resemble like two peas in a pod.

And what else? This gang of boys who have children and professions, doctors and lawyers, bank tellers and merchants, Ford executives, metallurgical workers, industrial magnates, and chemical technicians—all in all, the multicolor and mixed Argentine people of whom you form part—continue relating with each other as they had twenty-five years earlier: the leader, the fool, the Peronist, the steam-roller who chases girls, the smart guy with eyeglasses who knows everything. . . . Set in a different world, they recover that unmoving past by means of the glances of the others, Masonry of understanding only accessible to the initiates that share it. Estrangement caused by the passing of time and by death that, pathetically, they try to exorcise with old gestures and repeated jokes. You remember León and the recent meeting in the bar, that capturing of what was.

Who are you? You ask again. Through others you remember your painful marginality of those years, classmates always older who would not waste time with this bothersome "punk," except perhaps for mocking sexual lessons which put to test your street smarts and your lack of knowledge of the details. Until they came to accept you, toward the end, as if by habit.

Won't one of your original wounds be found here, one of those pains of childhood that, later, would try to scar over with help of memory, lost in an emotional shock and now recovered bit by bit, through the search and love for a past newly visited? "I need the neighborhood," you think.

POPLAR IN AUTUMN

He: Tiles laminated by the Moon, into a dark passageway that leads to Teresa's house. Some phantasmal sound, the squeak of a door, torn bits of paper that in the wind of early February, hot without exaggeration, go from here to there without desire. Your red hair, a hardly visible sign in that atmosphere of surprises; latticework left ajar, stain of light that penetrates, music-making from hazel-colored background, a frightening daybreak that resists arrival. In the chair made of green velveteen, Teresa and León whisper between stifled laughter; then she enters the kitchen to say something to her father, he crosses his hands on his chest and waits. You bend your long neck forward, curl up your nose, freckles that now dance around in a trace of penumbra, the raised hand. It is the first kiss.

She: You write on a piece of paper, on the night table: *I have dreamed a lovely mystery story / filled with suspense and poetry / I forgot it when I woke up / it went away like a column of smoke / before I could get out of bed/ finish opening my eyes. / Now the enigma is to find it / look for the trail. / The prize: life.*

If you stay in the night, the ghosts and the fears destroy you. You have to leave the sleepiness, David. Open your eyes. Encounter the day again. The first kiss, your unfolding love, the attachments to hope. After that, you will come to the accident, the crime, the loss of memory. Before you have to reconstruct yourself. Before the stone that has been pursuing you since birth catches you, smashes against the beautiful and minimal crystal of existence.

He: You want to find out what León told me a while ago, before he said good-bye. You get angry with this "manly silence," that adolescent shame that keeps him from repeating a tale of chamber maids, sighing under the weight of naked bodies, León's girl still asking for more, her back in the hallway and leaning so as to offer herself, insatiable. Those stories for boys alone are not for you. You arrange the tablecloth in the dining room. The face scrunched up by anger and silence. Little hands jut out from the cuffs of white lace.

She: You dream, David. You do exercises in Palermo park, with a group of adults. They are older, from the neighborhoods, not full-fledged adults. Night is falling, after a languid and slow-moving day; a lot of green, cuckoos, the smell of mushrooms and of recently cut grass. You practice in an open area which undulates off to the left, that rises a few meters and then goes down to a stream—perhaps a lake—of swampy water that damascenes its banks. Mud and moans from the coming and going of the liquid.

He: In your garret, that little room above the garage with a small window in the front, on a side street, dark and under the branches. Green gates that will open every night to spy on the one who leaves. A cement staircase that leads to the terrace, mixing of flower pots, here and there, will isolate you in moments of anger and sadness. You imagine a house with firewood and a lit hearth (fire that crackles), rain outside hitting the window panes, two children crawling on the rug. A broad river of tenderness permeating the atmosphere and hands held and lips on lips and the voice of your mother who, for the third time, yells for you to come down already, that the milk is getting cold, and that you have to go to school.

She: You run toward the group. You are wearing your gym uniform, blue shirt, white shorts, cotton socks, and sneakers. You are content, David. Very sporting. It is a beautiful night, and you feel pleased with your own physique that runs svelte and quickly through the open country. You measure your breathing, you breath in deeply the humid air. Proud that your body—in spite of your being an overly intellectualized sociologist—can move in a way that others admire it. Yes, it is a dream, it has to be. The indescribable world of the night, the drunkenness of the senses.

He: Your hands, your hands always, small and with the ring fingers curved from years of piano, that now play "Perfidia" at dusk. A cup of coffee with shortbread awaits on the table. Suspicious parents repeat, "Whew, how much longer?" and you hardly smile. You think of those fingers resting on yours, the kisses in the courtyard, the involuntary pressure on the neighbor's doorbell during the struggle, and the old man's head, with his rheumy eyes and his sleeping cap ridiculously pitched to one side, asking, "What's going on?" and "ringing the bell at this hour, have you ever seen anything like it?" It's nothing, you say, we just didn't realize, Don Clodomiro, good night, see you tomorrow. The fear is transformed into an irresistible laugh which you stifle against my chest, the half-awake old man having hardly closed the door, still not understanding.

She: With the nighttime emotion, you have hurried your run too much. For a moment, you stop paying attention to the path and now you are about to enter the muddy water. If you go on, you will sink in the slime and uncertainty. Neither can you suddenly spin on your heels and head for the group by the shortest route because, with the rapidity of the pace and the weight of your body, you can slip or lose your equilibrium, chancing a blow or looking foolish in front of the others (besides getting your uniform dirty). The night is arriving in the same dream, like an affliction, migratory pendulum in the labyrinth.

He: You say good-bye to your boyfriend—who will walk thirty blocks to the bus stop in the early Buenos Aires morning—and you follow him mentally while life plans accumulate that will overcome the family opposition, sleepless nights before each discussion, "subversive" newspapers that your father furiously tears up, nocturnal spells of fear and hope, this laborious present that you construct between hours of office work, bad tempered bosses, mornings of school and phone calls, always difficult, unfocused, from the service station where they let you use the phone. Questions that are almost angry: "When are we going to see each other?," your hair vibrating impatiently. That colored hank of hair that has merited several poems, one of which begins—quite unsubtlely—with the chromatic variations it suggests: *"Oranges, carmines. Vermillions / many-sided tongues that cross . . ."*

She: You opt for an intermediary action to avoid the water: you turn your body slightly, scarcely the foreshortening seen at a distance and, with long jumps, you climb the steep bank. The lashes of impulse keep leading you higher—you can't turn around now because you surely would fall—describing a parabola toward the highest part in order to, from there, continue in a smooth descent to the plain, when the group begins with gymnastic exercises that help throw off the everyday toxins of the big city.

He: And now the starry night, filled with light, summer again. Your father, Russian from Odessa, seated on the patio, sips maté, his gaze fixed behind his glasses. Your mother goes in and out of the kitchen, she wants to listen and, at the same time, she fears what is going to happen. You gesture, your face washed and without makeup, lips pursed, adolescent anger held back. Berna is the one who speaks, shielded by a fatherly and heated voice, while León sits at his side.

"We're only talking about a camp out, sir. We are Jews and Zionists, that's all. We are organizing a study week in Córdoba. An experience of joyful communal life. So that the young people can learn about the emotion of sharing, Jewish living around the campfire, songs and scouting games. The language of the heart. A new life for a better human being, healthier, less egotistical."

"My daughter will not go. She is a minor, and, in this house, I still rule."

"We don't mean to show a lack of respect. You decide. But she too should give her opinion. She has the opportunity to have an extraordinary experience, in a framework of Jewish education. I myself am a member of a kibbutz, I am here in Argentina, sent by the movement. We don't harm anyone, wishing only to better the world and every human being, speaking about Israel and the future."

Your father, inflexible, sips maté. The man with thinning hair, patient, unfolds with smooth gestures, the purity of a youthful utopia. You walk around, nervous: you don't know whether to intervene or keep quiet, you listen from the side, and you walk back and forth, a mix of nervousness and hope showing slightly through your middle teeth, so easily managed with the nacre smile.

She: It is the most curvy and difficult route. Continuing at a fast pace and concentrating, you would make it. For running faster, youth which is escaping you like the hand prints on a fogged window, now finds you leaping over a cornice of mud—after having been very near falling—and you advance bit by bit. You can't go back, you have to keep up the inertia of the sudden impulse to go upward without knowing, at each step. As if the soft earth under the grass will give way and you will land in the water. Hardly attached to that edge, with her herbivorous leaps that require strength and concentration from you each time, you grit your teeth and go on. You go on.

He: A neighborhood meeting hall in Paternal: damp, tiled floor, under the stars, the silk mantle covered a handful of excited faces. The rabbi insisted on the covering of the head because, from far down, it wasn't possible to see the *kippa* on the occipit of the groom. An elderly attendant brought out the *ktuvah* at the end of the ceremony, he refused to let it go—a ridiculous tussle over a stiff piece of paper—until some bills thickened his pocket. But all that has no importance. It's the color of the music that dominates the atmosphere: mentholated eyes, your face (Gingi) reddened from the dancing, blazes of flash bulbs, the embroidered white dress. With a childlike smile, you persist again and again until five in the morning, while the waiters put up the chairs and collect the silverware.

"I want my wedding party to go on, David. Please let it continue a little longer. Let's begin again from the beginning. Please. C'mon. You can do it."

A sun, mischievous and rubicund, struggles to show itself on the horizon.

She: Finally, you arrive at your destination. The Moon has appeared behind a tree and it lights up the dens of the Palermo night, reflections filtering through the foliage. By the most dangerous, most twisted way, but you arrived. You join the group of colleagues who are exercising their bodies—in monotone call out "one, two, three, four," again and again—under the aromatic presence of the manicured gardens.

He: A ray of light that penetrates the window allows you to pick up the photo before finding a place for it in this album that accumulates memories and makes possible the reconstruction of your memory. You are reclining on the full-sized sofa-bed (no more furniture, you have to live precariously, ideas and plans focused in a socialist agricultural commune there in Israel). Not to accumulate possessions or put down roots will make the disposal of urban cobwebs simpler. You are wearing white pajamas with red dots that fit you very loosely, they give you a comic aspect while you read the newspaper. Your face unwashed, as always: soft skin, warm velvet. Eyes not quite open in half-awakenedness, red hair, short and unkempt.

"It seems to be wake-up time," you say with a guilty voice.

She: Another danger, insignificant but certain. You run behind your daughter to some sandy mountains and you let yourself fall forward, toward the dark beach, where rippling waves dampen unhurriedly the acrid smell brought by whirling air. You turn. You wander a bit, playing where the foam of the sea roars softly. The waves tickle your back, you fall and stumble at times. One wave gets you wet, another covers you for an instant. Sleep, heaviness, a certain pleasure in that innocent flirtation with risk. Another burst of water surrounds you with caressing hands, it touches and is gone. "I'll get up now," you think. "I shouldn't tempt fate in this way. The sea can grow and become really dangerous, I feel like sleeping but I ought to stand up, let's go." Another wave makes your head wet. "Let's go, you have to get up." Another one covers you with water and foam. Don't stay, let's go, up. "Now I'll go."

He: You walk on the subway platform, white smock closed at the neck and book under your arm. "What a surprise to run into you," you say. The time had been calculated; you had let several trains go by, but your object was achieved. Your two companions a bit further off, watch without even pretending, to share their impressions later, among laughter and torrents of overlapping words. The portfolio goes from hand to hand, embarrassed, while you talk and talk, drawing in the air a seismic bridge that your partner wants to cross.

With the years, you will teach that love is the antidote to death. The only medicine that is truly effective in developing the good reasons, for being and to carry on life with dignity, without hatred, maintaining the capacity for amazement. Remembering you shakes the memory, as a broken door knocker strikes the passing of time.

She: Get up, let's go, lazy bones. To intervene in history you have to decide, beforehand, who you are (and who you want to be). The murder brought alive your wound—and your guilt—as a survivor. But you didn't kill that woman. It's necessary that you get rid of your

169

depression and become a witness to reality, not an unprepared spectator. You have to flee the night, wake up. Let's go. Up, up with this body. Let's go.

He: The paper says: *The Foundation of the Metaphysics of Customs in Kant.* Pencil in hand, you grasp it while the discussion around you rises in tone. When there is a pause, you return to it: on the back, a simple outline and a "shaggy line"—that is, in the "the way you shouldn't draw," as you have heard thousands of times—blossom into a little house with a chimney, two trees on the edges (they look like cotton balls mounted on toothpicks), a winding road that plaits itself like a used-up tube of toothpaste in the bathroom sink, two female profiles poorly designed, something that sluggishly attempts to show two chairs and a table, all carved with surprised and satisfied eyes, as if you had finished a masterpiece of contemporary art. Below the drawing you explain: "This gift is for you, silly."

She: The years have passed, it's true. Proof: You always find relationships by chance occurrence, and another that happened to you earlier. Self-referential analogy that only interests you yourself and your peopled history, but doesn't make any sense to anyone else.

Your son Eduardo mentions a demonstration of high school students who demanded "student centers" of the type to which their classmates of Buenos Aires National High School belong, in spite of having resolved the issue in their own place. Immediately, your monotone voice is reminiscent of the recent get-together of the graduates of "Reconquista" National High School: "The German Meter confessed to me that he, the only supporter of 'open education' in the famous discussion of 1958, took part in the strike that his twenty-seven classmates organized in favor of lay education because of a spirit of camaraderie with the group, although he didn't share their motives."

Eduardo looks at you, dumbfounded. You are a senile father who doesn't know what he is saying, whose imprecise digressions possess echoes that don't interest other people or modify the current reality. You pat his head and ask: "I'm getting old, ah? Repeating myself is the only thing missing."

He: Your texts vary in density and category: clippings, cards, notebook paper with hurried writing, everything conserved incredibly through some vague obsessiveness. The first ones reveal the *pathos* of the period, the romantic influence mixed with the neighborhood flavor: "To the ruler of my heart/from your eternal prisoner," or better "so that in the coming months/ we look into each other's eyes as intensely as we do now." Later on, letters, never sent through the mail (though personally delivered,) with curious addressees: "Mr.: sweet husband. Street: at a year from our engagement. Destination: When will the baby arrive!?" Of course, in the return address is written: "Wife, love. And also friend, eh?"

Ingenuity, at times, cedes to utilitarian feeling: If you don't wash the dishes, it shows that you are an exploiter of women, and it also means that "you are bad." Also, there is a "balance sheet of marriage" typed one winter afternoon, "where the expected difference between investments and withdrawals for this year will provide a balance of 6,000 pesos for the baby Eduardito" and, thereafter "Shh . . . Shh . . . don't say anything to anyone."

She: Neither old nor washed up. Your grandfather Moishe Burech, at sixty-three years old, had to learn everything again. You barely pass the forties line and it's difficult for you to know who you are, you drown in an autistic nostalgia. In the genealogical sense—and you've got to know it—your adulthood is the best age. Don't laugh, it's the truth. The cylindrical trunk of the tree is robust and, at the same time, permeable to certain changes. You still feel the pain and the flavor of your roots, which live extended under your feet, palpitating. And, at the same time, the branches have grown and are loaded with fruits that adhere to the source. You are a complete tree in your fleeting moment of integrity, before the maturation of the product, after the tender spines and indecisive blossoms. A tree that can remember and shelter the hope, speak Spanish and dream in Yiddish, support his extremities in Europe and America, to grow *mestizo* without shame. Like a poplar in autumn.

He: You write poems, the toy, the rainbow, the Moon that moves you and the eyes that when you look at them take away your sadness. In one of them, you asked forgiveness for "not knowing how to form pretty verses" and you offer, in exchange, the sounds that emerge from that piano that sings night and day, while the neighborhood birds gather in clusters by the window and, from the branches of the tree that touch the balcony again and over again, accompany with warbles an aquarelle rhythm.

Included are signs of repentance ("I didn't want to tell you what I told you, and I know that I was wrong, but you made me angry") and even a document—that you make your husband sign too—jumps out from a pile of photos and clippings—and that preaches, toward the end: "we promise each other for eternity to be better partners and to love each other like we do now and more so. With all the love that I can give you, I sign here," (there is a signature), "with all the love that you can give," there is another signature. Yes, Gingi, you are getting there. You say again: "Up, let's go, you have to get up, join life."

She: It is the moment of the year when the tree is the most beautiful, almost unreal. Its branches acquire three colors: green, ochre, and silver, with all the intermediate tones. The edges aren't rough, sharp-edged planes, the vegetation in one tone borders and invades the other: an emerald fist suddenly illuminates a yellowish bunch, behind an outbreak of shadow the color of green bottles appear silvered stains, shining leaves are about to fall, they doubt, they swing their locks. The poplar vibrates with pleasure.

He: The children arrive like first fruits. . . . There you are, lying on the bed, face up, the pregnancy is far advanced, a flickering light (from the street) crosses the darkness of the bedroom and disperses over a blanket. The blue bed jacket, hands crossed over that belly that kicks and moves, the overnight bag at the end of the bed—put together months ago—with booties and little outfits and towels and all that. There were many nights with the rivers running parallel, exploding at the same time while your hand would squeeze the other loving hand (almost lost in the hollow, small and with a curved ring finger), the skin covered with kisses, the fingers that softly tingle the sensitive places, your head at times resting on your husband's chest as when you were little—say you would say—the grown-ups protected you during the stormy nights of thunder outside. And now, the curled profile and the mischievous expression: you gather your legs, you raise them, repeat the straining exercise that they taught you in the "Childbirth without Pain" course, smile broadly and turn your head to say,

"Do you see? So easy. Tomorrow or the day after I do a 'Come on, baby' and the kid pops out."

She: This beautiful mixture of that which is born and that which dies, the brand new and that which leaves, the three generations—that are, have been and will be—constitute the tree's moment of splendor. Moved lightly by the twilight breeze, this multicolor plot that continually changes (the edge of tall naked poplars, standing close together) discovers easily its shape and size between the roots and the sky, the secret of the ancestors and the projection toward the heights, the speckless sky that divides the cosmos and its planetary dimension. You are like the poplar in autumn, David: green, ochre and silvered. And only in that beautiful time—the first autumn days—those who understand can join in the secret which is bashfully undressed.

He: New papers in the swirl of memories, a tailor's crate from the attic: "I don't love you any more and don't speak to me anymore. I was a jerk to tell you what I told you and I take back what I said. . . ."

Before, much before this, you get angry for no reason and you begin to pack your bag, taken noisily from some closet; Peppy, the little furry dog. Jerry the clown, the bottle of soda with its cover woven in a way to look like a bear. Toys, after all. Your riches. You run to the next block dragging the suitcase and, when going in, you slip on the waxed floor of the showroom, and roll toward the back, collecting bruises. Your father-in-law leaves his office and helps you get up: at least once a week you fall, befuddled, on the stairs at home, and it is necessary to massage you with alcohol and everything. You stay until dusk because, as you will explain later, the husband has to come to his wife carrying a bouquet of flowers, after the argument. You had seen it that way in the movies and that's the way you wanted it.

Another gift drawing appears here: three strange forms with the inscription "Little Duck" to identify them, eternal little house with a chimney, path, and tree; below two sailboats that navigate together with the supposed ducks and, lower yet, two figures that are very similar. One has the label "hen" to identify it and the other says "dog" but as both are very much alike, you add near the second one's mouth : "bow-wow."

More cards. "To live together forever" or: "To the clearest and most crystalline sky/universal and mine alone (always with rounded letters) joined with a "I love you a lot," another dedication that most certainly accompanied some present or other and says: "So that you wrap your heart up in mine"; and another unexpected declaration: "Despite the fact that you don't love me, not even a little, I still love you and now I'm going to the post office and to practice piano a little, no one hears me but it doesn't matter, I love you just the same." And in a green clipping, you ask, "Why is it so hard for you to tell me that you love me? Does everything have to be intellectualized and with rhyme?"

Capacity for amazement, to have faith even in the improbable. The fiery expression that children possess, free of skepticism—of that "know it all"—and retains the adolescent clumsiness of the fledgling.

The is a movie short about the Centre Georges Pompidou in Paris filmed in 1977. We were there in 1981 and, nevertheless, you wait happily and fully assured that we appear in the documentary. It's useless to try to explain it to you: at one moment, you believe you can distinguish Ruth, your daughter, from among the hundreds of faces that parade in front of the camera. You are absolutely sure that it is she, although formal logic says, "It's impossible."

They nickname you "Rogelia, the woman who thought too much," because your head always moved faster than the language and thoughts of others. That "I thought that you thought that I thought that you thought . . . " exasperated the others or caused them to laugh uproariously, depending on the situation. In the dialogues that you invent, the middle parts are always missing, the sandwich filling. Your sudden exits make them stop the conversation and look at you, in amazement. Unintentionally, you apply a rule of counter-physics: the response is never the expected one—especially in situations of conflict—and it provokes a continual starting over, rethread the tape of reasonings in order to figure out at what moment the thread was broken. "Rogelia," always "Rogelia," you smile again:

"It's so simple. It's you guys who don't understand anything."

That unaffected silliness maintains the freshness, helps in living. It is transmitted to those around you like a kind of contagion (your dog Galileo barks and plays with a porcelain dog that is behind a glass front, confusing it with a flesh and blood colleague). It is natural to trust in miracles, chance encounters, or conversations with a falling star. You simply reject as bitter those who don't believe in those everyday possibilities, without intellectual twists or linguistic tricks. "You have to live," you say. "Not understand. You have to wake up and embrace the day."

She: You begin to distinguish day from night, to feel instead of thinking with your head, rationally. The succession of those fleeting memories, lovingly held with nostalgia—why, if it were not so, you would be able to evoke them now, beginning with a pile of photos and papers strewn around the attic—shakes you into a necessary wakefulness, permits you to open your eyes to daily hope, to wake up. Dreams, fantasies, night fears, flee toward the temptation of madness—that mistaken door of literature—or early suicide, in the face of the apparent impossibility of ordering the chaos. That escape toward which you are dragged by the visions of your friend León or bookish dogma that asphyxiates you.

You discover, in sum, what are the *good reasons* to choose life.

He: You are falling asleep, with your hands crossed under your face. Then, you stand in the room's doorway, still half-awake with your eyes half open, and you begin to shout because of what you have just dreamt: "Yes, I know well that you went with her and left me by the road, abandoned and alone, because you tricked me. . . . " It is difficult to convince you that it is only a nightmare. You remain angry for a long time. That is what can't be shared, that which helps in remembering. They tell you of the visit to the childhood neighborhood, of Ignacio, and León and Teresa, but that capricious purring is worth more than all that: like a lantern light that vibrates between dullness, the minting of the day that infiltrates in the evenness of the memory.

So many papers and photos, so many memories and anecdotes, help in the recognition in the borders of your mirror. There, in one place, are the *good reasons* to love yourself and to love life, those that you must reread every so often to shake up the inertia of the passage.

family tree

Good Reasons

Because you chew on your left thumb and index finger
    when you hear something that makes you nervous
Because you have the right amount of surprise in your eyes
    like a stubborn bear
Because you are startled by the nocturnal sounds and the
    city wind
Because you murmur incoherent words just as you
    are beginning to fall asleep
Because a sweet fuzziness makes you dangerous to
    fragile and wide objects
Because you love the sun madly, blindly, furiously
Because you are distracted like a gazelle looking backwards
Because of your attacks of laughter that can last for hours
Because you never understand stories with double meanings
    and it is necessary to explain them to you
Because when you are sleepy, you get angry, and you walk hurriedly,
    and speaking to yourself you are capable of saying
    all sort of nonsense
Because of red hairs, because of your neck, because of your nose
    that scrunches up because of your caramel gesture
Because you are incapable of not loving others
Because you eat chocolate on the sly
Because you wrinkle your nose and hide your shoulders and you
    smile
    mischievously when you are surprised taking
    a nap in the middle of the afternoon
Because you cry in the movies when you are upset
    by a love story

Because of the effort with which you try, time and again, seriously
    and uselessly, to get interested in politics
Because you yell "intellectual" at me, and you shake a bit of life
    into me, and you help me wake up
Because you are one and irreplaceable like the first encounter with
    death
Because you take out the handkerchiefs, and you put the clothing
    in order, and I never can find anything
Because in the middle of a dream, the creases disappear
    from your face, and you almost always smile
Because I like to watch you sleeping
Because you alone know how to draw locomotives with violet
    smoke
    or little houses with chimneys
Because you close your eyes when you chew a bite, as if
    you needed to concentrate on that
Because without you I don't know my shirt size or at what time
    to eat lunch
Because you can be feminist while being feminine
Because you tremble with fear when I stare at you, and
    it's necessary to warn you that it's only a joke
Because you are completely sure of the most absurd things,
    and discussion is impossible
Because you stick out your tongue behind my back when you get
    angry
Because you hug the children, and it's difficult to know who is
    the most childlike of the three
Because you think that thieves can be chased away
    with a broom
Because your religion is the sea, the ducks, the tumbles
    on the grass
Because you insist that you want to be a bird and fly, although
    may it happen in a later incarnation, if that exists

Because when you hear the bed stays creak, you believe
　　that the ants are gnawing at the concrete,
　　and the building will fall down
Because you are capable of falling down a flight of stairs while
　　you are practicing yoga
Because you have a rounded hand like a student's
Because you learned in the movies that the man ought
　　to say pretty words to the woman before
　　kissing her, and you continue believing it
Because you fall asleep in the middle of a boring section,
　　with the book open on your chest
Because you hate jewels, war, racism
Because every day you befriend people on the bus,
　　while you travel
Because at fifteen years old, you would go up on the balcony and
　　you
　　would speak out loud with the Moon, asking it for things
Because you were brave when you had to be
Because I've never yet met anyone who could hate you
Because a necklace of mischief and bruises precedes you
Because you like fat-cheeked penguins
Because you speak like a little girl when you want
　　something very valuable
Because you are convinced that it is necessary to love
　　people
Because you suffer greatly from the cold, and you steal my socks,
　　and you wear them with embarrassment
Because when you get angry enough to fight you knit your brow,
　　and you make fists with your thumb inside your fingers
Because, in winter, it is necessary to force you to wash your face
　　in the morning
Because, at times, you converse with the birds or with beings from
　　other worlds that appear to you through the window

Because you possess, together, senses of reality and fantasy
Because every time you speak to me on the telephone, you are
    chewing a cracker
Because you disguise yourself in my pajamas, and paint a red ball
    on your nose, and you play the clown in front of the mirror
Because of all of this and because of a great deal more
Because I love you.

A GUIDED TOUR OF THE NEIGHBORHOOD

You get off the minibus at the corner of Nazca Street and Mosconi Avenue. Every paving tile, every door, every face half-seen in a window and every shop's sign bring sensations, waves of heat that rapidly rise through the body to invade you. The pasta store, that furniture store that also handles municipal paper work, then the little market.

In the first stall, on the left, you used to buy the Jewish "braids": that *challah* whose taste—when smeared with butter—is brought back to life in the saliva that now slips down your throat. Or the black bread, with the biting and manly aroma of rubbed garlic, knocking about on the tongue, throwing itself daringly at the palate. Vegetable stands and fruit stands repeat themselves, as if in a mirror, from the opposite side, in a circular way; in the center, the butcher shops, a fish stall and a chicken market.

Ignacio expects you before noon, but the fascination of recovered time is stronger than the need for punctuality. You advance over the grayish and slightly damp sidewalk tiles. A cold current of air, from the past, arrives from down below, where they forget to shut the door that leads to the loading docks. There works Salvador, the Italian with a small mustache and bulging eyes, who several times came near to pulling a knife on his competitors over clients: a bit balder, but everything else is the same. How many years since you've come through here? Twelve or thirteen. Since before traveling to Israel. These echoes that are now awakened are untranscendental for anyone else. But perhaps, isn't this nostalgia part of your story?

The next shop, you discover, is occupied by an older gentleman, unknown. Poor Armandito: you had heard that he died very young, it seemed to be a heart attack (the cold and all that, weighing on immensely sad eyes of a boy who never knew a family). You make a half turn. You are afraid that you may stay there all morning, sponging up your childhood mire.

You walk slowly: there are three blocks all told and there is no reason to run. At the corner of Argerich Street begins the religious School of Our Lady of the Orchard: a low and dark building, stunted. It takes up the entire block and, like a lightning bolt, evokes significant stories.

By the ugly big wall that faces Tequendama Street, one night, León swore before the entire gang that he had sex for the first time— the first of you, you looked at him with envy and admiration—with the little servant girl from the grocery store. You listen to his piled up, nervous words:

"I squeezed her and I frightened her a little. It was very dark, maybe that was the reason she loosened up. I took out my prick, and I tried to put it in her hand, but she said no. Then, with a few tugs, I pulled down her panties, I straightened her up with the other hand— turning her around, her face toward the wall, and I tried to screw her."

"Come on León, tell it straight. You're making it up."

"I swear to you on my life, Che. I was so hot that I finished too soon. It was curious that, just then, she seemed to get a little excited. All women are crazy."

"And then?"

"I took advantage of the fact that I'd gotten her all wet to lubricate her with my finger and I put it further in her. There, yes, she yelled and scratched the wall, but she had to bear it. We were like two animals."

This place was a pilgrimage site for the boys of the block. Even when León didn't come out to goof off because, stud and everything, his mother would yell at him and he had to stay at home to study. Dady and El Negro would play with little cards with sports figures on them near the wall—where, in the dirt, they always believed that they had discovered small stains, traces of the formidable coitus of their precocious companion—and you yourself, until it began to get dark, tired yourself out with the "Point and Flip" and, for a final game, an "On Top" that became interminable, with the little pieces of cardboard touching the ground (its body rounded by the patient work of the three fingers) flush with the vertical face, seeking to conceal those which were on the floor. But, above all, to scrape off some whitewash that, with infinite luck, had been witness to the scene that obsessed your nights, together with the image of Anchoíta's mother taking off her panties and wearing only openwork stockings, black garters and high heels.

You return toward Mosconi Avenue. In the middle of the block, two large doors with iron work, surrounded by files of pointed iron bars, expressive lances pointing toward the sky offering more than simply protection. The leaves from the trees pile up on the sidewalk tiles and a girl, a live-in student from the school—gray smock, thin hair, and a sad face ("nothing has changed about that," you think)—slowly sweeps the path. In front of this place, you walk with Gingi on a cold winter night, just married. The trees draw on the ground shadows of tortuous images caused by a very distant and solitary street-lamp, there on the corner of Juan Pascual Duarte Way (the name of which didn't come from that of Eva Perón's brother, as was believed for a long time.) From behind a thick tree trunk, he appears: a sinister appearance, bearded, very sickly eyes, and an aggressive attitude. The right hand, inside the bag, squeezes that which is about to be drawn to make an appeal to you: knife, revolver, something.

You are on your block, there you were born. Owner of these sidewalk tiles and corners, deserted avenues where any porteño would tremble from fright just to imagine a nocturnal stroll. But you are part of this bit of frontier between Villa Pueyrredón and Villa Devoto. Nothing bad can happen to you here, where all the neighbors know each other like brothers and use nicknames (Pechito, Angustia, Pelado, Azufre) translatable only in the neighborhood, where hardly anyone moves away and for years nothing of importance happens; where you played soccer in the streets and ran to see the bus that crashed into the awning poles of the Cuenca bookstore—there it was that Fool, the owner's daughter, was yelling, with eyes opened wide by the shock, and arrived, running, to this same Church of the Orchard to give thanks for still being alive—where the gangs of boys formed according to streets that are perpendicular (that of Mosconi and Cuenca, that of Campana and Carlos Antonio López) who are enemies among themselves, but who unite against others from farther away, for a football challenge or interminable skirmishes that begin with small stones and rotten peaches and always end with stick blows and someone bleeding. This is your place in the world, the set in which you are the principal actor, and nothing bad can happen to you.

So safe a womb, where one sips maté on the sidewalk and speaks about the distant Buenos Aires, belonging to others, about the perdition of downtown and about the bad influences who, moved by ambition, resound like deceitful sirens in the ears of those who do not yet understand the essence of that great family that is the neighborhood. Each one recognized at a glance. And it was in the small school on Tequendama that you climbed to the top of the flagpole, the first time that they chose you standard bearer of the light blue and white flag that put tears in your eyes. As with "Aurora" or the "San Lorenzo March," that music which despite daily repetition would never be tiresome for you.

All that, you think in a second—or that is how you relive it now—and you go forward without fear, your gaze fixed on the eyes of the man who is in front of you, wanting to assault you. You grasp Gingi's arm and you pass beside the figure—halted on the sidewalk, without making a decision—and with a firm step go on toward Helguera Street. You don't look back even once. This is your neighborhood, gigantic womb set forever in your memory. Here you are boss. You are somebody here. That will never be understood by the downtown hotshots, brought up in the undifferentiated heap.

You cross the street: from the sidewalk in front, one can see the wall with its filthy whitewash, solid and concealing until Tequendama. It grows upwards for five or six meters, scribbled with neighborhood inscriptions, red and black aerosols, hearts that declare eternal love or ingenious phrases ("God has a clitoris"), proper names, partisan slogans. The other memory, that episode that pursued you for years, to you, a young man supposedly hardened by the ideological formation and the activism in that socialism that, after the Cuban revolution, one became part of the ardent ways of rebellious beards and men who changed from the inside out and for always. But on that day you were an adolescent, politics mixed naturally with the sweet nonsense of the age. You argued with everyone and here was where you had your "first blood" of the street, the necessity to choose between (again) escaping and deciding to confront what life might afford. Those two gang members, Nario and Paco, helped you to grow.

Only ten more meters. Ignacio is waiting for you in his large old house and perhaps he will be able to clarify this absurd story in which León, unexpectedly appearing to help you (as he would have in the old days), finds himself involved. Mingo Castro, the newspaper seller from the kiosk, salutes you: he wears the same cap, the same mustache and eye glasses, the same maroon pullover—braided, knit by his wife—from time stopped in 1970, now as then. The only changes are a some small wrinkles on his temples, bags under his eyes, a trace of red color (perhaps a hemophage) in his tired face.

"What's up, David, my boy? Back here? What have you been up to all those years that 'no one saw hide nor hair of you'?"

You answer with some banality or other, but it is impossible to get out of it so easily. Two minutes hadn't yet passed and already Mingo—who used to get back issues of magazines ready for binding for you—is going on about his oldest daughter who is engaged and doesn't want to study any more, the second who has a remarkable head for numbers, the future son-in-law who . . . You hardly listen, preoccupied with your own and self-centered memories, with echoes that wake improbable traces in your sleeping insides. On the right side of the kiosk, where Mingo now puts the pornographic magazines, covered up by black wrappers, was that volume from the Buffalo collection, covers with red at the bottom and cowboys in three colors drawing their revolvers. You needed it to complete the collection and, after months or fruitless search, you found it in that corner, so hidden that Mingo himself forgot to include it in the returns to the distributor. You danced with joy that evening.

What was the title of the book? You try to remember but without success. The author, yes: Estefanía. He had a pair of initials in front of his surname. What were they? Yes, M. L. Soon after: with another volume by the same scribe, you would complete the information: Marcial Lafuente Estefanía. That's what it was. Read on rainy afternoons, when few customers came into your father's tailor shop.

Where would all those books be now? On the same corner, where Castro slides his little chair a couple of steps to continue taking the lukewarm morning sun, your son Eduardo (you remember) builds an imaginary barrier—with rough wood—that goes up and down to permit the passage of tricycles and of people. "Raise the bar," "Lower the bar," he repeats and sees the train approach as if it had a real existence; he nervously alerts any one who tries to cross that imaginary line. But there is something else. This corner evokes an evanescent tingling that you try to catch.

Yes, surely: the music teacher. You see it, ten meters away on the same sidewalk, the old house painted yellow with a garden out front. Juanita, the spinster who taught the rudiments of piano to the whole neighborhood. Small and vigorous in spite of an overwhelming shyness, flat shoes with low heels, worn out to an extreme. She always wore brown shoes. Why are you remembering that, now?

There is something else, though. Finally you are beginning to grasp it. It doesn't have to do with the music teacher or an imaginary neighborhood. Nor with your son but with yourself: driving a very primitive vehicle—it is called a hand mobile or something like that—you park next to the sidewalk curb. Your mother is sending you to buy something at the corner store, right in front of Mingo's magazine kiosk. You are there, your fattish face and you hair left a bit uncombed. Your large head accentuated by its "American style" haircut, wearing green overalls (the same ones that you once soiled, in Ignacio's house, when the emotion of a game of cops and robbers—between the chicken house and the high plants of the garden—made you forget the need for the john until it was too late). And Don Luis, the owner of the grocery store, says to you while he is packing soda crackers that if you don't behave he will lock you in the basement. He raises a dark door where nothing can be seen.

"It's full of rats down there," he says. You shiver with terror.

It doesn't have anything to do with your son or with the music teacher, then, but with you. You were born in this neighborhood. It is as much a part of you as "Lunfardo," the local dialect, or skin, or fingernails. You wore out sidewalks with your mother who checked your weight each week on the scale of the Dubin pharmacy—then alone, with friends, later with your fiancé, even later with your children, always living in the same house. Generations and generations of *porteños*, desperate love for Buenos Aires.

With effort you separate yourself from Mingo's torrent of words, because nostalgia can be interminable. A sweet and dangerous feeling invades you like a paralysis.

I never had to have left Mosconi—you think. Here everything was mine, sure, quiet, known. I would have lived happily on this block. Without blows or loss of memory, without wars or tough choices, always a child, with Mingo, Anchoíta, Ignacio, and the rest . . . What would have happened to me if I had never abandoned the neighborhood? I would have grown less; but, also, suffered less.

The Grimaudo brothers greet you, two of whom are standing in the door of the furniture store, like ten and twenty and thirty years ago, speaking of football and women. Also Miguelito, who asks why you are not going to visit him and, joking, curses you in Arabic while he rests a hand on his testicles. Dubin, the pharmacist from the far corner, inquires about your whole family (he tried to cure with dozens of injections your persistent sinusitis, in the little room where they conversed about politics and to reach it you had to walk around the side of the scale). In the café, the Portuguese man insists on inviting you to have a drink with him.

"You left the neighborhood, David. You did well. Certainly, you were able to progress, leave this backwater. I never found the energy and here you see me, always the same, vegetating."

You promise a visit for another day. You can't help smiling about the tricks played by the neighbors: he is very short of stature with a very fine mustache and nervous movements. He bought an enormous car, with the savings from the first years in the bar—where his wife cooked delicious dishes, although she never learned to speak Spanish—to impress the neighborhood. However, as he could not reach the pedals, he had to make two large pillows in order to be able to drive: when he went along Mosconi at full speed, it was hardly possible to see his little head sticking up over the steering wheel.

Raúl is seated at a table in the café. He tells you that one of the Grimaudos became a Fascist and spends his time doing strange things, perhaps with the death squads.

"I, as always, go on in the Party," he added, winking an eye at you.

A comrade. But you remember this same eye, half-closed and swollen. Raúl, three years older than the lot of you, drove your adolescent gang mad with tricks and humiliations. You told your cousin about it and he told your grandfather Moishe Burech. Since you don't know Yiddish, you need an interpreter. The fact is that Juan—your oldest cousin, the same age as Raúl—arrived on a visit soon thereafter. He traveled by trolley and then by local bus, because he lived very far away, in the Boedo district. In shirt sleeves, without a jacket, he drank some milk in your house and then asked, "Where is that Raúl?"

They went over to the other fellow's house. Everything happens rapidly. Juan rings the doorbell, Raúl comes out, they invite him to fight on the corner. The other one answers, "Fine, that way I'll kick the entire family's ass." He tells his mother he'll be right back and then comes with us. The encounter didn't last even half a minute: Juan gets him with a fierce punch in the left eye and Raúl lands like a sack of potatoes. The boys from the bar come to help him. They sit him on a chair that they pull out onto the sidewalk, they put ice on his eye. Juan, very correctly, greets your parents, takes the local bus and then the trolley and returns home. The family clan . . .

"Stay a while, Davicito. It's been along time since we've seen each other."

"I can't, Raúl. They are waiting for me. Another time."

You cross toward Ignacio's father's shoe shop. The two Jews on the block, until much later when León arrived. With Anchoíta and El Negro you used to form a solid defense in the pick-up soccer games; Ignacio played center and El Dady at goal. Edo and León, the fattest, in front, but only rarely did they score. You breathe deeply, filling your lungs with the neighborhood: essential language, innocence reclaimed, pieces of identity to fit the puzzle.

And your old house, now the home of a Yugoslav family that came to the neighborhood after purchasing it. You don't want to feel the pain of the loss. The home. Constructed brick by brick—you lifted up the buckets of mortar, playing with the masons—and then lost, burnt down, abandoned. In Poland, in Argentina, in Israel. Built with so much work, as your father, the tailor, tells it, on some Buenos Aires night where the day's good sales justify the purchase of a cold beer and quickly heighten his loquacity.

"A Polish landlord gave my father some bricks from his oven, to help him in building the house," the old immigrant said, half-closing his eyes. "We got hold of only one cart; two of us (Carlos and Abraham, the strongest) yoked up their chests as if they were draw horses.

We loaded the vehicle with bricks, and with everyone, pushing from behind, we dragged it to the plot of land. In those days we didn't have horses. I liked animals a lot: The milk man next door had a cart and horse with which he carried milk and cheese to Lemberg in the mornings. I waited for him at nightfall; he then took the harness of the animal and he allowed me to lead it to a small field, where it would graze during the night. I went on horseback and returned walking, alone. Riding was an enormous pleasure."

"And the house, papa?"

"For us, the house was a palace. For that reason also I liked to return home. We built it, bit by bit, over a long period of time. From our window, you could see the river, and farther on, the forest. On Saturday mornings we would hurry to bathe and then lie down, face up, looking at the sky. In the silence, you could hear the singing of the foliage, the musical dialogues that settle into the treetops, pushed by the wind. Listening to the trees, we too learned to sing. Without radio or electricity, imagine, the only way to pass twelve or fourteen hours sewing with the needle, stuck there, was with the songs in Yiddish and Polish which kept us company. Heirs of the wind and the branches, of the beautiful and natural air that surrounded us. And the house, that safe refuge that *was there*."

Also your house in the *kibbutz* was there, after a hard day of work in the fields. The garden of tended plants and colorful curtains that enlivened the narrow space punished by the eastern sun, so full of life and hopes. And now you return to the reality, in this frontier Villa Pueyrredón and Villa Devoto and the family dwelling that you observe after having rung the doorbell to the shoe shop: the two plate-glass windows, the center door, the mirrored counters with men's clothing for sale, the cutting table, and the tailor's great scissors. Nothing of that still exists. The modern front—rejuvenated by the new owner with ceramic tile of dubious taste—can't erase from your retinas that floor made of worn out ceramic tile where you played marbles, the clothes rack, the fitting room, the heavy green metallic curtain. . . . What did you and Ignacio, scarcely adolescents, do behind the tables, when you stayed alone for a while in the store? You blush right now remembering it: chats about women in hushed tones, mutual excitation, at times you masturbated in unison, sitting on high benches and looking at the street, distracted looks on your faces and your hands deep inside your pants pockets, reaching the invisible bulk. Shameful shaking that always ended with the same question: "Did you come yet?"

The balconies, on the other hand, are exactly the same, where every Wednesday and for several months your parents are waiting—resting their elbows on the railing—to see you appear walking, at lunch time. That was six, seven years ago. You were coming from Israel, from the war, and they had not yet accepted the immense conviction of the recuperated son. They touched you and kissed you, every day Wednesday. Like your grandmother Hettie, sleeping with Abraham when you returned from the trenches, fearing that sleep might carry off the son that they thought dead and who returned. That it was only a nightmare. In that balcony are your parents, repeating the story as you will repeat it with your descendants, taste and aroma of the fruits of the common tree. You want to shout, but just in that instant, your childhood friend opens the door.

Is it your sensibility, exacerbated by that pass through the mists of a memory that insists on recovering every instant and every wound, that causes you to note a certain discomfort on Ignacio's face as he tells you to come in, hangs up your jacket on the rack and moves toward the inside of the house without looking at you, as if he felt you guilty of something?

family tree

They are there in the middle of the block, against the thick wall: Paco and Nario. Unkempt beard and grimace on the owner of Napoleón—the dog ignominiously defeated by Alex, your German shepherd—the cigarette that hangs in the mouth of the hairdresser's assistant. You are afraid. Twice, last week, you went as far as the block with the convent and crossed the sidewalk to see them there, in the street. This cowardice humiliates you very deeply: they are big; they hate you. They are waiting for—you know it—any tiny reflection, a hidden reply, as cause to assault you.

But this time, León accompanies you, both of you are sixteen years old, you aren't babies. It embarrasses you to confess your fear. You don't have a choice. You walk together toward Doña Blanca's dairy, on Tequendama Street, staying close to the wall.

"We will drink cold milk from the bottle," he says, smiling. "We will buy three but, in fact, we will bring your mother two full containers and one empty one."

They are very close by. Paco comes nearer, swinging his legs. You see him come, and you divert your gaze: quickly, the autumn leaves scattered on the ground have acquired an unexpected interest. That makes him more self-assured, and he laughs.

He stops in front of you. He's less than half a head taller than you, he is pretty thin, but the evil that causes your terror is in his drunk's eyes, surrounded by little red veins and lacking in compassion. He watches you. You can't go forward or move sideways.

"How ugly you are, little Yid," he says, without raising his voice very much.

León looks at you and then at him. Nario also comes closer, murmuring, "What's going on, che? Is there a problem?"

One of your legs begins to tremble, and you can't control it. Your eyes move from Paco to León, then you lower your gaze. Now it's Nario who insists, "What's happening with those stinking Kikes? Did the Kikes shit in their pants?"

León hesitates a moment. Then he takes you by the arm and tries to pull you closer to the curb, to step over it onto the facing sidewalk. They are grown-ups, they are about twenty years old. You don't have to let yourself be provoked, they are too stupid. You move aside a couple of steps, but Nario raises his arm.

"One moment. Not so fast. If you want to pass, yell, 'we are stinking Jews. Long live Hitler, long live Perón.'"

León grasped his elbow in his hand, rigid. Your heart beats crazily. The hair at the nape of your neck stands up. Who made you so sensitive, what's it good for? The two of you take a step back, raise your heads, and in unison refuse. Nario thinks that you will turn and run toward Mosconi Avenue again and he will lose you. He insists: "Come on, Kike. Once. I'll make it shorter for you: 'long live Hitler and Perón.' Just one little time and you can go home with your bottles and drink your milk, your mother is waiting."

You two are paralyzed, but you don't you open your mouths. Paco spits, tired.

"Enough already, Nario. They're cowards. Let's go, let them go."

They depart, with broad smiles. When they are a few meters away, the spell seems to break. The air becomes clearer. You can breathe again, your leg stops moving, color returns to León's face. He looks at you: "He's right, David."

"Yes, we are cowards. What a shame . . . "

Force is the right of beasts and all that. You know it. But, how many times can you continue crossing sidewalks everytime you see them coming, feeling that terrifying humiliation—held like a disgusting cadaver that invades your nightmares—that hurts you as much as the imagined blows? You advance a few steps, and you call: "Eh, che, come here. You! Motherfuckers!"

Your voice cuts off. Your shaking stops the last words in a "stutter" that holds them in your throat. Nario and Paco figure out that you are referring to them.

"What's your story, asshole?"

It's León who is yelling: "Go fuck your mother the whore, stinking Nazis!"

There is a long, interminable moment of stupor. You think about your father, of your grandfather Moishe Burech, of all those who can give you courage in that instant. Paco is the first to react: he looks at León as if he had not understood and, suddenly, punches him fiercely on the face. You see the blood on your friend's nose and you want to respond, but Nario is coming toward you. Your legs are still trembling. You hit each other with hands and feet, bodies, heads, tangled up. The blows shake you, and, at the same time, increase your fury: you scratch, bite, begin to cry while you roll around embraced on the sidewalk, and you fall into the gutter filled with dirty water. León, you see at that moment, has gotten up and withstands, as well as he can, the blows from his opponent.

Shouts from other people, running. Doña Blanca, from the dairy, is the first to grab Paco's arm and pulls him away with one yank.

"Good-for-nothings! Have you no shame? In front of the Convent of Our Lady of the Orchard . . . "

Mingo, the newsdealer, now comes near. And Elías, the handkerchief maker. They grab Nario, whose eyes are burning with hatred and has spittle by his mouth.

"You're a Jew and a communist! You'll pay me for this, I swear it to you. I'm going to kill you. Today or tomorrow or some day, but I'm going to kill you."

You are beaten as if a truck had ridden over you. You have blood on your hands and gums, a thick taste that makes you want to vomit. León leans against the church wall: agitated breathing, disheveled clothing, a swollen eye. Both of you smile. Between the

wave of pain and the blow and the shame, you have begun to discover the secret language of courage. That which divides, you think
then, the men from the boys. That must be the reason you never
saw your father cry. Except one time: the day that your grandfather
Moishe Burech died.

"You and León always looked down on me a bit, isn't that right?"

Fifteen, twenty minutes of inevitable conversation about births, weddings, and neighborhood anecdotes have passed, when Ignacio took off his eyeglasses, and, out of nowhere, let loose with the question that gives life to a twenty-year-old past. Held, always, in the guts.

"No . . . Why do you say that? We were very young then. Everybody was interested in himself."

León, in front, always first, you next, admiring him and competing with him at the same time. Ignacio only played when there weren't any risks: not in politics, not in practical jokes, not in settling scores in high school. He had to "study" when the moment came to take on El Negro in El Dady's bar, or smoke a cigarette on the sly. The same Ignacio has deeper wrinkles, thicker lenses in his glasses, incipient baldness. As before, he doesn't know what to do with the sweaty palms of his little hands: he dries them against his pantleg, on a handkerchief, on the sides of his checkered shirt.

"He isn't very good-looking," you think. His recently discovered religious fervor softens his features: his hair grows over his ears, and, and although he hasn't gone so far as to roll up his sideburns (like the orthodox), it doesn't take much to imagine him at nightfall on *Shabbat* surrounded by candles burning in candelabras, sacred books, *mezuzot,* religious objects. He seems calmer in this recently discovered world.

"Adolescent problems . . . ," you say, raising your tone. "Then one grows up, stops putting importance on those little frictions . . . "

He scarcely smiles without answering. His eyes are damp, but it was always that way: it helped him have success with women. León was saying "You're the quiet one, Ignacio. Those of us who talk a lot don't do anything. It's the mutes who climb on top of the old ladies from the neighborhood, while we the fakers spend our time fantasizing and later jacking off in the shaking solitude of the bathroom. You, smart guy, Ignacio, don't get excited by what they say. You are from the race of winners, with those sensitive eyes you conquer them all."

The images mix: now there are too many details that flood your memory. You have to select them, put them in order of importance.

"Ignacio, I need your help. You've probably read about this unfortunate situation in the papers, and I suppose that the gossips in the neighborhood haven't missed an opportunity to comment on Señora Abud's murder on the corner of Campana Street and Mosconi Avenue, my partial amnesia, León's arrest."

He nods: he maintains his thin and ironic smile through half-opened lips. You explain Teresa's letters, León's plans in Israel, and the naming of Ignacio himself as the delegate in Argentina of his international organization. The words come out in bursts. He interrupts you.

"What is it exactly that you want to ask?"

"Señora Abud . . . "

"Don't you remember Señora Abud? You really don't know who . . . she was?"

The question falls like a mace blow. All the reality which, finally, you thought you had been putting together with patience and investigation to fill the empty spaces, totters. As when you were sure of beating El Dady, in that street fight, and the first blow sent you to the ground with a face red from pain and anger, undoing a sense of security patiently put together in the company of your friends.

"Señora Abud?"

You repeat to win time. While you gesture with the coffee spoon and your brain, like a crazy computer, splashes of light and questions in all corners. Nothing. If there was something, it has been erased.

"No, Ignacio. I don't know who she was nor do I remember . . . You must understand, the amnesia . . . "

Your hand moves toward the flower-patterned plate: pieces of black bread with butter, slices of borscht and pickles. Food of the Gods for your mestizo palate, full of eastern Jewish longings.

You point at the food.

"Your . . . mama?"

"Yes, Sara prepared it. You really don't remember Señora Abud?"

You give in. Also, you are red-faced: how did you forget that Sara is Ignacio's stepmother, that his mother died when he was a child?

"No, Ignacio. Help me, please."

"Samir and Elías Abud. The handkerchief factory, passing by the optician's and bumping into Pastor Maselli, the evangelist, the one whose son studied radio and built homemade units with which we listened to short wave. Can you place him, David?"

Something struggles to move ahead. You catch it.

Maselli! The one who worked with tiles. He caught our attention because he was a Christian minister without a uniform. And he wore overalls every day.

"Exactly, the Abud's factory was off to the side."

Another blast shakes you.

"Samir and Elías, the two brothers! What an imbecile I am! I didn't make the connection because we always called them by their first names. I had almost forgotten the last name. Abud. And the younger brother, Elías . . . "

The memories come together again in clusters, uncontainable.

"That's it, that's it! Elías was the unmarried brother, the one with an enormous nose and a mustache. Skinny, nervous, about fifty years old . . . A dirty old man for us. Samir's son once went to Maselli's place, to listen to short wave . . .

Elías was a bachelor. And Lebanese by birth.

"Now I remember everything. We noticed how they managed that business. He wanted an Arab girl 'direct from the factory.' The relatives made the arrangements in Beirut."

"Don't be so harsh, David. The man would have been lonely, an immigrant, a stranger in the country. He wanted someone similar to himself to marry."

"It happened this way: Elías traveled to Lebanon, paid a certain sum of money to a poor family, and brought a very pretty girl to be his wife. She wasn't more than sixteen and had enormous dark eyes, with long eyelashes . . . Sheila, she was called."

"Sheila Abud."

You hit your forehead with your hand.

"Obviously, how stupid! She was Sheila Abud. I remember what caught our interest, young and curious: she was covered with hair. When she raised her arms, she had a forest there. And large breasts, provocative."

"She was a piece, David."

"What most impressed me, she had hardly arrived—we were there with Maselli and Samir's son—was that she began to cry like a little girl, finding herself among so many strange people and not understanding the language. She was almost our age, and they had sold her like an object, foisted off on her an old and large-nosed husband."

"But what a babe, eh?"

"Yes, she was very pretty. She had two or three children . . . "

"Two. With the years her beauty increased, that's for sure, she was transformed into a woman. But she also became a part-time whore. She fucked half the neighborhood."

"I can't believe you, Ignacio."

"Yes, it was like that. A stinking whore. A sort of vengeance against her husband, it seems; but the truth is that he ruined this little girl's life. And she got back at him however she could."

"Señora Abud . . . "

You remain silent for a while, your head deep in your hands. So she was the poor woman who was shot down on a *porteño* street corner. Were you able to see her, before your head hit the ground? You close your eyes: impossible to reconstruct details. It was only a second, something very quick.

"Perhaps I wouldn't have remembered her in any case. So many years have passed."

Ignacio watches from behind his eyeglasses. You press on.

"And so, what's happening with León?"

A grimace passed across his face, disfiguring it slightly. You move around in your chair. Nothing is as it was, frozen in time as you wished. But, one never knows . . .

The silence goes on until it becomes uncomfortable. Suddenly, he grabs your wrist.

"What do you want to know: if I always admired León? Yes, he was my idol. Sometimes a bit less, sometimes a bit more . . . But that force of character, that powerful imagination that . . . Do you remember when we put up posters and the police came?"

A small street in Lanús, near the railroad station. The trees are there. Ignacio comes for the first time, it will also be the last—there is someone else there: yes, Teresa's younger brother. You ask: "What happened to Fito?" Fito, Teresa's younger brother.

Ignacio's grimace grew broader.

"They killed him years later, in 1975 . . . He was passing out leaflets at the corner near the high school. A pig took him away in a Falcon and beat him mercilessly. When they arrived at the outskirts of the city, he was already a pile of bleeding flesh. There, they tied him with a rope to the rear bumper of the car, and they made a few turns. There were neighbors who saw it. Teresa had to go and identify him, he was so disfigured . . . "

"Teresa has her reasons for not wanting to say any more about politics," you think. But Fito was a thirteen-year-old kid that night, in 1961, in Lanús. You were putting up posters in support of the Cuban revolution, against the mercenary invasion on Girón Beach.

"What a time," you say. "The party, those first years with the bearded guys in Havana, so pure and childlike. They inspired us with the desire to breathe utopia in one more generation. To know that it is possible."

The police car appears on the corner. León sees it turn, and he escapes. Fito and Ignacio are paralyzed with fear. You spin around, and you run too, you dive into the bed of a parked truck, you cover yourself with the canvas.

"And León came back."

Ignacio's voice sounds a bit distant. Sara moves through the kitchen dragging her feet. You remember family whispers about murky pasts, the *Migdal*, prostitution during the thirties, all of that. They brought them from Poland, promising marriage, and once they got here . . .

"León came back," Ignacio repeats, moving his face closer to yours and obliging you to pay fast attention. He had escaped, but when he saw that they grabbed us, he came back. So as not to leave us alone with the police. We were kids, we were really afraid. And he came back.

They talked about that in the neighborhood too. But respect for Boris, Ignacio's father, stopped them from looking too deeply into his second wife's history.

"I never forgot it. Since that day León was a teacher for me. Is that what you wanted to know? That's it: he was my teacher. But the disciple grew up: I'm not the boy I was then. I don't need protection or advice from anyone. I shit on teachers."

You don't understand these sudden changes of direction. He doesn't do or say what he ought to, according to what you remember. Old Sara ought to know, she was witness to all those years.

"I'm referring to something else, Ignacio: his plan to establish world communes or something like that. In a letter that he sent Teresa from Israel, I read that he had named you his personal representative."

There is a certain pride in his eyes, damp as ever.

"Yes, we both worked on that theme. I was in charge of the philosophical aspects, and León, as you might expect, the practical ones. Now, what does all this have to do with . . . "

"Don't worry. It helps me reconstruct a past broken into pieces.

The ellipses, the holes in the chronology don't matter: it's the sum of these small memories that rebuild the years I lost, the magazines that I stopped reading, the developments in which I didn't take part. Tell me more about that project, please."

Ignacio gets up to look for a couple of folders that are on the sideboard, together with dozens of books haphazardly arranged on a precarious wooden shelf. The telephone rings.

"Don't bother, Sara. I'll get it. David, you can take a look."

You spread some papers on the table. The first has an underlined typed title, "A Better Humanity Will Only Begin with a Better Individual":

> Better individuals will flourish when they feel motivated internally to wish to be better every day. For this to happen, it is necessary that the philosophies that explain these themes have an answer based scientifically and amalgamated with contemporary psychology, forming an international council from its representatives of varied orientations, so that they expiate the fundamental question that the individual always asks which is: the meaning of life. A real answer, not fantastic, not mythological, not dogmatic, can be in itself the seed which will foment the contemporary intellectualized individual, toward an unsuspected positive path.

The poorly done copy is confusing. What has happened over the years to the clear and logical discourse of Ignacio, of all of you? Is this a mystical delirium reached through unexpected paths, where political deception mixes with the crisis of the age, the consciousness of one's own finiteness? At random, you choose another paragraph:

> For this theme of the meaning of life to lead to realistic conclusions, we should analyze them from different perspectives, one of which is to not believe that a man has a soul, but rather that a

soul has a man, which is to say that the individual is a spiritual being (the other living species are too) and this, the material body, is only the vehicle, his school, for success in complementing the Law that rules the Universe which is: the law of evolution. It is not for now possible to prove it in the laboratory, but the causes can be observed through the causes of daily living, and we will see that it squares with reality.

With small steps, Doña Sara approached. She could hardly walk. She began to collect the leftover food on a single plate.

You are not getting anywhere, everything spins meaninglessly. And meanwhile, León waits, held for trying to help you, for trusting you. You show yourself to be absolutely useless. Ignacio returns, from the small room.

"You'll have to forgive me, I have to go out for five minutes. It's something urgent. What were we talking about?"

You raise the typewritten pages.

"Ah!, yes. Our theories with León. Earlier I admired him, I've told you that, especially for that will toward extreme experience, to touch the true edges of each thing, I loved León a lot, but . . . "

He adjusted his eyeglasses that had slid down his nose.

" . . . I don't know how I can help you in all this. I see that you are surprised. Perhaps you think that he went a bit crazy? I too, in the last period, considered him strange. Those trips back and forth to Israel, without deciding whether to live here or there. And that verbose, conceited tone . . . Almost messianic, isn't it so? As if he felt like a prophet."

"Ignacio, I don't know how to continue. This isn't helping. I began with my grandfather Moishe Burech and now I've come to the neighborhood, but something is missing, I don't know what it is, to solve this puzzle . . . "

He finds a way to change the conversation. And he takes advantage of it.

"Your grandfather Moishe Burech . . . Did you know that he wasn't named Schnaiderman? I never told you the story that my father would always tell me?"

You don't even have a family name? Somewhere a little light went out.

"No, you never told me."

He waved his hand, as if to lower its importance.

"Nothing special. Typical of the period. It had to do with your ancestors, not expressly your grandfather. I hope you won't get angry with me because of what I'm going to reveal to you."

Sara who is still there—although her silence makes her almost invisible—shakes the sleeve of your jacket, anxious.

"Eat, *eat*. You have to eat. Eat now while you can. Old things, no, they're not good for anything. Why tell? Afterwards remember, a man with a knife and all that. Evil. Death."

Ignacio blanches, but he recuperates immediately. He speaks with a certain pleasure, taking enjoyment from his knowledge in the bringing to life of ancient humiliations. "Why this bitterness? What could we have done to him when we were kids?" you wonder.

"In fact, your grandfather's last name should have been Grunbaum, not Schnaiderman. But it happened that he was the child of an unmarried mother—yes, that fair-going little old lady that you see in the family photo, above the sideboard in your home—and his father refused to marry the woman. That was the reason he adopted his mother's name, and he later refused to change it."

He paused to judge the effect of his words.

"This also has to do with the history of the Kuzars."

"The Kuzars?"

"A Caucasian tribe that resisted the Arab pincers—from the East—and Byzantine Christianity from the West. They lived between the Don and Volga rivers near the Black and Caspian seas."

"What does this have to do . . . ?"

"—We're getting there, David, just a minute more. Don't you

want to know where you come from? Moishe Burech once told it this way to my father Boris. Toward the year 700 that tribe converted to Judaism to avoid religious infiltration since, not having the power to defeat them militarily, they tried to conquer their spirit. Judaism unified them. They lived there some 300 or 400 years, until groups from the tribe immigrated toward the north and west, toward Poland and Austria. There they became the origin of Ashkenazi Jews. It's a theory."

"So."

"This would explain the lack in that area of features generally thought of as Semitic: black hair curls, aquiline nose. Like the Abuds or the other Arabs in our neighborhood. In families like yours, settled for many years in Lemberg, there is more ethnic similarity to the Russians and Poles than to Semites: they have long and dark brown hair. Light eyes, round faces. And they like to eat cheese and onion."

"That's for sure."

"Another variation of the story says that, around the year 1400, the Jews expelled from Germany and Austria arrived in the Lemberg area and mixed with the Kuzars. That is the genesis of your ancestors, according to what Moishe Burech used to say. You come from there, or in other words, confusion and mixture."

True or not, the theory expressed by Ignacio demonstrates—you think—that Judaism is a cultural and anthropological entity, before being an ethnic or religious one. It depends on your formation: after so many years of living as a Jew, you come to discover, suddenly, that in reality *you aren't a Jew,* but a Caucasian. And this includes, why not, being a child adopted by your family but the illegitimate child of a Christian seminarian, to talk nonsense. Would you, in that moment, cease to be a Jew, would you be able to walk away from your forty years of life, or, in truth, would you continue being a Jew because *you made yourself* Jewish during the course of all those years, and, with independence of birth, you incorporate those characteristics so that they cannot be separated from your personality?

The opposite reasoning would be equally absurd: Hitler discovering, before he died, that in reality he (and his real mother) were Jews.

Curiosity grows.

"What else did they tell you about my grandfather?"

"I'm sorry, David. I have to leave. I've already told you that they called me about an urgent matter and . . . "

"I need to know more, Ignacio. What else do you remember?"

He concentrates, thinks for an instant. He is playing cat and mouse with you, and he knows it.

"I don't know . . . something that has to do with religion."

"My grandfather wasn't very religious."

"That is your mistake: to the Jewish religion one returns, you'll find that out some day. That path was what helped me get myself together. Its riches are multifaceted, it doesn't exhaust itself in one way of being."

"Okay, okay, But you were talking about my grandfather."

"Yes, my father remembered how Moishe Burech taught religion to his older grandchildren, here in Argentina. They went back to the *cheder*, where they studied Torah with a rabbi, and he had lessons for them. He emphasized that the 'little dots' are the really important part, not the letters. In Hebrew only the consonants are written above the line, the vowels are represented with dots below . . . "

"I know Hebrew, Ignacio. I was in Israel for two years."

"Pardon me, at times I forget. It must be denial as the psychology books say. You and León went to Israel and I never . . . "

He interrupts himself, as if fighting with something very personal.

"Do you know, in truth, what I always envied you for? That sensation of silent dignity, almost of noncommunication, that those who live in Israel for a time acquire, in the relation with us, Jews of the Diaspora, as if there were something that, in spite of all the theories and religious rituals, we couldn't understand, not having been there, sharing daily life and not only words . . . "

You can't think of anything to say. Fortunately, the pause is brief.

"I'll continue with Moishe Burech. He taught that what's important is not reciting from memory, like a parrot, but to discuss *the meaning* of the phrases of the Torah. The 'little dots,' you understand; the tone, the meaning of the discourse, not the literal version. That was in 1940. My father told me that it is quite uncommon among people of his age. Your grandfather was a forerunner of the Lacanian psychoanalysts."

He got up.

"And now I'm leaving. Regretfully . . . "

The idea occurred to me in that instant.

"I ought to wait. My daughter is going to call me at this number to tell me where I should pick her up. She's at a friend's birthday party, and I don't want her to return alone. You know how kids are . . . "

He has put on his jacket, and he doesn't pay much attention to your words.

"As you wish, it doesn't bother me. Sara, close everything well, when David leaves. So long, old man, I'm sorry that I wasn't more useful. If you had been clearer about what you were looking for . . . "

You give him a strong handshake. He has become again the old Ignacio with that tranquil smile, relaxed, as if he had just done well on an exam.

Just as soon as the noise from the door to the street, as it closes, is heard, you turn toward the silent and diminutive old lady who is making balls of crumbs from black bread, taking it apart between her fingers.

"Doña Sara, you know who I am, don't you?"

The old lady's gaze passes through your body as if it were transparent. She has blue and watery eyes—incredible in their clarity—and an infinitely wrinkled face. Nothing to do with that lady who one day, unexpectedly, appeared as Boris's wife and stepmother to Ignacio (a miracle of the Jewish matrimonial agencies), after the poor Rebecca, whom you scarcely remember—thin, petite, curly hair—was taken by leukemia, in spite of the liters of transfusions in which your father, Boris's only friend in the neighborhood, participated (that you vividly remember).

Sara was always a bit strange: company at the end for the disconsolate widower, whose past that was murky and tied to the *Migdal* floated like a phantom in the air of your adolescent years. Your mother went as far as forbidding you to speak with her, because of an unknown resentment. But that happened many years ago, you are an adult.

"Sara," you persist. "Let's talk. I want to ask that you tell me what has happened in the last ten years. About your life, about Ignacio, Señora Abud. About that woman's children, Ahmed and . . . "

You stop. Ignacio spoke of two sons. In effect: Señora Abud, a Palestinian who had fled to Beirut, bought like a piece of meat and brought to Argentina, with her large and dark eyes of enigmatic gaze, had two sons. Ahmed is the oldest, the one who ran out carrying a knife when he saw his mother's cadaver. You never knew of the other. Sara responds all of a sudden, when you thought that she hadn't heard you.

"Leila. The younger one is named Leila. So they say, I don't know, pretty strange, a dancer. I don't to speak much in the neighborhood, many anti-Semites, knives, bad people. Before Germans, now Arabs, no one like us. I don't want to tell, for what, you speak to Ignacio. He knows."

"I should have patience," you think. The threads of the story are unraveling, capricious skein.

family tree

You advance up Mosconi Avenue, caressing with a light step the
river's edge of your childhood. Here are those who accompany
your memories: Don Raúl, the storekeeper, excitable companion
in the bar who backs the San Lorenzo team on autumn Sundays,
his French bread with butter in his hand and his ear stuck to the
old brown radio with a wooden case, listening to those incredible
mega-goals by the black Picot with which they win 3 to 1 over the
Yugoslavs. Further on, the diminutive auto dealer, Pucho, who insists that in Buenos Aires there will always be a sucker to buy a used
car no matter what bad shape it may be in. Doña María who lives
in the back of the same building and goes out to take the fresh air
of early summer, placing the Viennese chair on the sidewalk. The
Portuguese fellow from the bar, the Grimaudo brothers' furniture
store, the pillow makers' children who don't have the spunk to
mess with your sister during Carnaval, fearing brickbats, and they
run ashamed under the water toward the corner. Don Boris and the
shoe factory that was always dark ("come on, don, let Ignacio come
out and play,") the anti-Semitic butcher, the Italian's hair salon
where Nario works, and, right there, León's house. Your best friend
from adolescence, the anchor that ties you to this frontier between
Villa Devoto and Villa Pueyrredón: unrenounceable territory of
childhood, pretty place in the foreign world, paradise of feeling, if
such places exist.

And suddenly, as in a dream—could this be a dream?—
predating your real visit to the *porteño* roots?—past and present
come together. León is in the door of his house together with someone who must be his wife (Teresa?) and a couple of little children.
How many years have gone by! León looks mature ("this means—
you think—that in others' eyes I too will be older"), with a few gray

hairs in the sideburns, and, above all, the forehead very much wider: it has lost hair, and in its place some wrinkles appear, hidden by those extra kilos that are missing in the adolescent memory. He speaks with broad gestures and begins to walk toward Helguera Street. You speed up; you want to slap him on the shoulder, hug him, ask him about his family. Count on him to help you remember, begin again to live the sweetness of the years past.

He enters a construction site before he reaches the corner, and his wife remains outside. You walk even faster, you get to the place, and you barely glimpse the broad back entering through a corner of the half completed building. You decide to wait in the access way. Later, you conclude that the building may have an exit on another street, and you could lose him. You enter, barely hearing the swish of the silk dress worn by Teresa, who doesn't recognize you and remains standing, lost in thought.

You move around the construction area: passageways and half-built walls; spaces instead of windows, the floor muddied by the latest rains. You hear voices, but it's hard for you to place them. You call out "León" in a loud voice, a bit timid at first—the situation is pretty ridiculous—but no one answers. Nevertheless, he ought to be pleased at the meeting, after all these years.

When you complete the tour, you see León's back disappear through the entrance. You jog rapidly, and when you step on the sidewalk, he is moving away, without apparent hurry, without turning his head. He turns at the corner of Helguera Street: you don't know whether when you reach that spot, you will meet him again. This evasive walking seems absurd to you and somewhat disturbing. You want to reach your childhood, it is at your finger tips, but you're not able to touch it, as if it weren't possible any more.

You wake up, anxious. You are searching for something that stayed in this neighborhood: your image, dancing in the eyes of others.

3. extremities with HE

*You are not the one who must finish the work
nor are you free to take no part in it.*

—Jewish proverb

"How old are you Sara? May I ask?"

"Eighty-seven."

"Where were you born? Here in Argentina?"

"No, no, no: I borned in Lodz, in Poland. A big, big, big city."

"When did you come to Argentina?"

"Big, big. I was married to my husband. Before Boris. And he wanted to in order that I leave my Papa. And I says, I'm not giving up my Papa or my Mama, not for millions. I love my family a lot."

"But you got married in order to be able to travel? Some organization brought you . . . here, I mean, an organization helped you?"

"He wants to kill us with a knife. When my sister and I goes to London. He treats me bad, plays cards day and night, I work like a mule and he came and ate at home, without a jacket, which is to say without anything, I didn't want to have anything to do with those bums. He said they are his friends. Friends, he said, don't cost anything, a little while, you close your eyes and there you are. I don't lives with him, I separated from him. In London, in London. I many years there, twelve years. I was eighteen, sixteen years old when I go to London. But Papa saw me, and I tells him that he treats me bad, I, with my sister, takes our family from London. Have more *came*, it's delicious, with tea. He liked it, Ignacio, and Ignacio's father too, Yiddish food. Black bread with butter and cucumber. Very good."

"But, Ignacio . . . "

"He says, first husband, that I leave family and go with him. I said I don't gives up family for fifty millions. They can take me every where they like, I don't leave my family, I love my Papa and my Mama and all . . . "

"Are they . . . the *Migdal?* The organization? You met Ignacio's father there? Sara, think, it's important to me."

"Eat bread, David. Bread is tasty."

"But . . . why did you travel to London?"

"I married him. He was a soldier. He escaped the military and to fall in love with me, and later he wants to kill me."

"You traveled to London for him?"

"No, no, no. I got married in London, because he escaped soldiers. I and my sister was there. He worked, and they collected money from my whole family, before Hitler, before war, Papa, Mama, and everybody. After war, Papa writes that he wants to come to London, and we combine money with my sister, and we send tickets, and when my family comes, he comes too. And he wants me to leave my family, and Papa says: 'What do you want, you want to kill her?' and he said this, 'Kill me and the whole family, but don't touch her.' My Papa said that. He wants to kill, my sister sees this and says, 'I'll give you money and buy a ticket, go to Venezuela. I'm not going to return to Poland after the war, am I?'"

"Of course not."

"Go to Venezuela. Venezuela, *nu?* I arrived here later, I worked as a cook, at weddings, I sold tickets on the street, it wasn't enough. Very poor. There I meets those people, I here alone, poor, David, have a little more tea. I does all I can to get by. Every Friday I send Papa five rubles. That's all. What am I going to tell, I can't tell everything, you can't, it's a full life. Later, much later, I marry Boris and I come to live here. I can't say much. It hurts my heart. I was a little girl in London, very pretty. Everyone said, young girl and so pretty. Later the whole family went to *North America*. Papa died and so did Mama. I lived alone here, with God and good people who help, I was very pretty. I comes and sells tickets and I washes clothes and I does all kinds of work. In all the world, there are good people and bad people, I didn't know this language when I came. I married another man. Another. A young fellow that we worked together, fell in love, I liked youth, *nu?* He was very young then. I sold tickets, went right into the businesses, and it embarrassed me, tears flow from me for the first time. But I sold. Twice I sold the grand prize in Lomas de Zamora, because of the stores. And before Lomas, what is it called . . . "

"Andrógué, San Francisco . . . "

"No, no, no."

"Lanús."

"That's it! Lanús. I sold every sort of thing there, to many men. My husband was Polish too. From Warsaw, but I met him here. I married and I went to live with him. I was young and pretty, I came from London. *Better English and Jewish.* I know English better than Yiddish, I lived in London for twelve years. Two daughter, yes. One is in *North America,* in Indianapolis, Indiana, *nu?* Mine younger daughter in Paris. Family and all, spread out. Yes."

"I don't understand. You had your daughters in London or here?"

"London, of course. I was staying there. In Buenos Aires, I retired. I lived twelve years with second man, here. The good one, treated well. I lived in Córdoba Street in Avellaneda. He came to visit the lady. I lived twelve years with him. He thought I was Christian, *goy.* Downtown, on Córdoba Street. In Avellaneda later, at the end, before coming here."

"Yes, I remember you at the movement headquarters, Sara. On Córdoba Street."

"I didn't have children with the second man. Old, old house, more people live there, I don't know, I never got involved with people. Later he died. Everything died, we aren't here forever. We're passing through. Everyone is passing through. I don't much like living. Here everything Spanish, *I speak English well,* I understand everything said to me, that they call me, writing I can't do. That Ignacio, you. My sister is in *North America,* she writes English because I was in high school in London. I only speak: *Yes, I do. You want to speak English. I speak to you. I like to speak English. I like it.* When you know a language you can't forget, *you couldn't forget to speak English, I think.* I remember something of Polish also. And German. My sister more,

215

eight languages she writes, she speaks Japanese too. You see she learned in high school, she made it, she had a head on her. Two children she has, two boys. I, on the other hand, about my daughter, I don't know, she may be fifty-three years old now, or more, sixty-three. I don't know for sure, I forget. And the other one went to Paris . . . "

"Sara, I would like to ask you about Señora Abud . . . "

"She went to Paris because I was always angry with my husband. She can't stand it, she says, 'Mama, I'm leaving, I can't put up with what he's saying, if you want to, come with me. Let's go.' And she went alone to Paris, and I don't know anything more. She doesn't write or nothing. I alone in the neighborhood. I don't have nice things in my life. I was alone in the world here, what can I say? Nice things have never happened to me. Eat, David. Eat more bread. It's tasty bread . . . "

"But later you married Boris, a good man. And you have Ignacio."

"Always I speak like a little girl. Always. When I was alone, I cried. When I was with those people, I cried. I worked like a mule. Always. Boris good, but that child a bit odd, Ignacio. He told me why, and I can't see. Secret. What more were you asking?"

"If you don't want to tell me . . . I don't know, Sara, tell me about yourself."

"I sold tickets. And clothings. I sold and earned a percentage, later, when my second husband died. Because those years I lived well with him, we made a home. Lots of clothes, but I was always under his control. You can't understand, that isn't your business. I thought once about telling, but the organization very big, bad. They scarred Rifka's face, with a knife."

"Who were you going to report? Why?"

"He left a whole line on the face, better not to talk. I didn't have anyone to tell, not very religious. I go synagogue on *Yom Kippur*, nothing more. When I was a girl, Sabbath too, *nas keine simchas* in my family. Do you know what *nas keine simchas* is? Today young people don't understanding nothing, language or religion. Only crap,

216

sex, and drugs and all that. For that, Ignacio problem. For that reason, he is a bachelor and without a wife. A lot of crap, a lot of magazine crap, it perverts. I said to Boris: boy with a lot of garbage, going crazy with sex. He not paying attention to me. He says all the boys do that. You understand what I say, garbage, they masturbated, with a hand there all day and night. Many times I found magazines filled with filth, degenerate things. I threw everything in the trash, he very angry. He says, 'You not my mother, you can't do that.' I had to stop. Here. Don't you know that? From that comes craziness. Much putting his hand. Movies, magazines, filth, *nu?* Not like papa and mama. Better. Mama very Jewish, papa Yiddish with a beard down to here and mama had some thing inside, how do you call it? the cut hair, that was never seen, she wore a handkerchief. Wig. That's it. What, I'm going to tell about how my father became a clown. Those things are better not to say. I worked. I love my family, I sending five rubles every Friday. I came home, I bought my father a derby hat and a shirt. My mother arrives at a pretty synagogue, and there is a friend, friend asks why I don't play with her, she says that my eye hurts. I can't. I doesn't hurt. I didn't have visits, she doesn't want to go. Papa made boxes in Poland, he worked as a boxmaker, he makes boxes to send to Russia. For merchandise, for everything, packages. My Papa *tiranch a numen,* you know what that is, he had a beard down to here. I don't remember any more, I almost forgot what my name is. Nothing."

" . . . "

"I only remember that they spoke Yiddish at home. And among my father's clients were many *goyim.* Once a *goy* killed a Jew, I always tell Ignacio, so that he should know. On Friday, he left the synagogue. And we saw them come toward in the darkness. Yes, yes. And he cleaned off his knife. And I and my Papa see this, I tell him that I'm going to report him. He says he won't kill me, you kill me doesn't matter, I won't allowing, you kill me, I kill everyone. What do I do? I hit him in his middle, no? Nonetheless, Papa turned around and he says to me that I get behind him, *lovaia*. Do you know what *lovaia* is?"

"No, I don't know. Calm down, Sara, you're very nervous."

"We sing to death in Yiddish and carry it to the grave, no? And they say that to bring Death on *Shabbas*, in Yiddish it is to make the Sabbath damp. And he cleans his knife on his pant leg, with his pant leg. And he says to Papa, Papa says to him, you don't go and they kill you. He says, whoever kills me, who intends to, today he kills her, to-morrow he kills us. In Yiddish he said, that he isn't a good man. A big man, he went to *shul*. He kills Jews, and I report him, Papa doesn't want to report him, he's going to kill me. What do I care. Today he kills me and tomorrow you. Do you understand? I don't. I went one day where they were having a party. I forget what street it is. We went to the party and he also. He went, I was here. He went here. Do you understand, David?

"Yes, yes, Go on."

"I always told Boris. Ignacio listens, he's shocked, but he asks to hear it again. Then I said, 'Papa, I'm going there, he is going to kill me there with a knife. You know I don't want it, Papa cried. I don't say anything, I went there, I found him and investigators and police, all behind me, no? So that he can see that I do so, and he. He pushed my hand and gave it to me so. I said, I don't know, mister, he doesn't know that I reported him, but he was killing. Police. He killed Jews. After synagogue, Friday at night. So, he wanted to kill, what do I know, a secret society. Anti-Semite, that way. He says, I kills. He says the two of us going together. And they took him to the police station, and he says, they killed him there. 'We're going to kill Jews.' One said so, understand, to catch him. He lied to catch him. Lots of anti-Semites in Poland, after the war, but I don't know. I wasn't there. Before. Hitler. A younger brother of mine went to the war. He wanted to save Jews. Him alone. He used to be a tall, fat man, afterwards he was shrunken. In *North America*, they have cleaned up everything. From top to bottom. Poor fellow, he's sick.

I'm in London. Lots of fog there. No cold, not much; but fog yes; yes, in *White Chapel City, Chaynicrods*, it was like the Once neighborhood here or Villa Crespo. People all over the world, many Jews there. What did I care, I didn't want their money, I don't know. In London they sell potatoes in the street, I was there, I bought a potato, and he came by too, *Kin-gevengan*, you don't understand, the president of London. And this guy did like this, *give me a potato*, and he took out a check for fifty thousand grasped in his hand, he says: *I don't want a check, I want your name*. He wants to know my name, who bought from, who gave to him. Of course. He says: *I am the king of England*. The people there don't recognize him, he filled himself. This gentleman, with the eyes, he left behind so much money for the potatoes.

"You knew my grandfather, Sara?"

"I no remember grandfather. Grandfather. Little old man."

"Moishe Burech."

"Moishe Burech. Yes, now I remember. I didn't know him well, he came here to visit with the son, who is Boris's friend. He speaks Yiddish with me. He big, a bit sad. Once he said he, like me, didn't understand *argentinos*. He didn't know the language, didn't understand. Because of that he was nostalgic. He complained at times. But that's bad. He shouldn't have. Country over there always garbage, anti-Semitic Poles. Bad, bad life . . . "

"Over there, you didn't have to live so badly, Sara. In that little village. It's for some reason that it was missed. A life that was simpler, more natural, more . . . Jewish."

"You speak but you don't know. What do you know? You lived there? You experienced mud, you experienced ignorance, hunger, illness there? How nice there? Garbage, All garbage."

"But the memories . . . "

"Memories of garbage. Phooey! Men with knives, anti-Semites, cold you could die from, all garbage. All words, *nu?* Words. The reality was a miserable life. All say that they miss it, but no one wants to return. Bad life. Backwards. Jews all dead. What Jews are there? Dead ones."

"Nevertheless . . . My grandfather was content to be here, but he missed it. Saturday mornings, when he was cutting suits, he left early and he went straight to Cochabamba Street, on the way to the port. It was about fifty blocks. And why did he go there? He would stop and watch the ships that entered and departed, the advance of the shadows on the water stained with petroleum, the horizon that escaped with its sharpened line, very quickly, like a shot towards the infinite."

"You talk a lot, David."

"Moishe Burech, I think, looked toward the other side of the horizon. That mutilated Europe of which he could only dream, nostalgically, in a language filled with strange consonants, very far from the passersby who, most certainly without noticing his presence, walked by the bearded man who was suffering. As if they had taken from him his favorite story."

"Stories. You say truth, stories . . . Longing certainly; he longed for Yiddish, Jewish food, friends, houses. Long for, yes. But go back, no: life there garbage. No one says seriously that they go back. The reality was awful. Everyone says nice now, before, they didn't say it. Not even Jewish bodies remain there. Nazis kill everything, with Poles, they remain under the ground? Not even that. Burnt up. Like tentacles underground, at times I have nightmare, so they are moving underground. Above nothing good, only bad life. Miserable. Never there, never. Ask your father. He knows, I always said: nothing there."

"My father always was open to all kinds of ideas. He's very open-minded."

"Father of yours not broad-minded, father of yours nothing. Nothing defined, nothing. Not at all communist, not at all religious, not at all nothing. He says freethinker, that, but he doesn't fool me. He is a good person, hard worker, I don't mean that. But he never took a stand. Do you understand? He goes round and round, he could be, he doesn't say yes, that's the way it is. In this neighborhood, many Arabs, you know . . . "

"We played together with Lebanese kids from the block: those of the Abud's, those of the Syrian with the store, those from the hairdresser's . . . "

"Yes, many friends, for that reason, Ignacio confused. Boris always said that son of his liked Arab girls, but not men, you understand, because of Israel and all that. Pretty Arab women for Ignacio. He read a lot of books, always friend of León, always speaking friend in Israel. Letter, he wrote letters. He received too. From Israel. Now not as many. I said not to get involved in this. Anti-Semites, lots. Not like Jews and kill with knife. But I'm not mother, I can't say anything. Once I fought with Boris, after that no more, he's not my son, what do I know. Ignacio good boy but a bit strange. He suffered a lot because of something, I talked of knife and he was afraid at night. He is a fearful child but very good. Fearful. There are things that I can't tell. Secret. I always told Boris. Have more tea, David, you have to live, you have to eat. During the war, a lot of hunger, my brother so skinny, his bones stick out, you have to eat when you can, take advantage. Eat a lot. Always saying to Boris that these magazines are filth, but Ignacio only child, he not knowing what to do. Neither did my Papa, when I wanted to report the business about the knife. Do you understand? Ahmed also went out with a knife, the Arab, when they killed his mother. All with knife. All murders there in Russia, Papa said. They want to find the third eye in the forehead, third eye, *nu?* A lance. Wooden, sharpened, that's the way they did it in backward village there. With the sharp wood stick, they make a hole in the forehead of a person to look for the third eye and they kill him. Murderers, that. They opening head to take out special powers that are there. To take out, *nu?* To make people stronger. For that they kill. My father would say those murderers, like the one with the knife. Lunatics. Russian sect beasts too, many years ago, with disgusting things. Papa tells. Before: They cut off . . . uh, sexual organs off men, with a red-hot knife. With fire. Doing so to be saints, very religious, they were called *Skoptsy*. You know what it is? With a razor-sharp knife. Some cut off two testicles, another the whole of it, so that they could call themselves 'angels.' To avoid temptation from filth, that's it. I once said to Ignacio that if he continued with the filthy magazines, it will be necessary to cut off, you understand, so he wouldn't be tempted anymore. He shocked. They burn chest too, and forearm. Armpits they say, there they burned in the shape of the cross. Very religious. Stomach, legs too. There, in Russia, long ago. Not Jews, never: *goyim*. For that reason, I told Ignacio things about anti-Semites. Russians, Ukrainians, Poles, Germans, Arabs, all murderers. They kill Jews with a knife, they say. But I tell. My father knows."

family tree

He sits on the bench in the park. The confusion arises—he
thinks—from the need to find a line that explains everything, as in
the final allegations in a mystery story: each element in its place,
clean and correct. Here, nothing like that.

Perhaps the way may consist in accepting this lack of definition.
In the search itself is the secret, the permanent construction is the
essence of the incomplete. You can't tamper with the necessary
time. David lifts a branch from the ground and draws on the broken
red stone that leads to the corner of Helguera Street: a bird passes
even with the ground. It drags a bit of vine that resembles an enormous false tail or the vast trail of an airplane as it strains to gain altitude. Another bird sings invisibly in the branches and foliage.

He draws, now with a purposeful stroke, the form that orders his
thoughts: the figure of a tree. Arborescence. Knotted roots that
cross, almost all underground, weaving toward the sides to give
solidness to what is coming. The grandfather Moishe Burech, the
family stories, that natural and permanent Judaism that surges from
the herring with onion, the peculiar little Yiddish song, the voices
near the hearth that confer the warmth of the tribe, the notion of
belonging. Something higher than the parents, time of transition,
immigrants of uprooting and hope, condemned forever to tie themselves up among excessive vowels and near impossible pidgin. The
meaning ricochets on the little stones: the Guatemalans descend
from the Mayas, the Mexicans descend from the Aztecs, the Peru-
vians descend from the Incas and the Argentines descend from the
ships. Yes. Terrible irony: the immigrants replace, by their presence,
those who suffered genocide during the Spanish and Creole conquest, to constitute among all this particular American *mestizaje*,
this human mixture.

Hard and knotted trunk, with a strong structure, exposed to the wind and the wounds, penknives that draw hearts of love and parasites that hold on desperately to what can be carried away. There they are, in this poplar zone in autumn (as Gingi would say), the childhood memories of the neighborhood, León's delirium, Ignacio's fears and strange behavior, Teresa, erased from the past, the permanent presence of a cruel, skeptical irony. It is all that too. And Señora Abud, the crime on a Buenos Aires street corner, the insinuations that awake the demonic: rancor, prejudices, disputes between neighbors, erotic fantasies, acts of cowardice. And moreover, shameful parcels that will remain secret forever, buried.

Leaning forward from the bench, he traces—carefully—the lines that will reflect by analogy, an arboriform structure. The branches are not all the same, plain, alike in their nakedness: some have an unusual shape, a variation of perspective, a foreshortened view that belongs to them. The invisible bird sings again, a couple of chords.

The top part is yet to be done. To show the love climbing through the roots to the branches, toward the latest and tenderest buds. The extremities of the body, that unexpected filigree that is in contact with the sky, and where, above all, flowers are born. Inverted genealogy—from top to bottom—the passing of time permits the poplar to give its fruits, and then, implacable, it pushes it to the source of the story. First a tender trunk, then knotty, roots scarcely visible, finally veteran arms that advance, subterranean cords that give sustenance and solidify the future.

He draws, always upward. Children, friends of the children, scarcely bearded young men who build what is to come, say good-bye to what is leaving, advance while others only manage to staunch wounds. They should continue toward the sun without stopping. David stops sketching: branches in sinuous forms, always getting narrower toward the points; secondary arteries that spread out, fruits and foliage cover the free spaces, represent the natural harmony. And the sap through the inside, traveling noisily in the channels.

He straightens up, his back leaning on the rear of the bench. He judges the well-worked design on the red stone. A tree, almost completed. "It's pretty," he says out loud, satisfied. Another loafer looks at him, surprised, from a nearby bench.

THE DANCE CLASS

I. General Warm-up

(Duration: five minutes. Rhythm: cold, slow. Muscle awareness and lubrication.)

The weight of the gaze is an infallible translator of years lived. Gingi always maintained this thesis: hardness of eyes in direct proportion with "leveling" that the years—experience, annoyances, intuition of death, disappointments—pass over the body. David learned it during the visit they made to León.

He, now suspicious, preventively detained in the investigation, joked as always. But something had gone out of his tired, rigid gaze.

They remember him while they get ready on the beam that surrounded the dance floor. Ruth, there in front, moves in slow motion, together with half a dozen little girls and only one little boy, thin and drowsy. David referred to León's conversations, discovered facts, a certain discomfort that got inside of him. His friend was smoking, as if thinking about another matter.

"Very sad, David," he said finally.

He took a long pause.

"Yes, very sad. To shake up the past helps you find yourself, but also, to appreciate that which will never return. Teresa could have married me, but my pride kept me from acting at the right moment. When I reacted, it was too late."

David became impatient.

"How should I continue, León? The answers don't reach me. I don't understand Ignacio; his stepmother shocks me. I perceive that the bath of nostalgia is necessary, but . . . I can't keep living in the bathtub."

The other man didn't lose the coldness in his eyes. "Many scars," Gingi thought.

"The violence and the shots are confusing," he said. "Those blood stains on the wall . . . I would have understood a poisoning, or a rejected lover who turns on the gas. But this . . . "

David knew that he was talking about Señora Abud, but he didn't want to interrupt.

"Leila," he decided at last. "You have to follow that track: Leila. She is a dance teacher in the neighborhood. You can establish the relationship by starting with your daughter."

"You believe that . . . ?"

"I don't believe or fail to believe in anything: I'm an agnostic in spite of the *Ness International*. But she's a very determined chick: she was with "The Movement" during recent years. Her mother always feared for her life. As for Ahmed, on the other hand, you won't get anywhere: an impulsive boy, but the thread is cut with him. Yes, you have to continue with Leila. She ought to know something."

David was about to ask him how he knew the Abud family so intimately, but a touch from his wife on his arm (they used a code of minimal gestures, developed through many years of living together) dissuaded him.

"Leila," he repeated, pensively. "Agreed. Ruth will have a new dance teacher."

2 . *The Bar*

(Duration: twenty minutes. Intense exercise, perspiration. The personalities come forth. Pure technical work that cleans the center of the floor.)

My Dear Kings,

I am going to be ten years old and I would like you to bring me a ballerina's tutu (for me) which is found in the dancewear store (if it could be a color that goes well with light blue) or a doll called "queen of the dolls" (that is written on a little sash that she has, that is very little, that can be gotten on Mosconi

Avenue at Nazca Street) or a bride doll (that you can get in the same store as the other little doll), medium size. Thanks a lot for everything.

Ruth

I'll leave you water for your camels, and some leaves from my eucalyptus herbarium and two glasses of wine.

He passes the note to Gingi and lazes on the uncomfortable wooden bench. The instructor explains something about elongation and flexibility. Warm, simple language, adjusted for the pupils (nine to thirteen years old), indicates the movement of each muscle, the union behind the knee, at the point of equilibrium. The prohibition of skating, because it weakens the ankles. The possibility of opening, once the tensions were lessened. Skin that exudes liquid and the excited nerves that carry with their extensions the marvelous wisdom of the body.

"Are we doing okay?" Gingi asks. She returns the page from the striped notebook, written with letters that are very big and round, somewhat messed by erasures.

"Who would have thought. The Celebration of the Three Kings for Jewish children."

David changes position. His body sore from the hardness of the seat.

"We wanted them to be like the other children. That they didn't notice the difference. And, at the same time, they *are* different. Even the adults don't understand the limits of our *mestizaje*. In every instant, a delicate equilibrium is preserved. And Ruth isn't stupid: she goes along with the game, but she knows the rules."

Leila passes by and smiles. They have known each other for a few weeks, and a silent current of sympathy has been established between them. David can't avoid the feeling that he is using his daughter to attain other ends. He wants to say this. But from his mouth, without his knowing why, other words come out.

"Did I tell you the conversation, the other day, crossing the barrier?"

Gingi nodded. She always understands, everything is natural.

"With Ruth. Going to school. She asks me what it means 'to be Jewish.' Because a schoolmate spoke to her about Catholicism, and the teacher too. She lacks an element of judgment, as we 'grownups' would say. In the few minutes that it takes to walk those six blocks, I try to put together for a her a complete explanation: the one God and the Christian trinity, the difference between people and religion."

"For that reason you told her that . . . ?"

"Of course. As soon as the teacher brought up the topic, at mid-morning, Ruth got up and pronounced a discourse about the advantages of Judaism, the rationality of its beliefs and blah blah blah. With shouts and great gestures, the way she speaks, an actor."

The paternal complicity floats in the air.

"And Monday, when she awoke with big bleary eyes, I sent her to the bathroom and she says to me, 'All week we put up with that face-washing, but on Saturday at least let us rest from soap and water.'"

"And last night? I started to raise my voice, because she was play-ing and didn't want to go to bed. Then she says to me, 'You'll yell at me enough tomorrow morning, if I don't get up to go to school. Why do you have to start now, to get a head start?'"

The two of them laugh. David saves the paper written with child-ish handwriting in a jacket pocket. There he finds another two clip-pings, that he begins to unfold.

"Papers and scraps," Gingi says. "Don't let anything get away."

"I'm afraid to forget. The memory, sifted, by time, gradually moves away from the lived experience. Finally, you end up with the sensory impression of each anecdote and forget the event itself."

With concentrated expressions, the children repeat the exercises. Leila again crosses in front of the bar. She stays there, in a cordial mood.

"Ruth does very well," she says. "She has talent . . . "

It's not common for the parents to stay during the dance class and the instructor knows it.

"What is that paper?" she asks. The children perspire. The liquid falls over their cheeks and backs. Hand grasping the bar, they rhythmically raise and lower their legs, flex their upper bodies, sit down, as if testing the air's resistance. David picks up a piece of paper, unevenly cut, from notebook paper.

> ENTRANCE NUMBER 2. RESERVED SEATING. SEAT NUMBER 2.
> "TO SUPPORT THE CAMPAIGN FOR THE ORPHANS IS OUR LAW,
> THANK YOU." CONTINUOUS SHOWING. GENERAL SARMIENTO
> THEATER

Leila reads out loud and looks at the back cover.

> DINING ROOM. CASH ONLY. COOK: GINGI. WAITRESS: RUTH.
> CLIENT'S SIGNATURE: DAVID SCHNAIDERMAN.
> DRINKS: TWO KISSES.
> FOOD: TWELVE EMPANADAS — FIVE KISSES.
> FOUR FLANS — FOUR KISSES.
> TOTAL: ELEVEN KISSES PLUS TWO KISSES FOR THE TIP.
> PAID.

"What is this?"

He collects the messages that children write—Gingi hurries to respond—an obsession like any other. They aren't worth anything to anybody. Only to him.

David takes other clippings from his pocket: one has circles drawn with a dark brown marker, three cut-out hearts on lilac-colored poster board, below which is written: *"Love," "Friendship,"* and *"Work."* On the upper part it says in big letters: *"For Papa and Mama from Ruth, with love. With these accomplishments we will be a loving family."*

Another paper preaches:

Dear Daddy, I play a lot at school and I am the goalie and forward, and I am going to tell you how we did. My team is the one I put first. Atlanta 3, Boca 0, I was the goalie and I made 700 saves. River 8, Union 7, I was a forward and I made 6 goals. San Lorenzo 22, Union 1, I was a forward and I made 19 goals. I saw that it was your birthday and so I told Mama to buy you a very nice present, so we went and we bought the present for you, you earned it because you make me have fun and you work a lot, etc. I wish you a happy day and I hope that you like this present, Daddy, you were very good with us and you tell me stories. Is the part about the Mosconi gang true, did it really happen? Answer . . . . If you say "No," why do you lie to me? And here is the best part, the gift that you want so much. Do you like it or not? With a big kiss, Eduardo.

Leila stops reading.

"Very tender. But the handwriting is that of a ten-year-old boy. And Ruth tells me that her brother is sixteen. Moreover . . . "

One of the girls cries out from a pain in her ankle, a cramp. The instructor runs over to massage it, while the pupils work intensely on the lustrous gymnasium floor. She returns to the bar.

"My husband lost his memory not long ago," Gingi explains. "Those papers are a way of holding on to the past. To reconstruct an identity from the feelings. He was, also, the father to whom those notes were directed."

Leila looks at David, with more attention now.

"He lost his memory? How strange."

Another of the girls calls in an agitated voice.

3. *Stretching*
(*Duration: ten minutes. Individual exercise. Each one does it alone, seeking her own rhythm. Relaxed conversation.*)

"They are all beautiful," Gingi says, watching the cluster of girls that has begun stretching, as if identifying each movement. "They should never grow."

"The adolescents are very charming too. Eduardo told me what they organized yesterday for their teachers: to get at the Literature teacher, who is unbearable, they took the hinges off the door to the classroom. When the bell rang and she pushed the handle, she fell face first with the door and everything. She almost killed herself."

"It was worse with the old lady from Physics. They put all the desks together in the center and left only a pathway around them, at the side of the room. They explained to her that for reasons of pedagogical reform, that would be the new arrangement. The teacher couldn't give the lesson because the students weren't able to make it to the front of the room when she called upon them, closed in by a sea of desks, some stuck to others and without space between them. They climbed like monkeys. A joke."

"They always invent something new."

David shivers, in the midst of a smile: his father's voice now comes to him, through an unexpected association. It's a closed night in the large house on Mosconi Avenue, and the immigrant from Poland is talking about his school days.

"I went to the *cheder* when I was very young. Later on, my mother, so as not to send me, hired a *rebbe* . . . a teacher . . . to give me lessons in my home. The guy came, opened that book, always on the same little verse. Mama figured it out; then, one day, she tore out the page. He comes, asks for the book, begins to look and says: 'Hey, a page is missing . . . ' and right there, my mother 'dispatched' him. It happens that before, in the *cheder,* I was a troublemaker; the *rebbe* was teaching the children, and when they didn't know the lesson, he hit them with a riding crop. One time, he fell asleep on the table. He had a very long beard; I looked for glue and I stuck the beard to the wood he was leaning on. When he woke up and tried to stand, he was stuck, and . . . he hollered, in such a way. For he still couldn't detach himself. It was necessary to cut his beard, and they threw me out of there. For that, I later needed a private tutor."

David half-closed his eyes and, in an unorganized rush, his own mischief in the primary school on Tequedama Street where he attended, always the youngest in age, and therefore, the object of jokes and tenderness from his fellow students and his teachers. Everything is mixed up: Evita's funeral, marching with starched smocks through the upper gallery at the wake. The soccer games behind the fields maintained by the School of Agronomy, directed by the fifth grade teacher. (What was his name?) The fearsome entrance into the high school named "Reconquista," traveling in ancient trolleys that bounced around like covered wagons, dressed up in scarves and overcoats, enormous sandwiches wrapped in butcher paper and stuffed in our pockets. Worn-out stairwells, cigarettes in the boys' room, the pig they brought in through the window . . .

"There are bright spots," David says, aloud. "The personal memories. Like cartographic signs that reconstruct a map. The territory of childhood from which we unfold what we are now."

"Intimate maps, David. He who constructs them is lost in the mist and is seeking the way back. It shows that you are still sane: you plan your own trip."

"The bits of paper serve for something," he jokes. Moving the hand that holds them in his pocket.

The children relax by doing exercises of different speeds. Leila comes by.

"Don't you feel like getting involved? This is only physical expression."

David smiles and shakes his head. Gingi begins to get up.

"Why not?" she asks. "Can we join?"

"Of course."

"Not me," David insists. "My memory doesn't reach that far. I have to put up with a body that's pretty useless. At least, in expressing itself."

"Let's go! Come on!"

Gingi grabbed him by the arm.

"Don't be so Jewish. You've got to move a little with the music. That's all."

David refuses again, blushing. Gingi takes a few steps forward and begins to move with the smooth rhythm of the music. She follows her inner beat.

"I'm very Jewish," David repeats. "Jew from the previous generation. Now they are all rowers, fighters, dancers, sportsmen. The creation of Israel may have had an influence in this normalization. Or being native to the place, what do I know. To trust your own body. I, on the other hand, carry the sharp sensibility and unease of the elders."

4. Center

(Each one dances by herself. Forty-five minutes. There is no bar or point of reference. This period is subdivided into four parts.)

4.1 Warm-up

(Five minutes. New consciousness of space and direction.)

Gingi joins in happily and with good will. But she doesn't know the dance steps, learned with difficulty by pupils during the previous months.

"Excuse me . . . ," he says, directing himself to Leila who is slowly walking along the line. David moves around uneasily, anxiety climbing up his back.

"Yes, I hear you."

"I, we . . . would like to speak with you."

The teacher smiles, hardly showing her teeth.

"I guessed that you would come for that. It's also of interest to me. Ruth has told me about your experiences."

David bites his lip, trying to form a question. What has that blabbermouth—as they call her—incapable of keeping a secret, even

234

among friends, been saying? A streak of panic crosses his eyes. Leila seems to notice, and she leans her hand on his thin arm.

"We are—travelers on the same path."

She returns to her pupils. A gust of complicity passes through the atmosphere of the dance class. Like a ritual of initiates, a lodge of those who know themselves to form part of a minority, and together, accumulate strength for that which is to come.

4.2 Adagio

(Fifteen minutes. Slow. Highly demanding technically. Each dancer is permitted to show off.)

David hasn't figured out how comfortable he is. The children demonstrate long-studied movements one by one. A hand held high, head to the side, the other hand rising with heaviness, point of the foot braced so that the torso turns around it. Gingi tries to imitate them but loses her concentration before each error: she doesn't find the exact spot for the pause, the letting go, the harmony. The kids notice it and hurry, despite the music with its slow rhythm. Variations, monkeyshines, individualized details slide across the inlay wooden floor.

Then, they begin to circle around "the extra": each one oscillates as if following a plan, they move over to the right and to the left, until they put her in the center of the circle. Gingi has always danced well, but she never studied dancing. The initial sympathy dissolved as the childish joke grew with unimaginable perversity from the first moment. They smile among themselves. One girl, with greatly exaggerated movements, behind the older woman, imitates the awkwardness of her steps, more intuited than known. Attracted as by a magnet by that unexpected game, the pupils take advantage of the chance to avenge themselves of real or imaginary humiliations that their grownups, other grownups, all grownups had once inflicted upon them.

The situation begins to be unpleasant, but Leila doesn't move to interrupt it. Gingi surprises a couple of unintended glances, and re-acting rapidly, she makes a bow and returns next to her husband, among the ambiguous gestures is applause hinted at by the children.

"They're tough, no?" she says, sitting down, while she dries the perspiration with a towel. "They don't forgive anything."

"Nothing, that's true," David answers. "They make you sense very cruelly the very moment that you lose your place. So too, they make you 'be at home.' A delicious sensation, on the other hand."

"'To be at home,' what's that?"

The children form two lines, like a chorus.

"An image from Madrid. Yes, Madrid. From Israel, when you stayed with Eduardo and Ruth in the *kibbutz,* and I traveled urgently to Buenos Aires for a couple of weeks. So many comings and goings, so many planes and airports and Atlantic crossings confused me. I didn't know if I was coming or going, where I would sleep. . . . Noth-ing. There was a technical problem with the plane, and we had to spend the night during the stopover in Madrid."

"Yes, I remember."

"They took us from the airport to the hotel, to spend the night and embark the next morning for Tel Aviv. I was very tired, ex-hausted. We entered the city—I was carrying no more than a sports bag in my hand, something temporary. The luggage stayed in the air-port—and I looked through the small window, my eyes half-closed. Very soon, we were stopped by a red light. A street corner, a bar, two children playing with football cards. Another young man, muscular, wearing sneakers without socks—it was a summer night, very warm—he leans on the store's door. Bearded, bored, toothpicks in his mouth, hands in his pockets. Someone calls him from inside to play a game of cards. The man yawns, hesitates. Then, slowly, he turns around and enters the store. Do you understand?"

"No."

"He is at home! Nothing less than that. Ragged, simple, poorly dressed, perhaps with a starvation wage, but . . . *he is at home.* His language, his neighborhood, the tiles on the sidewalk. In that moment, I envied him profoundly: he doesn't have to travel in a plane, struggle with passports and strange customs, to learn codes and grammar that will never be like his mother tongue, circular coming and going through the world's confines without finding a place on the board. He is at home. I, impenitent traveler, wandering Jew, coming and going with that unease that undermines thinking and impedes, among other things, a good relationship with your body. As if it were a trainer who tames a dolphin and, in reality, it is the animal who holds the baton. He orders me to blow the whistle, to enunciate instructions, throw the coins. It appears that I control my circumstances, but, in truth, it's the opposite."

Gingi doesn't answer immediately. After a couple of minutes, she says, "You are a bit hysterical."

"And so?"

"I read recently: hysterical personalities are those who always believe that in another place, they would be better. They spend time making up stories about exiles and fantasies of trips, countries that are more developed, different ways of life. But, as soon as they arrive at the other side, they start over again. Hysterics."

David laughs.

"You're right. And I haven't told you yet about Ignacio and his library."

4.3 Vals

(About fifteen minutes. It incorporates spins and pirouettes. Half point. Faster. A competitive section.)

"What happened with Ignacio?"

The ballerinas spin now. Drops of perspiration oil legs and arms, shine under the florescent lights. Leila leads the march moving like one possessed, turning at every moment to control the steps of her pupils.

"The library. He burnt the library, almost completely: some

years ago when the repression was getting fiercer and we were all suspicious."

"And then?"

"Memory. The library is the skeleton of memory. It was necessary to make it disappear, in the same way that the dictatorship was kidnapping and disappearing people. Forgetting who one was makes it possible to survive."

David got up and walked around the wooden bench, nervous, missing a good seatback on which to lean his already curved back. He takes out a cigarette, but the climate of physical activity around him makes him hesitate, and he puts it away.

"He carried the books to the back of the house and made a bonfire. As during the Inquisition, without any direct threat. For terror. He burnt everything: Marx, Borochov, Realist writers, theoreticians of esthetics or the class struggle. . . . The texts that accompanied León, Ignacio, and me during our youth. He incinerated them. He erased all that, he was afraid of being the self that he had been until then . . . it's all right, I don't criticize him."

He sits down again.

"I never wanted to reject 'that,' to make my memory disappear. Therefore, I didn't burn my books. I put them in boxes which I stuck away in friends' houses, I hid them in the corners of closets, I hid them on an uncle's farm, I left some in my parents' apartment. I didn't throw away even one folder, not one page. But it was then when fear overcame me. That must have been the beginning of my amnesia."

"What happened?"

"Now the threads are coming together. Once they stopped me, three blocks from home."

"Why didn't you tell me . . . ?"

"I was carrying a briefcase, and I was going to my work. I had a beard. A little short beard, not very grown, of the sort we sociologists wore in those days. I was about to cross at the corner of Concordia

Street, and I saw a police car come closer; then I turned to step onto the sidewalk so he could pass. They interpreted my movement as something suspicious, and they braked. One of them, from inside the car, pointed his machine gun at me; the other one got out and pushed me against the wall, arms raised, a .45 pressed into my back."

"But you never . . . "

"I denied it, I wanted to forget it. There I began to lose my memory. There were two minutes where my life was at the whim of a nervous man with a cocked pistol, ready for any movement that *he* found suspicious. But I survived . . . "

The volume of the music gets louder while the children spin around. An interminable spiral of bodies and sweat.

"I too failed to tell you something. It happened three or four years ago."

She looks at the floor.

"It's the same terror. We prefer not to remember. It was when they took that young couple from the garage in our building."

"Yes, I remember it. They left a jacket behind. And blood stains on the floor . . . "

"They went through all the floors. Perhaps they got into the hall, escaping from the paramilitaries who were chasing them with a car. With the elevator, they got to the balcony, and then, they went back down, running. No one got a good look at them. They say that they were very young, seventeen or eighteen."

"How do you know?"

"Because they pounded on Graciela's door, the upstairs neighbor, asking to be let in."

"What?"

"Yes, yes. I never felt I could tell you about it. They called, desperately, screaming, 'Let us in, Madam. They are going to kill us.' And Graciela wouldn't open the door for them. That's how she told me: he stood trembling against the door, but she didn't open it. She was afraid of getting involved in something. Now, she tells me, she thinks that she could have saved them. I don't know. What is sure is that she didn't know them, and she was afraid. From then on, that question hammers in my head: what would I have done if they had beaten on our door? It occurred five meters from us, with less than a floor between. What would I have done?"

"Because of that it has been difficult to survive. We don't want to remember so we don't feel guilty."

Leila comes over, interrupting them. The ballerinas continue with their pirouettes.

"Can we get together after the class?"

"Yes, yes, of course. That's why we came."

She returns to the dance. Gingi is anxious.

"What are you going to say to her, David?"

"I don't know exactly. I will speak frankly about her mother's death, about León, about that diffuse past during the last few years. I want to know. I have closed my eyes for time enough."

4.4. Jumps

(Ten minutes. Jumps with complete, maximum reach. Twists in the air.)

"When I am anxious," David says. "I try to think of something about something that raises my spirits. . . . It's a good method."

"For example?"

"And . . . I am playing tennis, let's say, very tired and losing the game. Or in a very long line of humiliated candidates for a job. Then, imagine that Ruth and Eduardo are watching me from my side: on what I do in that moment will depend their future reactions, it has to do with something educational. That gives me strength, help."

The ballerinas jump. Each one tries to outdo the next, forcing herself up until she almost flies.

"Yesterday I brought Ruth to the school," David continues. "It was very hard to park the car. There was a very small space, I was entering at an angle, and I hit the curb. Finally, I made it on the third try. You know what the kid said to me?"

"What?"

"*'You passed with four, papa,'*" she said. "'You scraped by'"—"isn't she marvelous?"

An image, the closest thing to happiness, rises over the dance room. The four return from the beach under an improvised tarp, soaking wet and dripping mud, the sun umbrella like an imperfect umbrella-headcover that filters light in all directions. They enter the house after two hundred meters of steps that go deep into the sand, they bathe under the warm shower and the brownish spray runs down rapidly, across the floor, toward the drain. While he finishes drying himself with the red-and-white checked towel, David begins to sip a hot *maté*, his eyes fixed on this window from where, through the rain, it was possible to see the ocean smashing on the shore, and the grayish waves roaring, infuriated. That moment, now remembered, is worth years of tension and suffering.

The music roars, stronger yet, and the turns of each girl have repercussions in David's memory, they bring moments of sharp pain from that past that he needs to convoke. The corner of Mosconi Avenue and Campana Street; the games played with little balls in the dirt alleyway—was it called Agustín Alvarez?—that manageable spot of Buenos Aires that is still stuck in your memory. And Señora Abud's large and expressive eyes, which appear to you now, she was sitting in the beauty shop for hours, while they go back and forth to the garden near the commercial area, trading cards. Leila and Ahmed, the two little ones toward whom you scarcely look from the heights of your adolescence. What had been the secret plot of those years, the weaving of passion and vengeance that then you knew nothing about?

"I am with you now," Leila says, sitting on the end of the bench. "What did you want to tell me?"

David clears his throat.

"It's not what you may imagine nor does it have anything to do with Ruth or the dance," he begins. "It's about a question that is almost . . . historical."

"Historical?"

The young woman seems disturbed. A distrustful shine appears in her eyes.

"I will explain myself better: it has to do with your mother, the unfortunate event of her death, a couple of friends. I am very confused."

Curiously, she seems to be calmer.

"I don't like to talk about . . . that. I thought that we would discuss the experience that you had in the *kibbutz*. That topic, for me . . ."

"Yes, yes. We will talk about anything you wish. But I am anxious because one of my best friends has been involved in this, and I am sure of his innocence. You and Ahmed can help me."

The young woman nods.

"As you will understand, this isn't a pleasant topic for me. But tell me what you want to know."

There is a long silence, while David tries to formulate his question. Suddenly, he has a hunch.

"Do you know León? Have you ever heard him mentioned?"

"Of course I know him."

David squeezes Gingi's hand. Leila pushes her bangs away from her forehead and says, "León was my mother's lover."

family tree

"We are attending a graduation party or something like that, with Gingi and the kids. The event was taking place in a large covered enclosure that can equally be the auditorium of my elementary school or the collective dining hall of the kibbutz. Standing at the door of this building—and that is the curious part—you can see the Mosconi Avenue of my childhood, the neighborhood, the familiar sidewalks. There is confusion over the exact place where we were: it is my childhood home, my high school, and simultaneously, that commune where we lived, in the north of Israel . . . "

"The event in itself . . . is not clear. Something to do with fans. I stay out of respect for the organizers; the children have made an effort, so . . . I don't yawn, but I am bored. I move back toward the rear. There, a large dog appears, a German shepherd (I had a similar one during my entire adolescence), and begins to give me huge wet licks; he affectionately licks my arm. He is a puppy. I like him and he worries me a bit, I do not know that animal. Continuing to play, he holds on to my right wrist with his teeth, though without hurting me. I smile out of obligation; in truth, I do not really know what I should do. If I open his mouth with my other hand to get free, maybe he will bite me. He is an irrational, unpredictable being. I do not have assurances about what he will think of my attitude. I call to two companions from the kibbutz that are walking by, and they, who are his friends, open his jaws and free me."

David scarcely stops to breathe and then continues: "I thank them and I begin to walk toward the exit, but the dog wants to continue playing: he pesters me, he walks back and forth, wagging his tail, and suddenly, he takes me by the wrist again. It is an 'affection hold' and kind and . . . I am confused. I fear freeing myself alone, and yet I must do it to leave, to follow my path. Upset, I awake."

There is a very long pause until the other man asks, "What associations do you make to this dream, Mister Schnaiderman?"

"I think that . . . several, Doctor. To begin with, my right hand is vital to me; I write with it, travel, feed myself . . . I'm right-handed. I can't get around without freeing it. Therefore . . . it is as if the past (childhood, kibbutz) was holding me and leaving would be costly to me."

"But a good Talmudist wouldn't fail to point out"—and at this moment, he smiled slightly—"that the 'holding' takes place twice."

"That's true. I hadn't noticed that. In the first instance . . . let's see, there are my old friends (León? Teresa? Ignacio?) who help me free myself from that 'affectionate hold' of the past. But later . . . the second time, I have to do it for myself. Commenting on it now out loud, I understand it, as if I saw myself reflected in a mirror. Why do I wake up, before . . . ?"

"The dream is evidence of the desire, the unconscience never lies. And you wake up because life is not a dream. Here it is necessary to work: the title, the roles, the condition, the identity, everything. In reality, you work, you don't dream."

David congratulated himself for having given into Gingi's pertinent insistence that he begin treatment. The little pieces of the puzzle are coming together with unexpected revelations, evident truths that lose their opaqueness in barely a couple of weeks, starting with the laconic phrases that the professional interjects among your own associations. He relates a childhood anecdote—he once crossed over to the sidewalk on the other side of the street when he saw Nario and Paco advancing down Helguera Street—that is encrusted in his consciousness as a sign of cowardice that shames his family. It keeps him from the situations of greater risk—the pioneer, the one who goes to the front—that he would like to have in his life.

"You confuse prudence with cowardice," says the other man's metallic and assured voice, without emotion. "You tend to exaggerate the contradictions. And . . . from there is born the tension that exhausts you, the possible origin of your amnesia. The brain says 'enough,' preserves itself. At the same time, David, you want to incarnate the 'absolute goodness' . . . "

"Maybe you're right. They are the bad guys and I want to be the good guy in the movie."

"Avoid the fight with the toughs, if that's possible; that only shows good sense. Why should you be ashamed of it? Otherwise, if you consider evil as an absolute—and not an episodic, extreme situation that forms part of the total reality—the good that you pretend to stand for has to be absolute also, it becomes a symmetrical mirror. It's a somewhat course Manichaeism (you are the complete good, the others the complete evil) that then generates a . . . flashpoint of violence from extremely high self-demands."

David is irritated.

"But . . . that is pure theory. In my family tradition, we never lower our eyes before anyone else. They taught me that from childhood on. Look straight ahead. Don't be a coward."

"Yes, but another matter is the 'perfectionist demand' to not be a coward that you incorporate—as we have seen—through the myth of Moishe Burech. This doesn't exhaust reality, which is more . . . elastic and unpredictable."

"You can foresee an encounter. Prepare yourself physically . . . "

"You can never 'foresee' everything. You can practice karate, for example, so that no one can hit you with impunity and . . . end up cheated by the financial violence of an accountant. Then you study economics, and they will involve you in a lawsuit for which you are unprepared. Then law and . . . it is impossible. You would live always protecting yourself from others and preparing yourself endlessly for a permanent and inevitable conflict."

David discovers the lacerating doubt at last: why does he carry that compulsive obligation to always be first and to have to answer everything, that hypersensitivity that makes him experience every detail as a demand that requires a reply, under pain of having to re-live the anguished image of his childhood cowardice? For the first time, in this long search for himself, he relaxes. Not every minor occurrence is of vital importance, not every activity requires his controlling and vigilant presence, his inevitable and juridical action, his redemptive omnipotence. He smiles, relaxed.

"You know something, Doctor? There is also a family proverb that relates all this. My grandfather, would say it at times: *'Memish nisht ale jasenes ba sheinen, en ale meisem ba veinen.'* 'It's not neces-sary to be happy at every wedding, nor cry at every funeral.'"

He has a lot more to say. The adventure of getting to know himself, to construct his own tree, becomes engrossing. He remembers—at the instant that the psychologist consults his watch—that he has an appointment with Leila that same after-noon, in a restaurant. He wants to know more, more, more . . .

"We all ended up a bit crazy, after that. You don't cross with impunity the ways of Hell."

Leila has a nervous expression, strangely serious in a youthful face: well-formed features, front teeth attractively forward, green eyes that, from time to time, harden: the recently lit cigarette, the gestures, the legs crossed indolently, configure an image which is distinct enough from that of a couple of weeks ago, when she was giving the dance class. He said to himself that she attracted him—like almost all pretty women—with her innocent coquetry.

"There were always crazies," he answers mechanically. "Look at the neighborhood: the old lady Sara, who enters and leaves her delirium without realizing it. Ignacio's unexpected religiosity, Teresa's flight forward . . . León himself, with his ridiculous projects and those romantic comings and goings that keep him from holding onto a rock, a fixed point: those successive affairs, a continuous fluency where he loses his equilibrium. Each one trying to survive as best he can."

She doesn't answer.

"Does it bother you to speak to me about León and your mother? Perhaps . . . "

She denies it with a gesture as the waiter comes near. The bar is almost empty. A stifled horn blast comes in from the avenue. A couple of tears briefly moisten the greenish eyes.

"No, no. Nothing like that. It's that . . . I get emotional very easily these days. Perhaps to compensate for my hardness in the last few years."

She orders low-fat yogurt and a bottle of mineral water. David, a vermouth with flavorings and some spiced snacks on the side.

"León never bothered me," Leila says, returning to the theme. "To the contrary: he is a likable type, he can take care of himself. Brave. Not conventional, one could say. A man who is attractive to any woman. For many years he had a relationship with my mother."

David feels a little jealousy for his old friend León "Try Anything." "As always," he thought.

"Mama, as you will remember, was a woman of great beauty. Nothing special in terms of intelligence, angry enough with the world and worried about the length and polish of her nails. She was sold as a slave, hardly an adolescent."

"Yes, I know the story."

"She never loved my father. I understand her. The old man isn't a bad sort: a little older (really a lot older) and brutal, but with a good heart. Finally, the Arabs of my generation were educated in a manner so that . . . for us the women . . . "

She gestures again and again with the right hand, while she smiles, and her large teeth illuminate her face. David interrogates with his glance, without understanding.

"Nothing, nothing, a craziness. But I'm always left with a doubt."

"Craziness?"

"Or game. I don't know. The case is that . . . several times, in recent years, mama spoke with me about very delicate issues. And on one opportunity, she told me that . . . some day, before she dies, she will let me know about a horrifying secret. Referring to her children."

"And?"

Leila opens her hands, vanquished.

"They killed her, don't you think? Now we can only fantasize, But . . . I don't know . . . "

David surprises himself, suddenly, taking count. León now is forty-two years old, almost the same age as the Señora Abud's murderer. No, it's nonsense. He discards the theory for its absurdity. It sounds like a cheap soap opera, someone would know it . . .

The waiter arrives with the order. Leila looks with surprise at

David, who, after sipping a long drink, attacks the little onions enthusiastically.

"Do you always eat so much spicy stuff before supper?"

He finishes chewing. Then he answers, "I eat what I like when I want to. The memory loss that I suffered in the accident"—he was going to say "your mother's murder" but he was able to contain himself—"did well for me in that regard."

"Why?"

"I learned to find myself, not whomever the others knew."

"I don't understand."

"For example, with food. I've always liked garlic and spices, olives and *chimichurri sauce*, pasta with pesto and peppers, and in the same way I don't like candy or ice cream and I detest creams. But since everybody eats *in a certain way*, I had taken on the general tastes and customs, following the demands of my metabolism and my family background. My uncles, my grandfather Moishe Burech, my father, everyone ate spices, because they lived in regions with very low temperatures. And I, here, little salt, fruit and dessert, sugar, *dulce de leche* . . . "

He attacks the pieces of salami and cheese. She begins to enjoy herself.

"But you can't sustain yourself on spices alone."

"I didn't say with spices alone. I also like hard cheeses and meat from the grill. I wanted to explain: to eat what really appeals to me, not what the others suggest."

"Now I understand better."

"So it happened with my entire life: on weekends I like to rest, sleep, stroll in silence in a park or play a game of soccer. But the middle class to which I belong—I am a sociologist, although it may not appear that way—incites me to mix with the multitudes in the movies on Lavalle Street, to wait for a place in crowded restaurants or visit Country's, clubs in Greater Buenos Aires: three hours round trip, on highways clogged with millions of automobiles, under a burning sun, more tired when you return than when you leave, sweaty and with legs that have fallen asleep and your nerves agitated by the driving. Forty years of my life had to pass plus an amnesia for me to decide on the existence that I really want, without making explanations to anyone. I was an enormous idiot, wasn't I?"

Leila smiles again, forming that dimple between her freckles that attracts David so much. But he doesn't lose his head: he is conscious of the difference of age and situation, of the evil games made by that erotic and adolescent fantasy.

"One of the things that I most miss from Israel—I don't know if you are going to believe me—is a certain type of food. Hummus, for example. They are crushed chickpeas; you can get them here, but it's not the same. Over there, they serve it with two or three red sauces, very hot. You put everything together with a pita, an Arab bread . . .

"Yes, I know it. Mama used to make it."

"And then, you grab a piece of that bread, you form an opening with your hand and you drag the already spiced hummus to your mouth. That's how the Bedouins eat it in the desert, without place-mats."

She finishes the yogurt. A climate of mutual confession is in the air.

"Your references to Israel disturb me a bit."

"Yes, I understand."

"Evidently, Arab blood has its influence: Mama had relatives in Beirut and in the south, she cried every time there were engagements on the border. That stays in a child's mind, you know."

"Like the relatives dead in the gas chambers and in the pogroms in our house."

"And with it all, I was never able to hate the Jews. For my brother Ahmed, on the other hand, they weren't likable."

David figures ages again. It would be too absurd, León . . .

"I'll tell you more: it's a topic that never interested me much. Since I was a little girl, I was interested in social revolution, internationalism, not that cheap patriotism that stimulates the differences between people. Until . . . "

"What?"

Leila takes a long pause. David thinks that the conversation is spiraling, without defining itself.

"Until I had . . . a Jewish lover. Emilio. My great love. Is it vulgar to say it that way?"

The green eyes dampen again, only for an instant.

"It's a long story and I don't know if . . . I can tell it. They are terrible years and very recent ones, open wounds . . . "

David has an empty space in his stomach in spite of the spices just ingested. He fills his glass with vermouth, slightly diluted with a spray of soda and two ice cubes.

"You also like to drink, eh?" Leila says changing the conversation. He gripped her hand on the table.

"Listen to me: I'm trying to resolve the business about León and the murder, but I'm also trying to find myself, to draw my tree. It's a double search and I'm not fooling myself. Because my amnesia began before: when I hadn't learned to see what was happening in front of my eyes. Years of deaths and tortures and disappearances, the genocide that I couldn't imagine, the books that I couldn't burn. I want to know what it is that happened."

"And what can I . . . ?"

"Yes, you can."

David measures the pause, to produce a surprising effect.

"León told me that you were in the guerrillas."

Leila turns pale, stunned. She sits for a while, looking out the window.

"I don't know much about your first search," she says, finally. "León was my mother's lover. Many years. Everyone in the neighborhood knew, although they pretended not to realize. Papa (already resigned, it wasn't the first time), Ignacio who lived on the next block, that half-witch stepmother who was always at the door . . . I, I've already said, got along well with León. Ahmed, on the other hand, never accepted him. It seems that when he was just born, they were going out together."

"Your younger brother?"

"Yes, the one with the knife. He is a little punk, with bad influences. Some friends of his have put into his head the question of Arab nationalism and with it replaced a nonexistent family. He is in a theater group, he talks of becoming a Muslim. He never could accept that a lover of his mother was a Jew and had been in Israel. We are very different."

"But, he saw . . . ?"

"I don't know. He swore to me that he couldn't distinguish faces, he heard mama's screams, he took the knife and went out, running, but the murderer had already escaped. He didn't recognize anyone. I don't know if that is the truth or, with his buddies, he is planning some sort of bloody revenge. That is more or less all I can tell you."

"And León?"

"The business between León with mama had ended, five or six years earlier. As you may imagine, I don't know the details. Also, in that period, I was involved in another sort of problem."

"But she never spoke to you about . . . ?"

"How was my mother supposed to tell me about her lovers? León was a friend from the neighborhood, a friend of the family. He came over to visit from time to time, we would chat a bit. That's all. I was hardly ever at home during those years, and those at home were grownups, not kids. They weren't going to consult with me about something like that."

There is a silence that lengthens. Why did León send him to speak with this young woman? Would he have carried on his relationship with the mother, behind Leila's back? Would the daughter lie?

"I ought to speak with your brother," he said, to say something.

"I don't know if it will help . . . But yes . . . you can see him whenever you like."

"Now the rest of the story. You promised to tell it to me."

"I didn't promise anything. And it is in exchange for yours. We both had critical experiences. I want you to tell me about the *kibbutz*."

"But, I . . . "

"Your amnesia isn't that severe. I, David, have played for an ideal. Let's say social life; and I consider that I know what happens *afterwards*. If everyday life is more just and stable, if such adventure and such death has some meaning."

Leila needs to tell as well as to listen. It is difficult to live with the deformed fantasies of a limpid adolescent dream: León with the *Chama* communes, Teresa who wants to erase a painful time, Ignacio's mystical seekings that are confessed only before God. How to undo that ideological prolapse, fallen web of individual destinies, the fascination and the hope of the sixties, to explain it to a young woman who only came to know the horror of a generational breakdown and never the celebration of an imagined future, arriving any moment?

She quickly looks over the deserted tables in the bar. The humidity cloys on sticky hands. She hesitates for one instant more.

"It's not a pleasant story. It hurts a lot to tell it."

"I'm listening to you. Please."

Leila lights a cigarette. She half closes her eyes. She leaps like a leopard toward the past.

"I was thirteen years old when I went to Ezeiza Airport to greet Perón. Before . . . I had hung around a socialist center for a few months, but I quickly tired of it. Then, in high school, in 1973 in Buenos Aires, it was a whirlwind that dragged you in. Though I can't say 'they convinced me, they forced me' . . . No, I chose on my own, I got involved, I sought what happened next."

She turned the yogurt package with her fingers, without putting the cigarette down.

"They are like disconnected scenes in an action film," she says. "At times, I believe that I saw them presented in the *Acongagua Theater*, instead of remembering them as lived experiences. Do you understand what I'm saying?"

"No."

"I can't put them together, construct a linear path. They are like flash bulbs going off, needles in my memory, partial images."

TECHNICAL SCRIPT

Setting

Bridge near Ezeiza airport. Exterior. Day, when the sun is setting.

Action

Demonstration with flags. Shots and dispersion begin. People running, many, many people. In the confusion, Leila loses her bag. They separate her from her group of classmates.

A man who comes running by grabs her arm. A bullet hits the man in the left side. The impact is violent and he falls backward, covered with blood. Confusion.

Leila runs between fallen bodies and shoving. Gestures of desperation. Unexpected face, close-up of a military officer. A patrol. Leila, frightened, squeezes the identity card that she carries in her pocket. She continues running. She finds again some of her classmates, farther down. They get away beaten, the camera opens into a wide angle and shows again the field covered with injured bodies and confusion.

Dialogue

(*Voice Off camera:*) It seems that they shot from a riser, I don't know. They say that there were hundreds killed.

(Shots, screams, orders.)

Man's Voice: Run, come on, girl, run or they'll kill you!

(Bullets screech.)

Man's Voice: Run, girl. Don't wait. They'll kill us all.

Military Voice: Halt there! Papers! (Background of shots and screams, farther away.)

Voice Off Camera: I should have taken pity on them, they seemed so young to me . . .

They let me go.

SCENE 2

Setting

Patio of a high school. Interior. Day.

Action

Group of young people. Foreground a folder that passes from hand to hand. Polemic in the school patio. Members of different groups are coming together, attracted by the yelling. A boy with eyeglasses, thin, shakes a flyer in the face of another, dark-skinned and with curly hair.

From shouting it escalates to shoving. Threats of exchanging punches. Closeup of Leila's face, admiration for the curly-haired boy. She comes closer to him when the discussion ends.

Dialogue

Voice Off Camera: Later, the events were very fast. I approached the Peronist youth. I saw that they were more active. They mixed militancy and life. They took risks to change things. They weren't leftists from the club.

(Background of many speaking at the same time, can't be understood.)

Young Communist: What you are doing is objectively reactionary, because the involvement of the working class . . .

Young Peronist (voice over): You don't know what Patria and Perón stand for, you are bums . . .

SCENE 3

Setting

Various places in the city of Buenos Aires. Outside. Daytime.

Action

Rapid shots of demonstrations, lightning speed action, riots, clashes with the police.

Panning. Over the road to the emergency station, new sudden attack, clashes. *Panning*. A close-up of Leila distributing newspapers and talking to people.

Dialogue

Another Young Man: They spend their time discussing revolution, and they never do anything . . .

Voice Off Camera: At fifteen, I was already involved in the movement. I wanted to have that permanent contact with the masses, with the people.

SCENE 4

Setting

Plaza de Mayo. Outside. Daytime.

Action

Demonstration advances toward the central plaza, flags unfurled. Columns of excited young people. A close-up of a girl wrapped up in the Argentine flag.

The dispersal begins. Leila is up on a building that is under construction, the camera zooms in on her while she peers through factory pillars in order to get a better view of what was happening.

Dialogue

(Background of shouts. Later, noise of shooting.)

Voice Off Camera: Once, they began to shoot at us from some tall buildings. Those from the Organizational Command, the Fascist right wing of Peronism. The bullets whistled by from all sides. They shoved me down.

Scene 5

Setting

Idem. Plaza de Mayo. Outside. Daytime.

Action

(A scene from a documentary.) Perón speaks toward the plaza. He shouts and gestures. Columns of young people begin to pull back, taking down their flags. The plaza is left half-empty.

Dialogue

Voice Off Camera: During that period, Peron kicked us off the plaza.

Peron (pre-cut fragments of the speech): "Youngsters . . . " Those stupid ones who just know how to yell.

Scene 6

Setting

Ladies' Room. School. Interior. Daytime.

Action

Leila converses. Broad gestures, with a friend. Close-up of a printed flyer. Same place, discussion between two adolescents.

Dialogue

Voice Off Camera: There I felt that Peronism didn't have anything left, it wasn't going anywhere. I tried to find something else.

Scene 7

Setting

Meeting in an apartment. Interior. Night.

Action

Group of young people, gesturing. The one who seems to be the leader tries to control the discussion. Shots of folders, mattresses on the floor, cigarette butts overflowing the ashtray.

Pan that ends with the two interwoven hands of a couple.

Dialogue

(Background sound doesn't coincide with the image: political riot. Fragments of lectures. A shot.)

Voice Off Camera: It was very difficult to make contact, the secrecy was absolute. For reasons of survival (pause). I knew of a girl who sympathized; I searched several times, I was being allowed but with great hesitation.

SCENE 8

Setting

A field of high pasture land. Exerior. Night.

Action

A row of young people with their eyes blindfolded, Leila among them, moves forward, holding each other's shoulders. Half view of Leila, shooting, knee on the ground, toward a target. Camera in telephoto until it shows the group that is practicing and the instructor. Close-up of Leila's weapon, hand holding tight to the groove.

Dialogue

Voice Off Camera: At sixteen they gave me military training. I didn't have an adolescence, I skipped that step. I went out with an 11.25 pistol that was very heavy. It was even difficult for me to turn the barrel, to reload it.

SCENE 9

Setting

Entrance to the factory. Exterior. Stormy day.

Action

Workers are arriving at the establishment, almost dawn. Faces marked by exhaustion. A boy runs, carrying a red flag, climbs up the flagpole and ties it on the top. Another improvises a short harrangue.

Wide-angle of Leila and another adolescent girl. Hands hold something inside the jackets; they move because of the cold and nerves.

The camera moves away in a choppy fashion; it follows the talk and goes on a ladder rising above the factory.

Dialogue

Voice Off Camera: I remember the surprise attack that they made at six in the morning, when the workers were entering a factory.

Man's Voice: Comrades!

(Murmuring of surprise.)

Man's Voice: . . . to follow the road to a triumphant revolution, in the face of imperialism and reaction . . .

Voice Off Camera: My comrade and I were the security team. If the police cars appeared, we were supposed to shoot until the boys escaped.

Leila's hand trembled slightly.

"I'm going to the Ladies' Room, and I'll be right back."

She got up quickly. "Some memory," David thinks, while he swallows saliva. Like a collection of slides that go back and forth, the large *kibbutz* dining hall during a veterans' meeting appears, filtering itself through depths of memory.

The trees, outside, sway with the wind of a nonexistent autumn, in that corner of the world, where the seasons change brusquely, the climate molds the character of the inhabitants. Soft undulations of the field that can be seen beyond the windows, green and energetically cut, serve as paths for the steps of the commune's children, who now walk to their collective houses so that they can go to bed.

Abi, the kibbutz *secretary, introduces the theme directly. Israeli style.*

"We need volunteers who would be willing to put off for two years their

move to the new housing, so that we can receive immigrants here who arrive with their children, lack of stability, unresolved situations. We all know, comrades, that we're not dealing with something simple. We have worked very hard, since we drained the swamps of this valley forty years ago, to achieve the material equilibrium that we possess. And it would mean almost beginning from zero, from the start."

"We've already done our part," replies a man of undefined age and thin eyes. "We deserve to begin enjoying something of the terrestrial paradise, after a generation of sacrifices."

"It's true," Abi answers. "It's true, Amnon: from a personal point of view your claim is just. But at times we forget that which brought us to live in a commune: the idea of solidarity, to help the comrade, superior to the cannibalism of mass society."

"Words!" Shaul shouts, a bald and thin old man. "These living quarters belong to us. We wait, our turn arrives, and we ought to occupy them."

"None of this can be imposed," Abi insists, while he begins to raise his voice. "But let's not get upset about a piece of bread, a television set, a new house. We are men who don't want to feel ashamed of our youthful ideals, full of illusion, but men, finally. Not accumulation machines nor unfeeling walls."

He pounds on the table. The murmuring ceases.

"Why are we here? Do you remember? We wanted to be pioneers of a new society, leaders of love and hope, militants who exposed their own bodies to the risks and advantages of socialism. Let's rise for a moment above the everyday! And those hope filled nights that we shared when we founded this kibbutz? What happened to the generous qualities that helped us overcome cold, hunger, war, hostile neighbors? What happened to the disposition toward the common good that justified our adolescence, filled the dreams of our youth, gave meaning to life?"

Silence cracks. All of them seemed to remember.

"In some corner of our hearts, we keep that generous flame. Let's not let it die! We have to take care of it as part of our faultless childhood, that moment in which we decided to try to change the world and modify ourselves, to construct ourselves as people. We should purify ourselves of material anxieties, pass beyond this concrete animalism that contaminates the solidarity that humanizes. *Let's try to look at ourselves as we were twenty years ago. And let's not betray that image too much, please.*

We test our valor on the battlefield or raising the orange harvest under the shooting, in defining situations. Now, reality offers us a time that is gray and silent, anonymous, without history. The courage to continue being human.

There is a tense silence, Amnon raises his hand.

"I'm a volunteer," he said simply.

Another half dozen comrades offered.

"Me too."

"And me."

David, who from a corner deciphered the Hebrew with some difficulty, finds his eyes have become moist. Everything is not lost, in spite of the prophets of doom.

The sound of the chair being moved wakes him from his dream state. Right there are Leila's recently washed hands.

"Tell me," David picks up the conversation, as if it hadn't been interrupted. "Weren't you afraid during that time?"

"Of course we were afraid. But we were in a frame of mind to fight, to be tortured, to die. I was convinced that I wouldn't talk, even under the worst torture. And the same thing, I think, happened with my comrades. Like the night we were held in the police station."

Her expression now has a certain fanatical hardness to it.

"It was quite absurd. A girlfriend, her parents weren't in Buenos Aires. There were seven comrades at the meeting, and we knew each other only by nicknames, no one knew the real names or addresses. I was Sabina or The Turk, all were that way (except in school with your usual classmates). You tried to change your identity continually, to have, at the most, relationships with the members of your cell and

one or two outside contacts, I mean to say, those people on the pe-
riphery, close to our ideology but less involved. A neighbor heard
noises in her apartment and thought that we were thieves; she
locked us in from the outside—with a copy of the key that the girl's
parents had left with the woman when they left on vacation—and
called the police. When we heard the whine of the Ford Falcon in
front of the building, and we saw the cops jump out of the cars and
climb the stairs, I thought: 'Okay, my turn has finally come.' I was
scared to death, but with the absolute conviction that I wouldn't
speak, that I would withstand the test for which I had prepared myself for so long and that, all at once, had arrived. They weren't words,
I really believed in that."

She took a sip of water, raising the suspense.

"Luckily, we were aware of what was happening a few minutes before they had locked us in. So we made up a small story, we revealed
our real names. We tore up all the folders and magazines, and we
were throwing them down the toilet until it got plugged up. The police were coming up by way of the stairs and, desperately, we were
putting our hands in the toilet, pushing the papers, we flushed it time
and again. Our lives were going down with that. That time we were
lucky and we got away with it. They interrogated each of us sepa-
rately to verify the story, and we all said the same thing: we were
meeting to plan a summer camping trip. Gloria loaned the apartment
to us so we could organize it, we were students from good families, we
didn't know anything about the neighbor's key."

She is suffering through all that again. He voice waivers.

"Meeting was more and more difficult. We would go with everything covered—a meeting point was set and from there the 'owner of
the house' made us take several turns, walking or in a car, head down
and looking straight ahead—so as not to notice houses, directions,
floors in the elevator, nothing. Once a comrade was imprisoned, and
they informed me by telephone: 'Pato got sick, and he's not coming

over to study today.' When I went to tell the parents, they reacted with anger, shouting, 'I told you that this bum is going to get us into trouble.' I didn't know what to do. We had to clean out his home of materials, but we turned the corner without making ourselves enter right away, it could be a trap. It was easier when the organization rented apartments on Brasil Street, and we had the ideological seminars there, just as if they were summer vacations. But that was over quickly. As the repression intensified, houses, public plazas, set places, everywhere is dangerous. At the end, the meetings were arranged so: we went walking on Monroe, to name a street, you from Cabildo Street and I from Tejar Avenue, and where we meet, we stop to speak. You understand, it wasn't an arranged spot. They taught us to watch the store windows to see if we were being followed and all that. It was like a paranoia, a perpetual tension, something very difficult. And in it were our lives. It wasn't a game. Do you know what they did with the comrades who they arrested in Tucumán? After interrogating them, they put them in an airplane without doors that took off, turned over the wharf El Capital, and the thing leaned so that the tied up bodies fell into the emptiness, still alive. There was nothing left of them. Not even bones."

David lit another cigarette for her, as if to help the evocation. But Leila's voice had returned to normal.

"I was rising in the organization. A bit because of the losses in combat and a bit for the level of my involvement. I was always ready for anything. My neighborhood or zone chief was ascending in the combatant structure and he, in turn, named his replacement. Perfect democracy in those conditions is very difficult, but also, in that kind of organization, we would have been infiltrated, since in the midst of battle, it's impossible to have anyone in observation for very long. The organization asked me to abandon my studies. It was the only time that I refused: I only needed a few more months to complete the fifth and I wanted to complete that cycle, even with all the irregularities of my parallel life as a guerrilla. At heart, I was always petit-bourgeois, that is the class from which I sprang."

She is quiet for an instant, while the waiter takes away the coffee cups from a nearby table.

"Later, I ascended to neighborhood chief. My boyfriend, Emilio, was also in the organization, but his involvement and intelligence were far above the average of the militants. He was Jewish, I told you. He had contact with the workers, because he had voluntarily joined the proletariat: delivery boy on a soft drink truck of the type that leaves crates at the grocery stores. He liked movies a lot: when he got excited about a movie, he would speak endlessly, making me seek unexpected nuances, developments, antecedents of each director. He also wrote reviews of shows, in a morning newspaper. And he studied, he studied everything: one day I found him with a book of Political Economy, something difficult and abstract. I said to him: 'Why are you reading this, if you don't understand anything,' and he dared me to open the book to any page and ask him, who just recently read it, questions. All afternoon, I opened the book randomly and questioned him, and he answered with precision, he had an extraordinarily retentive memory. And an enormous sensitivity, of course, for the suffering of others, for the necessity to change an unjust society for a better one."

Leila becomes quiet, looks at the floor, seems to have finished, but no.

"They took him away, I figure, because of my director. A slippery sort of guy. I told Emilio that I didn't like that person, he was capable of breaking down and ratting as soon as they put a little pressure on him. I had good intuition for that. There were many questionable types among us. I myself was brought up in a somewhat unusual household: my father so much older, my mother an adolescent, economic difficulties . . . My childhood nightmare is that every six months we had problems with the house, and they sent us with our suitcases to sleep in the street. My father was always very pretentious, he liked to brag about nonexistent riches. Once he was convicted of fraud, and he spent two months in jail: no one in the neighborhood found out; we said that he traveled to Lebanon to see an uncle, and meanwhile, we took care of the business. For all practical purposes, I grew up in a household without a father and with a mother who hated him for having brought her over so young, tearing her away from her family. In an Arab family, that is terrible. There wasn't money or a strong character, my mother looked elsewhere—with León or with others—her compensations. All in all, these antecedents don't succeed in explaining everything, but starting with them, I can understand my Olympic jump over adolescence, my early entry to a maturity that I now regret. If I had a daughter, I would make her play with dolls until she was eighteen, those dolls that I didn't have time for. Other kids in the neighborhood, in those days, had as their goal becoming swimming champions in the neighborhood club, while I . . . "

Tenderness invades David. Leila continues:

"I remember other strange cases, with problems at home. Petete was an archetype: a middle-class boy, bearded, long hair, always disheveled, he even smelled. Imagine that he had managed to understand how grimy he was. Right away, I said: 'I don't like this guy, he has more personal problems than ideological conviction.' And it was that way."

"One night we went out to do a 'painting.' It was organized like this: two with the red aerosols, two guarding, two in the corner to warn; if a police car comes by, we escape by this way. Did everyone understand? Yes, yes, we understood. We're in the middle of the 'painting' and a green Falcon comes up, without a license plate. We all leave by the way we had agreed upon and Petete slides away in the other direction. As if looking for a reason to run smack into the police, as if wanting to end that story in which he had placed himself, dirty and unkempt."

"They brought him in to give him the machine. And Petete sang immediately: the chief of the cell fell. But Petete continued; he told them things they didn't even ask for, he spoke too much. At times, I think about how terrible it must be to have an acquaintance that has been kidnapped, disappeared, and to learn that he was a collaborationist in order to hunt down his own comrades."

Leila passed her hand across her eyes, as if scaring something.

"They should have liquidated Petete too. The chief of the cell, whom later they freed by one of those miracles, told us that he admitted only to being a contact and to sympathizing with the organization, but he didn't direct nor was he the head of anything. They gave him electric shock and he held to his story. Petete, on the other hand, insisted: 'Yes, it's him. It's him.' And since the other kept denying, they gave more 'machine' to the big mouth, those cowardly stool pigeons disgusted them—in spite of the work. And the more Petete screamed that the other one was the chief, the more they hit him with. For being a squealer."

David plays with the ashtray, without taking his eyes from Leila.

"Emilio, on the other hand, didn't talk. Because of that, I'm still alive. When he fell, I had to permanently leave my home, even my grandmother's apartment, where at times I spent the night and which I had converted into a storage place for the movement, with magazines and folders and arms. I slept a few nights in the all-night movies or in my aunt's car on the street. During the day I was always moving from one place to another. I don't know why or how I saved myself. Luck, chance, I don't know."

"Emilio didn't talk, poor fellow, because at that time he knew how to find me, and they would have grabbed me . . . He's surely dead; I hope that he hasn't suffered too much, so intelligent, sensitive, good person . . . *They* were crazed looking for me: they knew my nicknames and my job. They were more interested in the big picture, not the low-level militants. They kidnapped a Paraguayan family who were friends of mine, a couple with their two daughters, fourteen and sixteen years old, who knew where I was. They raped the two savagely, and they tortured them, until they almost killed them, but they didn't talk. Because of that, I can tell about it. I was somewhat crazed but alive. And I began to react on a day in which, traveling on a minibus, I grasped the hand of a baby who was traveling with his mother and who was bothering me. Getting off the bus, the light went on about my state of being: I was nuts about kids, I adore them. How could I have assaulted that little thing? I understood that I was half crazy, that I had to cut away and begin again if I wanted to recover. Others had died and suffered so that I could continue to live. Dancing helped, too: I had studied it as a girl, I took it up again and I could . . . "

This time it was difficult for her to continue, although she had almost finished.

"This is not a story of the disposition to die or to be censured for the cause. I don't tell it for my own benefit, but for those who didn't talk, thanks to them I can, now, tell all of this. I don't know if this is what you wanted to know. I was part of a generation that was sacrificed by History, and it is necessary to go on living, to think about tomorrow, to make plans, because something of us will remain in everyone. We can't remain frozen in the past. I'm certain that Emilio would have thought in the same way, as full of life as he was. You have to continue."

Now Leila is crying, in silence. And David notices, with amazement, that his cheeks too are wet. Naturally, without fuss, he has just finished with that story about "every day courage" and omnipotence, and his tears run effortlessly together with those of the young woman. He cries, without knowing why.

family tree

"It was all darkness, the dead of night. The dream developed in a place without lights, without colors. You couldn't see anything. This unexpected blindness makes me shiver. I feel around myself, horrified by the possibility of losing my eyes."

"Do you associate this with anything, David?"

"The night of the Military Process, let's say," I go on. "I am getting used to surviving there, I hope for the dawn that will come. After the initial blindness, the other senses acquire greater importance: touch, the modulation of the voice, the differences between your own rubbing and a noise made by others . . . I become more subtle. I begin to live in the darkness, acting as if nothing had happened, *adapting myself* to the nonlight. I discover the way to cook: I go back to spicy salads and eggplant, with garlic. I discharge in a meal the anxiety that this new way of vegetating produces in me. A certain day, a faint light comes in through the window, and I can recognize the place where I live."

"Does it have to do with your home?"

"I don't know. I think so. The walls are covered with distorting mirrors, like those that are found in amusement parks. The illumination is very weak. All that keeps me from knowing who I really am, from recovering my true image. The lines break, turn, recede in unexpected angles. Like the silent movie *The Cabinet of Doctor Caligari*, from the German expressionist period, where the image on the screen comes from the retina of a madman and, for that reason, passes through a lens that disfigures it before it puts it together."

"What do you do, then?"

"I go on breaking the mirrors, doctor. One by one. I tear off them those sheets of silver that reflect me, I check every corner, and I take off the bits of glue. Once I finish with all of them, I go outside the house."

"Outside?"

"Yes, the outside. I don't have mirrors there, but neither do I have distorting eyeglasses. So I can begin to search for myself in another manner. I am in a special place, a mixture of Paris and Macondo, an underdeveloped banana republic that contains paternalism and backwardness, living together, mixed in with groups of marvelous people and universal talents, the prettiest countryside on earth, a good climate. Strange country, my Argentina. Here I am, I recognize my limits, in this river course and my need to decide in the darkness that is almost absolute and without mirrors. I save my interior view, to call it that. And then I wake up. Anguished and at the same time content, as if my condition contained not only problems, but also the possibility for enjoyment. What can you tell me, doctor? Am I dramatizing what happens to me during the day, like kids do with their toys? Why that search for the root and sense of each word, of each phrase, of each subject or event, as if there I might find the explanation for the survivor's anguish and the happiness of being alive and able to talk about it?"

"And what do you think?"

SURVIVORS

The man with shaving cream on his face looked at him and said, "I didn't want to remember a long story. like the old folks, who need to know the origin and the anecdotes that make our every event; to apply hard-won lessons of the age where they don't fit. But I can't avoid pointing out that it deals with a family matter."

He put the machine under the stream of water—as if greasing it for what was to come—while the steam rose in spirals.

"All of us are survivors. This sensation grows in every member of our clan, as the years pass. It is transmitted like baldness or good humor, but not in a rigorous way: it is here, waiting. And, in each generation, we seek hesitantly that thread of color that distinguishes us until we run into it. My father, so as not to go any further, survived the First World War—in the center of fire, with rifle shots that came through the windows of his house and famines that finished off the majority of the children of his age—and he escaped from that zone of Europe, perhaps instinctively, a few years before they besieged his neighborhood. His town was destroyed to ground level. Do you understand? Nothing was standing, not even a miserable wall, without mentioning the people. They even annihilated the plants."

He began to slide the sharpened razorblade over his chin.

"And my son? He wasn't yet two months old, when he fell from a table; he'd been playing on for an instant. What a shock! And at six months, sleeping in his baby carriage, a closet door fell on him—one of those that open downward, like the bar of a piece of modular furniture—and the thick wood slammed against the sides of the carriage with a terrible crash, but he remained below, where the blow didn't affect him, a couple of centimeters from death. At three, a cup of boiling tea fell on his shoulder, and it left an indelible mark on his skin, and four years later he spent the *Yom Kippur* War in a bomb shelter, where he spent thirty-five days under the bombardment. You don't understand me, do you?"

He blandished the shaving instrument in his hand, the face covered with foam and half-obscured by the hot steam, but the movement was more one of affirmation than of threat. Or, at least, that was how it seemed to David.

"It's not about being omnipotent. We live and we die like anyone else. I'm talking about that which goes on growing inside of us, that strange mixture that produces the feeling of being a survivor. And the consequent necessity to transmit our history before . . . No, I see that you don't understand."

He went across with the razor, back and forth, both cheeks, He seemed pensive. Unexpectedly, he raised his voice, as if during the long pause he might have been talking to himself silently.

"They drafted me for military service in 1962. A tough year for Argentina, huh? 'Blues,' 'Reds,' revolutions, all that. I was assigned to the cavalry because of my height and my physique (I, who never even learned to ride a horse!) And not even my flat feet could save me. Almost through inertia—or so that I could feel that I had done everything possible—a few months earlier, I filed a request for an exemption because I'm deaf in one ear. That file arrived at headquarters the same day I was to enter the service, during the last and ridiculous physical examination, where the noncommissioned officers straighten up those who claim they couldn't walk well by stabbing them with sharpened wooden sticks."

"I was the only one of the two hundred boys assembled there, who ended up P.U.M.S (Physically Unfit for Military Service) and I wasn't drafted. From that group, El Dady went to the La Tablada regiment, and they took him, almost without training, to fight in a neighborhood of Buenos Aires against other boys from Villa Pueyrredón, who were in the 'blue' gang by the absolute chance of fate. They gave him a *Papi*, a type of small bazooka, and he shot into the air to try not to hurt anybody. Told like this, it sounds like an operetta, but it was a tragedy."

He took a very short pause, but without giving the other time to reply.

"Anchoíta was in a barracks that the other group attacked. He didn't know how to use weapons. He stayed, pressed to the ground in the Portuguese's bar at Cuenca Street and Mosconi Avenue—while the shots sounded, without raising his head. He took a shot in his leg and ended up lame with a nervous tremor that never went away. And El Negrito, Leon and Ignacio's buddy, didn't have any better luck: he went to practice in a special battalion, which they trained toward the end of that year to invade Cuba, I don't know if you remember, David. They drove him crazy making him drag himself between thorns and bushes, climb mountains at a full run, withstand tortures . . . all in all, 'elite troops.' They killed other boys from the neighborhood in this encounter, they ended up crippled, one became a drug addict. By chance, I saved myself."

"I didn't complete what they called 'rifle training,' would you believe it? I don't like firearms; I try not to . . . They gave us old and very heavy Mauser 1908s, which if you didn't brace them properly, kicked back on your shoulder with each shot and left your bones sore. But nothing. I was okay. In the demonstration that protested the American invasion of the Dominican Republic, they killed a high school student with a shot, twenty meters from where I was. And so many other acts: the marches for 'lay' education in 1958, the Nazi groups, the disturbances . . . At the height of it, I broke my collar bone, practicing self-defense with my buddies. Isn't that splendid? I went for two months with half of my body in a cast, but I had broken it myself. When will the thread be cut?"

He smiled, raising his arms and spitting a bit of soap. David waited the return of the hand with the razor to its habitual position and was about to open his mouth, but the other man kept on talking, and it didn't seem prudent to interrupt him.

"Survivor, yes. I'm afraid to speak about this. Superstitious, bah!: you can't rationalize everything with your head. They say that if you provoke destiny . . . We lived through the 1973 war in the Golan Heights, right on the Syrian border. My neighbor dead of a bullet between the eyes, the one farther down also, in an ambush; a friend seriously wounded, several others in shock, all on the front. And to us, essentially, nothing. Except, perhaps, some glandular modification—it's strange, I sweat much more since those days—and the guilt of having remained whole in the midst of so much destruction. And now here, in Argentina, during the last few years: The Military Process, the thirty thousand disappeared . . . I wonder, often: how do we survive so much massacre, without having taken even elemental precautions? Death was in the streets; disgust and terror formed part of daily life. The children in elementary school used to sing in those days, in all of the school cafeterias of the country, as if they had agreed upon it:

> We want to eat, to eat, to eat/Coagulated blood/mixed
> into the salad./Hot vomit/from a very recently dead man./
> Exploded frog/mixed into the stew./Very green snot/from a
> disgusting old man . . . "

He raised his hand to interrupt him, although David hadn't said anything.

"No, don't answer. You believe that you know everything, but no, . . . My acquaintances cleaned out your libraries, burnt even the most innocent books, forged a new image of neutral, elusive, somewhat stupid men. Just as the regime wished. I, unconscious of what was happening and shipwrecked in time, was incapable of shooting or destroying absolutely anything. I know what you are going to say, it was nonsense. Suicidal obsession, lack of contact with . . . Not only did I write 'inconvenient' articles, in community periodicals that spoke of human rights; neither did it occur to me to shave my beard. Now it seems idiotic, but in those days, to go into the street bearded and looking suspicious, while around me thousands and thousands of young people disappeared for less than that . . . Did I tell you about the time that . . . ?"

He began to shave the throat, every once in a while blowing the steam that was rising like mist of memory, perhaps so that he could continue seeing himself.

"I was leaving a minibus stop, I a saw a patrol car coming. Yes, I remember: he took out the .45 and he told me to stand against the wall. In those days, I carried a small portable radio for listening to music at my boring job as office clerk. It occurred to the cop that it was an apparatus for sending signals, or something like that. He wanted to take it apart into little pieces . . . He's seen many movies on television, I'm sure. So. If I had crossed the street or made an un-called-for gesture, he would have killed me right there. I'm ashamed to have remained alive, that's all. It doesn't matter being innocent of any charge that might have been made: it's a recurrent feeling that returns with the Malvinas War—last year—or with the accidents . . ."

He laughed sardonically and repeated, "Accidents? Every time that I think . . . I don't know if the same thing happens to everyone. When I was fifteen, I was returning from the 'Reconquista' High School in a minibus of the 107 line; I was traveling in the front section, right behind the driver. The vehicle veered, went out of control, and, moving very fast, crashed into a tree. It was like an ac-cordion: dead, wounded . . . I remember that I got out through the destroyed bus body, jumping between broken windows and bent metal. And in the university, one rainy night, when another car hit us on my side; we were riding in an open jeep, made of scarcely a few pieces of fabric and metal, without any protection. And I could al-ways tell the story: a gigantic truck, the type that drags a tow, hit the Citroën I was driving from behind, and pushed its way in up to my back, destroying the trunk and the rear seat, but didn't hit me. Does all of this really have importance?"

He seemed to have finished his task because he washed the razor under hot water and the steam that rose from the sink had clouded around David's silhouette, making it blurry.

"Some time, the family tree should be shorn of survivors. I'd even go further: I don't want to make this memory public, because I perceive that the day that I do . . . chaos, the conjunction of chance and will is over. For that reason, too, I talk so much about facts and people: the grandfather Moishe Burech, the parents, the nostalgia for certain personal stories . . . Seeking them, I seek myself (in Europe, in Israel, in my *porteño* neighborhood), so as to be able to understand and prolong our survival. This digging around in submerged memories is a search for time lost, which wins out over that of space. Only, I identify myself with the mythical corners of a Villa Pueyrredón . . . that no longer exist as they were. And this is something very Jewish, David. Yes: the uprooting that the roots transmit. No place on Earth is safe for us, immune to anti-Semitism and persecutions. We survive in time, rather than in concrete space."

It seemed that he was hiccuping. Perhaps a small annoyance, soap in an eye.

"It must be for that reason too that I never keep the rough and rewritten originals from my college class notes or my doctoral thesis or the interviews from my work as a sociologist: once a final copy is made, I collect all the scribbled originals, covered with stains and notes, and I throw them in the waste basket. It's like beginning again, you know what I mean? What is left is a provisionally final text, without blemish and printed. A certain exterior order that brings into balance the disorders and searches of memory. Who cares about this boring trail full of missteps, back and forth, renunciations and encounters? There is already enough bound paper. It means offering the most synthetic result possible of the search. Do we really have something to tell to those who come after those who went through these Argentine years? Our meaning develops behind the scenes, it appears from time to time, shows signs like a wink used for identification. The repetition serves to fix the memory and attention of the one who comes along trying to reconstruct that illusive and nontransferable form that constitutes all other life, whose components resemble a tree, although the architecture can only be observed in a fragmentary way: utopia, madness, desire, delirium . . . Nuclei of fascination that, at the same time, attract and repel."

The voice, now without a visible source, sounds in David's head.

"What most scares me, in truth, isn't the physical disappearance, but rather the possibility of an unexpected death. Not wanted, absurd. To be distracted for a tenth of a second while on the highway and end up as debris under a bus that will only leave a pile of bent metal and a puddle of blood. To leave a gas jet on in the kitchen and fall asleep sweetly. To suffer from dizziness and fall from the balcony during a family get-together. To contract a raging and sudden illness; to bleed from a deep wound. To be trapped by an earthquake, a landslide. To roll, tearing yourself to pieces, down the slippery side of a mountain that you visit as part of a package deal, to drown in the ocean, dragged down by a wave. To argue a traffic dispute or an insult with a stranger in the street and end up with a knife deep in your intestines, the cerebral mass shaken by a blow with a club . . . To trip and fall backward, hitting the back of your neck. Thousands of ways, most definitely, to die absurdly, outside of the statistics of time and place, leaving inconclusive, the parabola that we began very early and whose meaning we don't know, generally, until the end. For that reason, survival fascinates us: to elude those tricks of destiny, to be able to stop the car centimeters before it smashes against the columns to the bridge under Libertador Avenue, in that uncontrollable and very fast skid that your vehicle took skating over a rain puddle and going out of control, a wild animal throwing itself forward with the inviolable laws of physics of weight, inertia, speed, and definitely, chance. So, your hand trembles slightly, and you cut yourself while shaving."

The water continues running in the sink, unneeded.

"It doesn't mean committing suicide, either, to know the exact date of your death. Or to try to guess, even if it be an approximation (dizziness, nausea, loss of self?), so that it becomes an intolerable torture. No. Really, we hope for something more modest: that the end may be unexpected, as most are, and in not knowing the exact date is found a secret that helps you keep on living; but, at the same time, that 'that' doesn't come before its appointed moment. That you can survive sufficiently long to end the saying that you have begun to chisel in. That you may say the whole word before breaking, that you may possess the great fortune to try to understand and transmit what is yours, that which is unique and nonrepeatable that makes you into an individual human being who seeks to transcend, as a happy and proud *Mestizo*. In a word: to live a dignified life. And to be able to recount it in a beautiful way before you leave."

David tries to dissipate the steam with his hands because he can't see anything anymore. He turns off the faucet, he listens as a movement of his arm turns off the light switch. And he remains without a conversation partner, without a mirror, in the darkness, alone as he came into the world, without more company than his shaved insomniac memory. Surviving.

family tree

"There is a difference, Gingi, between experience that is sought after and that limit which, having been crossed, gives up its place to horror. It's the crossing guard that separates words from that which is vital, the intellect from common sense. With violence, for example: a neighborhood brawl where manliness is born—as it happened to me, to so many other adolescents—or the film death of a murderer at the hands of a family's avenger, circulate by means of another aerial tramway (or the same one, but changed) as the horrendous tortures inflicted in the detention center, as they are now being made known by the press. Do you understand?"

"Not very well, David."

"The political disquisitions of a group of studies, to cite another case, and on the extreme opposite, the concrete scenario of a leader who should decide, though overwhelmed by the limits of reality: because he is responsible for what happens, not for writing a book. The little glass of liquor that helps bring on sleep is not the same as the glorification of alcoholism as a kind of bohemia of the creative spirit. Or the experience of the artist with a psychedelic drug— which allows him to expand his visions, to enter hidden and symbolic worlds—and the sick dependence of an addiction that ends in destroying the brain. Or the sexual games of an adolescence that affirms itself in multiple experiences, decanted to a promiscuous adulthood where the momentary pleasure is not distinguished from respect for the other member of the couple."

"Your son would say that you have become bourgeois."

"Yes, it is a generational question. When young, we intend, legitimately, to break everything. As Huidobro would say, we feel like 'little gods,' immortal and all-powerful. But it's necessary to put these plans into practice as quickly as possible, because after a few decades, physical decline and the closeness of death—one's own and that of others—will get in the way of completing them. The birds of finiteness are growing within us, without our realizing it. Like love, changing and always the same. I think of León, of Ignacio, of Teresa: those friends whom I loved so much, separated by paths that, often, are incomprehensible to me. That fatso León, for example, I admired him for so long . . . "

"You always said so."

"Yes. But the same thing happened to me with him as with reading the life stories of some great revolutionaries, like Bakunin. In every day matters, he was a difficult being, unscrupulous with other people's money, a poor worker, sexually impotent . . . A dubious, tragic private life. Neither could León maintain a stable family, raise children, finally . . . He redeemed society and destroyed his own life. That does not suggest that they be disqualified: they unite ideals of justice and truth, of the best of humanity. But limits are needed."

"A revolutionary who speaks of limits?"

"A dialectic equilibrium. Between the centrist and routinized majority and a decentralized and rebellious minority. These later create the ferment necessary to produce change, and without them, advance would be impossible. But it is very, very dangerous to hand over to them the *totality* of power, since their jumps of the imagination, in each discipline, could not be directed at the right time through the rest of the society. They convert themselves, in a paradoxical manner, into destroyers of the entire social fabric. And so they make possible the growth of conservative reaction, which comes to restore order. In sum, it's a delicate balance."

"Then, you and León . . . "

"I love León, for everything that he signified for me. But, today, I also feel fear: his fantastic plans, the pride that . . . would you like me to confess something to you?"

"Tell me, David."

"I'm starting to have doubts about the role that he played in the business of the murder. He is involved in too many threads: He was Sheila Abud's lover, he has a mysterious relationship with Ahmed and Leila, only parts of his life are known about . . . I don't know, but . . . I could imagine him, without much effort, pouncing on a lover of so many years who had decided to abandon him. It's a fantasy, nothing more. But I have my doubts."

DREAMS AND HATREDS OF YOUTH

He arrived early, as his anxiety dictated. A commercial gallery in the windy street with hardly any passers-by. Dirty papers blow down the sidewalks. A couple passed by his side, in a hurry. David found, at the back of the passageway, the theater. In the small bar with two lights turned on but without customers, a man, bored, was looking through the pages of the newspaper. He bought a ticket for *Palestine, Song of Love and Liberty*. A middle-aged woman with unexpressive eyes took the money, without asking which seat he preferred. On the counter two sold tickets could be seen.

He read with attention the reviews stuck to the boards. They were giving five or six shows so that he had to look patiently until he found two newspaper columns—one in Arabic and the other in Spanish—that referred to what interested him.

He checked the cast list. There he found, almost at the end, "Ahmed Abud." In fact, it's pronounced *Achmed*, he thought. Leila had not been mistaken in telling him the facts about her brother who for a few weeks now had not been living at the paternal home (the "new company" that he now keeps . . .). The program and the notes in Spanish (David had learned Hebrew with great difficulty during his stay in Israel, but he didn't dream of expressing himself in Arabic) spoke of a "choral work," based on "poems, scenes, and songs by Palestinian authors." Other people arrived: an older couple, an isolated young girl, another girl with accentuated Semitic features and long black hair with an old man who must be her father, judging from the gestures.

Gingi wasn't able to accompany him, and, moreover, she didn't have any great desire to meet the son of Señora Abud. Instinct, she said. Avoid that which is unnecessarily disagreeable. A wise decision which he envied.

Another woman appeared, alone: there were now eight specta-tors forming a line near the entrance. Bravo. He remembered the in-dependent theater of the sixties in Buenos Aires, those enthusiastic multitudes in little rooms in the back, where young casts worked for free to produce culture, to bring art to the people and all that. Sil-via's face appeared to him, with her big light-blue eyes, short red hair, and her little dark-blue suit, seated beside him at a production of Molière's *The Imaginary Invalid*, surrounded by students and re-tirees. Did he stroke her hand? Yes, but without bringing himself to do anything else. The irreparable timidity of being sixteen years old, Jewish.

Further back, even:—the performances of the Club in the Polish village, which the father would remember with an ironic smile—like conquests from the past, of which good taste impedes taking de-light—while your mother, without malice, made fun of the "leading actor" and the girls who hovered around, including Nachem's wife, that near-sighted one with the siphon nose, so that you can get an idea of the type of beauties who would trail along behind your father. And Moishe Burech, in attendance, amused (and somewhat scandal-ized?) at those functions systematically repudiated by the religious people, captained by Sholem, the butcher, of the long beard and thick eyebrows that hid eyes streaked with little red veins.

They entered the theater. Each chose a seat. He tried to reread the program, with the scarce illumination from the aisles: he didn't remember Ahmed well and he wanted to make sure of the characters that he played. First, a short piece—*Return to Haifa*—then a pair of folk dances (*Dabka*, he read) and then alternating stories and songs: Mahmoud Darwish, Tawfiq Zayyad, Ibrahim Abdallah. . . . The last names of the actors were Hispanized, or considerably shortened for production reasons, since Arab names could be hard to read.

"Prejudices," he thought. "Other people are filled with prejudices toward us, the Jews, for their difficult and, more important, strange last names (he remembered García, that clerk with whom he had an exchange of words, when he went looking for work). And now, I my-self recoil when faced by these unusual names. As if today's Pales-tinians were the Jews, discriminated against a couple of generations ago, seeking their land with laments and heroic shouting, incompre-hension, and solitude."

They turned off the lights and the show began. Long and ener-getic speeches, against a background on national conflicts. Thick mustaches, dark faces, eyes that were brightened with poetry, but also fanaticism. Texts of combat, death, struggle. Dust brought from the desert, *keffiah* of the combatant fallen on the sand, freedom songs and scenes that, little by little, are rising in tone: in the first, the Is-raeli soldier is fat and a bit brutal. In the fourth act he rapes women, steals ornaments from poor Arab farm workers, and lets them slip though his hands again and again, his eyes filled with greed. He mur-ders without mercy or motive innocent young people who confront, unarmed, his wildness. An elderly Palestinian, sick of it all, throws himself grasping a grenade against the ruthless invaders and dies along with them "to pave the road toward a free homeland."

"A lot of hate and little love," grunted David, gradually disen-chanted. The brief show culminated with a final hymn that the actors sang from the stage, inviting those present to clap hands in ac-companiment, "for the triumph over the Zionist invasion" of "that land that calls to us, sown with martyr's blood."

The girl with black hair and the older woman sing, excited: the couple clap their hands lightly, almost as a compromise. David feels watched and somewhat uncomfortable, imprisoned between his nat-ural sympathy toward all those who are persecuted—the Palestinians were creating their own mystique—and the memory of terrorist at-tacks against civilian buses and schools, the destruction of a passen-ger plane, that absurd and bestial massacre of the Israeli athletes in Munich (that he heard, bit by bit, from his work station in the fac-tory of the *kibbutz,* among the worried faces of his comrades). The horrors of the war, the bombs and the lives of the refugees, scenes that his head refused—healthfully—to remember and that only persisted in a smell, an instinctive reaction, the unexpected shaking caused by a surprising thunderclap or his children's psychoanalytic sessions. And the neighboring *kibbutz,* the one that produced sandals, where two crazed Palestinians had come in firing, broke into the children's house, and carried out a slaughter of the little ones before they were shot down.

No. David neither applauded nor shrunk down during the song. They watched him with puzzlement—there were more people up on the stage than in the audience, so that all were perfectly identifiable, and they couldn't avoid noticing his hard expression, his pensive eyes, his arms clutching the seat—but he refused to push aside his own story. "I'm not someone neutral," he thought, "but a human being filled with passions and tales. I can't annul my past and agree with the glorification of any such killing: Poetry doesn't erase unacceptable bitterness."

Even less so with Jewish life. Above all when he is in his home, in Israel. Those occasions in which, as Moishe Burech would say, "even the walls punched." The *pater familias* told how it was on a Sunday, after work, when they were resting. Hettie knits, seated on the bed, Moishe Burech thumbs through a book, Carlos—who is fifteen years old—runs about the room. Suddenly, hell: a violent kick opens the wooden door and Rebeca and her family enter. An old rivalry between families that has dragged on for years. Rebeca jumps on the mistress of the house, takes her by the neck with both hands, and tries to strangle her, throwing her on the bed. Father and brother of the invader—large men, close to two meters tall—throw themselves on Moishe Burech: chairs fall, blows break jaws; bones smash against each other, blood flows over the coarse faces. Carlos takes Rebeca by the back of her neck, struggles until she lets his mother go, and sends her to the floor with a couple of magnificent punches in the face. Moishe Burech hits with his two hands together, like implacable pile drivers; their movements collect teeth, bruises, bits of skin from those huge men who, finally, escape on the run toward the police station in order to report the tailor.

There are the war days, when life is not worth much. A Polish soldier, involved in police activities, came over to the house and took away Moishe Burech and his adolescent son. They go walking in the street, toward the detachment, arms high and the soldier behind them, brandishing his rifle. They meet another Polish soldier.

"What happened, Andrej?"

"These Jews were fighting each other," answers the first. And I'm taking them to the barracks."

The other, surprised, opened his eyes wide.

"Why waste time with these *yudi?* Come on, I'll help you: We'll shoot them here and throw them into the ditch."

The policeman hesitates.

"I don't know . . . I would have to carry them there . . . "

"Don't be silly. It's about four hundred meters to the detachment. We'll kill them here and be done with it. They're only a couple of miserable Jews."

"No, Cibulski, I can't."

The Jews listen to their fate, which depends on the Pole's whim. Finally, he decides not to pay attention to his comrade and begins the march again. Finally in the police station, the commandant interrogates them. He doesn't understand.

"You're saying that these two went to your house to attack you. And the daughter too?"

"Yes, sir."

"And you want to make me believe that you alone, beat these big guys, each one of them a head taller than you?"

Moishe Burech answers, without hurrying, with the parsimony of always.

"It's that . . . when they attack your own house 'even the walls punch.' I was sitting there, in my place. And a man defends himself in other ways when he is in his place . . . "

"Even the walls punch." Wise old man. Israel is the home of the Jews: that is the only thing not contemplated in the work. He waits briefly in the hall of the theater, tired. He has slept poorly for the last few nights and his eyelids hurt him. Ahmed goes out almost immediately, wearing a scarf around his neck. His eyes watch with mistrust when David begins to explain. Other actors pass through the half-opened door.

"Come on, Ahmed. We're going to eat, brother."

"I'm coming. Right away."

The young man has light blue irises, a thick though not unpleasant nose, very large lips, bony and somewhat clumsy hands.

"I'm very sorry, sir . . . "

"David."

"That's it. David. As you must see, I have to go with my comrades. I don't know what it is you want from me and I can't attend to it now."

"Listen to me, Ahmed. I know you since you were very little, since you were born. We were neighbors in the neighborhood, years ago."

"I'm quite pleased that a former neighbor would come to enjoy the play in which I'm working. Now you will have to forgive me, because . . . "

David takes him by the shoulder. The young man pulls back and in his expression a flash of anger appears. He lets him go, understanding his error.

"I have to talk with you," he says, measuring his words. "Respecting . . . your mother."

"It will be another time. Now I have to go. Good-bye."

"Your mother . . . and León. It's very important, Ahmed. Tell me where we can talk, at what time. It's urgent."

A bit of curiosity shows in the boy's voice.

"Okay. Come to see me tomorrow night."

"I can wait . . . "

"Today is impossible. David Schnaiderman, you said? Tomorrow night. At ten. In the cantina called *Zorba,* on the corner of Tacuarí and Carlos Calvo streets."

"Agreed," David gives in. The boy would want to find out something about him before meeting. He still has to tolerate an ironic twist.

"At ten. I hope you like Arabic food, right?"

Without saying goodnight, he rolled up his scarf, and, walking quickly, he left.

According to what Ignacio, whom he called as soon as he woke up the next morning, informed him, that cantina was frequented by sailors and prostitutes.

"It's a trap, David. That boy, besides being an imbecile, is an anti-Semite. I don't know what you'll get from him."

"Neither do I, Ignacio. But I thought that he would be able to help me in my search, León is still in prison and . . . "

"You didn't answer me as to what it is you are looking for."

"My memory, where the face of the murderer of Señora Abud is inscribed. And I'm also looking for myself. You and I haven't seen each other for years, and for that reason we don't know about part of our lives. Isn't that right? Imagine something similar on a personal level: not to know who you really are."

There is a long silence from both sides.

"Ignacio, are you still there?"

"Yes. I was thinking about what you said. It reminds me of the Biblical story of Cain and Abel. Perhaps I'm responsible?"

David had a sudden inspiration.

"Would you go with me to the Zorba cantina? I can't go with Gingi and . . . I'm sure that this aspiring actor knows more than he is showing. Will you come?"

Another long silence on the phone. Finally, Ignacio answered.

"Agreed. I'll go."

"Nine thirty at your place. Don't have supper, they have Arabic food there."

In fact, they met at nine and they arrived at Zorba a half hour later. The two of them were anxious. During the trip, David tried, without much success, to draw out facts about personal life, love affairs, and jobs from his former buddy. Ignacio had always been that way, of few words. Schnaiderman tried to shorten that distance imposed by the years. He was a bit brusque.

"Why didn't you ever get married, Ignacio?"

The other man scarcely hesitated.

"By ten centimeters," he said, as if the reply had been prepared beforehand, as if the identical question had been repeated many times inside himself.

"Ten centimeters? I don't understand."

Ignacio gave a little nervous laugh.

"I was ten centimeters short, David. I said that."

"I don't . . . "

"If I had been ten centimeters taller, my back would have been ten centimeters wider and my penis ten centimeters longer . . . then my relationship with women and my entire life would have been different. Do you understand me now? Nature was unjust with me."

David looked at his buddy's thin body, and he didn't know what to say. Everything was, suddenly, too cruel.

They entered by some stone steps. Some thirty round tables and rustic chairs were spread around the room, surrounding the central space. On the stage, four musicians played strings and drums with a rhythm that went beyond the apparent monotony of the pieces. The smoke floated in large spirals and made vision difficult. A waiter came over to wipe with a rag the place they had chosen, and he asked, looking in the other direction.

"What can I bring you?"

"Hummus," David answered. A puff of smells and condiments affected his salivary glands: he was in the Middle East again, even if it be by means of its gastronomy.

"What else?"

Ignacio made a gesture, indicating that anything would be all right with him. He looked very nervous. David quickly searched his memory.

"And tahini. And cucumbers. And that hot sauce that . . . I don't remember the names exactly."

"I'll bring you an assortment, a little of everything," the waiter decided.

"That's it. Exactly. And white wine."

All the while looking in the other direction, the waiter asked, "Are the gentlemen alone?"

At that very moment, David noticed some women who circulated through the aisles, the incessant movement of couples, the lights that are too weak. He answered reflexively.

"No, we're waiting for someone."

In fact, he wasn't lying: he had an appointment there with Ahmed. The waiter nodded and left quickly, advancing like a consummate rocket through sailors and families that were beginning to fill the room.

Near them, two women were arguing loudly, while a fat man with a prominent belly and large bags under his eyes waited off to the side, with a genial expression. "Don't do it for less than twenty-five thousand," they heard. Several couples got up to dance. Greek music with its quick, linked, sharp notes that get under the skin, invaded the area. David was hungry.

"Is it ten o'clock yet?" he asked, just to say something.

Ignacio shook his head, without looking at him. A very thin woman was smoking in silence at a table in the back, her pupils hardened in the emptiness. There was something attractive in that fragile profile that was lost in strange ways, grotesquely distorted by her makeup.

"This boy won't show up," he said finally. "He made an appointment with you here to get you off of him last night in the theater. An irresponsible fellow, like all of them."

"You're a reactionary," David answered, touching him. "You talk like an old man."

The waiter arrived with the order and laid out a dozen different small plates on the wooden surface. They began to chew enthusiastically. The gathering had become animated, and now, a half dozen men were dancing on the floor, holding shoulders, with that camaraderie that excludes women. Young and older women, excessively made up, of varying ages, were permanently circulating near the bathrooms, followed at a certain distance by some potential customers.

"They agree on the price for fornication," Ignacio said. "They disgust me."

David raised his gaze from his plate, surprised. Another proverb from his paternal culture came to his memory, when he noticed something a bit out of place: "The stupid one doesn't realize, the clever one realizes but doesn't say anything."

"How do you know so much?"

"You're innocent, David. You always were, the absolute truths are denied you. A young terrorist makes a date with you in a strange place like this, and you come, without taking any precautions. Smiling, you put yourself in the lion's mouth. You are preoccupied with the folkloric color of the business, the hummus and the Eastern music. Lots of the past, but you don't realize what's happening around you. Did you know how Pedro died? Pedro, the one from the furniture store on Bermúdez Street, who traveled to Israel in 1970. He was in our movement, in a youth group . . . "

"I remember him vaguely. What happened to him?"

"They killed him on Mount Hermon, during the *Yom Kippur* War. Do you want to know what he was like when they found him? Tied to a post, barbarically tortured by the Syrians, with eye balls burst open. They cut off his genitals and stuck them in his mouth. That's how they found the cadaver. And you want to have a discussion with these savages? Don't trust them. They're all murderers."

"But, then you must have . . . "

"I came prepared. As always. Or perhaps you don't know that Ahmed is a member of those Palestinian attack groups which go out at night to deface synagogues?"

He moved a few centimeters from the table and pushed over a bag. David caught a glance of the wooden handle braces of a .38 short revolver, holstered at the waist. He felt like an imbecile.

"I'm afraid that, in effect . . . I only wanted to help León, but these complications . . . "

Ignacio didn't answer, giving him time to check out the room again. Several older men, bald and with big mustaches, broke crockery against the wall, around the dancers, to the rhythm of the music. From the table where steaming plates overflowed, an old man asked for a song. Another, short and somewhat clown-like in his exaggerated gestures, successively asked to dance all the very numerous members of a family, together to celebrate some intimate occasion. All of them speak in shouts, mixing interjections in Greek and Arabic, Mediterranean lingua franca that spread through the air the flavor of sea, nostalgia, distance.

One of the women from the establishment, somewhat older, with red hair and a prominent abdomen—although her full curves hadn't lost a certain attractiveness—invited a very young man from the group table, apparently the favorite. Interwoven like two lovers, they danced to the music, while the little brothers ran around the couple noisily throwing plates, the pieces of which splashed on the dance floor. An inexpressive old man with heavy eyes passed among the chairs, selling little cloth dolls in vivid colors.

"Ahmed won't be coming," David said.

"I told you: he's a cynic. Just like all of that family of crazies and fakers."

The orchestra came to the end of its set. The guitarist, a very young boy, was playing the instrument with a lighted cigarette tightly held between his ring finger and his little finger, from which he took a drag whenever the chords permitted him. Sailors with white and bright blue uniforms were crossing the parquet, seeking the women who hung around in groups. Two of the women danced together: one was tall and thin, with small eyes and an aquiline nose; the other dark-skinned, with short hair and a black dress, watched the smoke that rose in spirals, as if lost in contemplation while she moved to the beat of the music.

"Look at that chick," exploded Ignacio. "Didn't I tell you that they're all whores?"

A girl who was about fifteen years old, very smooth skin and red shoes, was dancing alone—as if a bit ashamed—hiding her face behind long and oily hair that swung right and left with her movements and covered her features. They were so fascinated by her that they didn't notice Ahmed's arrival.

"Good evening," his voice said, strangely calm.

Ignacio took a start and moved backwards in his seat as if to get up, but he controlled himself. David's face brightened.

"We thought that you wouldn't be coming. It's—" he looked at his watch— "ten thirty."

The other man didn't answer. The members of the orchestra were descending from the stage—thus completing their performance—and the sound of some records of Arabic music entered the environment. David searched Ahmed's eyes to celebrate the coincidence, but he remained immutable.

"It's okay. Sit down."

The young man did so. The maitre d'—a young man wearing a white jacket and a dark tie—came by, and Ahmed spoke to him in Arabic, ordering something to drink. There was a certain tension at the table. Ignacio had his hand draped loosely on his bag, on the side where he carried the pistol. On the floor, a gentleman of advanced age danced with one of the girls of the house, the one who, very scantily dressed, moved her lips and hips lasciviously toward him, while the old man, almost without moving, turned around and snapped his fingers, very effectively carrying the tune, and pointing out his companion, who was paying . . .

"Those Arabs are sharp," Ignacio commented provocatively. "They command and the women obey."

Ahmed didn't respond. The waiter brought the drink, and the young man took a large swallow. Then he sighed, as if he were tired of something.

"I am waiting, gentleman. Didn't you want to speak with me?"

"Yes, yes. Of course."

David moistened his lips, without knowing how to begin. The tension grew, and he decided to go to the heart of the matter without evasion.

"You don't remember me, Ahmed, but for a while we were neighbors. I am the son of the tailor, who lived near the Portuguese's bar, beyond Cuenca Street. You were very young at that time. I know your family and I have learned of your mother's misfortune . . . "

Ahmed did not seem to be paying close attention. The dancer, now free of the old man, danced close to the family group's table. While David continued his explanation, she made an almost imperceptible gesture toward him.

"I had a memory loss, and I can't remember in detail what happened that terrible night. You came out running, behind . . . "

"Yes, but behind," Ahmed said, as if returning to the conversation. "It was a few seconds later, and I didn't see anything, if that is what you wanted to know. I've already told the police."

"But you, did you know León?"

The veins in the young man's neck tensed up, and for a moment, David remembered his absurd fantasy. But Ahmed controlled himself.

"Of course I knew him. What's happening with him?"

"He's in preventive detention. It's based on a confusion, but if we could demonstrate . . . "

"Why do I have to demonstrate anything? What does that . . . Jew, mean to me?"

Good, it's done, David thought. The cards on the table. Ignacio straightened up. David hoped that he didn't hurry.

"You're an anti-Semite, right?"

The fellow didn't waiver. He looked back and forth from Ignacio to David and responded, "No, I'm not an anti-Semite. I'm anti-Zionist. But I have nothing against anyone in particular: you, for example. It's a question of power groups. The world is a continual struggle, some try to dominate the others. And we're on opposite sides."

"Right," Ignacio said, gritting his teeth, while his glasses were sliding down his nose. "And there isn't room for everyone on this earth. Some win and others lose. You hate the Jews, and then . . . "

Ahmed shook his head, without losing his calm.

"No, it's not like that. I am a person without phobias. I don't feel anger nor do I discriminate against anyone in particular because of his origin. As a child, I didn't know many Jews: I lived in a neighborhood where there were very few of . . . you: we called all the shopkeepers 'Russians,' even if they were Turks and smoked *narguile*. But when I speak with a Jew, *the others* are always the gentiles and anti-Semites. Your sick sensibility tries to make me take on a role. Mercilessly, you present yourself as a Jew. You tell me, for example, 'I bought myself this tape recorder during my trip to Europe, but I won't sell it to you for less than double what it cost me.' Boris, your father, always made fun of me with that. He wanted me to assume the role of the gentile and think 'what a dirty Jew' or something like that."

"I won't permit you . . . "

"In that way, the roles were made clear. He knows how to handle himself before the image of the non-Jew whom he has stereotyped. I was surprised; I thought that Boris could have said to me, 'I won't sell you this tape recorder because I like it a lot' or something like that. But it's always that way. That mentality belongs to you, the Jews: it is the phobia of the gentiles, the need to label them."

"But today's anti-Semites are called anti-Zionists," David interrupted. "And you . . . "

"That business of anti-Semitism is a myth, like many tales told around here. There is a kind of atemporality about the Jew, because the history repeats in a contradictory fashion: the Jews kill Christ, but, at the same time, they save humanity, because Christ's death saved man. Or, said in another way, it made his salvation possible. The Christians ought to be, at the same time, opposed and thankful to the Jews. Something similar happens through history, the Jew is a mystery, the atemporal entity that 'pays' for the salvation of the others. He is distinct. For that reason, he is always in the gunsight."

David interrupted again, nervous. The young man was too sure of himself for his age.

"What you are saying is antihuman. All human beings are equal . . . "

"Not so," Ahmed said. "Some dominate others. Today the Jews on the Palestinians. Tomorrow, who knows . . . "

"But we are fighting to achieve a better world. Like your sister Leila, even if she used mistaken methods."

"What do you fight for? Why do you do it?"

"For . . . love of my fellow man. For humanity."

Ahmed laughed loudly.

"That's shit. Words of weaklings and homosexuals, as I explained to Leila more than once. Lies. No one does it for that. You fight for power, to dominate others, to be superior. It's always been that way, in the whole world. Force is the final triumph: everything else is intellectual constructions created to give you a motive for that hatred, so that we don't see ourselves as simple murderers. I don't know why I'm wasting my time arguing with the two of you."

The music was louder. The violins went higher, interwoven with the incessant beating of the percussion that invited the body to move. The woman who was dancing had come closer to the table on Ignacio's side, and now turned stomach and hips, grazing him while other customers applauded. Ahmed grimaced.

"You have to give her something," he said.

Ignacio was paralyzed, his face very red, wild. David had watched the fat man at the family table, and he imitated him, taking some crumpled bills from his pocket and offering them to the dancer, who, without stopping her movements, took them between two fingers and made them disappear between her breasts, under a modest sequined bra. Everyone smiled, including Ignacio, getting through the uncomfortable moment. With a final spasm, the one who was dancing touched with her buttocks the shoulder of the "chosen one" and went on toward another table.

"It was a joke," Ahmed clarified; he appeared to have regained his good humor. "Before I sat down, I told her you were American tourists and . . . "

David nodded, but Ignacio was still agitated.

"We're wasting time. I don't even know why we came here."

Ahmed watched him harshly, without answering. Ignacio held his gaze, his hand resting on the bulge in the sack.

"You don't argue with a Nazi," he continued. "There's nothing between us that can be arranged through philosophy."

The young man got up.

"I agree," he said.

He left without saying good-bye. David cursed his silence. Perhaps he could have avoided the brusque end to the conversation.

"Everything's ruined," he blurted out. "But this business with Ahmed turned out to be nothing more than an immature joke."

"You're very stupid, David. Which joke are you talking about? We use different languages and different codes. We were saying something, but we were thinking about something else."

They paid and went to the exit. Ignacio climbed up the front steps, he let his friend pass while he took a look at the dimly lit area and closed the door. His hands trembled.

"Did you notice the table on the left-hand side, behind the family group?"

David was surprised.

"No. I don't know what you're referring to."

"People from the Syrian embassy. I know them well: those short mustaches and plastered hair can't be confused. So are their noses. They came for me, I'm sure of that. They were in agreement with this bastard Ahmed."

David didn't answer, suspecting a joke. Ignacio felt the bag again.

"It's not going to be easy for them. I'm going to shoot back. León taught me: the one who is frightened first loses everything. Backing away has no limits. That ideological purity is what has always fascinated me, David. I was a coward for many years, do you remember? I wasn't worth anything. But one day, I said 'never again,' and that was it. Never again a step backwards or turning my gaze away from anyone."

They took a taxi. Ignacio got off at Mosconi Avenue, and David continued the trip. He felt sleepy and tired in that cold Buenos Aires night. Gingi was staying up waiting for him, and Eduardo wanted to tell him something about the student center. Papers and clippings are piled on his desk, waiting to be deciphered.

"Ignacio doesn't look good to me," he said. "We haven't been in contact for many years, but there's something in his eyes that . . . Perhaps I am affected by the conversation with Sara. But that fanaticism . . . I don't know. Something frightens me."

He went to bed almost immediately. He hardly had the strength to tell Gingi the latest happenings. He and Eduardo agreed to talk during lunch the next day. The interview in the cantina had gone badly: that violence that at another time might have fascinated him—by means of the self-defense youth groups or the Cuban experience—now seemed to him to be disturbing, upsetting, through Leila's stories or Ignacio and Ahmed's aggressiveness. He went to sleep upset.

Gingi woke him suddenly, in the middle of the night. Old Boris, she told him—while he tried to focus, opening his eyes with difficulty—wanted to know where he and his son had been the previous morning. He didn't understand. His wife had to repeat it to him a few times, through a dark half-awake state from which she refused to emerge. That a while ago Ignacio had shot himself in the head with a .38 revolver that belonged to him, lying in bed. And old Boris cried desperately for an explanation for that absurd death. And that Sara was walking around screaming in her home.

family tree

The story, which seemed cryptic, was told by León off to the side of the room. He had obtained permission to attend the funeral—discreetly accompanied by a policeman in plain clothes—and he intercepted David, the moment he entered the room. The mirrors had been covered and the tightly kept silence was broken only by murmuring.

"Ignacio died twice," León said, as a way of greeting. "I understood only recently. For that reason, he deserves compassion: he never really lived, he couldn't even make himself tell a woman 'I love you' without getting tongue-tied . . . "

"He was a shy kid," David protested. "That's not his fault."

"A member of the living dead," León insisted. "It was useless to try to change him."

"I don't understand what you mean."

"A metaphor will help you understand; it's the best way to tell it to you. It deals with a story that they told me last year, on the Brazilian border."

The protruding eyes frightened David. What could León have been doing in that area a year ago?

"The man pilots one of those boats that cross, daily, the Iguazu River near Foz," León began, without a transition. "The river is broad, but with a strong current. It was almost nightfall, the crew—about fifteen—started out on what would be their last trip. A sharp, humid breeze covered the murmur of the waves and got inside the colored shirts."

He lit a cigarette before continuing.

"The compass was magnetized, and mistaking the direction, in the dark, the vessel moved quickly toward death in the gigantic falls of the cataracts: fifty to eighty meters of sudden, vertical geographical break, noisy and splashing remains of a two-hundred year-long volcanic eruption. With a cut-off at the level of its navel, suddenly amputating its natural course, the Paraná River—which comes down from the north of Brazil—seeks desperately to place its feet in the emptiness that opens as if by magic and plunges, with an infernal din, in several dozen cascades. Whenever it can, wherever it's permitted. An enormous mass of water, thundering, drops between rocks and trees, whining like a beggar, bringing up blows of foam."

David saw Boris go through the bedroom door, reeling.

"By day, an immense rainbow, completing a perfect circle of droplets with light passing through them. At night, the noise of the cataract, a deafening moan, immense mass of water that doesn't stop falling and falling, brownish and tenacious. The boat, now uncontrollable, is trapped by the whirlpools. The crew members shout and cry, but they can't do anything. They arrived at the first falls, like a crazed Russian mountain, and they felt the vertigo that sets in instantaneously. The vessel falls, turning over and over, smashes its timber work, drowns, with death sighs, broken bodies and unfulfilled hopes."

"But, I don't . . . "

"Wait. You'll understand. The boat straightened up for a second and then fell down the second cascade. Fifty vertical meters of water and horror that chew up objects and people. Only one, one of the fifteen crew members, our man, can, by instinct, hang on to a rock that stood out, wet and brilliant, with strange bushes that dig in their roots and resist being torn out. He succeeds in somehow climbing up, and he embraces the hard rock, without time to notice how the brownish white cascade carries with it the remains of the shipwreck. In the weak moonlight, he sees outlines, not colors. In two seconds, it is as if nothing had happened. The water continues draining."

David listens more attentively.

"The man holding on there recovers his breath a bit. The cascade roars at his sides, above and below. Would he have cried, laughed, begged God, thought of his mother in that instant? Would he have converted, suddenly, into a believer in an all-powerful force that could save him? All night is a shaking of lips, of body, of hopes. Dawn breaks. He keeps hanging on, with plant-like tenacity: perhaps someone will come to his aid, perhaps they're looking for the missing vessel, perhaps . . . "

He inhaled forcefully on his cigarette. David remembered Sara, Ignacio's changes in behavior. Is he referring to that?

"The whole day passed, and night fell. The swollen body, now without tears, the man resigns himself to his fate. He is isolated, with that gigantic root and without feelings that can be expressed, sleepless, water around his arms. He prays. He can't do anything, except let himself die. But he has the bush in front of him, that won't give in."

"Señora Abud . . . "

"With the new day's sun, thirty-four hours after his fall, the man hears a motor. As if in a dream, something appears that he can quickly identify. A helicopter. His cries have been heard. The rotors fly over the rock he is tied to. He makes signs with one hand, without letting go. The machine returns an hour later and lets down a rope from its golden underbelly; at the end of the rope is a life jacket."

León puts his cigarette out. The last thread that unites him with life, David thought. To fall in love with his teacher's wife. Was it that?

"Burnt by the wind and the sun, in rags, our man feels life like a gallop that runs through his guts. He should proceed slowly, after so many hours of suffering and weakness. The jacket reaches his level, and, with infinite care and shaking hands, he surrounds his body with it. He looks upward, to where his rescuers indicate, thumb pointed upward, to show everything was okay. The helicopter gains altitude, carrying away the only crew member rescued from the sharp fingernails of the cascade, which, mad with rage and roaring, while its prisoner escapes, hurls violent masses of foam impotently into the aquatic and never ceasing falls."

"The metaphor is clear," David said to himself. "Why complicate it so?"

"The aircraft ascends. It covers some eighty meters when, perhaps too burdened by the body that it holds, the life jacket slips upward—did it take advantage of the psychological numbness of our worn-out protagonist?—and it kept rising, now by itself. Everything occurs in a second. Like the repetition of a horrible lived nightmare, the crew member falls from that height above the center of the cataract, is torn to pieces by the impact, avidly swallowed by the raging mass of water."

León interrupted the story for a moment, breathed deeply and asked, "Why *die twice*? Why this absurd and unnecessary punishment? Would our man have had time to ask himself? Would Ignacio or anyone else been able to tolerate the suffering that led him to return to Hell when he finally believed himself free of the ghosts that accompanied him since he was a child? Do you understand, David?"

From Boris's sobs and Sara's shouting, he put together the basic facts of the tragedy: it had happened between three and four in the morning, in an unplanned fashion, without any message that might give away his intentions. Everything pointed to a sudden conclusion, surely motivated by depressive processes of long duration that no one had seen. Ignacio utilized the same revolver that he carried in a holster at his waist the night before, when they visited the Middle Eastern cantina and met with Ahmed.

David thought he perceived in León's sudden revelation and his metaphorical story about the man who died twice, a certain repentance for an unexpected chain of events, the idea that the end could have been modified. Or, as he suggested to Gingi, his old friend was involved in "something else."

"He plans gigantic projects, while this new tragedy is already part of his past."

"You are saying that, really, he's an adventurer."

David meditated for a moment before agreeing.

"Exactly, I believe something like that. He's very desensitized to pain."

During supper, the table blossoms with discussions. Eduardo is active in the High School Students' Center. During the terrible years, in that same high school, a half dozen adolescents disappeared. Their babyish faces search for an answer to their absurd fate, from the photos with which, each anniversary, their schoolmates and teachers remember them in the establishment's patio.

"They had done the same things that you are doing now," Gingi says. "Organize the Student Center, ask for a student pass. Little things. And for that, they took them away."

Eduardo disagrees, angered, and his curly long hair waves from side to side. His head leaning forward toward his plate, not looking at the others. A mixture of timidity and determination.

"But they prohibited our Center magazine. They censured us."

"What did you expect? Also, that drawing . . . "

"What's wrong with it? It happened this way: the caretaker saw Raúl and Fabiana kissing in the rec room and scolded them. Even love they won't allow . . . "

"That's okay, but . . . the caricature that they put up was very coarse. A disheveled old lady shouting, 'Where you study, you don't fuck.' It seems pretty obvious to me."

"It's what they deserve. You have to hit them where it hurts. What do you want, that we hang around watching television or that we go out to dance to disco music, like the mindless adolescents that they wished to create?"

"But I'm afraid . . . ," Gingi insists.

"All of us are afraid. But if we don't act, this will never change. It's 1983, we're awaiting elections that may permit a return to democracy, and allow us to turn, with our own hands, the direction of history. And do you want me, at seventeen years old, to stay at home . . . ?"

David couldn't argue.

"Eduardo, you're right. I, too, at your age, was in a Student Center that . . . "

"'At your age, at your age . . . ' Simply put, you've become a member of the bourgeoisie. You are an old reactionary, who's going to vote for Alfonsín because you are afraid. You're over . . . the hill, Dad."

"It's that the other options vindicate death. And I want to love life, I'm sick of so much violence. It has contaminated us. You yourselves . . . "

Ruth intervenes, from the other corner of the table.

"What happens to us?"

"You don't understand, you're too little. I'm telling your brother that the years of the military dictatorship didn't pass without effect.

They made all of us a bit Fascist: authoritarians, mean-spirited, bad-humored. We don't listen to each other, we like to control . . . "

"Now you say that?" Eduardo replies, pushing his empty plate toward the center of the table. "You speak of authoritarians, and you don't stop telling your daughter what to do."

"That's different."

"It's the same thing."

"It's not the same. Kids always belong to one of two categories: when they go to school, some kids always get their book bags stolen, their erasers, pencils, and every day you have to replace the stuff for them. Those are the kids like you: for that reason, we fear for your life. The others, in contrast, never lose anything, they always find, they come out well in the worst situations. You are one of those who say 'hit me.'"

"Nonsense from an old gorilla. Everything is part of the fear. And that fear corresponds to your generation, not mine."

"But, they're going to . . . "

"Don't include me. Today we must demand the maximum, break everything, change the world. We won't put up with half measures."

The history that David had tried laboriously to reconstruct slips down the alleys of time gone by.

"What's that about my generation? What's wrong with my generation?"

Eduardo directed an accomplice's glance at his sister and his voice took on a professorial tone.

"That time passed you by, old man. You speak some Yiddish, travel to Israel, listen to romantic boleros . . . but always in the middle of the road, neither here nor there. Perpetual doubt. The historical opportunity has already passed you by. We are more direct, we are sure of what we want: if something doesn't work, it's broken, and on to something else. You have to change everything from the roots up, to make it from the start. We are young, we have time. You, on the other hand, are pragmatic: up to this point, yes, further, be careful, you can get hurt. Bullshit. 'Don't be insolent, you punk.'"

The young man breathes hard. Gingi and David understand each other through a glance: almost the same words filled the years of their courtship, back there in the sixties. The militancy, the adventure in the *kibbutz* . . . Why be surprised?

"Eduardo," she says, placing her hand on his head. "Perhaps we are the mistaken ones, trying to put excess importance on personal experiences. You need to follow your own path. But I am afraid for you, that's all. I'm afraid that they will kill you, afraid to lose you, because I am your mother. Politics doesn't have anything to do with this."

David repeats, in a loud voice, that familiar phrase that Moishe Burech would say as his father had: "Since this business of death appeared, life is no longer safe at all." The tension eased notably.

They eat dessert. Eduardo mentions his last nights, full of nightmares.

"You're nervous about next week's march," David reflects. "It's the first in many years, the hope that this passage through the inferno may be coming to an end. I'm also afraid."

"It's not *your* fear. Let's not begin again!"

"Agreed. What did you dream?"

Gingi appears, running while carrying the coffee, protesting because they never wait for her to share everyday experiences.

"We were in the camp, and I was teaching you how to walk in the air," Eduardo said, directing himself to his father. "I realized that by moving my arms toward the side, as if they were wings, one rises and *can fly*. That beautiful sensation to plane and see everything from above. I was telling you not to hold back, to get the spirit and to come and fly with me."

"I want to go too!" Ruth shouted.

They took the plates from the table. David mentioned next Sunday's event at the Plaza Congreso.

"There will be a festival of popular music, with many important artists. Does it appeal to you? There will be rock stars and things like that. Later, we will march down the avenue."

"And in which group will you march?," inquired Eduardo, kidding him.

"Group? Which group? I'm going alone, with your mother."

"No, Dad. Don't you understand anything? That was before, in your time. The independents of your style don't fit anymore. To demonstrations, especially if they have to do with human rights, you go together with an organization. Among other reasons, for security, do you understand? You can choose whatever banner you like: the Mothers of the Plaza de Mayo, the Jewish Movement for Human Rights, some political party. Anyone. But, how are you going to go, given your way of thinking?"

They agreed to attend a soccer game the next day. David remembered that when his son was five or six years old he took him, regularly, to follow the campaign of the San Lorenzo team, from the cheap seats. Those were other times, when the picture stories filled up the weekend (with the excuse that "the boy" would like to read them.) That graphic language that might have fascinated his adolescence. The small neighborhood plaza, at the corner of Holguera and Habana streets, entire afternoons, teaching Eduardo to kick with the *empeine*, the *sobrepique*, the *chilena*, the *olvidarse*, the ball behind your ankle, to do the *autopase* and run to the side of the defender. All these little tricks are transferred like precious treasure, ineludible experience of the young colt.

"Do you remember?" Gingi says. "Since he was very little, you made him into a fanatic with tables of positions, scores, collections of miniature players . . . Bah! *Soccer crazies*."

The evocation revives in his contemporary backbone the lost paradise of a youth that will never return, those years without gray hairs on the temples or tension in the knuckles or dandruff or psoriasis or all those unpleasant novelties of the forties.

After lunch, they arrive at the stadium where San Lorenzo plays. They are playing Tigre, a team from the lower group, without much in the way of pretensions. Vehicle traffic is stopped, the multitude occupies the streets, parading like a continuous strip. Thousands of fans comment on team formations, backgrounds, rumors . . .

The eyes (again adolescent) of father and son enjoy the spectacle, perhaps more attractive than the game itself: fans with drums that resound incessantly, long banners crossing transversely the popular grandstands, songs and yells, clouds of confetti that rise like cosmic dust. There are boys hanging on each cornice, in the advertising signs, on the flag poles. They jump onto the wooden planks, which flexed dangerously, catching the enthusiasm.

From Tigre's decks, located behind one of the goals, some hundreds of enthusiasts let out with *Ay, look, look! What a bunch of jerkoffs! They're going to put the stadium up their asses.* But the answer from the crowd of San Lorenzo fans is demolishing, drowning out their opponents and alternating the mythical *Bo-e-do! Bo-e-do* with the *San Loreeeenzo! San Loreeeenzo! San Lorenzo! San Lorenzo. . . .* There are twenty San Lorenzo fans for each backer of their opponents. The sensation of father and son is gratifying, compensating for the struggle to enter past the horses of the mounted police.

The "San Lorenzo" loyalty overwhelms that of the rivals. "Lories" who, before that day, had never met, now hug each other, discuss the style with which the penalty kick was executed, ask for information about other games from those who are carrying radios, plan.

"San Lorenzo fans, we're the most, and we're the best," David says proudly, while they walk triumphantly through the streets. He relives afternoons of joy and fervor, the goals by the black Picot or the proud free kicks of Facundo and Sanfilippo, stuck to the old, worn radio on the dining room table, before the first television set arrived in the neighborhood.

"Dad," Eduardo reflects. "It's something very strange."

"What do you find strange?"

"To be part of San Lorenzo, here and now. To have won."

1. David and Eduardo choose to sit on the upper deck.

"Coca-Cola! Ice cold Coca-Cola!"

"Hot dogs! Hot dogs!"

2. The teams enter the stadium.

Next row

1. The feeling of seeing it from here is different. It's not like television. You're right, old man. But let me watch the game.

2. You understand the mistakes. You have a complete picture of the game.

"The game is getting boring."

Lower box

"Tigre is holding back, you can't play like that."

"Come on, asshole! Run after it."

"We don't have the spirit. That happens sometimes."

"Who put number 7 on our team? The enemy?"

"Kick him, asshole, this referee doesn't catch anything."

[*Banner*] GO CYCLONE!

1. "Good, skinny. Kick it in!"
2. At ten minutes of the second period, there is a quick encounter
   in the middle of the field, a long
   pass to the side, number 7 comes
   out.

THUMP

Bar:
"GOOOOOOOOOOOOAL!!!!"

Next row

1. "Great goal! Great goal!"
"San Lorenzo! San Lorenzo!"
"I told you, buddy, that number 7 is
   A BEAST!"
2. "Our boys!" "Our boys!"
"Boom, boom, boom!"
"Boom, boom, boom!"
"Your mother's a big whore!"

1. Suddenly, the unexpected happens, number 3 of Tigre escapes down the side, brings the ball to the center, bumps off a defender's leg, sets up.

Bar:
"GOOOOOAL!!!"

next row

1. There are a few seconds of silence . . . and then the restrained anger erupts.

"Tigre!" "Tigre!" "Tigre!"
"Let the 'santos' cry in church."

[banner:] TIGRE CHAMPIONS

2. The yelling and the threats increase. The action seems to have shifted to the spectators.

next row

1. "We're going to tear it up."
"We're going to tear it up."

2. "We've got to teach them who owns this place."

"Let's smash them. That will shut them up."

"Don't they know they are a second-class team. Who've they beaten?"

"Bunch of bums. Last year they were in division 'b'."

Shouts:

"Nothing happens."
"Nothing happens."
"When it's over . . . "
"We'll beat the shit out of them!!!"

1. Suddenly . . .
2. Penalty

next row

1. "Gooooal!"
2. "What a faker!"
"What a faker!"
"They're dancing for the television!"
"Yes, yes, gentlemen."
"I'm from Boedo."
"Yes, yes, gentlemen."
" . . . . . . heart."

3. Borombom-bom, bom, bom.
"We've been robbed!"

next row

1. There are some pleasures for the San Lorenzo team, while the game was coming to an end, the reduced group of Tigre fans had become quiet and started to leave. The songs of the majority are now condescending, the good humor revived, life is good.
2. "Prrrrrit" [ref's whistle]

"And what's strange about that?"

"To be in the majority, Dad. It's the first time that's happened to me. We could have done anything we wanted with the Tigre fans. Did you realize that? Take away their flags, hit them, allow them to live, kill them, quiet their songs with our shouting, crush them . . . Didn't you feel good?"

Images overcome David: Jew, intellectual, sociologist, immigrant in Israel, unemployed, social bastard wherever he might remember, always condemned to be a minority. Now, for once—and his son was right—it was like a bit of heat in winter, when a liquor circulates inside and warms the innards. To be one of those who win, of the majority, of those who decide. For the first time.

"It's true," he says. "I didn't think of it before, but it's true: I felt part of the majority."

"How strange, huh?" the young man insists. The 'others' must always feel that way, members of the majority. Letting us live and all that. Choosing to be a minority—for example, when we play against River—and not ending up members of a minority by fate, like us."

He doesn't know what to answer, except to intuit the fortunate completion of that second San Lorenzo goal that avoided a massacre, where they might have been considered "from that side." In the corner of the stadium, a boy wearing eyeglasses is thrown to the ground, twisting, spitting saliva from his mouth. Many people surrounded him, but no one intervenes. David speaks to the police agent who is watching from the sidewalk.

"Sir, it must be . . . an epileptic seizure. He has to be moved."

The uniformed cop, very young, almost beardless, has shock in his eyes.

"Here comes the officer. He will take care of it."

A corporal, short in stature with a mustache, approaches without hurrying. One of those present shouts, "give him air," and the circle begins to disband. David takes the boy's tongue between his thumb and his index finger and pulls it out of his mouth, until the convulsion passes.

The fans lose interest, shouting sarcastic phrases toward groups of Tigre supporters that are leaving in silence.

"It's nice to be in the majority," Eduardo repeats, looking at them.

A fuzzy drawing completes itself. Through the foreshortening that reduces the length of the body according to the laws of perspective, David achieves oblique views of every remnant of light, every piece of the brain teaser that constitutes his interior life. The repeated themes—violence, minority, survivor, the figure of Moishe Burech, the voices from the past and nostalgia about the neighborhood—integrate themselves into a central metaphor: the inevitable *mestizaje* of that family tree where his portrait is born. But something is always missing: the blow against the sidewalk, the terrified face of Sheila Abud, the blood that splashes on the wall, a story in police court that brings to the surface his own sense of his life at that crossroads of forty years old.

He returns to Ignacio's house. Boris has left, apparently in the direction of the Portuguese's bar, where he pours out his troubles to anyone who is willing to listen to him. Sara stays in the living room, and David feels uncomfortable. He has never known how to pay his respects, to say "I'm so sorry . . . " and all that; so this time, he limits himself to reach silently to the nervous hands, splotched with marks of advanced age of that old lady whom he kisses on the cheek.

"You. All of you had something to do. Poor boy, he always suffered. He cried at night, I heard. He said that since he was a child they made fun of him, because of his eyeglasses, women. Garbage. My father's razor did well. It killed."

"Who did it kill, Sara? What are you talking about?"

"Everyone wants to kill. So papa said, 'Kill me and all my family first,' he says so when he sees a knife. Everybody wants to kill sometime. To be a bad human, to make others suffer, you never?"

David tries to string along the conversation.

"Yes, Sara, me too. Everyone, at some time, we've thought about committing suicide. Especially when we were young, in the adolescent years."

"Ah! You, too, know what that is. To suffer a lot, pain in the soul, worse than sick body. There is no treatment. You want to burst, to put an end to everything, to sleep. To rest."

"I understand you, but, why Ignacio? Why did he shoot himself?"

Sara's eyes leave again. He holds her hand.

"Answer me. Why?"

"You say yes, but not able to understand. Ignacio from child always problems, eyeglasses, friends say ugly things, 'asshole,' 'homo,' that. He to suffer a lot, to be ashamed, to think women don't to like him. A shame, *nu?* Always friend León, bigger, strong, kills others. Wipes his knife on his pants, I thought he would kill me, but papa didn't let him. In Yiddish he tells him . . . "

"It's all right, Sara. Let's go back to Ignacio. What happened to him?"

The old lady gets up and walks toward the kitchen.

"Ignacio with fear. That's why he bought revolver. Arabs and Nazis, always were following, he said all in the neighborhood were against him. Not a knife, he was afraid of cutting himself, for that reason, he surprised the Arab boy, son of the owner of the store that they killed. Ahmed carried a knife to kill him. Ignacio not to like Arabs, you understand. He didn't know Yiddish either, he was a Jew like those from here, more or less. I didn't know what he to want to be. I much worked, always, I can't do everything. He got tired and said *chau, chau, chau,* I'm going. He had already died inside, now another time. What else do you have to understand?"

She closed the door, leaving without saying good-bye. David remained standing for a moment, confused. He returned home and ate a great deal, going to bed immediately thereafter.

He awakes, with a start, in the middle of the night. He promised a thousand times (and Gingi was his witness) to eat light suppers. But the anxiety of the last days made him eat and eat. The nightmare was lengthy and complicated: he remembers some of it, a trace imprinted on the mass of his consciousness, a joking and incoherent remnant. He is driving down a Buenos Aires street. With the gearbox in first gear, he begins to accelerate more and more. He passes a car, then another. There is little traffic, and he continues leaving others behind.

His foot presses the accelerator all the way down, he continues in first; that is to say, the motor has all the inertia from the start, but little "oomph" for when it enters in a rhythm and quickens the rapidity of the explosions. The car creaks, whistles, purrs, deputing in the absurd mechanical struggle between the quantity of gasoline sent to the carburetor—David continues pressing the pedal to the floor—and the technical limitations, those gears that, on their own, can't turn any more rapidly. The uproar is infernal. The speed too increases, but very slowly. He doesn't perceive the necessity to shift to second with the gearbox, to establish an equilibrium between force and acceleration.

Finally, the box jumps into the air, in pieces. The car stops. David walks to an automobile repair shop: the broken and twisted piece hangs from his fingers, in the other hand, he holds the shift. He is upset, thinking of the price of the repair. He doesn't understand how he could have been so distracted, that he didn't direct in a harmonic manner an apparatus and its distinct parts, insisting in resolving it with a single element.

Sitting in the bed, the night-time darkness—Gingi at his side, sleeps placidly—that half-awakened state makes him strangely lucid. He doesn't hear noises, blasts from car horns, the garbage truck that passes by collecting trash, a siren that is not far away. There is, on the other hand, an interior cracking sound that causes him to shiver: the *puzzle* has taken on a perfect form. Roots, trunk, branches, spiraled leaves, and rugosities of wood converge very fast, as in a movie on fast forward, in front of the arborescent center of your eyes.

Everything reaches a scale that makes the reading possible. The role carried out by León, perhaps in spite of himself: the extreme necessity to have all or nothing, the rigor to throw himself forward always, voluntarily, first row, pioneer, unique and perfect castrating father. He loves Señora Abud, somewhat older than he. For an image, he imagined them, rolling around in a dark room, fucking her savagely on the kitchen table or behind a door, a few meters from where her children and her husband were watching a television program, their excitement increased by the danger. That desire for grandeur, to do what no one has done before: the car's accelerator always all the way, pedal to the floor, roaring like a desperate animal, while he sought his limits.

Ignacio lived each adventure second-hand, recreated on a table with coffee by León, just as when they were adolescents, with their nocturnal stories on the convent wall. He functioned like the gearbox of the vehicle: he wanted to increase that acceleration in the race for life without preparing his own changes, he arrived at the extreme point, and he broke up.

The rest could only be conjectured: perhaps erotic stories that crazed the disciple, little brother on excursions, eternally behind. In that binary love-hate relationship that structures every human being, it fell to Ignacio to play in the worst extreme: injured in his capacity for tenderness, without children nor lovers to pour his affection, solitary accumulator of frustrations, all this petrifies in the recipient and generates resentment self-destruction, and madness, León always "speaks" of the extreme experience, but he "acts" with one foot placed in reality, knows how to measure his strengths. Ignacio takes too literally each word from the master, each delirious plan or sexual fantasy, fanatic monk at the precipice. "Wouldn't I myself," David thinks, "perhaps have followed that path of madness and violence, if I hadn't found the love of Gingi and the kids to calm my permanent unease, control it, and make me a respectable man?"

He moistens his dry lips with his tongue and closes his eyes, so he can imagine what comes next. An unbalanced disciple attempts to repeat situations for which he is not prepared: to fight, to love, to kill, to be another person. Now comes the true story, that in which can be seen a correlation among the subjects of the narration, psycho-sociological and the linguistic facts.

"I," "you," and "he" begin to identify themselves with real beings.

Like a little image that forces its way through the memory to put itself on the highest level, the changed outline of Ignacio pushes out the shouts of neighbors and passers-by that go on fading away, covered with the amnesiac veil that has just run off with the pain and the desperation of the inevitable, by means of a "we" that succeeds in placing us in reality and as an expression of modesty, replaces the generic "they." Including David, León, everyone, it helps to eviscerate the memory, to participate in history and not only observe it from a comfortable distance.

family tree

ARGENTINA 1983

Hope is a promenade
harsh and uncertain as the flicker
of fire over mosaic
and in the end unable to decide
whether to turn into tongues of smoke
paintbrushes shading reality
a play of sheathed sparks
from bitterness to guesswork
lukewarm oracles of the ordinary
or, quickening, now
a hot, arborescent whirl
and those small flames
breed subterranean fires
burst of lads and lapidary
shards tumbling through the air
to grip hands that
are unity, warmth, flight of shadows
are a swath carved by the enamored son
are soft rockface of the morning.

4. tree, WE

The pronouns are a mirror
in which are reflected the system
of social relations
—A. A. Leontiev

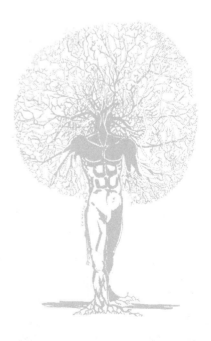

MEMORY PORTRAIT

Moishe Burech lived with those nerves, always, he spent all day at the sewing machine, sewing and cutting, you have to imagine such a large man with so much energy, keeping it all inside, every so often he would explode. One time two large fellows, Polish grenadiers, came to pick up a suit. I remember that it was a Sunday morning, and the work wasn't ready. So one of them pounded on the table and shouted, "What do you mean that it isn't ready yet," and he cursed my father.

My papa, without showing any emotion, said to my mama, "Hettie, efnmer of detir."

She opened the door—the others hadn't understood, of course, because Moishe Burech spoke in Yiddish—and my papa grabbed the first one by the lapels, raising him into the air, then with one punch he knocked him out of the house. He gave the second fellow a terrible beating. The two of them had to escape through the rear of the house, because people were returning from church, they'd been to Mass, and those fellows were embarrassed— they were just teenagers—that people see that they had taken such a beating, their faces, their noses covered with blood.

The story stayed with us. We would say, "Hettie, efnmer of detir." And everyone knew the rest. But he wouldn't pick a fight, never. He only defended himself and didn't let anyone put him down. He had his pride, that was it. He didn't like to fight.

When the army began to recruit men for the war, they made them show their ability with a rifle. They told my father to shoot in any direction or pretend to be near-sighted, he was just at the age limit—forty-five years— and with a pile of kids to support. But he was very proud, everyone knew that Moishe Burech wouldn't be a coward in any way; then he hit six bulls eyes with the rifle, and they took him immediately. He had never carried a gun before. He left his wife and kids, and they sent him to the Russian front, in a company that had Hungarians and Czechs. He didn't under-

stand anything, so he bought a pair of dictionaries, and he began learning two languages, so he could speak to the other soldiers. They kept him until 1916. At first, he dug trenches, and that caused an illness in his legs, rheumatism or something like that. When he returned from the front, he was still sick—and then he went to work in a tailor shop and made the uniforms for the officers and for the army in general.

He began and ended as a private. He never liked stripes, military salutes, parades, and all that. He couldn't put up with any fanatic.

It was near the end of the war, in the central plaza of Yarchev, when they killed this Bolshevik boy. I saw him. And everyone was talking about him in the village and in my family, many years later, in 1918 immediately after the October revolution. He was hardly more than an adolescent, he would have been about seventeen; he lay hurt on the ground, dirty and bloody with feverish eyes. A boy. A Polish officer approached him, with a revolver in his hand, and pointing at him, he said, "What are you doing far from your country? did you come to fight here?" And the boy answered him, "Svobodoi." It meant "For Liberty" in Russian. The Polish officer got angry, many people in the village were watching him. He hit the Bolshevik in the head with his revolver and threatened him, "If you say that again, I'll kill you. Why are you fighting, you Russian dog?" The fellow looked around and shouted, "Svobodoi."

And the officer squeezed the trigger and blew his brains out. The story was long told in the village. We were very impressed by it—and especially in Yarchev, there were not many communists, I think the only one was the wigmaker, perhaps two or three more. There were more Zionists.

We were always in the middle. When the Russians came through, they burned everything, then the counterattack came from the others, and they burned the village again. A no-man's-land.

The day of the pogrom, many hooligans met outside. We had a large iron door in front that wasn't at all easy to open. All the men met in the first-floor apartment with hatchets, knives, sticks, whatever there was for self-defense. We women and children stayed upstairs on the second floor.

Just then, he came, the owner, who was at a son's house, at about that time. The Poles wanted to get inside. They threw a grenade against the door, and they blew a hole through the metal, but they weren't able to open it. Next door there was a store that had an open area. I remember that it sold kerosene, candles, soap, it was a general store, it was part of the house, and it had a door that opened to the premises. Do you remember? Eleven o'clock at night. He was a Yid too. It was nighttime. He didn't realize what was happening, and he wanted to go inside. They said to him, "Ah, you have the key." Then they opened the divider, and they stole or broke everything in the store. And they got into the house through the back room.

We were horribly frightened. When they got in, they went directly to the first-floor apartment and the fight began. Everyone was shouting, and we were crouching on the floor upstairs, trembling. The arm of one of our men was slashed with a saber, but our guys killed a soldier, a Polish officer, they were all Polish volunteers who did the pogrom, they were brutal.

I was a five-year-old boy, but I still remember the fear we felt, the butcher's blood-covered cleavers and knives, the alarms, the sweat and the noise, the blows, insults, someone who cried for God.

After all, they weren't able to get upstairs. We defended ourselves well, and the others left. Then the Jews themselves formed a militia to protect the building.

I remembered that when, soon thereafter, a tailors' strike began. I am in among the leaders . . . I don't know the language well yet, but there is a great deal of suffering, a man can't see that without reacting. In that period, I wasn't really communist, but socialist, I read Di Presse. The others weren't the same, the cuénteniks and other businessmen read the Idische Zeitung, were more to the right. But I am a worker, my place was there.

It wasn't a partisan thing, everything was mixed together, from several parties. Spaniards and Argentines and Jews and even Italians. We were all tailors, that united us. We called the strike, but there were "big shots." It was for an indeterminate period of time, until they raised the price, seven pesos for a jacket was too little. A pittance. When the strike began, I boycotted my older brothers too, since they gave me part of the work, but I couldn't betray the others, nor let myself be seen working. A strike is a strike, isn't it? That caused me a problem with my brothers.

We went on strike and in order that the "big shots" couldn't enter, we set up a picket line. I was one of those who made sure they don't go though. But the bosses called the cops. As soon as I step forward to stop a strikebreaker, and barely grab his lapel, three or four policemen jump me, grab my arms, and put me in the paddy wagon. The "big shots" didn't understand that, if they didn't break the strike, they would have to raise our commission.

They took all of us from the union leadership to what was called the Special Section. I believe it was on Urquiza Street at the 600 block. I was held for six days and from there they sent me to the Police Department. On Moreno Street. As we were incommunicado, they separated us into halls, those bunk beds hanging on the walls, one on top of the other, mixed in with common criminals. Like it was in the ships, that's the way it was. Bunk beds, a dirty blanket, rats. As I was a foreigner, they threatened to send me back to Poland. I answered with gestures, I didn't even know the language well. There I met "the Russian Sow," Jacobito who worked for them and took the statement in Yiddish.

The "Russian Sow," a fat guy, a Jew who had sold out. He came and began to speak Yiddish, getting friendly, so he could find the truth in the lies, but we already knew, we were warned that you didn't have to say a word to him, because the guy was a sellout. He belonged to the police, they paid his salary. He gave me "advice." He told me that not even those "things" that were going to sell "for me," that was for my own good. And, years later, they came to see me from the same Special Section, because of another ad in the Party daily. They said to me, "So you're still fucking around, communist?"

He stops in front of you. He's less than half a head taller than you, he is pretty thin, but the evil that causes your terror is in his drunk's eyes, surrounded by little red veins and lacking in compassion. He watches you. You can't go forward or move sideways.

"How ugly you are, little Yid," he says, without raising his voice very much.

León looks at you and then at him. Nario also comes closer, murmuring, "What's going on, che? Is there a problem?"

One of your legs begins to tremble, and you can't control it. Your eyes move from Paco to León, then you lower your gaze. Now it's Nario who insists, "What's happening with those stinking Kikes? Did the Kikes shit in their pants?"

Force is the right of beasts and all that. You know it. But, how many times can you continue crossing sidewalks every time you see them coming, feeling that terrifying humiliation—held like a disgusting cadaver that invades your nightmares—that hurt you as much as the imagined blows? You advance a few steps, and you call, "Eh, che, come here. You! Motherfuckers!"

Your voice cuts off. Your shaking stops the last words in a "stutter" that holds them in your throat. Nario and Paco figure out that you are referring to them.

"What's your story, asshole?"

It's León who is yelling, "Go fuck your mother the whore, stinking Nazis!"

There is a long, interminable moment of stupor. You think about your father, of your grandfather Moishe Burech, of all those who can give you courage in that instant. Paco is the first to react: he looks at León as if he had not understood and, suddenly, punches him fiercely on the face. You see the blood on your friend's nose and you want to respond, but Nario is coming toward you. Your legs are still trembling. You hit each other with hands and feet, bodies, heads, tangled up. The blows shake you, and, at the same time, increase your fury: you scratch, bite, begin to cry while you roll around embraced on the sidewalk, and you fall into the gutter filled with dirty water. León, you see at that moment, has gotten up and withstands, as well as he can, the blows from his opponent.

He: And now the starry night, filled with light, summer again. Your father, Russian from Odessa, seated on the patio, sips maté, his gaze fixed behind his glasses. Your mother goes in and out of the kitchen, she wants to listen and, at the same time, she fears what is going to happen. You gesture, your face washed and without makeup, lips pursed, adolescent anger held back. Berna is the one who speaks, shielded by a fatherly and heated voice, while León sits at his side.

We're only talking about a campout, sir. We are Jews and Zionists, that's all. We are organizing a study week in Córdoba. An experience of joyful communal life. So that the young people can learn about the emotion of sharing, Jewish living around the campfire, songs and scouting games. The language of the heart. A new life for a better human being, healthier, less egotistical.

My daughter will not go. She is a minor, and, in this house, I still rule.

We don't mean to show a lack of respect. You decide. But she too should give her opinion. She has the opportunity to have an extraordinary experience, in a framework of Jewish education. I myself am a member of a kibbutz, I am here in Argentina, sent by the movement. We don't harm anyone, wishing only to better the world and every human being, speaking about Israel and the future.

Your father, inflexible, sips maté. The man with thinning hair, patient, unfolds with smooth gestures, the purity of a youthful utopia. You walk around, nervous: you don't know whether to intervene or keep quiet, you listen from off to the side, and you walk back and forth, a mix of nervousness and hope showing slightly through your middle teeth, so easily managed with the nacre smile.

The children arrive like first fruits. There you are, lying on the bed, face up, the pregnancy is far advanced, a flickering light (from the street) crosses the darkness of the bedroom and disperses over a blanket. The blue bed jacket, hands crossed over that belly that kicks and moves, the overnight bag at the end of the bed—put together months ago—with booties and little outfits and towels and all that. There were many nights with the rivers running side by-side, exploding at the same time while your

328

hand would squeeze the other loving hand (almost lost in the hollow, small and with a curved ring finger), the skin covered with kisses, the fingers that softly tingle the sensitive places, your head at times resting on your husband's chest as when you were little—you would say—the grownups protected you during the stormy nights of thunder outside. And now, the curled profile and the mischievous expression: you gather your legs, you raise them, repeat the straining exercise that they taught you in the "Childbirth without Pain" course, smile broadly, and turn your head to say, "Do you see? So easy. Tomorrow or the day after I do a "Come on, baby" and the kid pops out.

She: *This beautiful mixture of that which is born and that which dies, the brand new and that which leaves, the three generations—that are, have been, and will be—constitute the tree's moment of splendor. Moved lightly by the twilight breeze, this multicolor plot that continually changes (the edge of tall naked poplars, standing close together), discovers easily its shape and size between the roots and the sky, the secret of the ancestors and the projection toward the heights, the speckless sky that divides the cosmos and its planetary dimension. You are like the poplar in autumn, David: green, ochre, and silvered. And only in that beautiful time—the first autumn days—those who understand can join in the secret which is bashfully undressed.*

Abi, the kibbutz secretary, introduces the theme directly. Israeli style.

We need volunteers who would be willing to put off for two years their move to the new housing, so that we can receive immigrants here who arrive with their children, lack of stability, unresolved situations. We all know, comrades, that we're not dealing with something simple. We have worked very hard, since we drained the swamps of this valley forty years ago, to achieve the material equilibrium that we possess. And it would mean almost beginning from zero, from the start.

"We've already done our part," replies a man of undefined age and thin eyes. "We deserve to begin enjoying something of the terrestrial paradise, after a generation of sacrifices."

"It's true," Abi answers. "It's true, Amnon: from a personal point of *view your claim is just. But at times we forget that which brought us to live in a commune: the idea of solidarity, to help the comrade, superior to the cannibalism of mass society."*

"Words!" Shaul shouts, a bald and thin old man. "These living quarters belong to us. We wait, our turn arrives, and we ought to occupy them."

"None of this can be imposed," Abi insists, while he begins to raise his voice. "But let's not get upset about a piece of bread, a television set, a new house. We are men who don't want to feel ashamed of our youthful ideals, full of illusion, but men, finally. Not accumulation machines nor unfeeling walls."

He pounds on the table. The murmuring ceases.

Why are we here? Do you remember? We wanted to be pioneers of a new society, leaders of love and hope, militants who exposed their own bodies to the risks and advantages of socialism. Let's rise for a moment above the everyday! And those hope filled nights that we shared when we founded this kibbutz? What happened to the generous qualities that helped us overcome cold, hunger, war, hostile neighbors? What happened to the disposition toward the common good that justified our adolescence, filled the dreams of our youth, gave meaning to life?

Let's try to look at ourselves as we were twenty years ago. And let's not betray that image, very new comrades? For that they call us pioneers: for everyday heroism. We have always been a minority.

"San Lorenzo fans, we're the most, and we're the best," David says proudly, while they walk triumphantly through the streets. He relives afternoons of joy and fervor, the goals by the black Picot or the proud free kicks of Facundo and Sanfilippo, stuck to the old, worn radio on the dining room table, before the first television set arrived in the neighborhood.

"Dad," Eduardo reflects. "It's something very strange."

"What do you find strange?"

"To be part of San Lorenzo, here and now. To have won."

"And what's strange about that?"

"To be in the majority, Dad. It's the first time that's happened to me. We could have done anything we wanted with the Tigre fans. Did you re-

alize that? Take away their flags, hit them, allow them to live, kill them, quiet their songs with our shouting, crush them. . . . Didn't you feel good?"

Images overcome David: Jew, intellectual, sociologist, immigrant in Israel, unemployed, social bastard wherever he might remember, always condemned to be a minority. Now, for once —and his son was right— it was like a bit of heat in winter, when a liquor circulates inside and warms the innards. To be one of those who win, of the majority, of those who decide. For the first time.

"It's true," he says. "I didn't think of it before, but it's true: I felt part of the majority."

"How strange, huh?" the young man insists. "The 'others' must always feel that way, members of the majority. Letting us live and all that. Choosing to be a minority —for example, when we play against the River team— and not ending up members of a minority by fate, like us."

And now we are all here, we are the enormous majority, that applauds together for a stranger, intones anthems to life, against the flag-bearers of death. We look at each other's eyes, while our mouths sing the recently learned phrasing. The insistence on a long syllable, the intended tone for the final repetition. For an instant, and possibly for all times, we are brothers, although we may never see each other again. We recognize ourselves in the others, exposed philatelists, militants of hope.

We have with us, seated on wooden benches or beach chairs, elderly people and women with buns on their heads, scarves tied over their shoulders, a thermos under the arm, the always present maté cradled with a warm hand. Adolescents with nervous gestures and acne on their faces circulate among the rows offering partisan periodicals, human rights publications, petitions to sign. We are different, with tastes and wardrobes, ages and gestures, curious or concentrated expression, but what does that matter? We are in the plaza like the vessel that quenches the thirst. A boy in old jeans, long hair in a pony tail has climbed the statue of the woman with the large jar under her arm, white and opulent like a perfume bottle, and he embraces her like a desperate lover so as not to fall.

We circle around that expanding boundary, rings that encircle the center. Intoxicated, we clap hands. Small kiosks, placed at points which are tangential to contact with the undulating masses that are coming and going—taking the stage as center point—give out balloons, drinks, hot dogs, party flags. There are white overalls on the children and jackets of the same tone on the women, as if these chromatics indicated a way of purity. Children who cannot see the spectacle climb onto the backs of their fathers or play with the dogs that, with the line moving happily, circulate among the demonstrators.

They sing "Ode to Life" from the loudspeakers. A young man faints, perhaps overcome by emotion or the heat. Another adolescent holds his head downward and asks that others not worry. "It's low blood pressure," he says. A similar problem invades us: to shake off the generational tiredness that weighs on the shoulders, to give the baton to those who just recently begin. For them, everything is possible: change the world, modify life, to revolutionize the experience on Earth. The Universe continues spinning, we have yet to see thousands of dawns and everything is ahead of us.

We need unity, life and not death. We are many, and we want to be many more, because the "we" is not only a grammatical subject, the plural of "I," but contains other added questions, conditions of intentionality, beyond the grammatical. It represents a determined configuration in the relation of speaker-group-listener-action, one among the possible. Tired of aggressions, we know how to behave. We, the people, all together, we defend ourselves from the tyrannies of urgency, the beam that crushes crumbs, the calls of the nonsensical. Because we want the best of everyone, the pluralism of the minorities is what we make flourish contagiously, sympathy, example. That portion of neighborhood tenderness and humor, of good porteño quickness, that makes up the common code.

The march begins. A group of young people moves among flags that have begun to wave in front of us, about fifteen meters away, unfurling the immense street banner that identifies them as members of the Engineering Student Center: concentrated faces, dark glasses. The poster, light blue with red letters, is lower than the rest—given that its bearers are located in a pendant, lower in the ravine of grass—and it obstructs the view of the scene for those of us who are behind. Nervous little councils, angry gestures, spindly protests are now heard. Until one, voice of the people, shouts with affection: Let's see how the engineers run! The tension is lessened—adolescents who carry the flag laugh over the honorific mention of a far-off future—and the groups get settled again. The enemy is elsewhere, not among us. Let's not lead aggression in the wrong direction. The same thing happens in politics as in art and in daily life: those who really change reality develop in a logical manner, the others with unplanned capricious, cheating routes. It's difficult to differentiate: we end up assimilating originality to nonsense, if we only let ourselves be carried along by our impulses.

The plaza has gone on filling up. Open spaces between movements and posters are being closed. The pressure starts, light gas that envelops cisterns and pitchers, without forcing itself, but persistent. We go on squeezing together a little further, joining with the comrade, the passion of the multitude in the air, an essence that enters our throats. Thousands, tens of thousands, we already are hundreds of thousands. Forever the majority in favor of life, elbow to elbow, inspiring each other with pushes, hugs, and clapping that resounds, new, on the survivors' backs and hearts. Gigantic popular assembly, fiesta of color and emotion, each with his own and all together. We are the multitude that frightens those who would make a coup, single and multiple identity simultaneously, topaz and ashes, violin and sweet flute, great orchestra that plays the polyphonic symphony without conductors. With this, "we" orders cannot be given, since the speaker himself is included in the work and characterizes it as "collective," of all.

The different threads have wound around the plaza where we hear the last concert—not by chance, Schiller's "Ode to Joy," later utilized by Beethoven in the last movement of the Ninth Symphony, a moving song of love for the explosion of living nature—now we separate, in columns, toward the great demonstration. Many of us protect our militants, chains of grasped shoulders; others belong to more open and massive lines, or to small, isolated groups, like those of the National School of Dance and the Conservatory of Dramatic Arts, figures with long red hair and informal clothing, their pupils filled with great amounts of life while we pass by, dancing, we turn somersaults once and again, holding arms, surrounded by accompanying refrains.

We snoop around the surroundings: one side and the other, fragments of a banner, a face with a white handkerchief, the hint of what will come. And we let ourselves slide through the multicolored human sinusoid, excitement that rises and falls.

The crowd continues its march, a strip that effervescently snakes between and statues of the plaza. We experience that ambivalent sensation of loss and gain, of blood vessels that press the outsides of ourselves, among faces in which we recognize ideologies, loves, experiences, gestures, common solidarities. And those others with which we reencounter the taste of the roots, the essence of nontransferable codes that define us as individuals, family and intimate histories, not shared, that precisely because they round off a rich and satisfied specificity, permit the integration of the group from which we are, were, and we make, not from an anonymous multitude. With past and trunk and branches that extend out to the newest fruits. The same and different. Like a game of billiards with two cushions, what we gain in Judaism, Hebrew language, Israel, fighting in your own trench, we are losing in Nicaragua, internationalism, relations with the good people of Mozambique and Holland, Italy, Costa Rica, El Salvador, and Switzerland, Russians and Scandinavians, happy Paraguayans and Africans of copper-colored complexion. Perhaps gentle and poor little men, taken one by one in terms of life experience, insignificant particle compared to the magnitude of the Universe, with his limited life, the necessarily scarce experience of a possible incarnation. But we are large, enormous, when together, as now, we march holding arms, shared mystique, beautiful and wise multitude that occupies streets and sidewalks, insignia waving like birds that sing of the joy of being together. And together we will be able to turn our backs to look straight at the future, not to forget the past, but neither to stay there frozen, without return.

We don't lose anything, then: for once, our ways of communication coincide, the lack of global replies does not condemn us to a limiting ambiguity. The differences fade into a common carpet of humanity. While Ignacio loses himself in the mystery story or León in the solitary adventure, we find the rest in the "we," the voices heard by the fire, the mythical figure of Moishe Burech, father and mother and friends, brothers, comrades in struggle and loves, somewhat quarrelsome students, attitude of pride facing the anti-Semitic Cossacks and tailors' strike in Buenos Aires of the thirties, improvised oratory in front of a factory or in the assembly of the commune, the love that scars over the wounds and the illness of resentment that makes reconstruction possible, that understands the initial "big-bang" of the Universe as a cosmic orgasm.

The ill-considered (and brave) youthful fascination for the rapid and violent changes, the passion for life, the care of nature, and the pacifism necessary in a world that charges toward holocaust, all, all, and all of us are here, majorities and diverse minorities in this group of faces that are filled with hope and white ker-

chiefs that, like a new and definitive hymn to joy, unites memories and portraits in the trees built by our heart. Because all History (construction of the tree) will only be a metaphor for the central meaning: mestizos and survivors. We start to advance down the wide avenue singing, singing, always singing, the rest of life ahead of us, and the memory of the identity (Jewish and Latin American blossom, plural and yearning) found in us, recovered for all times.